ALL IN

A NOVEL

ELAINE EVANS

Book Cover Design by Get Covers

Edited by Nevvie Gaine

First edition 2024

To Lisa and Steve,
The road was bumpy,
but you're back where you belong.

Author's Note

All In is a second chance, closed door romance that spans twenty-seven years. The novel, although a love story, contains elements that may be sensitive for some readers. The following list is present in the novel. Physical and emotional abuse, alcoholism, sexual harassment in the workplace, mental disability, talk of postpartum depression, parental abandonment (off the page), and death of a family member are present in the novel. Readers who are sensitive to these themes, please take note.

Prologue

Dear Sam,

I'm all in. Meet me at our spot. I'll be there.

Waiting all day if I have to.

Love always,

Maria

Chapter One

1995

∞

Maria

M y life is officially over.

Nothing in this world could prepare me for what I am about to do. I'm going to break Sam's heart.

More like smash it into a million pieces. I know this because my heart is in the same condition. I am an awful person, and I take full responsibility for my actions. Sometimes, life throws unexpected curveballs our way, forcing us to adapt and make difficult choices. Including hurting those we love the most.

And for me, that person is Sam.

The only man I will ever, or could ever, love.

My life is being pulled in two different directions right now. It's a tug of war in my heart, a battle I never expected. A battle that I have chosen to lose.

As I run my tongue along the flap of the envelope, the faint trace of glue almost gags me while a single tear falls and lands on the crisp, white paper.

Then I close it shut. Sealing my fate in place.

God, I think I'm going to be sick.

The nausea pit in my stomach is threatening to surface, but I use all my strength to hold it down. I can't lose it. Not here on my living room couch, waiting for Sam to pick us up for our date tonight. And not with *him* sitting next to me.

Why am I going to break up with Sam if I love him so much? Great question. And I will always give the same answer to anyone who asks … it's complicated. Which is the answer you give to a question you want to avoid. This is more complicated than anything I have had to handle in my twenty years of life. And that complication is my father. My disabled, selfish, money-hungry father. I don't fault him for being disabled. But the choices he has made, well, they have far-reaching consequences.

Sam's strength is in stark contrast to my dad's weakness. I hope and pray he has enough strength to endure the tidal wave of emotions I'm sure he is going to go through tonight.

I can't believe I am about to do this.

Sam and I have been in love since our sophomore year. It was amazing to me that the oldest (by one year) and cutest boy in our class wanted me. I never looked back after that day.

Even though I always had a crush on him, I fell hard and fast. Mostly because he treats me with respect and in the way that makes me feel valued as a woman. There isn't a single thing I wouldn't do for him. And that's why what I'm about to do is tearing me apart from the inside.

Not that I haven't hurt for the last six weeks. The decisions I have made led to that little voice in my head letting me know what a terrible person I am. I should have told Sam what was happening. But I was ashamed. My constant need for people pleasing, especially my parents, has brought me to this place.

Out of habit, I look at my wrist to get the time from the watch Sam gave me, and I remember I'm not wearing it. Because of *him*. Instead, I glance at the clock on the wall, its ticking echoing throughout the heavy air of the room, weighing me down. Sam should be here in fifteen minutes. I bite my nails down to the quick as I think about my life and what got me to this place.

Being an only child, with a father who suffers from a traumatic brain injury he sustained during a terrible car accident, brings on a lot of challenges. I put a lot of pressure on myself to be the perfect obedient child at home. My mom couldn't be worrying about me messing up when she had Dad to take care of after his accident. She needed to concentrate on helping him get better, not on me. I was twelve when it happened, and his recovery was long, hard, and traumatic.

Which led to a lot of loneliness for me, lack of friends, and stress at home as my dad lost job after job. Then, to help us financially, Dad thought turning to gambling was a brilliant idea. It quickly became a full-blown addiction. I stayed out of my parents' way during this time, causing distance in our relationship.

But when Sam came into my life, suddenly, a future felt possible. I wasn't alone anymore.

Now, though, as I wait for Sam, I feel more alone than I ever have in my life.

I keep envisioning the look on his face when I hand him this envelope. I lower my head in shame at the thought. All of this is shattering my heart and, once again, the tears pool in my eyes. Pushing down the sadness, I release a breath as the couch shifts beside me.

I have been a shell of myself these past six weeks. I haven't been eating or sleeping. And I know Sam has noticed these changes. I'm sure he senses something is wrong. Whenever he asks me if I'm okay, nothing but love and genuine concern fill his questions. But I lie and say I'm fine.

If he only knew.

"I'll be right back," I choke out to *him*, not wanting to make eye contact. Before he can protest, I stand, sit the letter down on the coffee table, and make a beeline to the bathroom on the other side of the house. I need a moment to be alone.

As soon as I shut the door and turn on the faucet, I brace myself against the icy surface of the sink with clutched hands. Raising my head, I peer at the mirror, and I hate the person staring back at me. She's a liar. And she deserves to live a life full of misery and pain.

Before I can stop it, the weeping begins. I cover my mouth to stifle the sobs as I crumble to the floor and curl up into a ball, hugging my knees to my chest. Then, my whole body starts to tremble uncontrollably. The emptiness and coldness that my life has become are bubbling to the surface. The tears flow, and I can't make them stop.

I'm not sure I even want to.

In the background, the opening and shutting of the refrigerator and the clanking of dishes lets me know *he* must be making something to eat.

Wow! This is no big deal for *him*, I guess.

It breaks my heart even more to know that for *him,* this is just another ordinary day.

My grief is overwhelming, and the sobs become uncontrollable.

I don't give a crap if *he* hears me.

As I cry like a little girl, I mourn the death of my life with Sam. The realization of the pain I am about to inflict on the man I love only causes more tears, and I weep for the consequences of my actions. I don't know if he will ever be able to forgive me. The weight of my decision hangs heavy in the air of this small bathroom.

I have no clue how long I have been sobbing on the cold tile. I realize, though, that I need to get out of here and back out there to *him.* On unsteady legs, I peel myself off of the floor, step onto the blue shag bath mat, and look in the mirror. My face is red, blotchy, and my eyes are puffy from crying. As I splash water on my face, the coolness instantly jolts me, and I reach for a towel to pat my skin dry gently. I glance at myself one last time and try to memorize the face of the girl that still has Sam in her life. Because in a few minutes, that will all change. Sam will be here any second for our date, with no clue that a bomb is going to blow up his life.

Hopefully, one day soon, I can explain. But for now, lies need to be told.

I need to do this for my parents.

Because I am always the girl that makes everyone happy. I am willing to bear the burden, regardless of the cost to both myself and Sam.

The boy I fell in love with that day in the cafeteria.

Chapter Two

1995

∞

Sam

The black velvet box is in my front jean pocket.

With force, I shoved it only seconds ago, trying to make it fit. The last step in getting ready to meet Maria for dinner. Tonight, I'm aiming for a nice, casual look, and I think I nailed it. My outfit consists of black loafers, a button-down shirt in black with the sleeves rolled up, and dark denim jeans. There's only one problem ... it's pretty obvious that I have something tucked into my pants. There's a huge side bulge.

God, this looks ridiculous. I yank the ring box from my pocket and place it on the hand-me-down dresser. When I pause and step back, I admire it sitting on the chipped wood, and one thing is clear. It's glaringly out of place sitting next to my deodorant, aftershave, keys, and watch. But it's the one-and-a-half-carat diamond inside that I know will fit.

I grab my watch and clip it onto my wrist. My palms are sweaty because of the nerves coursing through me, so I instinctively wipe them on my jeans, then run my fingers through my dark brown hair. I take a deep, exaggerated breath, feeling the air fill my lungs, and my body relaxes.

Better.

I have never been this nervous in my whole life. Throughout the entire day, my heart has been beating so fast that it feels like it's trying to break free from my chest. All day long, I couldn't help but open and close the box repeatedly, half-expecting the ring to get up and walk away. I mean, it's not every day that you get on one knee and utter those four life-changing words to someone. "Will you marry me?" Then hold your breath for that one three-letter answer.

The plan is to ask Maria to marry me after dessert while we are at our favorite spot. Point State Park in Pittsburgh, right at the fountain. At night, the city skyline sparkles, while the three rivers flow peacefully. The mist from the fountain adds a touch of magic as it shoots up into the air. It's always been the place where we make big decisions, and now, it will be where I will ask her to be my wife.

Nothing could be more perfect.

A surge of excitement courses through me as I daydream about the moment. Maria isn't flashy. One quality I love about her is this alluring, sexy, yet understated vibe she has always put out there. She's witty without sounding full of herself. She is kind to every single person who crosses her path. Plus, she has no clue how unbelievably gorgeous she is. Honestly, I love everything about her, even her flaws, because they contribute to who she is as a person.

In high school, she was a little shy with not a lot of friends. All the guys in our class wanted her—but she chose me. Boring, looks-like-your-everyday-dude Sam. Not knowing that she had a crush on me, I took my chance one day in geometry sophomore year. I asked her to eat lunch with me. To this day, we call that day in the cafeteria our first date. We became a couple after and have been inseparable ever since. It's not lost on me. I am dating way above my station.

While planning this whole evening, I knew she wasn't interested in a flashy, over-the-top proposal. Kind of like the ones you see at NBA games.

That's not my girl.

Plus, I wanted intimate and unforgettable. It's going to be a moment so special that we can't wait to tell our grandchildren about it. A story we will never tire of retelling over and over again.

Now this massive ring box won't fit in my pocket, so I need to redirect things. I mean, I guess I could just put the ring in my pocket and not use the box. The thought of losing it scares me to death.

But I have to chance it. There is no way I'm not asking Maria to marry me at our spot.

I carefully take the ring out of the box and place it on the bed while I rush to the bathroom. With a quick motion, I yank three tissues from the Kleenex box, their softness playing between my fingers, before returning the ring to securely wrap it. Carefully, I shove it into my pocket, then glance down, satisfied and praying it doesn't fall out.

There, better.

After I propose, we can come back here and plan our lives over a half-eaten tiramisu (Maria never finishes her desserts) in the living room of my new apartment.

The one I plan on sharing with her.

When I toured it a month ago, vivid images of carrying her over the threshold flooded my mind. Visions of us snuggled up on the hand-me-down couch, wrapping ourselves in a cozy blanket, enjoying *Friends*, while sipping on wine. The one-bedroom space is compact, but I don't care because this is going to be our first place together. It will just force me to be closer to her.

No married couple forgets their first shared space as man and wife. I'll let her decorate it to her heart's content. Even if she decorated the studio with pink and lace (no lace because it's not her style, but she loves pink), I'd still be happy waking up next to her every morning for the rest of my life.

Over time, I'm sure we will move into a house, have babies, and watch our kids grow up behind a white picket fence. We have our entire future mapped out, down to the smallest details.

However, my nerves also stem from another source.

And that's Maria herself.

For the past six weeks, she has been a mere shadow of her former self. It began when she accepted the position as a secretary at that bustling warehouse. She's been pulling away from me, slightly, ever since. I've noticed the little things, the subtle details that often go unnoticed. Like not returning phone calls under the excuse that she is tired. Canceling dates because of a paper she has due. The shorter kisses and stiff hugs are the worst. I've asked her again and again if she is okay. She always reassures me she is.

I didn't want her to work in that kind of environment. You know what I mean, right? Those types of places are a breeding ground for inappropriate behavior. Gross men making unwanted advances, secret hook-ups in storage closets, suggestive comments, and sexual harassment. Not that she would cheat on me. I trust her one hundred percent, but what boyfriend in their right mind would want their girl subjected to that kind of stuff?

Not this guy.

I need to keep reminding myself that it pays way better than it should, and it works with her school schedule. The manager hired her on the spot when she interviewed and met all her demands. He paid her as if she had years of seniority and experience. I mean, of course she accepted the job.

She always tells me it's a means to an end. This job will help us save up some money so that we can start our life together. And she's right. After college graduation and getting her bachelor's degree, she can pursue a career in exercise science, her passion. I'm so incredibly proud of her. Her striving to get her bachelor's degree inspires me to upgrade my associates.

But I can't shake this sense of dread I have. It's strange and unlike me to doubt Maria and what we have together. I've contemplated asking her about it, but then I figure she must be going through something, and I need to be there for her. She would talk to me about it if anything was really wrong. That I'm sure of. I pray that I'm overthinking and this proposal will solidify our future together. No more fear or second-guessing.

I check my watch for the hundredth time. Six forty-five, which means it's time to leave. I swipe my keys from the dresser, turn out the lights of the apartment, head out the door, down two flights of stairs, and to the carport. My beat-up Ford Taurus is waiting for me as I slide into the driver's seat, the ripped upholstery pulling away and making the hole in the seat even bigger. I cleaned this sucker inside and out to prepare for tonight. It's old, rusty, and has over one hundred thousand miles on it, but it's shining pretty for me on this special night. I put the key in the ignition, and it sputters to life. A Michael Bolton cassette tape is in the middle console, so I pop it into the player, his smooth voice singing to me. I tightly grip the steering wheel, trying to ease some of the tension coursing through my body.

The rest of my life starts tonight.

I throw the car into drive and pull out onto the street, the soft glow of street-lights guiding my way. Throughout the entire drive to her house, butterflies swirl in my stomach.

The only thing that will ease my nerves is one three-letter answer to my question from Maria.

The woman I have loved since that day in the cafeteria.

Chapter Three

1990

∾

Five Years Prior

Maria

G od, I hate geometry.

Or math in general, if I'm being honest with myself.

I roll my shoulders as I ready myself for the next forty-five minutes of torture. I grasp the old copper doorknob of room 213, Mr. Madison's geometry class. A gust of air that smells like mold and chalk dust smacks me in the face as I swing it open. None of my friends are with me in this class, so not only do I struggle, but I have no one to help me through it. Or pass notes to. Not that I'm close to any of them, but it helps. The only saving grace is that my lunch period is right after.

With my books clutched to my chest, I walk over to Mr. Madison's desk and drop my homework into the black plastic tray that rests in the corner.

"Hello, Ms. Bryant. So *nice* of you to join us today." His comment is dripping with sarcasm because side note—I skip this class from time to time.

He looks over his dirty glasses at me with a sneer, his greasy nose shining like a disco ball. "Should we expect at least a C today?" As usual, he smells like mothballs. He's wearing another ugly 80s sweater, and his toupee is two shades lighter than the natural hair that he has. He looks like the uncle you can't stand to be around at family dinners.

I hate this teacher.

I lower my head and murmur back to him, "Mm-hmm." Pretty sure that paper will get me a D at best.

On heavy feet and with an anxious heart, I make my way to my seat, last row, corner desk right by the window. This seat is perfect because it allows me to blend into the background, making me feel invisible. Plus, I can look out the window and let my mind wander instead of focusing on how to calculate the distance of a triangle.

As I approach my desk and tear my eyes away from the floor, my heart skips a beat and I stop dead. I'm met with the most beautiful brown eyes I have ever seen, staring at me, following me as I land at my desk.

It's Sam Harper.

He's the one guy that I've always had a little crush on. Okay ... a big crush. Huge crush. We've never spoken, but when he's in the hallway, my eyes always find him somehow. He's the type of guy that exudes confidence but isn't cocky, nice without being fake, and gorgeous without being too full of himself. Also, he is one of the oldest in our class. Sixteen.

He's kinda perfect.

But right now? Well, he's sitting in the seat right beside mine, which is weird because it's been vacant all year. I know he hasn't been in this class—trust me, I would have noticed—so I can't seem to figure out what he's doing here. My eyes dart around the room, still trying to process what's going on and also looking for an answer. I find none. Obviously.

Our eyes meet again as I shift my focus back to him, and he responds with a gentle smile. The moment his attention lands on me, my face becomes warm, and my knees turn to jelly. Which causes me to stumble into my desk as it shifts, scraping against the floor. He snickers.

Way to be graceful, Maria.

Settling into my seat, I shove my books into the tray below. With a tired exhale, I grab my math book and open it, dreading the next lecture full of equations and formulas. I'm also trying my hardest to regain my composure because the air has escaped my lungs. How in the world one small smile can affect me this way is mind-boggling, to say the least.

His eyes are on me as I tap my pencil on my notebook, looking straight ahead at the chalkboard because if I look at him, I may melt.

"Hey," he says. His voice is husky and masculine, like I knew it would be.

Oh, God! He's talking to me. Sam Harper is talking. To me!

I turn my head, which feels woozy, and offer him a nervous smile. "Hey." He pivots in his desk to face me. He stares, not talking, which is unnerving, to say the least.

It is intoxicating.

Finally, I can't take it anymore. "Have you always been in this class?" I ask out of pure curiosity because I'm sure I would have seen him.

"Nope. Just transferred yesterday." He extends his hand across the aisle. "We've never actually met. I'm Sam."

He wants to shake hands? Who does that? What are we, thirty?

After sitting my pencil down, I reach out and grab his hand to shake it because what else am I supposed to do? What I wasn't expecting was the jolt of electricity that surges through me when our hands connect. My breath catches because it's like nothing I've experienced before. He must feel it, too, because his grip on my hand tightens. We study each other, our eyes locked across the aisle.

Now that I have a second to take him in, I do. Sitting behind the desk, his tall frame is concealed from sight. Sam's height is perfect, making him appear both confident and approachable. He isn't basketball tall but not the average girl height either. I haven't been close enough to him to know if he towers over me. I wish I knew, though. His hair is dark and cut close to his head and styled perfectly. His shoulders are broad, and his grip on my hand is firm and not letting up. Which I like.

With a sly smile and his eyes filled with mischief, he asks, "Is it okay that I sit next to you, Maria?"

Wait. HE KNOWS MY NAME!?!

I open my mouth to answer him and tell him he can sit here every day just as Mr. Madison starts class. "Alright, people! Let's get started!"

I moan internally at the interruption. Sam clears his throat and drops his hand, releasing his grip. The warmth of his touch lingers as he turns in his seat to face the front of the class, looking completely unaffected by the events of the last two minutes.

Class begins, and Mr. Madison drones on and on about … something math-related. The chalk is gliding over the blackboard as he explains equation after equation. I have no clue what he's trying to teach us because I can't stop thinking about something as simple as a handshake and how cute Sam's smile is.

And how intense his stare was.

And how it made me feel.

The minutes tick by and instead of paying attention, I doodle. It's no wonder I'm struggling in this class. Suddenly, I'm taken aback when, out of nowhere, Sam's hand extends across the aisle to my desk, gripping a pencil. He's jotting down a note next to my flower doodle. I watch as his hand pulls back, and I scan the words on the page.

`You didn't answer my question.`

I glance up at Mr. Madison to make sure he isn't looking, then my eyes dart to Sam. He's playing the part of the star student, paying attention as if geometry is his favorite subject. Mr. Madison's back is to us, oblivious to what's happening in the last row of his class. I take my pencil and reach across to his notebook. Sam slyly slides it closer to me. I write.

`You can sit here. I don't mind.`

He reads it and gives me a quick side glance and a slight smile, checks Mr. Madison, then reaches over and starts writing again. His words appear one at a time as the anticipation grows in my belly. I'm mesmerized by his masculine hand manipulating the pencil as I swallow the nervous lump in my throat.

`I have lunch next period. Care to join me?`

I smile when I read the words and glance up to look at him. I know his lunch is next period, like mine, since I always try to find him in the crowd. His stare is pleading, as his brow furrows, a clear sign that he genuinely cares.

I mouth my answer. "Yes."

Relief floods his face as he lets out a long breath. He sits back in his seat, a look of pure satisfaction washes over him.

I think geometry is my new favorite class.

The bell rings, and the entire class stands up and leaves like it's on fire as Mr. Madison spews off our homework assignment.

Mr. Madison is no one's favorite, apparently.

As I bend over to gather up my stuff, Sam lightly grasps my elbow. "I'll meet you there, okay?" I turn to face him, and his eyes tighten. It's like he thinks I'm going to change my mind.

I'm not. "Okay," I choke out and plaster on a nervous smile.

He grins, grabs his books, and practically runs out of the classroom. Honestly, I was kinda hoping we would walk down together, but whatever.

After a quick stop at my locker to grab my afternoon books, I weave through the crowded hallway as the next bell rings.

As soon as I cross the threshold of the open cafeteria doors, I hear my name from across the room.

"Maria!"

My head snaps up at the sound of my name, and I see Sam waving me over from a table in the corner. It's the most coveted table in the cafeteria because it's out of the way and private.

My heart thumps, quick and hard, as I wave back and maneuver through the other students to reach him. He continues to watch me as I pass the popular table, the band geeks, the burnouts, and the nerds. A knot of nervousness tightens in my stomach. Once I get closer, I spot him clenching and unclenching his hands. He's nervous, too. Why in the world would he be nervous? It's only me. Boring Maria. Unless he actually cares.

Now that's a crazy thought.

I reach the table, and the first thing that catches my attention is the colorful floral tablecloth. One that looks like it belongs on my grandmother's dining room table. Gently, I place my books down, and my eyes immediately focus on a handmade tented sign.

Reserved.

Also, in the center rests a small vase with two fake red roses in it. Two pieces of rolled plastic ware lie in front of our seats.

I shake my head, trying to process what is going on. Then, it clicks into place. The reason he rushed out of class now makes sense. He was here ... doing this.

For me.

All the commotion of the cafeteria fades into the background, and I can't help the huge smile that stretches across my face. I study him as he comes around and pulls out my chair for me.

I'm pretty sure I'm going to die because this feels like a date. In the cafeteria. During school hours.

It's a first but I'm digging it.

I want to appear confident, so I round my shoulders and raise my chin. "I was hoping you wouldn't have changed your mind." The words come out hoarse as I sit and he scoots me closer.

With a playful snicker, he circles the table and pulls up a chair, positioning himself across from me. "Are you kidding me? Not a snowball's chance in hell. I have been planning this for months."

Wait ... he's been planning this for months? Sam. Cute, adorable Sam that I have always watched and admired from afar. The boy that always seemed too far out of my league. The most beautiful guy in the entire school has been planning this. For months. For me.

Impossible.

I can feel the blush creep onto my neck and face at this revelation.

He continues. "I'm sorry. I shouldn't have rushed out of class like that." He shrugs. "I was just nervous, I guess."

He was nervous? I can't process that statement, so I turn my head downward and wipe my palms on my jeans.

Out of nowhere, Sam snaps his fingers, causing me to jolt upright. Ricky Holland comes scurrying over ... wearing a freaking white plastic apron. The same ones the cafeteria ladies wear.

I suppress a giggle, barely audible. Ricky is the class clown, and this whole set up fits him to a tee.

"Hello and welcome to Cafe Fitch," he starts, his eyes darting between me and Sam. I look across the table at Sam, bewildered at what is happening.

He winks at me. My stomach flips.

Ricky continues. "Today's selections are Pizza Noodle Casserole with a side salad. For dessert, we are offering a chocolate brownie smothered in icing." He whips out a small, spiraled notebook from his back jean pocket. "What can I get the lovely lady to drink today?"

I glance at Sam, not sure if I should play along or not. "You heard him," Sam gestures to Ricky. "Order whatever you want to drink. I wish there were more menu options, though. We may have to dine elsewhere tomorrow."

I can't believe this is happening. Nobody has done something this sweet for me. Ever.

Ricky stands tall, his eyes fixed on me as he patiently waits for my so-called order, pencil and notebook in hand. "I'll have a Sprite."

"Certainly." Ricky writes this down as if it's hard to remember. For him, it might be. "And for you, sir?" He shifts his attention to Sam.

"I'll have a Coke."

Ricky scribbles down Sam's drink and bows to us. "I will be back momentarily with your drinks and entrees. In the meantime, would you like to order an appetizer? Today, we are offering bags of chips and pretzels."

"No, thank you. We're good." Sam replies between gritted teeth. I'm thinking Ricky may have taken his duties too far because his grin is playful as he turns and gets in the food line.

This whole thing is surreal. And pretty darn amazing.

I lean forward on my elbows. "What did you do to talk him into this?"

"I have to pay for his lunch for the rest of the school year." Sam leans back in his chair, resting his forearm on the worn wood. "Totally worth it."

There is an awkward pause after this loaded admission, and now it feels like we are the only two people in this noisy cafeteria. My whole undivided attention is on Sam.

"You said that you have been planning this for months." Sam nods his head in agreement. "Why?"

He cocks his head to the side, as if I should know the answer to my own question. His face softens.

"Because I have been wanting to ask you out for so long. I never had the nerve. So, I figured, start small with a cafeteria date."

"Is that even a thing?" I can't contain my amusement as a soft laugh bubbles up from my throat.

"It is now." Sam's hand stretches across the table, his palm open and inviting. With his eyes locked on mine, I ease my hand inch by inch to meet his as the tablecloth moves and shifts. The thrill of feeling his touch is growing with each passing second. I'm pretty sure I won't be able to eat my lunch due to how many butterflies are swarming around in my stomach. My breath is quickening as Sam's fingertips lightly brush against mine.

"Here you are." Out of nowhere, Ricky reappears, causing us to jerk in surprise and tearing us away from the moment. On instinct, I pull my hand away, as does Sam. Ricky now has a white paper napkin draped over his arm. He must have forgotten this part of his costume earlier. He gently places the trays on the table. "Please be careful. The trays may be hot. Is there anything else I can get you today?"

"No, that's all," Sam counters. "You can go sit with Brittany now. Thanks, man."

Ricky pulls down hard on the plastic apron, and it snaps in half. "Thank God!" He balls it up and throws it at Sam hitting him in the face. We watch as Ricky trudges off in a huff to his girlfriend Brittany a few tables over. As he approaches her, he leans in to kiss her on the cheek, but she jerks away. "How come you have never done anything like that for me?" The disgust on her face matches her tone.

Sam and I turn back around, laughing under our breaths.

I take a bite of my casserole, which is by far one of the best things on the menu. "You've set the bar kinda high now, Sam. For all the guys."

"Possibly." He takes a bite, chews it, and swallows. "But if you really like a girl, you need to go full throttle." I stop mid-bite and look at him as he winks at me.

What is he saying? Plus, that wink is going to be the death of me.

I lower my plastic fork. "You like me?"

With a slight lean forward, he utters in a quiet whisper. "I've liked you for a really long time."

This can't be happening.

With every ounce of courage, I muster the strength to ask my next question, feeling my entire world spiraling into chaos. "Why didn't you say anything sooner?"

"You were with that loser, Max." He takes a bite of his food as I watch him, trying to take this in.

He's right. I did date Max for a few months, and he did turn out to be a world class loser. But if I had known that Sam was interested ... well, I would have broken up with Max *way* sooner than I did.

I take a drink of my Sprite, using the few seconds to compose myself as the bubbles coat my throat. "You said that you have been planning this for months." I need the details.

"Yep. I was just waiting for the right day. The right time. When I requested to switch to your geometry class, I knew today was the day."

"Wait." I shake my head in disbelief. "You switched to my class. On purpose?"

I can't breathe.

"We didn't have any classes together." He says it so casually as he drinks me in with his eyes. It's the same intense stare he gave me in class and when I arrived here. A stare that is doing crazy things to my emotions.

I glance away to break the connection. "So, is this our first date?"

He shrugs. "Sure. Why not? But I really want to take you on a proper date if you'll let me."

"Are you asking me out?"

"I am."

As I smile, I can feel my cheeks heat. I glance at my pizza noodle casserole, now cold and unappetizing, as I try to gather my thoughts. I can't bring myself to look at him because my nerves are completely shattered by now. The words are bubbling up inside me, ready to burst, as I know exactly what I'm going to say. There is no other way to answer this. My eyes slowly meet his again.

"I would love to go out with you."

The last fifteen minutes of lunch fly by due to the ease of our conversation. It flows. So relaxed. And so good.

The bell rings, and we both frown, not wanting this to end. He gathers up our trays and slips me a piece of paper with his number on it. I give him mine as well, and a promise to eat together tomorrow.

We reluctantly part ways as we each head to our next class.

I leave the cafeteria, walking on a cloud, and I can't help but wonder ... if my life just began.

Chapter Four

1995

∞

Maria

As I wait for Sam to arrive for our date, I'm resting on my couch, feeling like I want to vomit. I've composed myself after my bathroom meltdown. My knee bobs with nerves as I steal glances at the clock, each passing minute heightening the suspense of his arrival. I'm turning his Dear John letter into my hands. More than likely, this will be the last letter I write to Sam.

Because that's what Sam and I do. We write letters to each other, and we live only ten minutes apart. There was nothing better than the jolt of excitement that would pierce through me when I would open the mailbox and find one waiting for me. Sam's words would act like a warm blanket around my heart.

I'll miss those letters more than anything.

A flash of light streaming in from the window from his headlights breaks up my memories, followed by tires crunching on the driveway. A wave of anxiety washes over me, making my stomach twist and turn as if I could hurl any second.

He's here.

Standing on shaking legs, I clear my throat, the only sound in the quiet room. The moment he lays eyes on me, he'll realize something is wrong. My long blonde hair is in a ponytail, I have no makeup on my green eyes, and my tall, slim frame (which has gotten thinner thanks to stress) is in pajamas. Definitely not date-approved attire.

I slide back the curtain that overlooks the front of the house and watch him stride up the walkway to my parents' split-level home. My heart aches because he looks incredible. The sight of his hopeful smile is like a dagger to my chest, causing a dull pain to spread throughout my whole body.

He has no clue what is about to hit him. And for whatever reason, he looks extra nervous tonight. He keeps running his hand through his hair, and he appears restless.

Strange.

I regain my composure, trying to steady myself. I use my free hand to grasp the cool door handle while keeping the letter hidden behind my back. The door creaks on its hinges as I slowly open it, trying to prolong the inevitable. The cool night air hits me as well as his smile, which was there a moment ago, but vanishes as soon as he sees me.

He lets out a small gasp as his eyebrows pinch together. "Maria, are you okay? Why aren't you dressed? Are you sick?" His face is a canvas of concern. Concern rooted in nothing but love.

I think I'm going to pass out.

I lay my hand on my stomach and try hard to keep my composure and not cry. "No, I'm not okay, Sam. And I'm not going out tonight." My voice cracks.

His head cocks to the side as he tries to gather his thoughts. "Wait, what? So, are you sick?" I don't answer. A few seconds pass. "Maria, you're scaring me. What is going on?"

God, this is harder than I thought it was going to be.

With a trembling hand and a quivering voice, I pull the letter from behind my back and hold it out as my chest tightens. "I explain everything in here." The wind picks up slightly, brushing a loose piece of my hair into my eyes.

He takes the letter from my outstretched hand and stares at it, his brows furrowed. "Maria, what is this?" he questions, his eyes narrowing as he examines the envelope. He tears his attention away from the letter and walks up the first step toward me. My feet have a mind of their own, and I recede backward toward the door, grabbing the handle from behind me.

If I get any closer to him, I'll collapse. I can already sense my resolve crumbling; the intensity of the moment is overwhelming. Tears are forming in my eyes, and the thick night air is weighing me down. "I'm so sorry, Sam. Please forgive me." As quickly as I can and without looking at him, I turn and bolt into the house, leaving the love of my life stunned and confused on my front step. As I shut the door, I rest my head against the cool metal. The tears are threatening to spill over, so I close my eyes tightly, trying to hold them back.

Because I can't let *him* know I care.

"There. That wasn't so hard, was it?" The conniving voice cuts through the thick tension. I open my eyes and Chad, my supposed new boyfriend, is on the couch, both arms stretched out on the back cushions, his ankle resting on his knee. He arrived this afternoon and made a point to stay until it unfolded.

My anger is building as I lock eyes with him. The side table lamp casts a glow on his face, revealing a victorious smirk and a menacing stare. I scoff and quickly shift my eyes to the carpet to help quell my anger. Starting an argument right now wouldn't be the smartest idea.

His footsteps grow closer as he stands and walks toward me, stopping inches from my body, his cheap aftershave assaulting my nose. As he leans into me, his warm breath tickles my shoulder, fueling my anger. He trails soft kisses up my neck until his mouth is right next to my ear, every smack of his lips making my skin crawl. "I can make you so much happier than he ever could," he says in a low whisper.

Out of nowhere, his grip tightens on my chin, forcefully slamming my head against the door, causing an excruciating pain to shoot through my skull. His face and black rage-filled eyes are mere inches from mine. "You will *not* contact him again, will you, Pookie?" His tone is seething and full of venom. There is no mistaking the threat in his question. For my safety and Sam's, I give him the answer he wants.

Why, you may ask again? Because it's complicated.

Taking a moment to compose myself, I prepare to feed him what he wants to hear. "No. Never. It's over." His lips crash into mine, and I can taste the turkey sandwich he ate right before Sam arrived. He forcefully breaks our connection and lets go of my face. Then—acting as if he didn't just assault me—he places a gentle kiss on my forehead.

"That's my good girl. Now keep being a good girl, and I won't have to act out again. Understood?"

As his question lingers, a sudden pounding at the door jolts me out of my thoughts, the vibrations reverberating through my body.

Chad's palm covers my mouth, and he presses his finger up to his lips. "Shhhh..."

Chapter Five

1995

∞

Sam

What in the world just happened?

Left standing on Maria's doorstep, tension builds with each passing second. The contents of the mysterious envelope hold my sole focus.

A letter I'm not sure I want to read.

The world comes to a halt, and my racing heartbeat fills my ears. When Maria walked out of the house with her shoulders slumped and her expression full of sadness, I knew something wasn't right. Plus, my girl looked exhausted. The first thing that caught my attention was the dark circles under her puffy eyes, which is why I assumed she was sick. That coupled with her coming to the door in her PJs when she knew we had a date tonight.

Thoughts are swirling around in my head like a tornado. I look back at my car, wondering if I should stay or leave, and that's when it catches my eye, making me pause and take a second look. I notice a vibrant red Corvette parked on the street. The streetlights reflecting off of its polished surface. My nerves were so shot when I arrived, I didn't see the obnoxious car.

Clearly out of place in this middle-class neighborhood.

Whose car is that?

What is going on?

I have no clue how to reconcile this in my head, so I do the only thing that makes the most sense. Mustering up the courage and with a swift motion, I tear open the envelope. Paper ripping fills the air, mixing with the crickets as my eyes scan the words written on the letter.

Dear Sam,

I am so sorry, but I have to be honest with you. I've met someone. Chad, my manager at the warehouse. I am in love with him.

I hope you can find it in your heart to forgive me and move on. I want you to be as happy as I am. You deserve to be happy.

Regards,

Maria

My throat has gone completely dry, and heat is rising in my body. I'm pretty sure my head is going to explode, and I'm suddenly weak in the knees. I stumble backward, running my fingers through my hair.

Wait. Did I just read that right? Because there is no way.

As I read and reread the letter, the words seem to blur together, leaving me more and more confused.

She's met someone?

Chad?

She's in love with him?

None of this makes sense.

Yet, it does. This would explain why she has been acting strangely. The distant behavior, the shorter hugs, the quick phone calls. But why? Why would she throw this away? Two months ago, we were talking about baby names for our future children while I cuddled her on the couch.

I pinch the bridge of my nose, trying to ease the instant headache I have. *This can't be it. I need more answers.* The light is on, so I know she is still in the living room. Breathing heavily with determination, I march up the remaining steps and knock on the door.

"Maria! Maria, open the door and come out here so we can talk."

Nothing.

I pound on the door, this time with my fist, the metal cold on my flesh. "Come on! I know you're in there." *Why isn't she coming out?* "Maria! Please don't do this!"

Silence.

I continue to beat on the door, the force jolting through my body. "MARIA!!" I scream, not caring who can hear me. More pounding. "Maria, please!"

Crickets.

I'm out of breath as I rest my forehead on the door, my hand sprawled on the cool aluminum, unsure of what to do next. Suddenly, I'm shrouded in darkness as the porch light goes off. I take a step back, peering at the door. The click of the lock follows, then the living room goes dark.

Well, there you have it. Message sent and received.

Fifteen minutes ago, I was pacing back and forth in my apartment, trying to calm my nerves at the thought of proposing to this incredible woman.

Now, I'm standing on her porch ... and she's gone. She's left me in the dark, both literally and figuratively. Just like that.

I look down at the letter, fold it in half, and shove it in my pocket. As I turn to leave, I glance one last time at the house. A house that minutes ago felt like a second home. Now, it will forever be the crime scene that is my life. And all I can think is ... she's behind that closed door with someone new. Someone better. *Chad.*

With my heart and entire future shattered in one fell swoop, I walk to my car, feeling the weight of rejection in every step. Hanging my head in defeat, I get into the rust bucket. I mean, what else am I supposed to do? If she doesn't want me, I'll leave. I'm not about to make a fool out of myself and beg. Even though I feel a pull to do just that ... beg. Force her to tell me what is going on. But I won't.

Honestly, I think I may be in shock. I'm numb.

Once I start the car, Michael Bolton's voice blares from the cassette player, singing about love. With force, I jab the off button. He's the last thing I want to hear right now. I reverse out of the driveway and yank the gearshift into drive. As I inch forward, I pull my beat-up Ford Taurus alongside the shiny red Corvette and stop.

Chad's Vette.

The contrast of the two cars mirrors the two men who own them. Rich and fancy versus poor and regular. As I stare at the car, the reason for her choice becomes obvious.

Maria wants shiny. And I am dull.

Who wouldn't choose the Corvette?

Maybe I didn't know her at all. I guess some things I'll never know.

With that thought, I angrily press my foot to the gas pedal until it hits the floor. The tires screech on the blacktop road, and I race away, wishing my Taurus was the Corvette she wants.

As soon as I step foot into *our*—I mean, *my* apartment—I throw the door shut, causing the walls to shake. Anger is radiating off my body. Kicking my loafers off, I head straight for the fridge, grab a Heineken, and pop off the cap. The cold iciness of the beer coats my throat as the first swig goes down. It does nothing to help the dull ache in my heart. I chug the whole thing practically in one gulp as I pace the floor. Frustrated, I tug at my hair, hoping to find some relief from the intense emotions that are coursing through me. I plop down on the couch, not knowing what to do next. With this night *or* my life.

I slam the beer down on the stained, used Formica coffee table, which shakes on impact. I reach into my pocket and pull out the letter to read it again.

Then again.

And again.

One more time.

I can't take this anymore.

Anger swells in my chest as I ball up the letter and crash it down on the coffee table. The force of my fist causes the legs to give out on the piece of crap. The table breaks and crashes onto the old brown carpet. Along with my beer. I stare and watch as the alcohol pours out, soaking the carpet.

Something about this dumb coffee table breaking sets me off.

With force, I grab the bottle off the floor and throw it at the wall. It shatters, sending shards of glass all over the living room.

I need to release this rage—or heartbreak—that consumes me. I throw my arms and head back and scream. "AAAAHHHHH!" The primal and rage-filled sound that erupts from my throat causes my voice to strain. I fall to my knees, the beer puddle seeping through my pants.

Then I cry.

I cover my face and let it out. I cry like I'm a toddler who just got their favorite stuffed animal thrown away. Because that's what happened. My favorite person in the universe is gone.

I give myself the time I need to cry this out. Alone. Because now, that's what I am.

After a few minutes, I pick myself off of the floor and wipe away any evidence of my breakdown from my face. Then, I make a promise to myself.

I will never cry a single tear for her again.

And I mean it. Not one tear.

As I walk over to the fridge to get another beer, my legs feel as heavy as my heart. A wave of emotional exhaustion takes over. Having a total freak out takes a lot out of you, I guess.

I open the door, the light from the inside illuminating my dark apartment. I peer down, and I'm met with a package of wrapped processed cheese, a box of baking soda, and a questionable carton of milk. No beer in sight. I'm out. Because, of course, I am.

I slam the door shut in anger, and it shakes on its hinges. Stepping over the debris of the broken coffee table, I reach for the phone and pick it up. I would go to the store to get more, but I don't trust that I won't drive to her house and break Chad's face. So, I call the one person who I know will be here with a six-pack in hand. No questions asked.

I dial my best friend Ricky's number. Ricky and I grew up together on the same street, two houses away from each other. Since I have three sisters, he is the closest thing I have to a brother.

The phone rings a handful of times before he picks up.

"Hello."

"Ricky, it's Sam."

"Sam!" he exclaims. I jerk the receiver from my ear. Loud music and commotion radiates from his end of the line. No doubt a party at his place. "Why are you calling me? Wait, are you wanting me to be your best man? Because, of course, the answer is—"

"She broke up with me."

Silence.

"I'm on my way."

"Bring beer."

The line goes dead.

Twenty minutes later, there's a knock on my apartment door.

"Come in!" I yell from the living room. I parked my butt here as soon as I hung up the phone, and I haven't moved. The apartment is pitch black, and I'm staring off into nothing.

Like I said, numb.

The creak of the door echoes throughout the quiet dark space, along with his footsteps. He's approaching slowly. "Sam, you in here?" Ricky calls out. The clanking of glass follows as he sits the beer on the kitchen counter.

"Yep."

He flips on the light switch, and I shield my eyes from the brightness. His footsteps grow louder as he gets closer. Out of the corner of my eye, I glimpse him surveying the room. "Dude, what the heck happened in here?" He takes in the scene laid out before him. Broken coffee table, spilled beer, broken glass littering the carpet.

I take in my surroundings, trying to see things from his perspective. *It looks bad.*

"I had a moment." My voice is void of any emotion and a little hoarse. I screamed it all out, I guess. This must be what heartbreak feels like.

I stand and walk to the kitchen counter, zombie-like. He brought two packs of beer. *Outstanding!* I grab one, rip off the cap, and drink. The alcohol lingers on my tongue, a reminder of my worsening mood. But I down it anyway. Maybe if I drink enough, it will dull this ache.

"I guess so," he mutters, his eyes lingering on the destruction, finally shifting to me. He gives me a once over. "You look like crap."

I salute him with my beer. "Thanks."

"What happened?"

With the bottle in hand, I gesture toward the crumbled-up letter lying on the floor, my motions robotic. He reaches down for it, as I grab the handle of one of the six-packs and sit down on the couch, resting the beer at my feet since my coffee table is now a goner. Ricky grabs the letter and sits as well, the couch shifting with his weight.

He holds out the letter, now crinkled with a wet spot in the corner. Probably beer. "Please tell me this isn't what I think it is."

"I call it '*The Chad.*'" His brows furrow in confusion. "Read it and find out."

He unfolds the letter and lays it on the couch cushions, smoothing it out with his hands. I down the rest of the beer as he reads. Which doesn't take long since the letter, or I mean, *The Chad*, is short and sweet. But, man, does it pack quite a punch? He looks at me, then reads it again.

"She's in love with him?" His eyes scan Maria's words, which shattered my heart.

"Apparently so."

"So, like what? Did she fall in love with him at work?"

"No clue."

He rubs his hand down his face. "Sam. This makes no sense."

"I know. Trust me, I know." Visions of his hands on her makes me grab another beer, open it, and take a swig. I should feel better soon. "And to add insult to injury, he was there."

Ricky's jaw drops. "He was there?"

"Yep. Him and his shiny red Corvette."

"Geez."

The story spills out of me from start to finish, and he listens, nodding every so often.

"*The Chad* is a good name for this piece of crap," he says as he shakes the letter.

"Yep."

"So, what are you going to do now?" Curiosity fills his question.

"Well, right now"—I look around on the floor for the remote to the TV. I find it resting next to the couch, pick it up, and press the power button—"I just want to dull this ache in my chest with some booze, share a beer with my friend, and watch the game."

Ricky scoots his body down on the couch. "Well, okay then." He discards the letter back onto the floor, and my eyes track the last piece I have of Maria as it soars through the air and lands on some glass. Looking away, I hand him a beer, and we watch basketball.

As the time passes, I try to pretend like Maria's not at her house with Chad. Kissing him, holding him, loving him.

I grab another beer.

At some point during the evening, perhaps at around beer number five, or maybe it was six, I passed out.

The closing of my door jolts me awake, and I find myself on the couch, only wearing my shirt from last night and boxers, reeking of my poor decisions. The light streaming in from the window isn't doing much for my pounding headache, so I shield my face. Slowly, I sit up, rubbing my eyes, allowing them to adjust to the brightness. I survey the room, and I can't believe what I'm seeing.

It's spotless. As if nothing happened here.

After I passed out, Ricky must have fixed my coffee table, cleaned up the broken glass, thrown away the empty beer bottles, and vacuumed my carpet. I was out cold.

How drunk was I?

Scratching my head and standing on unsteady legs, I walk straight to the bathroom. After a shower and a glass of water to help with my obvious dehydration, my focus and current situation come roaring back to me. The breakup letter is lying on the counter next to a note from Ricky.

A fuzzy memory flashes in my mind. *Wait ... did I nickname her letter?* The events of last night after I called Ricky seem to blur together in my mind.

I did. I glance back at *The Chad* letter, then at Ricky's note, written on the back of the electric bill envelope.

```
I ran out to get us some breakfast and coffee. You
really need to go grocery shopping. Your milk was
spoiled. I know this because I took a swig before
looking.
    P.S. I cleaned up but wasn't sure if I should
throw it away.
```

By *it*, I'm assuming he means her letter. On impulse, I pick it up and read it ... again. The entire night comes flooding back into my brain.

Turns out I still have a broken heart, which is now coupled with a hangover. A fun combination.

Did she wake up thinking about him? The thought makes me sick to my stomach. I crinkle up *The Chad* letter again (it's a miracle it's still in one piece at this point) and walk over to the trash can, opening the lid. Broken glass and beer bottles stare back at me as my shaking hand hovers over the can.

But something stops me. I don't know what or why, but I can't bring myself to throw it away. Maybe it's because it's Maria's last words to me. Or I am a glutton for punishment and want to hold on to the hurt.

Whatever the reason, I smooth it out, fold it up, and walk to my bedroom. As soon as I open the door, my eyes land on the black velvet box still resting on my dresser. It's staring at me, taunting me. Which causes another thought to pop in my head.

The ring!

I head over to the hamper, grab my pants from last night, and fish out the wad of tissue paper. Gently, I unfold it and watch as the ring appears, looking as beautiful as it did the day I bought it.

But instead of it being on her finger right now, it's resting on a bed of tissue in my palm. Remembering the promise I made to myself, I force down the tears that are starting to form. With an unsteady hand, I gingerly place the ring back in the velvet box. It snaps shut as I grab it, and along with the letter, I walk to my closet that's missing a door. On the top shelf is an orange Nike box that has all the letters that Maria has written to me. Years' worth of letters. I grab it, open it, and place inside *The Chad* letter and the ring.

Is it unhealthy to keep them both? Probably.

But that ring and letter are all I have left of Maria. And I'm not ready to let go.

Not yet.

So, before Ricky gets back and tries to talk me out of it, I grab a pen and a piece of paper and I write one last letter.

Chapter Six

1995

THREE DAYS LATER

My Dearest Maria,

It's been less than twenty-four hours and I already miss you. I'm not telling you this to make you feel guilty. I just want you to know. And if I'm being honest, you never gave me a chance to tell you how I feel about this whole thing. You took the easy way out. And maybe that's because Chad was there. He was there, wasn't he? I know he was. I saw his obnoxious car parked out front. I mean a Corvette for crying out loud. You always hated flashy sports cars. Anyway, after you gave me the letter, I bet you went right back inside and the two of you celebrated.

That was mean. Forget I said that.

I can't for the life of me figure out why you would do this to us. I'm sure he's richer and better looking. But I know he can't possibly treat you better than I did. There's no way. And I know I can't give you everything materially, but I would have died for you. Given up everything for you. I can't help but wonder if Chad would part with his Corvette for you. Doubtful. If this is about the money, then I guess I had no chance.

I am so mad at you. Yet, I'm so in love with you. I'm not used to feeling this way. Granted, we've had our arguments, but this. This new feeling of anger I have towards you. Well, I don't like it. And I don't know how to fix it. There is no fixing this. Because you broke us. I'm sitting here seething, knowing that you are kissing and touching him. I don't understand. And I never will. No explanation will be good enough. I'm not sure I can ever forgive you.

Anyway, this is probably the last time I will get to communicate with you. I mean, I'm not going to beg you to come back to me. I have some dignity and pride. Your letter told me all that I need to know about where you are in life. But I want you to know how I feel. Maybe I didn't tell you enough. God, I hate all of this self-doubt and questions that are swirling around in my head.

So if I can't get answers, I'm going to tell you what I need you to know. Maria, loving you felt impossible. It felt surreal. It felt explosive. It felt illogical. But it felt worth it. You were the one woman that was worth it. I know that sounds weird to say but, when I'm with you, I lose all rational thought. You are the one thing in my life that I would give up everything for. Everything I thought I knew or wanted to be. Everything I own, or would own. Everything I needed or desired. I would have traded it all for you. I love you, Maria. Now and always. I truly hope you are happy. Because your happiness means more to me than my feelings for you. But mostly, I'm sad that this is the last letter I will write to you.

Yours,

Sam

Maria

As tears stream down my face, I delicately fold up the letter, holding it close to my heart.

In the darkness of my room, I sit on the edge of the bed, overwhelmed by the weight of the pain I've caused Sam. When I got home from work, I saw the letter resting on the counter, waiting for me. It's been three days since I broke up with Sam. Three days of lying and pretending like this is what I wanted. Three days of packing up my things because, after Sam left, Chad handed me a key and *told* me I was moving into an apartment he was going to rent for me.

Essentially, Chad will have control over all aspects of my life. My job, my schedule, my money, and now, where I will live.

I don't want to move, of course, but I have to. But for reasons that I am not yet ready to accept responsibility for, I am going along with it all.

Whenever Chad touches me or kisses me, it's like needles stabbing my skin, and I have to fight the urge to run. It's like a death sentence and a constant reminder of the choice I made. My flight or fight response kicks in, but I push it down. His touch feels foreign and borderline painful. Nothing like how Sam feels.

And honestly, since that day, Chad has been treating me with kindness and tenderness. The intimidating, scary person who was there that night seemed to disappear. I mean, why wouldn't he be happy? He got what he wanted.

Me.

But that doesn't mean I want any of this.

Despite the blur of tears, I force myself to read the letter again, trying to fully grasp what Sam has said.

He thinks I want money. *It's of no importance to me.*

He thinks I don't love him. *My love for Sam will endure until my final breath.*

He will not fight for me. *Why would he? I broke his heart. I wouldn't fight for myself, either.*

Looking at his handwriting is unbearable. I can't take it anymore, so I get up from my bed and walk to my closet, the old blue carpet from my youth soft under my feet. I slide open the door, and I'm met with empty hangers and some odds and ends that I'm not taking with me. But there is one box that's staying.

With a heavy heart, I navigate to the back of the space, lowering myself down onto my hands and knees. Along the back wall is a small door that looks out of place. This door serves no purpose and was here when my mom and dad bought this house when I was a kid. It was my secret hiding spot for the things I wanted to keep hidden as I grew up.

As I turn the gold knob, the door opens with a creak. Resting on the floor is a floral box. I open the lid, and years of Sam's letters stare back at me. As I place this letter on top, a sudden pang of sadness grips my chest, knowing that this is the last time I will place a letter in here.

I kiss the tips of my fingers and then rest them gently on the stack of letters. "Goodbye, Sam," I whisper. With a gentle tug, I unclip his watch from my wrist, the one he gave me as a gift at graduation. I flip it over to read the inscription on the back for the last time.

The etching stares back at me. *Yours, Sam.* Tears pool in my eyes at his words. I place the watch in the box, effectively closing my time with Sam. But I hesitate as something stops me.

The memory of the day he gave it to me fills my head, replaying like a vivid movie. There's no way this watch is going in that box. It doesn't belong there. So I shove it into my front jean pocket. I'll hide it from Chad. I'm not ready to shut the door on Sam.

Not yet.

Sitting cross-legged in the middle of the living room floor, I sift through stacks of CDs, feeling the smooth plastic cases in my hands. Keys jingling and the door opening alerts me Mom is home from work. She walks through the threshold with heavy footsteps, looking tired from a long night. She's a janitor at a local hospital.

"Hey, sweetie," she greets me in a weary tone. She places her purse on the chair and sits on the couch facing me. The dark circles under her green eyes are visible against her pale skin, and her dirty blonde hair is a mess. Proof that she worked her butt off. She's also looked thinner lately. More than likely, she's not eating much because of stress. Like mother, like daughter.

"Hey, Mom. How was work?" I ask, even though I know the answer. She cleaned up vomit, poop, and blood. I'm sure it sucked. But she won't admit to that.

"Good. Not too busy tonight." She sounds exhausted, and yet I can feel her intense stare on me.

"Mm-hmm," I murmur in response as I study a Celine Dion CD, trying to decide if I want to take it with me. Chad loves Celine Dion, so it's staying. I sit it back on the CD rack.

"So, did you see the letter that I left you on the counter?" She knows I saw it.

"I'm not doing this tonight, Mom." I keep rummaging through CDs, hoping my curt tone gets my point across.

"Maria, you know you don't have to do this. I'm working, your father is looking for work. I'm sure he will find something soon. We will be fine."

I stop what I'm doing and toss the CDs onto the floor in a pile as they clank together. Frankly, I don't want any of them. I stand and head to the kitchen, trying to send a message that I don't want to talk. She doesn't take the hint. "Maria, honey," my mom pleads, following me, "you don't need to take care of us!"

My mom and I have had this same argument for the last few days. It started when Dad gambled away my parents' whole financial means of living. And by that, I mean they have lost everything. Their current savings, their retirement, and now they are drowning under a mountain of debt. They may even lose the house. The house I grew up in. On top of it all, my dad got fired. Another job, gone. So yes, now my mom has been working as a janitor. It's gross, back-break-ing work that she wouldn't need to be doing if it wasn't for my selfish father.

Thankfully, it's only temporary. My mom started taking night courses at Ohio Northeastern about a year ago to be an LPN. She knew she needed to work outside the home since my dad was in and out of jobs all the time. She should graduate soon, and when she does, hopefully, she can find a good-paying job as a nurse. But as of right now, this is where we are at.

Thanks, Dad.

I've never blamed my dad for losing jobs due to his disability. Employers can be cruel and not very understanding. They would always view my dad's slower processing and memory loss as him being lazy. But he's not. Far from it. When you give my dad a job to do, he will give two hundred percent every time because he wants to prove himself. But sometimes, his brain has other plans.

However, instead of trying to find more work, what does he do? He gambles. My mother would always defend him, even though the gambling caused a lot of tension in their marriage. It's the wash, rinse, and repeat of my life, and I'm so over it.

This time, he has gone too far.

Which leads me to my current life dilemma. Chad came onto me soon after I started at the warehouse. Obviously, I rejected his advances, but he didn't stop. His sexual harassment was intense and constant. I didn't dare tell Sam. I was embarrassed and scared. Plus, the money was good—great actually—and I was trying to save for our future. One I knew was coming.

But then he threatened to fire me if I didn't date him at the exact time my dad screwed up. There is no way I'm leaving my parents destitute. Even if that means making the ultimate sacrifice in losing Sam. I hope someday I can explain it to him. And that he will understand.

In anger, I turn to face her. "Yes, I do, Mom! Who else is going to help? I'm your only child, and I refuse to watch you guys lose this house, your car, or struggle to buy food and medication. Medication Dad needs. And how else am I going to pay for school? You know it will take Dad a while to find work. It always does. Chad pays really, really well, better than I deserve, and if I can do this for you, please just let me!" The words come out strangled.

My mom places both of her hands on my face. "Not if it means sacrificing your happiness," she whispers. Hearing my mom say this causes my chest to break open. And that's when the tears flow. I fall into my mom's arms and let the loss of Sam come out in a way that I haven't allowed to happen yet since the bathroom the day I gave him the letter. Mostly because Chad is always by my side, and he can't know how much this hurts.

"Maria, look at me, please," my mom demands. I pull my head away from her work shirt, now wet from my tears. "What did the letter say?"

We walk back to the couch. I lie down as she guides my head down onto her lap and rubs my hair. Just like when I was a child. "He thinks I left him for Chad's money. He said the most beautiful things about how he felt about me. I hurt him deeply, Mom. I've ruined him and the life that we had planned." The sobs become louder.

Her body stiffens, and she stops rubbing my hair. "Does Chad treat you well?"

What an odd question to ask. But then I realize why she's asking. She is reluctant to fight me on ending things with Sam anymore. It's pretty obvious that I've made my decision, and she feels as trapped as I do. As long as he treats me well, she is okay with allowing her daughter to live a life that she won't be happy in. For money.

My parents will never look the same to me again. Ever.

"Yes," I lie. My mom tenses up because she knows I'm not being truthful.

But what else am I supposed to say? If she's willing to go along with this whole charade, then who am I to tell her that Chad is manipulative and emotionally abusive with tendencies toward violence?

"I'm always here for you if you need anything," she whispers as she continues to rub my head.

"I know." Another tear falls.

She nudges for me to sit up, and as I face her, tears stream down her cheeks. "I'm going to go shower, and I'll come back down and help you pack, okay?" She kisses me on the forehead, then she disappears up the stairs.

I peel myself off the couch and stand up, feeling the weight of my life choices in my bones. I kneel back down in front of the CD rack and weed through them again. Wondering what Sam is doing right now.

Wondering if I will see him again someday.

Chapter Seven

∞

Six Months Later

Maria

"I think this is all of it," Dad says, his arms straining and sweat rolling down his temples as he carries in the last box from his car.

"Thanks, Dad," I reply. "How are you feeling?" I ask as I rest my hand gently on his forearm.

He gives me a small smile as he squeezes my shoulder. "I'm fine, sweetie. Just knowing you are safe is enough." I can't look at him or I'll burst into tears, so instead, I scan my old bedroom, trying to figure out how to put my life back together again. Boxes are everywhere, clothes on hangers rest on my bed, and garbage bags full of what, I don't know, rest at my feet.

My mom walks in, holding out a glass of water for both my dad and me. I happily take it. "Do you need help getting anything unpacked?" she asks, looking around the room as I gulp down the cold water. I hold up a finger as a signal to give me a second. The water feels so refreshing after packing my stuff up from the apartment Chad rented for me and then hauling it up the stairs to my room. Sweat beads on my brow. My arms and legs feel like Jell-O, yet I have never felt better in my whole life.

"Ah!" I exclaim as I sit the glass down on my dresser. "No. I'm good, guys." I zero in on a box and open it. We had no time to label anything, so I have no clue what's inside. For the first time in a long time, my parents have been there for me. But honestly, I need to do this alone.

Earlier today, Chad and I broke up. And it wasn't pretty.

Our relationship was never a relationship. Granted, he thought it was. Once I broke up with Sam, Chad was sweet and kind to me. He would shower me with gifts, he would take me to expensive restaurants, he gave me a beautiful apartment to live in. But also, in exchange for these things, I was at his mercy. He controlled my life. And he knew it. Slowly, he alienated me from my parents.

These last six months have been an endless cycle of misery, and I've despised every single second of it. I did it for my parents, despite my suffering.

Do I regret it?

That's a hard one to answer.

My biggest regret, the one thing that will forever haunt me, is the pain I caused Sam. I'm sure I shattered him. The overwhelming feelings of loneliness and sorrow that consumed me during my time with Chad were deserved.

However, the money Chad paid me helped tremendously in getting my parents somewhat back on their feet. Paying for my schooling was the last thing on my mind. All I wanted was to help Mom and Dad.

In time, my mom graduated from nursing school and got a job at the hospital, where she worked as a janitor. After that, I knew the time had come to leave Chad, but I needed to formulate a plan to make that happen. He would not let me go easily.

Unfortunately, I didn't come up with a plan because Chad spotted Sam's watch resting on my wrist last week. I was stupid enough to keep it on one day. I always tucked it away in an old pair of shoes, hidden at the back of the closest. But Sam must have been on my mind (as he always is), and I didn't take it off. Putting it on makes me feel as if he's right there by my side.

Obviously, Chad demanded to know where it came from. I think deep down, he knew. When I didn't answer right away, and before I could register what was happening, he punched me. Never in my life have I seen someone change in the blink of an eye. When his fist came into contact with my chin, it felt like my head blew off of my body. As the pain shot through my head, tears welled up in my eyes. It was a bone-chilling, hair-raising moment that left me trembling in terror.

As I stood there, holding my cheek, I knew right then that I needed to get away. Of course, he apologized and swore that it wouldn't happen again.

Typical abuser.

As soon as he got in the shower, I called the police. They were waiting for him when he stepped out into the living room with only a towel wrapped around his waist. I'll never forget the look on his face when he rounded the corner and saw two very large police officers standing in the middle of the apartment. My favorite part, though, is what the police heard him say.

He was walking, shoulders bent, out of the bathroom and was rounding the corner toward me. Staring at his feet, he said, "Sweetie, I am really sorry. I will never hit you again." He faltered backward as he looked up and saw the police officers step out into the living room.

He backed himself into a corner and couldn't lie his way out of the hole he dug for himself.

The police escorted him out of the apartment (they wouldn't even let him get dressed) as I frantically packed up my things. I called my parents, and they arrived soon after to help. In twenty minutes, flat, my car and my dad's became filled with the things I brought with me into this relationship. He can keep the rest. I don't want one reminder of my life with him.

Chad never said a word as I walked past him, my head held high, and proclaimed, "I quit."

We are going to start the protection order process first thing in the morning.

Chad is out of my life for good.

Steam from my shower fills the bathroom as I wipe away the mirror. My hair is up in a towel, and my pink robe clings to my wet body. Leaning in closer, I inspect the area where Chad's fist contacted my chin and cheek, trying to get a better look. The bruise, once purple and prominent, is now barely visible. What remains I can cover up with makeup.

Almost two weeks have passed since that frightening day, yet it feels like longer. It's amazing how quickly I could leave Chad in the past. Even though I didn't file charges, the authorities issued a protection order against Chad, which stopped him from contacting me. I haven't heard from him since.

Good riddance.

Being back home has also given my parents and me a chance to talk, reconnect, and get closer, which has been nice. It's the best our relationship has ever been. What happened, though, six months ago continues to strain my parents' marriage. They try to hide their arguments from me, but they forget I am a grown woman now and not a child. I know what's going on.

Despite my dad's ongoing job hunt, I was fortunate enough to land a waitressing job at an upscale restaurant. The money is decent, the tips are amazing, and my boss is a woman who doesn't harass me. A total win-win.

Mostly, things in my life are looking up.

There is still one lingering matter that continues to haunt me. It's been on my mind since the day I moved back home.

I have to try to mend things with Sam, maybe repair our broken relationship.

It's Friday, and with the night off, I can finally set my plan in motion.

Honestly, it's not much of a plan, but I gotta try.

My so-called plan is to drive over to Sam's, sit down with him, and tell him every detail of what happened, and plead for his forgiveness. Forgiveness that I don't deserve.

I'm not above begging.

I have no idea how this is going to go. He could shut the door in my face. There's a good chance he may tell me to go to hell. Or it could go exactly how I've imagined it. Will we get back together?

"God, I hope so," I mutter to myself as I dust on some eyeshadow.

But if not, at least I can finally lift this weight off of my chest by telling him the truth. I have planned out what I'm going to say and replayed it repeatedly in my mind. The visuals of him at first being mad but then understanding and embracing me play in a constant loop. Our lips would meet in a passionate, earth-shattering kiss, bringing us together again.

The mere thought of his lips on mine again causes a rush of warmth to spread across my cheeks.

I knew ending it with Sam and not having him in my life would be hard. But honestly, I did not know how big of a void it would leave in my life. I miss his touch and his husky voice. I miss his strength, how his arms would encase me and make me feel safe. I miss his optimism and his honesty. And, of course, I miss his lips.

Nerves erupt in my stomach as I leave the bathroom, ready to get this show on the road. Operation Get Sam Back is in full swing!

Peering into my closest, I chose an outfit that Sam always loved on me. It's a basic black dress that showcases my legs. After taking way too long on my hair and makeup to ensure they both look perfect, I cast a final glance at myself in the full-length mirror.

Wait, I forgot something!

I walk over to my vanity, grab his watch, and slip it on my wrist. It snaps into place. A feeling of relief washes over me as I realize I will never have to hide it again.

Satisfied, I grab my purse and car keys and head out the door.

The fifteen-minute drive to his apartment feels like an eternity. And you know how it is. It seems like fate is against me tonight as I hit every red light and get stuck behind every slow driver on the road. I may have honked my horn a few times at some innocent senior citizens.

I can't help it. The feeling that the rest of my life starts tonight is making me impatient.

Finally, I pull up alongside the curb of his apartment complex. Sam's place is in the building's front, and his car parked in the carport, so he's here. There's a light on in what I know is the living room on the second floor. The high hopes causing my stomach to churn is almost too much to handle.

Being back here, a pain of regret erupts in my chest because this was supposed to be our first place together. I sit and stare at it, lost in daydreams of the different path my life could have taken if only I hadn't been so foolish and stupid. We could be in there together, the smell of popcorn wafting through the air, as we snuggle on the couch and map out our future while enjoying a movie. A future I destroyed.

Finally, it's time to regain what we lost. I only pray he wants the same thing.

"This is it."

I have never been this nervous in my whole life. Thankfully, I didn't eat any dinner, or I may have puked it up right here on the street. After taking a big breath for courage, I grab the door handle but then decide to check my makeup and lipstick before I go. Lipstick that I hope ends up all over his face at the end of this.

The light on my visor broke last month, so it's hard to see. The street light casts a dim glow, the only light in an otherwise dark surroundings. As I press the tip of the soft red to my lips, laughter rings out from the complex.

That's Sam's laugh.

But it's not just Sam's laughter that fills the air.

I turn my head and let out a gasp. Sam and Jennifer Snow are stepping out onto the porch from the complex entrance.

He's helping her put on her coat, pulling her curly hair from the back. Their laughter rings out into the night.

Oh, my God.

Sam and I went to school with Jennifer. She was the type of person who was friends with everyone. I don't think she had one enemy in all of Fitch High School. She was kind, genuine, and funny. I would venture to say that we were even friends.

Did she like Sam in school? Probably. All the girls liked Sam. But that is where Jennifer stands out as different. There were plenty of girls who let Sam know that if we broke up, they would be waiting. But if Jennifer liked Sam, she would never have said. He was in a relationship, so she wouldn't cross that line.

That's how good of a person she is.

As I watch them, I wonder how they connected. He's single, so I'm sure she made her move.

I can't say that I blame her.

Or worse yet, maybe he pursued her.

And, naturally, she is just as gorgeous now as she was in high school.

With rapt attention, I watch the two of them laughing, thoroughly enjoying each other's company. Jennifer is eating up his every word as he says something, laughing and touching him with each giggle.

I scoot down in the seat of my car because I can't risk him seeing me, even though I am shrouded in darkness here on the street. The porch light casts a soft glow on the happy couple, giving me a front row seat to the end of my world. My mouth goes dry as my insides churn.

Their conversation stops as he whispers something in her ear. He runs his hand up her arm, and she inches closer to him. Their eyes lock as she nods in agreement with whatever it was he asked her. My hands tighten on the steering wheel as I watch Sam with another woman unfold before my eyes. And not just any woman.

Jennifer Freaking Snow. Quite literally, the nicest person in the whole wide world.

Taking her 'yes' as the invitation it is, he grips her arms, and in one quick motion, draws her closer, their lips colliding. I feel queasy as a pain shoots straight to my heart.

I turn away and cover my mouth to control the sob that is bubbling to come out. One thought flashes in my head almost instantly. *He used to kiss me that way.*

After taking a second to compose myself, I look back at the porch.

They're gone.

My head whips to his car, which is still there. So that means only one thing.

They went back into his apartment.

The sob that I was suppressing comes out, along with a scream that I can't stop. My stomach aches, and I clutch it as tears steam down my cheeks. I'm crying so hard that I can't catch my breath. Both hands land on the steering wheel. I need to ground myself to something as this overwhelming feeling consumes me. My forehead falls forward, colliding with the black vinyl as my breaths increase.

"How is this happening?"

Wait, I know the answer.

Me. This is happening because of me.

I let Sam go. I drove him into the arms of Jennifer Snow.

The blame falls on me.

My life is a total disaster. Tears are pouring out of my eyes, streaking my mascara, wetting my dress. I'm trying to get my breathing under control because I need to get off of this street. I can't take the chance of him seeing me. Although I'm fairly certain his attention is on something else. Or *someone* else.

I gasp for a breath, and I can't fill my lungs with air. He's in there right now, kissing her, touching her, loving her.

"Oh, my God, I'm hyperventilating."

Focusing my attention on the car parked in front of me, I draw a huge breath in. I slowly let it out. I do this a handful of times until my breathing is stable. Raising my eyes to the visor mirror again, and with a shaking hand, I wipe away the black marks that are running down my face.

After a few more minutes, I have myself under control enough to start the car. Before I drive away, I glance one last time at his apartment. The living room light is out.

I lost him.

He's gone.

Forever.

I pull away from the curb and start the drive home. Amidst the chaos of my racing mind, there is one undeniable truth.

This is my fault, my mess, my mistake. I have brought this upon myself. I deserve to be miserable.

And I hope Sam is happy. After what I did to him, I want him to find happiness.

Even if it's with Jennifer Freaking Snow.

The nicest person in the whole wide world.

Chapter Eight

FALL 1997

❦

DEXTER'S

Sam

"**D**ude, this night is going to be da bomb!" Ricky exclaims as he shuts his car door. He takes a step back to admire his horrible parallel parking job. "Not too bad, huh?" He looks over the top of his car at me, satisfied with himself.

As he rounds the car, I walk up onto the sidewalk and take it in. It's awful. "Um, it's terrible, man," I say, laughing under my breath as I look at the back tire up on the curb. Ricky can't park to save his life.

He makes it to my side, studies the tire, and slaps me on the shoulder. "Doesn't matter. We are here, and that's what counts. Let me just feed the meter, and we can head inside." Excitement is radiating off his body.

The inside he's referring to is the country bar we are going to spend money in tonight. And I need it. Desperately.

Because as luck would have it, I lost my job today. The small communications company I was working for went under. They announced it first thing this morning and told us we had two hours to clean out our desks.

Fun times.

I walked out with a tiny box full of what little things I had in my cubicle and immediately called Ricky as soon as I walked into my apartment. Which I have no idea how to pay for after today.

Two years ago, my life was in shambles. I lost Maria, and it felt like I was living in some kind of black hole. In time, I picked up the pieces again. But now … I'm jobless. It feels like I can't catch a break.

I turn around and glance at the half-lit neon sign that hangs above the door of this dive I love.

Dexter's.

The 'x' is completely dark, while the 'r' flickers on and off every few seconds. When I call this a dive bar, that's being generous.

I have no clue who Dexter is, nor do I care. But he serves cheap beer and killer chili cheese fries, both of which I need to help me cope with the crap show that is my life right now.

And it seems I'm not the only one that needs a night out because this place is packed. People are streaming in as I stand and wait for Ricky. *What is taking him so long, anyway?* Whenever the white door with chipped paint creaks open, Garth Brooks's crooning voice, mixed with very happy bar patrons, fills the night air. It's the sound of fun, and I'm itching to get in.

Finally, Ricky makes it to my side. "Stupid meter won't take my quarters. I'm probably going to get towed," he says with exasperation, looking around, trying to decide what to do next. "I'll meet you inside. I'm going to have to find another spot."

With a nod, I reach for the door handle, ready to take on what lies on the other side. When I open it, a few people view it as a kind gesture and stroll inside. "Cool. I'll meet ya at the bar."

I'm already half-way through the entrance when I hear him cry out, "And you better have a honey on your arm when I get in there!" As I shake my head and grin at his demand, I glance around the crowded bar. It's wall-to-wall people, which is to be expected on a Friday night. The dance floor is alive with the sound of boots stomping and glasses clinking as line dancers hold on tight to their drinks.

Not a single high-top table is available, leaving only one empty seat at the bar. Which I decide has my name on it. I weave through the crowd and sit down on the stool that has a huge tear in the plastic. Within seconds, Big C, my favorite bartender, makes his way over to me. And he is just that ... big.

Big C (no clue what his real name is) is Samoan and used to be a linebacker for Georgia Tech before a blown-out knee stopped his career. He's six-five and at least two-sixty of pure muscle. No one messes with Big C. Since I'm a regular here, Big C knows more about my life than just about anyone. The best bartenders listen and will take your secrets to their grave. Since getting to know him, I've discovered how awesome he is, and now we're friends.

"Sam! My man," he charges toward me from across the sticky, lacquered bar to give me a slap handshake.

"Big C. Huge crowd tonight." My raised voice pierces through the noise and music so that he can hear me.

His eyes scan the dimly lit bar, taking in the various patrons. "No kidding. I haven't stopped for longer than two seconds since I got here. The usual?"

I flash him a thumbs-up, and within seconds, Big C slides a Heineken over to me. I grab the bottleneck, and the chill from the glass is already making me feel better. So does the cold beer as the bubbles coat my throat. I turn around on the stool and rest my elbows on the bar as I scan the room. Maybe Ricky is right. I should try to meet someone and have some fun. I'm not looking for anything serious, but a few dances and friendly conversation with a woman could definitely brighten my day. The excitement of that being a reality gets my adrenaline moving.

I zero in on a table of ladies who look to be having fun. They appear to be my age, or a little older, which I'm not opposed to. That could work. I'll wait until Ricky gets in here and we can approach together. Knowing Ricky, he'll be okay with it.

As I scan the room for more prospects, I lift the beer to take another swig, but the bottle tip stops on my lips as my eyes land on ... *her*. My heart stops. I slowly lower the beer because there she is, in the flesh.

My Maria.

Saddled up against some preppy-looking dude at the table in the far corner. His arm is tightly around her waist in almost a possessive way. I could spot her from a mile away, anywhere. Her blonde hair is still long, cascading down her back. She's wearing a yellow cropped shirt, which shows off a sliver of her bare skin. Her long legs are on display with a black skirt, and she's wearing black chunky sandals.

She looks incredible.

My stomach is in knots as I do a double take, then take another swig of beer before I rotate on my stool. I need to get my bearings because I haven't seen or heard from Maria since I read *The Chad* letter two years ago. Who would have thought a simple piece of paper could hold so much power, but it destroyed me with just a few words.

I glance over my shoulder to get another look, and as I study her, I notice something is off. Maria was always so full of light. She's shy but could brighten any room with her smile. But the Maria I see right now is not the Maria I knew and loved.

Well ... *love*, if I'm being honest with myself. Which the beer is helping with.

With her shoulders slumped over and her eyes locked on the floor, she seems to carry the weight of the world on her back. She's not laughing. She's not talking. She just looks ... sad.

Preppy guy laughs at something one of his friends says. He removes his arm from her waist, wraps it around Maria's shoulders, and pulls her towards him. She turns to look at him, and he slams his mouth onto hers.

I look away as I clench my beer. *Is this the guy she dumped me for?*

Chad.

I have read and re-read her letter so many times that I will always hate that name.

Ricky returns and breaks up my thoughts. "There you are!" He takes the now empty stool next to mine. "I had to park in no-man's-land. This place is jamming tonight."

He raises his hand to get Big C's attention, then looks over at me. I sit motionless, my brows furrowed, disgusted. The clinking of glasses, blaring country music, and chatter are all around me, but my eyes stay fixed straight ahead on the rows of liquor behind the bar. "What happened to you? I thought you were excited to come here tonight. Why does your face look like that?"

Right then, Big C comes over with a Budweiser for Ricky. He notices my change in mood as well, his eyes narrowing with curiosity. "You okay, man?"

I turn the beer in my hand, no longer wanting it because of the nauseous feeling that has bubbled up in my gut. "Maria's here," I reply, emotionless.

Both Ricky's and Big C's mouths drop open. They both know the story and what she meant to me.

Means to me.

"You're kidding me!" Ricky exclaims. "Where?" His eyes scan the room, searching for her.

I take a small swig, savoring the taste, and motion with a subtle flick of my head. "Over on the far side wall." Ricky and Big C turn their heads in unison.

"Dang! She looks hot!" Leave it to Ricky to point out the obvious. I shoot him a sharp sideways glare.

"Dude, come on," Big C says, tilting his head in exasperation.

"What? She does." Ricky shrugs as he turns back around. I'm too thrown off kilter by seeing her to care that Ricky checked out my ex, who I'm still in love with.

Big C chimes in. "The guy she's with is a complete jerk. Do you think they are a thing?"

This catches my attention. I snap my head in his direction. "I'm assuming, since he just shoved his tongue down her throat. Why is he a jerk?" My heart speeds up, waiting for his answer.

"They came in about an hour ago. He had his arm around her shoulders, as if she was a piece of property. She looked uncomfortable. I'm pretty sure him and his buddies were already lit." He points in their direction. "He demanded we scrub that table before they sat there and had the nerve to check and make sure it passed some sort of inspection. Then he threw his gold card at us and said, 'Money is no object. Run this when we leave.'" He lets out a puff of air and shakes his head as he wipes down the bar. "He's running poor Maggie ragged. And seriously, who dresses like that at a bar like this?"

I take another quick look. Preppy has on white chinos, a pink collared shirt, and penny loafers. I pinch my lips together.

"So basically, an entitled rich brat, spending Daddy's money," Ricky proclaims.

"Would appear so." With that, Big C is called over to another paying customer.

I glance over my shoulder again. "Do you think I should go over there?" I squeak out.

"And do what exactly?" Ricky asks. "You would piss off her boyfriend, and I'm not in the mood to break up a fight tonight. It will only end badly, you know that."

I abruptly pivot, choosing not to answer his question because I know he's right.

We both sit in silence for a few minutes, the eager energy of the room not doing much for my mood.

Ricky tries to knock some sense into me. "Seriously, man, what purpose would it serve to talk to her? That was two years ago, and you were horrible to be around after that day. I don't think I could endure that again." He shakes his head as he finishes his beer and slams it down on the bar.

"Gee, thanks." He's not wrong. I was a bear that day. And every day after for months. But Ricky was there for me, like best friends should be.

Big C hands him another beer as Ricky continues. "Look, we are here tonight to let off some steam and have some fun." He lifts his beer to the table of women I noticed earlier. One of them wiggles her pinky at Ricky. An evil grin crosses his lips. "You can sit here and sulk all you want, but I'm going over there to talk to that redhead in the black dress."

And with that, I've lost my wingman. He cuts his way through the crowd and is standing next to the fiery redhead within seconds. He's already making her laugh with one of his cheesy pickup lines, while she rests her hand on his chest.

I don't have Ricky's charisma, charm, or bravery with women. In the past, I didn't need it, since I had the one person I could ever need or want. The beautiful blonde that is sitting only fifty feet away from me. It's the closest I have been to her in two years.

This is what small towns do to you. They force you to run into people you least expect to see at the exact moment you don't want, or need, to see them.

But I can't stop staring at her.

So many questions are swirling around in my head that I'm feeling dizzy.

Is that Chad?

Is she still in school?

Does she live at home?

Why? Why did she destroy us?

I finish my beer as I stare, willing her to look in my direction. The minutes tick past as song after song plays. The dance floor is a revolving door of people, while more patrons come and go out the entrance. A fight breaks out near the front as the bouncer grabs a guy by the collar and throws him out.

But the commotion fades in the background as I watch Maria. I can feel Big C's eyes on me as he serves customers, watching me, probably wondering what I'm going to do.

Just when I decide to take off because this is pure torture, preppy guy whispers in Maria's ear. He gets a small nod from her and then leans in to give her a tender kiss on the forehead. I track him as he leaves with his friends, weaving through the crowd and right out the front door.

Leaving Maria alone.

She's swaying to the music and looks lighter now that he's gone. I'm watching, spellbound by her presence. As the tacky disco ball in the middle of the dance floor comes to life, beams of light bounce off of something gold resting on Maria's wrist.

Oh, my God. It's *the* watch.

The watch I gave her at graduation. The watch that I saved our entire senior year for. The watch I gave her in Pittsburgh, at our spot.

I can't believe she still has it. And wears it.

This realization forces me to look away so that I can get my bearings. I still don't know why she ended things. I know what her letter said, but for two years, something has always felt off about how it went down. It continues to haunt me. There is nothing I want more than to hold her in my arms again, one more time. Maybe ask for answers.

And as if I willed it to happen, the music changes to a slow song. I glance at Big C, and he shakes his head in warning, knowing what I'm thinking.

But I can't help myself.

Taking a swig for some courage, I place my beer on the bar and head in her direction.

I'm going in.

Chapter Nine

1997

∞

Dexter's

Maria

"Have fun tonight, Maria," Nate says as he kisses me on the forehead, his breath reeking of booze. I give him a fake sweet smile as I watch him and his friends leave the overcrowded bar.

God, I hate this place.

Nate and I have only been here one other time since we started dating a few months ago. It's always the same scene. Drunk guys and girls downing beers and exchanging numbers after they dance up against one another. Loud country music blares as line dancers stomp and turn in unison with the beat of the music. Nate picked this place for our guys' and girls' night out.

I didn't get a say. I never do.

Which I know sounds awful, but it's what I need in my life right now. School is kicking my butt, and my parents' marriage is deteriorating at a rapid rate. I don't have the energy to make decisions ... with anything. That's why Nate and I work.

He leads the way, and I follow.

Am I happy? I gave up on happiness two years ago.

Nate enjoys showing me off and parading our relationship around like I'm a prize he won. And I admit, deep down, I like the attention. And he likes the arm candy. There's no denying it, we look good together. Our friends say it all the time.

"You two are the cutest couple."

"I want a relationship just like you guys have."

"I wish I had someone that loves me like Nate loves you."

If they only knew how profoundly sad I am.

Nate and his buddies left to play poker while I wait for the girls to arrive. I hope once they get here, I can convince them to leave because this place is not my scene.

I glance down at my watch. A quarter after ten. *Ugh.* They were supposed to have been here fifteen minutes ago. I'm standing here alone in this dive, hoping no one approaches me. Out of the corner of my eye, my gold link watch catches a ray of light from the lamp at my table, and it looks just as beautiful as the day Sam gave it to me.

When I glance at this watch, memories of him flood my mind. I broke him, so I don't deserve to have any feelings for him. I know I shouldn't. But I do, and I always will. The guilt I harbor in destroying his life will always stay with me.

On instinct, I cover the watch with my hand after I look at it to get the time. It's almost like covering it holds in place the time we spent together. I never want him to escape my memory, so I cover the watch. To protect what we had and hold it close. It's comforting. Almost like he's here with me as I wait alone.

A Shania Twain song plays as couples slow down and hold each other on the dance floor.

"May I have this dance?" a deep voice asks, and a calloused hand appears under my nose as I stare down at my drink.

I knew it! Now I have to tell some drunk dude 'No, thank you. I have a boyfriend.' There is no way I'm dancing with some stranger. I turn my eyes up to this man to give him the death glare. "No, thanks, I'm wait—"

My breath hitches in my throat.

It's Sam.

I'm frozen in place. My heart drops, and heat rises to my head as I'm met with the brown eyes that I know so well. Eyes that I could stare at for hours.

This can't be happening.

I look around the bar frantically, praying that Nate is gone and not seeing this. My girlfriends aren't here yet either. He knows about Sam, but he doesn't know it all.

"Sam, what are you doing here?" I ask, as if this is my bar and he's on my turf. I have a feeling it's the other way around.

He doesn't answer my question as he takes my hand in his. This is the first time we have touched in two years. An instant spark pierces through me from his touch. He leans down and whispers in my ear, his lips grazing my hair. "Please, Maria, dance with me?" My knees wobble at the sound of his plea, and I have no clue how I'm going to move.

But I can't resist.

I never could.

"Okay." The word comes out in a whisper as I struggle to catch my breath.

Before I know it—or control it—my feet are moving, and I'm following him to the dance floor.

God, he looks incredible. The same, yet different. Older, perhaps. We dodge the swaying couples as we make our way to the middle of the floor. He pulls me to him, resting his left hand on my lower back while grasping my other hand. I place my palm on his shoulder, which feels broader. The moment I'm in his arms, a sense of comfort and familiarity washes over me, as if I've returned to where I belong. We fit together like a puzzle. We always have.

With Shania singing from the speakers, our bodies naturally sway to the music. I take a step back, keeping a distance between us.

"So, was that Chad?" His eyes are practically burning a hole into me with his stare, waiting for an answer, but I can't look at him, so I glance around the room.

"Um ... no. That was Nate." I pause before I tell him the truth. "My boyfriend."

Now it's his turn to look away from me. We continue to sway in tune to the music. With his hand touching my back, it ignites a burning sensation that spreads like a fire through my whole body. A fire that was non-existent with Chad or Nate.

"What happened to Chad? Or are you seeing both of them?" My eyes dart up to his as he grimaces at his attempt to hurt me.

"Chad and I didn't work out."

"Shocker." He huffs out.

I survey the room, looking for Jennifer Freaking Snow. She's nowhere. "Things didn't work out with Jennifer?" I squeeze my eyes shut, shocked the question poured out of my mouth.

Sam's head snaps back in surprise, causing me to glance back up at him, a puzzled look etched on his face. "Jennifer? Who is Jenni—" Realization flashes in his eyes as he shakes his head in disbelief. "How did you know about Jennifer?"

I guess it's time to confess, but I can't look at him, though, as I admit to it. The shame and embarrassment are too much, so I lower my gaze.

"After Chad and I broke up two years ago, I went to your apartment to try to win you back. That's when I saw you and her on the building's front porch. You took her inside, so I left."

As I continue to focus on the floor, his eyes burn into me while he stays silent at this revelation.

Seconds tick by. "You came to win me back?" he asks in a whisper. I nod my head.

Neither of us says anything as we continue to sway to the music, lost in the moment. With each passing beat, the dance floor grows more crowded, the rising temperature of the room adding to the heat that always existed between us.

I can't take the silence anymore, so I speak up. "Sam, why don't you say what you want to say? I know you want to. I deserve it." He should give me a tongue-lashing. I broke up with him over a letter. A letter that was full of lies. A letter Chad forced me to write.

"I never dated Jennifer." As he reveals the truth, our eyes lock. He studies me before he continues. "Her and I connected, here actually, about six months after *The Chad,* I felt like maybe—"

Suddenly, I'm very confused. "*The Chad*?" I question.

A wicked smile crosses his lips. "I nicknamed the letter."

This makes me snort out a laugh, which causes Sam to chuckle, adding some lightness to an otherwise heavy moment.

Sam continues after we get ourselves under control. "Anyway, I ran into Jennifer here, and we started talking, so I asked her out. She confessed that she always liked me in school, so I thought, why not?"

I turn my head away again because this is harder to hear than I thought it was going to be.

"We went out only once. That night you saw us, apparently." I nod in agreement and let out a slow breath, mentally preparing myself. He pauses, and his grip on my hand tightens, steadying me for what he is about to say next. "She met me at my place, and we went to dinner, then here for some drinks. We had a good time. She was nice, like she always was in high school. I drove her back to my place and—"

"Stop. I don't need to know the rest," I interject, because this is pure torture.

"I couldn't go through with it, Maria," he continues. My head jerks up to meet his eyes, hollow and empty.

"Why?" I choke out.

The mutual affection we always shared passes between us as his eyes soften. "Isn't it obvious?" He whispers.

As we continue to dance, on instinct, our bodies gravitate toward one another. A tingling sensation erupts through my whole body as we come dangerously close. The electricity humming along with nowhere to go.

He's peering down at me now, and I know what he wants to ask. Finally, he does. "Why, Maria? Why did you do it?"

I quickly avert my gaze back down to the dusty dance floor as I ready myself to lie to him. My voice trembling, I force out the words. "It was complicated." It's the only response I offer to anyone brave enough to ask.

I can't tell him the truth. How my manager sexually harassed me for weeks, leaving me feeling cheap and small. How he forced me to date him, or he would fire me. How I wasn't brave enough to stand up to him. How I desperately needed the money, even though I can't tell him why. Then how Chad gave me a raise, one bigger than I deserved. How Chad sat next to me as I wrote the letter, then kissed me after I finished. A single tear ran down my cheek as my new reality came into sharp focus. The story of why I left Chad.

I can't tell him any of it. I don't want to ruin what feels like a perfect moment here in the bar I hate, but now, never want to leave. Plus, too much time has passed.

Does he even want me anymore? After what I put him through, probably not.

Thankfully, he doesn't push as we continue to dance. Sam could always read me like a book. I'm sure he can pick up on the tension in the air, the silence heavy with unspoken words. My shoulders are tight, and I'm biting my lower lip. If he wasn't holding my hand, I would be biting my nails, so I pick them instead.

All my tells.

Sam knows this because, out of habit, he strokes the exposed skin on my back with his thumb. He pulls our interlaced fingers into his chest as he nudges me toward him. I follow his lead, and before I know it, my head is resting on his chest, his racing heart, thumping away. Bob Seger's "We've Got Tonight" plays as the entire room fades to black. The commotion, the chatter, is gone.

It's a surreal feeling to be back in Sam's arms, a place that was a distant memory, and I'm going to relish in it for as long as I can.

He slowly releases his hand from mine and runs his fingers over my wrist and down to the watch, staring at it, studying it, and moving it around. Goosebumps erupt over my arm. "You still have it," he chokes out, not taking his eyes off it as he runs his fingers under the band, lightly grazing the skin on the inside of my wrist. The intimate touch causes the passion we always felt to pass between us. I force down the tears.

"Maria, can you look at me, please?" I do as he asks. As soon as our eyes connect, we stop dancing. He stares at me intently, scanning my face, memorizing it, the way he always did. I wonder if he misses this, misses us, as much as I do. The darkening of his eyes tells me he does.

His eyes drift to my lips as his part slightly. If he tries to kiss me, I know I'll let him. His hand leaves my back, landing on my hip, and squeezes. His desire matches mine, and I can sense the internal struggle he's facing. Our mouths are inches apart, our heavy breaths warm with hunger. I tilt my head, part my lips, and close my eyes, waiting for it.

Which is why I don't see Nate coming.

"HEY! GET AWAY FROM MY GIRL!" In a flash, Nate grabs my arm and tears us apart. He shoves Sam away from me as I stumble backward, slamming into a couple behind me.

Sam puts his hands up in surrender as he gives me a quick, knowing glance. "Sorry, man, I didn't know she was taken," he says, covering for me.

Nate looks at me; his face is red and, his eyes glassy. "Did this moron force himself on you?"

That would be a no.

But I can't say that. I also can't tell Nate who this is. In his current inebriated state, I don't trust that he won't do something stupid and try to hurt Sam. I can't let that happen. I grab onto Nate's arm, pulling him toward the exit. "Nate, it's fine. Let's just get out of here," I plead with him. "And why are you back?"

"We hadn't left yet and were still outside. The girls arrived, and Jenny came out and said that she saw some guy with his paws all over you on the dance floor." I glance over to my table, and there sit Jenny, Kim, and Valerie, looking stunned by the scene that just played out.

I was so caught up in my Sam haze, I didn't notice that my friends had arrived and saw the whole thing.

Lovely.

Nate takes three determined steps towards Sam and points his finger right in his face. "I better *never* see you in here ever again."

Sam shakes his head in disbelief and huffs out a snicker as he takes a step closer to Nate. They are nose to nose now. "Or you'll do what?" Sam asks through gritted teeth, his voice low and dripping with anger. I have never seen Sam full of this much rage.

Out of nowhere, the massive bartender inserts himself into the chaos. "Do we have a problem here?" His big, booming voice reverberates throughout.

Sam turns to the giant, takes a step back, and puts his fisted hands in his pockets. "Nope, no problem." Another guy—this one I recognize—rushes over. Ricky. Sam's best friend and our supposed waiter on our first date. A piercing look filled with anger locks onto me.

He turns to Sam. "You okay, man?" Sam nods.

The big guy looks at Nate, then at me. He narrows his eyes. "I think it would be better if you left." I have a feeling he knows exactly who I am because he addresses me and not Nate.

Nate shakes his head in disgust as he grips my hand tightly. "Come on, Maria, let's get out of here. This place is a dump, anyway." He leads me towards the door as my friends abandon the table and follow behind us.

Before I exit, I steal a glance back and see Sam standing alone in the middle of the dance floor. Bob Seger's voice fills the room with a question that mirrors the expression on Sam's face.

"Why don't you stay?"

I wish I could, Sam. I wish I could.

Chapter Ten

1997

∞

Sam

Walking into my dark apartment, it's as if there is a lead weight holding a vice grip on my life. I still don't have a job, and my rent is due in two weeks. And the $57 in my checking account is not enough to cover it. I yank the tie from around my neck since it feels like it's choking me to death, and I whip it on the floor. Neatness? Who cares?

It feels like a Heineken is in order after the interview I endured. It was for a manager's position at a grocery store. A job for a middle-aged man, in a loveless marriage, with two bratty teenagers and a beer gut. Definitely not me.

Although, if I keep up this beer habit, my gut won't be far behind.

The interview went well, so I can't complain. Do I want to work in a grocery store? Absolutely not. Have I found only a few options, and this is one of them?

Yes.

Which is depressing, to say the least.

So, if it's offered to me, I'll take it. It pays well, which means I'll be able to pay my bills.

The lack of viable employment in this town has left me considering whether it's time to move on and start over in a new state. It's hard to comprehend that I'm considering that as a life choice. Two years ago, my life plan took a detour I wasn't expecting. I felt lost for so long after Maria. But after some time, it seemed like I was finally getting a grip on things again. Work was good, I was dating again, more or less, and I had a solid friend group. Then, out of nowhere, last week, I lost my job and saw Maria (and held her in my arms), all in one day.

And my head hasn't been straight since.

The feel of her skin, the smell of her hair, how she kept and still wears the watch I gave her. That sentiment alone almost made me want to carry her over my shoulder like a caveman and bring her back here to the apartment we were supposed to share.

What almost broke me was when I learned she came to my apartment to try to win me back. But of course, she picked the day I went out with Jennifer. I can't believe Maria saw us on that porch, and what she witnessed was nothing. I pulled Jennifer into the apartment with no plan in place. At the moment, I thought it was what I wanted. Jennifer is amazing and gorgeous. But kissing her felt ... wrong and off.

I wasn't ready.

So, I sent her home. She understood and was really sweet about it.

But to think that Maria saw the whole thing and then to know the conclusions she had drawn, well, it makes me sick.

Then, to make the dance at Dexter's more complicated, and like the idiot that I am, I almost kissed her. But reality came crashing back in the way of a preppy rich boyfriend named Nate. Who she left with. Not gonna lie ... I've been back at Dexter's every night since, hoping that she returns.

She hasn't. It's just been me, Big C, Ricky, and my friend Heineken.

The thought of that unexpected night at Dexter's sends a pain of uneasiness straight to my gut. There's this knowing feeling I have that Maria isn't being honest with me. I've known her long enough. Something's off. I just don't know what.

I forcefully unbutton the top collar of my dress shirt, open the fridge, and grab a beer. Future beer gut? I'll worry about that later. And yes, I understand that I'm drinking in the middle of the afternoon. Don't judge.

Honestly, I need to get this beer problem under control.

As I sit down in my favorite chair and settle in, I realize I haven't got the mail yet. A loud moan escapes my lips because I know the only thing waiting for me is bills. Bills I can't pay. But I also can't ignore them, so I sit my beer down, hoist myself up, grab the mailbox key, and head back downstairs to the main floor. I insert the key into the mailbox labeled 2B and open it.

Okay, so maybe it's been a few days since I got the mail. A massive stack of long white envelopes and ads comes cascading out of my box and onto the dirty lobby floor.

"Son of a—" I mumble under my breath as I bend down to pick up the mess I made. Then, out of the corner of my eye, I notice a pair of purple-painted toenails peeking out of black heels step on the envelope that was in my hand, preventing me from grabbing it.

"Hey Sam," a female voice purrs.

As if this day couldn't get any worse. It's Cara. My neighbor, who lives right above me, has let me know frequently that I am welcome to visit her apartment anytime I want.

Not interested. Which she's been told, on repeat, yet here she is.

Pinching my lips together, I glance up at her, careful not to look at her legs, which I know she will notice since her skirt is extremely short. I'll admit, Cara is hot. I may not be interested, but I'm not blind. "Hey, Cara," I mutter.

She stoops to help me pick up the mail mess on the floor, bending over so that her cleavage, which is hanging out of her crop top, is in my face. She's desperately trying to make eye contact with me, which I purposely ignore. "I got it. Thanks." We both stand as she whips her long, sleek black hair behind her shoulder and hands me the mail she picked up. She rests her other hand on my forearm. *God, I can't stand overtly forward women who can't take a hint.*

"So, do you have any plans for this afternoon? I'm free. If you would like to get lunch or a drink, maybe." She takes a step closer and is batting her fake eyelashes at me. As if that will do the trick.

It won't.

"Can't, Cara. I'm busy," I reply while turning to walk away and shifting through the pile of mail in my hand.

She follows me as I take the steps to my floor, her heels clanking on the concrete behind me. "Busy doing what? I heard you lost your job. Come on, Sam, it's just a drink. As friends."

Yeah, right.

I don't answer her as I turn toward the hallway that leads to my apartment and walk to my door. Her cheap perfume is filling the air in the hall, which means she didn't continue up the stairs to her place. *Why can't this woman take a hint?* I intentionally ignore her, hoping the silent treatment will do the trick as I rifle through the pile in my hand.

Phone bill.

Electric bill.

Visa bill. (We sit that one aside for now.)

Cable bill. (Going to be canceling that soon.)

OH, MY GOD!

Only feet from my front door, I come to a sudden halt and zero in on the white envelope in my hand. It's addressed to me, written in Maria's delicate handwriting.

She wrote me a letter.

When did she send this? I zero in on the post stamp, and it's dated three days prior. Holy crap. That means she wrote this the very next day after seeing me at the bar. Which also means, if I wasn't so forgetful about getting my mail, I could have read this three days ago.

That same euphoric feeling I would get when we dated and wrote to each other frequently bubbles up. Letters that were full of love and feelings. Butterflies erupt in my stomach, and my hands immediately feel clammy. I can't contain my excitement. I have to share this with someone, and Cara is the only person around. "This is from Maria!" I turn and exclaim with wide eyes, bursting with enthusiasm.

Her nose crinkles as her lips curl upward. "Who is Maria?" she asks, popping her hip out and resting her hand on it.

"My ex," I say, staring at the letter. "I can't talk, Cara." The words spill out of my mouth as I turn and fumble with my keys to open my door. Eager to get inside and tear this open.

"So, what about lun—" I slam the door in Cara's face. Now maybe she will take the hint.

I throw the rest of the mail on the kitchen counter as I walk to the couch and tear open the envelope. My stomach churns with each step. I sit down and try to compose myself. A thousand questions are swirling around in my head as to what she could say. I peer at the folded letter, her written words in ink peeking through the blue-lined paper. I have no idea what meaning will be behind them.

With my heart full of both fear and hope, I unfold it and read.

Oct. 4, 1997

Dear Sam,

I really hope this is still your address. I know it's been two years since we communicated this way, so you could have moved. God, I hope not. If this isn't Sam, throw this away, because this is private and none of your business.

Sam, if this is you, and you got this far, please keep reading because I have a lot to say. And apologize for.

Last night at Dexter's was surreal, wasn't it? I'm not going to pretend that being with you again didn't affect me. It did. More than I anticipated. Then again, you always had a certain way about you when it came to me.

After Nate and I left, I pretended to not feel well, and I went home. I needed to think. About everything. I decided that I owed you the truth. You deserve it. The truth about why I broke up with you. So, I hope you are sitting down, because I think you are going to be surprised.

Here it goes.

I never loved Chad. He harassed and bullied me into dating him. He was emotionally and physically abusive to me. I was miserable and alone the whole time we were together. And I hated every second of it.

Take a minute, sit this letter down and breathe.

She's right, I need a minute. I can't help but notice that she has an uncanny ability to understand my needs. No one knows me better than Maria. Her voice in my head is so clear as I read her words, it's as if she's sitting right next to me.

I do what she says and sit the letter on the cushion beside me. Leaning forward and resting my elbows on my knees, I run my fingers through my hair. Whenever I think back to that day two years ago, all I can remember is the overwhelming anger I felt towards her. How each time I thought about them together, romantically, I almost punched a wall because I thought she wanted it. Now I know the truth. She was miserable.

The desire to punch a wall again is back, but I can't lose focus because I need more details.

I pick up the letter, hoping to get those answers.

Are you back?

I'm sure what you just read was a shock. So let me explain, from the beginning, what happened.

You remember when I got that job at the warehouse, right? What am I saying? Of course you do. I told you the news, and we went to the mall to buy me some work clothes, then to Olive Garden for dinner and, of course, their breadsticks. You looked so handsome that night.

Anyway, Chad, who was thirty-two years old ... wait, did I ever tell you that? I don't think I did. I remember when he asked me in my interview why I wanted the job. I told him the truth, because you and I were starting a life together. He looked almost angry at my answer, which confused me because I just met the guy. Remember how he offered me the job on the spot? Well, I found out later through my workmates that never happens. Normally, the interview process is long. And don't even get me started on how much he was paying me. Way more than I deserved. I thought this was a blessing for us. I was so excited that I didn't see at the time what he was doing. God, I was so naïve. I knew you were leery of the work environment. And at the time, I felt safe. Until I wasn't.

I hope you're ready for this next part.

Almost immediately after starting, he asked me out and I refused. And that's when the harassment started. He was relentless and a pervert. I didn't say anything to you because I needed the job and I thought I could handle it. But it took a toll on me. I'm sure you noticed that I was distant. I was trying hard to not show it, but no one knows me better than you. When you would ask me if I was okay, I should have told you. But I was so scared.

About six weeks after I was hired, Chad scheduled me an afternoon shift. I never worked in the afternoons, but he assured me that there was no one to cover the shift. It wasn't until everyone left for the night that he cornered me in the break room and forced me to kiss him while pawing my whole body. I shoved him away and threatened to quit. He laughed at me and told me that if I didn't date him, he would fire me. I ran out of the breakroom, to my car, and then home to call you and tell you what was happening. I was shaking the whole car ride home. I even pulled over and threw up. At the time, I thought I was never going to go back.

Once I got home, I walked through the door to find my mom and dad fighting. That's when I found out that he lost everything gambling in Vegas. He lost his job right before that and he never told my mom. Instead, he lied and told her he had to go to Vegas for a work conference. He thought that he could help us financially by winning big. So stupid. The opposite happened. It's all gone. And this included not just my college tuition, but their entire life savings. All of it was gone, Sam. They almost lost the house. We were broke. And not just broke, but wildly in debt. My mom wasn't working, so we had no money coming in. Except mine. And we both know how long it takes my dad to find work.

I felt so trapped. And you know me, Sam. You know I wasn't about to abandon them. I felt like I had no choice. Even though I did.

I didn't dare tell my parents, or you, what happened with Chad. In the blink of an eye, my life changed. In that moment, in my living room, after being assaulted by my boss, I had lost you. And you didn't know it yet. The next day I went to work and lied to Chad. I told him after thinking about it, dating him was what I wanted and needed. Little did he know that there was no want. Only need. I needed the job.

I was so stupid for not telling you. But I was ashamed. I felt guilty, like maybe I was leading him on somehow and I didn't want you to think that. And if I said something, I knew I would have to quit, and all I wanted was to save money for our life together. I could have gone to HR, but one of my workmates said that was pointless. Plus, he was my boss. He had all the power. And he made sure that I knew it.

Honestly, I thought he would take the hint and forget about it. But I was wrong. I am profoundly sorry for hurting you. There will never be enough apologies in the world to cover my remorse. Sometimes the guilt I feel is so overpowering, it's hard to breathe.

But I need you to know that I was miserable. You're probably wondering how I could do it. How could I be with Chad if I hated the whole situation so much? I don't know how I did it. I was numb and dumb. I only knew that I had to put my parents first. I had to choose. You or my parents. It was an impossible choice.

Chad knew about you and me. He demanded I break up with you immediately. So, I did. I wanted so badly to see you on the sly, hoping it all would blow over. But that would have been cheating. And I loved and respected you too much to do that.

And you were right. He was there that night. He sat next to me and told me what to write in that letter. Those words you read that day were his, not mine.

Then, after that went down, he rarely left my side. He told me what to wear, who I could see and talk to, what I could eat. And with him being my boss, he controlled my schedule and my income. He owned me. And he told me as much. The final straw was six months later when he found your watch and then his fist found my face. That's all I'm going to say about that part. I don't want to talk about it. Sorry. I left the same day and he was served a protection order. I never felt braver in my whole life.

I am so ashamed of myself. I should have told you what happened. I should have stood up for myself. I should have seen the danger. I have a lot of regrets. The biggest being you.

I carefully place the letter back down on the table, needing a few more seconds to grasp what I read. I knew something wasn't right with how everything went down that day.

Honestly, I don't know who to be upset with. Maria, for not trusting me enough to tell me and giving us a chance to work as a team and figure out a solution. Or her dad, for being an idiot who always gambled too much and putting her in this position. But more than anything, my heart breaks for the only woman I love. I know one thing for sure: I better never cross paths with Chad. The thought of him laying a hand on her makes my nerve endings stand on edge. I'm fuming right now, and I need to do … something.

Before I continue reading, I walk to my closet and grab the box that contains Maria's letter. *The Chad* still sits on top. I walk straight to the kitchen sink, open the junk drawer, fish out a lighter, and I set it on fire. There is no way those man's thoughts or desires will stay in my life. I watch the paper go up in flames, grateful that I will never read it again.

Once the ashes wash down the drain, I return to the couch and keep reading.

It took me a while to heal from everything. But I knew I needed to see you and explain. So I waited until the bruise was almost healed and I went to your apartment to try to win you back. I saw you with Jennifer and I thought I was too late. Seeing you with her broke me.

After that day, I buried myself in work. I got a job as a waitress and took every shift I could get. It was a nice distraction. Plus, there was school, which helped. And school is where I met Nate. I know you don't want specifics about him or us, but I feel like I need to tell you some things. Especially after what happened on the dance floor. Nate and I have been together for a few months now. I like him; I do. He's gorgeous and makes me feel special, but if I'm being honest with myself, I don't love him. I think I could, though … someday.

Anyway, my dad was in and out of work during this time. Nate's dad owns a huge manufacturing company. So he offered my dad a job. Nate's dad took pity on my dad and gave him a really good-paying job that is low risk. My dad is comfortable there, helping with the maintenance on the building. He can work by himself and at his own pace. It's the kind of job he has always needed and wanted. It's perfect for him.

My dad getting work didn't help my parents' relationship. Get this. They are getting a divorce, Sam! After everything, my dad is leaving my mom. The whole thing makes me so mad!

I really wish you were here to talk to me about this. But I guess a letter will do for now.

After Dexter's last night, I realized something. How much I miss you and how much I miss talking to you. We didn't talk much last night, but being with you again was amazing. Was it that way for you? I know that we can't talk on the phone or see each other in person, but if you're up for it, I would love to continue to write. Your letters were always one of my favorite things. When we were a couple, you weren't just my boyfriend; you were also my best friend. And if I'm being honest, I have no friends. Those girls at the bar are Nate's friends' girlfriends. God, they are so fake, I can't stand them honestly.

Can we write, Sam? Can we please be friends again? If I don't hear from you, I'll have my answer and I will accept that. Mostly, I wanted to give you the truth. After our time together, I owe you that.

I hope to hear from you soon. You can write to me at my old address. Nate won't see them if that worries you at all. Take care, Sam.

Love,

Maria

P.S. If this isn't Sam, shame on you.

This is a lot to take in. Out of nowhere, it feels like Maria has bulldozed herself back into my life. With only an envelope, a stamp, some ink, and lots of words. Words that I'm struggling to process.

She didn't want to leave me.

Chad abused her.

She's with preppy guy.

She misses me.

She wants to keep in touch.

The answer to the last question in her letter comes to me fast. I frantically scan the living room for some paper and a pen.

Nothing.

I lift stacks of old bills, feeling the crispness of the paper beneath my fingertips.

No paper.

The handle to my junk drawer almost falls off as I open it with force. Among the pile, I find the lighter, loose batteries, random playing cards not part of a deck, screws, and three pairs of scissors. AH-HAH! A pen! I click it and pray that it works. I scribble on the stack of bills and grin in relief when the blue ink appears.

I turn and head toward my bedroom and beeline straight to my nightstand. The drawer practically falls out of its track as I yank it open. I can't shake off this sense of urgency because it feels like I'm running out of time. There's no deadline to write this letter and no point in rushing this. But the desire to communicate with Maria is so strong it's like I'm running a marathon. And I'm only looking for paper.

Finally, a notebook shows itself at the bottom of my drawer. I grab it, head to my kitchen table, brace myself, and write.

Chapter Eleven

THE LETTERS

Oct. 10, 1997

Dear Maria,

Thank you for the letter and for explaining everything. I have to admit something though, and it may be hard for you to hear. But I am so mad at you, And I know that's awful and selfish considering what you wrote to me. So let me explain.

First and foremost, I am so sorry you went through all of that. It must have been so hard. I can't really think about it, because I may go and find Chad and I would rather not get arrested. But, and this is where I get kinda mad, because while reading your letter, all I kept thinking was, why didn't she come to me? We could have worked through that together. I would have been there through all of it and then maybe I wouldn't be here writing this letter without you in my life. Because you were my girl, and in some ways, you still are, and always will be. I could tell in your letter that you were holding back from saying certain things, since you are in a relationship. But I'm not seeing anyone, so I'm going to tell you how I feel. It may be my one and only chance.

My feelings haven't changed. I still love you.

That's it. That's what you need to know. Because it is, well, it was, everything.

To answer your question, yes, I would like to start writing to you again. But from this point on, our letters need to be nothing but friendly. Because that is the only way I can allow myself to think about you. In Dexter's, holding you in my arms, well, my head hasn't been the same since. So, if you are with Nate, and there is no chance of us getting back together, I can't have these letters become romantic. I can't, Maria. Besides, I won't pursue you if you are with someone. That's not who I am. When we were together, I always felt that we were two insecure people who were secure in each other. So maybe talking to you again will give back that sense of security I lost two years ago. I guess we'll see.

Since you caught me up on your life, I think it's only fair that I do the same. After the night you gave me The Chad, I struggled for a very long time. I had huge dreams for you and me. And that all came crashing down, so obviously I needed time to adjust to my new reality. Eventually I did. I started dating again, as you saw. There have been other women, but nothing serious. Although there is my neighbor, Cara, that lives above me. God, you would hate her. She is so pushy. It drives me nuts. I still hang out with Ricky, as you saw. Also, that bartender that helped diffuse the situation on the dance floor has become a friend as well. Big C has been a nice sounding board for me when it comes to you. I dare to say that I trust him more than Ricky, if you can believe it.

That night at Dexter's, I was there with Ricky, letting off some steam because I had just lost my job. It sucks so bad, let me tell you. And you know how this area of Ohio is right now. There is no work. Today, I had an interview as a manager in a freaking grocery store. Writing it down makes me laugh because it is funny actually. But I think if they offer it to me, I will take it.

But it makes me feel like such a loser.

That's it. That's my life. Pretty riveting. Anyway, I hope to hear from you soon. I guess I'll find out if you were serious about this whole reconnecting thing. I look forward to your letter, Maria.

Yours, Sam

Oct. 13, 1997

Dear Sam,

Of course I was serious about writing again! And I have to admit, I was so excited to open the mailbox and see your letter. It felt like old times and it let me know that you were open to communicating with me again as a friend. So, thank you for giving me a chance.

But I have to start off by saying that you ARE NOT a loser. Please don't say those things about yourself. Taking a job, no matter what that job is, to support yourself is never a bad thing. You know that I never cared what you did for work. As long as you did it with integrity. So, if they offer you the job, take it and run that store like the badass you are!

Life has been pretty boring my way. Just school, Nate, dealing with my parents, which is a huge headache. They don't divorce well let me tell you. It's been a lot of fighting and since my dad works with Nate's dad, I think he kinda expects me to take his side, but I can't and I won't. Do you remember that episode of Friends last season? I guess I should be more specific, huh? Haha. Well, there was an episode last season that reminds me so much of my situation. It's the one where Rachel's parents are divorcing, and they have the two parties in the apartments. She keeps going back and forth between the boring Monica party, where her mom was and the fun party at Joey's, where her dad was. Ross helped her navigate the whole thing. That's how I feel. Kinda like I'm being toggled between two apartments. And Nate doesn't help me the way Ross helped Rachel. It's frustrating and lonely.

Do you still watch Friends? You know me; I was and still am addicted. Nate hates it! He says it's "brain numbingly dumb." Whatever that means. Remember when you and I watched the pilot together after that random Thursday we spent in Pittsburgh? The one where we walked and talked about our future. We came home and thought, hey what the heck, let's watch this new show and see if it's any good. And we ended up loving it! It's still on the air, so I guess other people love it too. I wonder how many seasons it will last?

Write back soon!

Love, Maria

P.S. Stay away from the trashy girl upstairs. I don't like her. She sounds like trouble.

Nov. 2, 1997

Dear Maria,

Well, I took your advice, and I accepted the job. But a funny thing happened. I've been there for two weeks now. Learning the ropes, getting to know the employees and such. Then today these two really tall dudes knocked over a huge display of beans. It was a mess. They couldn't have been nicer, though. They felt so bad and even helped me clean it up. Well, we started talking, and they told me about the construction business they had just started about a year earlier. Givens Construction. They are cousins and are trying hard to get this up and running. One of the owners, Scott, just got married like two years ago, I think he said. And get this...they are looking for people to train.

They offered me a job on the spot!

So, I took it! Life is so funny sometimes. In a matter of less than a month, I was working in IT, gainfully unemployed, then a grocery store manager, and now tomorrow I'm going to learn about how to read a blueprint. I'm sure some people would say that it was fate. You know how much I hate that new age BS. However, my faith in happy accidents has been restored. I couldn't wait to come home and write this letter to tell you. Ricky and I are heading to Dexter's to celebrate. Big C has the night off, so he is going to be joining us. I think Ricky wants to introduce me to this girl he works with. Well, I guess I should say woman. I don't trust his opinion about women, so I'm scared if I'm being honest.

Also, I wanted to ask you how school is going? You mentioned it in your last letter. I know the situation with your dad and Chad (GOD I hate that name) made things worse for you, I'm sure. I know what getting your degree meant to you. I'll never forget the look on your face when you got accepted to Ohio Northeastern. Let me know.

Yours, Sam

∞

Jan. 16, 1998

Dear Sam,

School is okay, I guess. I'm still majoring in exercise science and I decided only recently to minor in Psychology. And that's because of you. You were always interested in psychology, so I thought, what the heck! Why not! It's hard, but I'm dealing with it. I know that you always wanted to be a psychologist. Did you ever think about pursuing it? You should!

Oh yeah! Congrats on the construction job. That's great! I love it when things work out like that. And I'm proud of you for taking that management job. I know you weren't thrilled about it. And see how it worked out. If you wouldn't have listened to me, then you wouldn't have been there when those guys knocked over the beans. You're welcome.

Sorry it's taken me a couple of months to write back to you. Things have been hectic on my end. Nate and I just got back from a vacation in the Keys. He hates the winter, so he was ready to get out of dodge. I tried snorkeling and scuba diving for the first time if you can believe it. The colorful fish we saw reminded me of the fish that you had in your fish tank when you lived at home. Remember those? I used to love it when we would watch a movie with the lights out and the tank would be lit up. It was so pretty. We used to always talk about getting one once we got married. Did you ever get one? I asked Nate if we could and he said no. He said that they are too much to take care of. Maybe he's right. I hardly have the time to sleep lately, let alone take care of any kind of living thing.

So how did the set up go with Ricky's friend? Was she nice?
Love, Maria

∞

Mar. 9, 1998

Dear Maria,

I'm glad you had a great time at your vacation and yes I remember the fish tank. You never knew this, but I named your favorite fish after you. It was that rainbow fish that looked almost iridescent. Maria the rainbow fish. Here's some irony for you. Maria died three days before the night you gave me your letter. I should have taken it as some sort of sign. If only I believed in that sort of thing.

Ricky's attempt at setting me up was a complete fail. Turns out the girl, her name is Jasmine, was more into Big C than me. I mean, it's fine obviously. They are a couple now and my friend is really happy. Which is great.

And that leads me to the next development in my life. I know you told me to stay away from the girl upstairs. Well, turns out that Cara isn't that bad. She's kinda cleaned up her image and stopped being so forward with me. Even going as far to apologize for being so in my face before, which I felt took a lot of bravery on her part. Eventually, we started talking when we would see each other in the lobby and I realized she was pretty cool. She is kind and compassionate. She takes care of her sick mom and is the greatest aunt to her niece. She's loyal toward those she cares about. So on a whim one day, I asked her out. We've been dating now for the last two months. She's kinda great. Actually, her sense of humor is what I like the best about her. This is why my letter has taken so long. Between working and spending time with Cara, I've been busy.

And there's something else. After your last letter, you got me thinking. You're right, I have been interested in psychology for as long as I can remember. I read your letter and my wheels started to turn so I checked out what would be involved. Well, since I already have my associates, I would only need two years to get my bachelor's followed by two years for my masters. The hard part is after. I would need to apply for a PhD or PsyD program which is roughly five years. I guess I need to ask myself, am I ready to commit to nine years of schooling? It's a lot of food for thought.

I'm going to have to cut this one short. I have to get Cara for date night.
Sincerely, Sam

Mar 16, 1998

Dear Sam,

I will be so mad at you if you don't pursue this, Sam!! You know you can do it! I know you can do it. Could you imagine? Samuel Harper, PsyD. I mean, you have to admit, that looks pretty cool, right? Just so you know, no matter what you decide, you have my full support. I'm always rooting for you.

I'm happy that you found someone. If Cara is as wonderful as you say she is, then I'll take your word for it. I only cautioned you to stay away based on how you described her. But hey, if she's cool, then cool.

I never thought we would find ourselves in this kind of weird friend zone. I guess we could call ourselves pen pals. But that makes us sound like we are twelve. I mean, I know we are friends, but I never imagined that is all you would be to me. We were always Sam and Maria. Maria and Sam. Through high school and after. You couldn't see one of us without the other. Now, we just navigate this kinda long distance friends from afar scenario.

Oh well, I'll take what I can get. I really wish I could see you again, though. Is that something you would be up for? Just maybe some lunch or a coffee? Think about it and let me know.

Love, Maria

∞

Mar 19, 1998

Dear Maria,

I'm sorry, but I can't meet you for lunch or coffee. And I think you know why. It's best that we just stay, as you called us, "long distance friends." That's all I can give you right now. I would love to see you also and maybe we will run into each other somewhere someday. But intentionally meeting you for lunch or coffee, that I can't do.

I'm pretty sure Cara or Nate wouldn't like it.

Sincerely, Sam

Mar 31, 1998

Dear Sam,

You're right. I shouldn't have asked. I know that you wanted to keep these letters strictly friendly. I promise to do that from now on. And you're right. Nate would be furious if he found out I met to have coffee with another man. Especially if that other man is you.

Love, Maria

Aug 1, 1998

Dear Maria,

I have to start off by apologizing for not writing for a few months. I think it was a couple of things. You asking to see me kinda felt strange, so I needed to distance myself for a while. Also, and you are going to like this one, I decided to take the leap and go back to school. I started in the spring and I'm taking classes through the summer because I really want to get going on this. When I finally made the decision, I honestly couldn't wait to get started.

And my bosses Scott and Johnny, remember I told you about them. The bean guys. Well, they have been so cool about it. I really thought when I approached them they would say that they couldn't work with me since I assumed their kind of work only happens during the day. Here, they hire guys to run security at night at the different jobs. So that's what I'm doing now. School during the day, working security in the evenings. And of course, there is still Cara. Life has really, for the first time, felt good. Great even. And I have you to thank for that.

I'll try to not let so much time pass between letters this time. I hope your summer is going well.

Sincerely, Sam

∞

Aug 13, 1998

Dear Sam,

I AM SO HAPPY FOR YOU!!! I have no doubt that this will be everything that you need it to be.

School is going slowly for me, to say the least. At the rate I'm going, it looks like it will take me approximately seven or eight years to complete. I've already been going for longer than four and I'm only a sophomore. It's frustrating but I won't quit.

So you and Cara are still together?

Love, Maria

Aug 16, 1998

Dear Maria,

Please don't ask me about Cara. Never once in my letters have I asked you about Nate. I think we need to make a new rule. We don't ask the other about our relationships. If the other wants to bring up their boyfriend or girlfriend, that's fine. But we can't and shouldn't ask.

I'm sorry if that sounds harsh, but it has to be that way, Maria. If we want to continue to keep in touch, we have to do this. I know it has to be hard for you to think of me with someone else. Trust me when I say I know that feeling.

Sincerely, Sam

Sept. 6, 1998

Dear Sam,

You're right and I'm sorry. It's really none of my business what your relationship is or isn't with Cara. I won't ask again, I promise.

I've literally sat here for the last ten minutes wondering what to write because now, for the second time, I've made this weird. Ugh! Why am I like this? I drive myself crazy. You know me and you know how I am. I obsess about things that I can't control. I also tend to get jealous easily. Heck, you know this about me. Do you remember when Mrs. Durcy assigned that pretty new girl Rebecca to be your chem lab partner? I know you do because I asked you about her every day all of junior year. And it's not that I didn't trust you. It was her I didn't trust. Because let's face it, you were a catch and she was a knockout.

Okay, I'll stop now. Honest.

Anyway, I wanted to let you know that my parents' divorce was finalized on Friday. They finally stopped the fighting and came to an agreement on things. Funny thing, after the court date, they went and had a drink together. Nothing romantic, just as friends. It was nice, actually. My dad is still working at Nate's dad's company and that has led to some tension between Nate and me. I won't bore you with the specifics, but him and I don't get along the way we used to, or the way you and I always did. I feel so trapped in this relationship. I know they will fire my dad if Nate and I break up. And my dad is in a really good place right now. His gambling has stopped and he's dating someone. Plus, I'm just hanging *on, hoping things improve. Maybe this is just a rough patch with Nate and me, ya know? All couples have one. Right? Although, we never did. Since you said that it was okay to bring up our relationships, (I promise to follow the new rule) I hope this is okay, Sam, because I need a friend.*

Nate doesn't treat me the way Chad did. But he ... well, he can be controlling in his own way. I guess you could say I love him. I don't really know though, because any relationship I have from here on out will always be compared to ours.

Why do I put this kind of pressure on myself? Why? I don't think I will ever know.

Anyway, thanks for letting me vent. I hope I haven't ruined this long-distance friend thing we have. Write soon.

Love, Maria

Jan. 19, 1999

Dear Maria,

I'm surprised you don't hate me. I've let another four months go by without writing. I'm so sorry.

So, about Nate. I won't ask the question I'm dying to ask because of the rule. The rule I made. I'm so stupid. Anyway, all I'll say is, I hope you and Nate are doing okay. What bothered me the most about your letter, though, is your unwillingness to put yourself and your feelings first. You have always been that way, Maria. Please don't do that to yourself. I mean, that's why you lost me in the first place. You let one relationship go because of your dad. Don't stay in another one because of him.

I'm going to change the subject. School is kicking my butt. It's so much harder than I thought it was going to be. I'm burned out. I know that it will be worth it in the end, but man. I am beat.

I promise to write more often. One other thing, Big C is getting married. It's the same girl that he's been dating. The one Ricky was supposed to introduce to me. Maybe now, I will find out what his real name is. I have a clue, but I really don't know.

Sincerely, Sam

∞

March 7, 1999

Dear Sam,

That's great news about Big C! That night at Dexter's, even though I had no clue who he was to you, he seemed like a friend. You'll have to tell me all about it!

You are going to crack up when you hear this! I know that you hate pop music. I went and saw NSYNC in concert! I'm sorry, but I love them. Nate got me tickets as an anniversary gift. Front row!! It was insane! You're laughing right now, aren't you? I can totally see your face in my head. You're rolling your eyes and smirking at the same time. If I was right beside you, you would have started to jokingly make fun of me because I like a band that is supposed to be for teenage girls. I'm right, huh?

Sometimes, I sit back and wonder if you've changed at all. You seemed the same at Dexter's, but that has been almost two years now. Do you still like to watch Friends, Frasier, and ER? Do you still like country music and Michael Bolton? Do you still smell the same?

WOW! It just dawned on me that we have been writing for almost two years. Time flies when it's spent with those you care about.

Love, Maria

June, 10, 1999

Dear Maria,

Big C is moving back to Georgia. I don't think I told you, but that's where he is from. The wedding was this past Saturday, and it went well. It was small. It was just in his backyard, then a dinner after. I liked it. It reminded me of when we would always talk about our wedding. Something small and intimate. That's what Big C had, and it made me think of you.

You know me Maria; I am a simple guy. I haven't changed much. I still like Thursday night TV, Michael Bolton is still a favorite and in case you're wondering, Polish food is still a staple. I could eat halushki morning, noon and night.

Your writing about change made me wonder if you have changed at all. Your horrible taste in music is still the same, but do you still have an aversion to reading books? Do you still watch cheerleading competitions on ESPN? Do you still tape Days of Our Lives if you aren't home? I wonder about a lot of things with you. All the time.

Yours, Sam

P.S. Cara and I broke up. And Big C's name is Clerance. He HATES it. So funny.

Sept, 9, 1999

Dear Sam,

I'm sorry to hear about you and Cara. Is asking what happened part of "the rule"? I won't risk it. Anyway, if it was for the best, then I hope you are at peace with it and are happy. Your happiness has always meant everything to me. I know it's been a few months since I've written. Have you started seeing anyone else?

I have a confession to make. I saw you the other day on campus. You were coming out of Regency Hall talking to a few guys. It took everything in me to not go over and talk to you. I wanted to, really really bad. I wasn't sure if you would be comfortable with that. So, you know what I did instead? I stalked you. I know, I know. It's confession time here. I followed you as you walked to your next class over at Glayson Hall. God, writing this down is making me sound like such a creeper. You and the other two guys were joking and laughing, which was nice to hear. I miss your laugh. You haven't changed much. Your hair is a little longer, and I liked the shirt you were wearing.

Being that close to you was hard. I understand now why you felt the need to approach me at Dexter's. Why is there still this magnetic pull between us? I really wondered if I should tell you this. I hope you aren't mad. Please don't be mad at me. I don't think I could take it.

Love, Maria

P.S. can you believe this Y2K stuff? It feels kinda over the top, but should we be worried? If the world ends and I didn't go talk to you, I'm going to be really mad at myself.

Nov. 20, 1999

Dear Maria,

Let me start off by saying this. The world isn't going to end. The clocks will flip over and nothing will happen. Mark my words.

I wish you would have come up to me. It would have been okay. And I'm not mad at you. Even when I felt like I was mad at you before, I don't think I ever really was.

Do you and Nate have any plans for the next few months? Nothing on the books for me. More than likely, I will just still be at school, still working, still studying. Pretty boring stuff.

I get what you mean. Seeing you that night and once I saw Nate leave, there was no stopping me from going over to you. I still regret the way the night ended. I'll always regret it.

Yours, Sam

Feb, 11, 2000

Dear Sam,

You were right. The clocks flipped from December 31st to January 1st and nothing happened. The whole thing was ridiculous.

Now it's my turn to apologize for taking so long to write. I had a nice start to my new year. Nate surprised me with a trip to Europe! That's why I've been a little quiet. I mean, you know how much I've always wanted to travel. He told me about it on New Year's Day and we left the week after. We visited England, Ireland, Spain, and France. We were gone for a month and spent a week in each country. It was amazing! And I feel like Nate and I got closer on this trip. Which has made me feel better. He seemed more relaxed and playful even.

Anyway, it was nice and I hope to go back someday.

Love, Maria

March 2, 2000

Dear Maria,

That's awesome, Maria. I'm really happy that you have got to go to Europe. I hope you got to go to the Eiffel Tower. I know that was always something you wanted to see. Plus, I'm happy you have someone that can afford to take you to the places you have wanted to go.

I'm going to be honest here. I went back through and reread our letters. Even the ones that we wrote to each other when we were together. It brought back so many memories and feelings. Truth be told, I probably shouldn't have done it. I was with Cara for a whole year, and she never made me feel what I felt for you.

Okay, I'm traveling into the romantic zone. You literally just told me that you and Nate are doing well and I have to go and pull this. I'm so sorry.

But I am going to ask you what you asked me before. Do you think that we could meet for coffee? I don't know ... should we meet? Let me know what you think.

Yours, Sam

March 12, 2000

Dear Sam,

If we are being honest, then I guess I have to be as well. I read your letters all the time.

Yes, I would be okay with us meeting up for some coffee. My schedule is pretty busy, but does the beginning of April work? Nate and I are going to go to a Cavs game that first Saturday of April, but maybe we could meet the next day? Nate always takes his mom to church so we could maybe get brunch that morning. Let me know if that works for you. If it does, I'm looking forward to it.

Love, Maria

March 18, 2000

Dear Maria,

I honestly can't believe you said yes. April 2nd sounds perfect. I don't think I have any plans and even if I did, I would make sure to be there. How about we meet at Bistro 1845 around 11:00? I hope that works.

Yours, Sam

P.S. sorry this one is short. I have a huge paper due and I'm really behind. We will talk soon, though. In person.

∞

March 22, 2000

Dear Sam,

I'll be there!! I'm sitting here grinning from ear to ear. I can't believe in a little over a week I'm going to get to spend some time with you. Writing letters is one thing, but being together and talking face to face is something completely different. Plus, I miss my best friend.

Also, I've been dying to eat at Bistro 1845. I've heard they have amazing pancakes! I wonder if they are as good as yours? I guess I'll find out!

Love, Maria

P.S. T minus nine days and counting.

Chapter Twelve

JUNE 2001

THE SHED

Sam

M aria didn't show.

Over a year has passed, and the memory of that day still lingers, haunting me. April 2nd, 2000. I waited in Bistro 1845 for three hours. The hardest thing was deciding to leave, fully aware she wouldn't be coming. I lost her again, and the ache in my chest became unbearable.

As soon as I walked through my front door, I felt an overwhelming urge to write her a letter, and so I did. I knew there had to be some sort of reasonable explanation for why she stood me up. Her letters sounded so hopeful and full of excitement at the idea of seeing me again. I mailed that letter and a letter every week for two months ... with no reply.

I have no clue what happened. Time has passed, but the ache remains fresh, more than a year later. Thousands of questions plague me.

Why did she change her mind?

Did Nate find out about our writing to each other?

Has she finally moved on?

I eventually decided that I had to stop torturing myself, and it took me the entire summer and fall to clear my head of what happened. To let her go ... a third time. In the new year, Cara and I reconnected and started dating again, until she took a job in California. I can't blame her for leaving the area. Saying goodbye to her was difficult, and the allure she holds over me will always be there. She was a pleasant distraction from the hurt.

But now I understand I need to concentrate on my future. Move forward. Which is what I'm doing. I recently got my master's in science, which gets me one step closer to becoming a psychologist. I have also applied to doctorate programs. Amazingly enough, three accepted me. Ohio State, University of Michigan, and Georgia State. Who would have thought that I would go from a grocery store manager to a PhD student? Certainly not me.

Big C's excitement about Georgia is over the top, and he is really pushing for me to accept there. Who knows where I will end up? More than anything, I wanted Maria to be the first to hear this news. The letters I sent to her never made their way back to me. Which means her mom must still live in the same house.

So many times, after she stood me up, I thought about driving over there to fight for her.

But I didn't.

The desire to see her faded and morphed into a need to talk to her and share with her things about my life. Nighttime was the worst. That's when she would only exist in my occasional thoughts and linger in my dreams.

Gradually, I sensed the door to my heart closing. But not completely. Maria will always be able to open that door. Also, I kept the same promise to myself.

I haven't shed a tear for her.

And I won't.

"So, when can I get your room ready at my place?" Big C asks me as he saddles up next to Ricky. He's in town visiting. I'm at Dexter's with both of them, blowing off some steam on a Friday night. Just like old times, except Big C is on our side of the bar.

Before I can answer, Miles, the bar manager, races over to say hi. "Big C! Nice to see you, man!" They grab hands and lean into each other for a semi-bro-hug above the slick, lacquered bar. "We are slammed tonight. I could use you!"

Big C lets out a hearty laugh. "No way, man. My days of slinging pints are over. I just want to hang with these two losers tonight," he says as he waves his finger between Ricky and me.

Miles shrugs. "Suit yourself. Nice to see you again, though." He points to us. "If you fellas need anything, let me know. In the meantime, the first shot is on me." Before I know it, three shot glasses filled with whiskey materialize in front of us. As we raise the glasses, the scent of alcohol wafts into the air. "To new beginnings," I say and down the amber-colored liquid as the burn coats my throat.

Ricky's eyes lock on mine, filled with excitement. He turns to Big C. "Cool! So you told him." Big C winces and lowers his head. Ricky turns back to me, his inquisitive eyes searching for answers. "I'm impressed! You're taking it better than I thought you would."

I look at my two friends with their two different reactions to what Ricky said. I pause, taken aback. "Told ... uh ... told me what?"

"You know, about Maria"—just hearing her name stirs my curiosity—"*and* tomorrow," Ricky retorts as if I should know what he's talking about.

As I sit here, my bewildered expression must be apparent because Ricky mirrors my confusion, realizing finally we aren't on the same page. I peer past Ricky and catch a glimpse of Big C, his eyes fixed straight ahead, his jaw clenched. "Dude, what's going on? Is Maria okay?"

"Maria's great," he replies, without bothering to make eye contact. "She's getting married." As he turns his attention to me, I notice a slight crease forming on his forehead. "Tomorrow."

The blood drains from my face. Heat rises to my head, and the usual Dexter's commotion fades to black. My unanswered questions from the past year are now getting resolved with those three words. 'She's getting married.' It explains everything. Why she didn't show. Why she stopped writing. Why she never answered any of my letters.

More than likely, Nate proposed that night at the Cavs' game. What other explanation could there be?

"Dude, you look pale," Ricky says.

I stare down at the bar, my throat tightening as I struggle to find the words. "How ... um ... how do you know?"

Out of the corner of my eye, I glimpse Big C reaching into his back pocket and retrieving a folded-up newspaper clipping. He tosses it my way, and I watch as it glides effortlessly down the bar, slipping past Ricky. I quickly halt it with a firm hand. I hold it, feeling the weight of curiosity with what I know lies inside. A thick tension hangs in the air. With Big C's and Ricky's unwavering focus, they wait for me to make a move.

"We were going to tell you tonight," Big C starts. "The plan was to get a few beers in you first, you know, to soften the blow. Maybe make it hurt less."

We remain silent, creating a palpable tension in the atmosphere. My head pounds against my skull, the thumping rhythm blending with the boisterous bar noise.

Finally, after a few minutes, Ricky speaks. "Are you going to read it?"

I nod, but before I open it, I turn to my two closest friends and a surge of gratitude for their unwavering support. However, I need to be by myself. "I think I need to read it alone."

They both nod and turn on their bar stools. I don't feel Ricky's presence anymore, more than likely disappearing into the crowd. Big C's imposing figure stands only a few feet away, allowing me the space I asked for, yet watching.

The newspaper clipping crinkles as I unfold it. My fingers graze over the raised lettering on the paper that has started to yellow. It's only half of a full sheet, the edges uneven from this portion being ripped from the rest. As soon as I look at it, my eyes lock onto the clearly displayed date at the top. It's from two weeks ago.

How long has Big C hung onto this?

I shake the thought from my mind because it doesn't matter.

I turn it over and staring back at me is still, to this day, the most beautiful woman.

My Maria.

But in this black and white newspaper photo, she isn't mine. She belongs to Nate. Both of them are smiling ear to ear, leaning into one another. Maria's left hand is resting on Nate's chest, and on her third finger rests the biggest diamond ring I have ever seen.

They look perfect. The All-American couple. Pristine, polished ... and engaged.

Before I read the announcement, I flag down Miles. He sets a beer in front of me. I take a long swig and begin to read.

Bryant - Connelly

Lily and John Bryant of Youngstown, Ohio, are pleased to announce the engagement of their daughter, Maria Lynn Bryant, to Nathanial James Connelly, son of local businessman Roger Connelly and his wife, Rosemary Connelly.

Maria is a student at Ohio Northeastern, where she is studying exercise science. She is currently employed as an EKG technician at St. Augustine's Hospital.

Nathaniel received his bachelor's degree in engineering from Ohio Northeastern and is currently employed at his father's manufacturing firm, R&R Conn.

The wedding will take place on June 9th at Riverside Garden in Madison Creek Park, with an invitation-only reception to be held at Avon Grand Pavilion.

I lower the article as I hang my head. The loneliness I felt, first when she left me for Chad and then when she didn't show at Bistro 1845, is back with a vengeance. The sea of unanswered questions I have seems to stretch out endlessly.

I will not let her take the easy way out again.

Hell, at least I got a letter last time.

She doesn't get to shut me out without at least an explanation. I ball the newspaper up in my hand and slam it down on the bar. With determination, I yank my wallet out of my back pocket, fish out a ten-dollar bill, and toss it on the bar as I stand. Big C must be able to read minds because he stomps over to me, knowing what I'm about to do.

"Sam, don't do it," he says. He grabs my arm as I try to walk past him.

"Let me go, C."

"I can't do that." His grip tightens.

We stand face to face, and I know I'm no match for his massive frame and strength. So, I appeal to his humanity. "What if it was Jasmine?" I ask. He doesn't answer right away. Without warning, his expression softens to one of understanding and his grip loosens.

"Fine, but I'm going with you and driving." He lets go of the vice grip he had on my arm. "Where's Ricky?" We glance around the bar, he's saddled up against the back wall, chalking up a pool cue, talking to a beautiful woman.

"RICKY!" Big C's booming voice pulsates through the loud bar, and Ricky looks in our direction. He salutes us and nods.

He knows where I'm going and what I need to do.

With that, I make my way out of Dexter's and into the night.

On my way to Maria.

I obviously haven't thought this through because I have no clue where Maria could be. I'm assuming since it's the night before her wedding, there must have been a rehearsal dinner. But where ... no idea. I also don't know where she is living since my letters went to her mom's house. Is she living with Nate or on her own, maybe?

God, what am I doing?

So, I direct Big C to the only likely place she can be.

Her mother's.

Big C pulls up alongside the curb in front of the house. Through the windows, the soft glow of lights is visible, and a row of cars sits parked in the driveway. But is *she* here? I scan the cars and another realization floods my brain … I don't know what she drives. It dawns on me how little I know about her current life, yet no one knows her better.

I'm in a really weird head space right now.

Big C and I both sit and stare at the split level for longer than we need to. He glances at me, waiting for me to do or say something. "Her old bedroom window is at the back of the house," I start. "Maybe I should go check it out?" I look to C for validation—or permission—I'm not sure honestly.

"If they call the cops on you for trespassing, then I am out of here, and you are on your own. Got it?"

I nod in acknowledgement. "Otherwise, good luck. I'll be here when you're done."

I open the car door as it creaks on its hinges. The warm night air hits me in the face as I race up the walkway, crouching down like a thief, looking around to make sure no one is watching. I make it to the shrubs that line the side of the house and round the corner to the backyard. I look up to find her window and, sure enough, the light is on. *YES!*

The craziest thought pops into my head, and I can't believe I am about to do this. As I search the ground for a pebble, I shake my head in disbelief at what my life has become.

Because I am actually going to throw pebbles at her window. Like I'm in a freaking movie.

It's my only option because I am not about to knock on the front door.

With a handful of pebbles in my hand, I position myself so that I'm not too far away. I was in baseball in high school, so my aim is decent enough. As I stare up at the window, the white sheer curtain that always hung there is a cruel reminder of the past.

Alright, here goes nothing. I throw my arm back and heave a pebble at the glass.

Tink.

I wait. Nothing.

I toss another one.

Tink.

Nothing.

I try again.

Tink.

This time, I decide to wait and see if anything happens. I look around to the darkened back yards that surround me, making sure none of the neighbors are watching. My breaths are heavy with adrenaline. I look down at my palm and stare at the two pebbles I have left, turning them as I think.

If she doesn't answer after these two, I will walk away. Forever.

Before I can talk myself out of it, I throw my arm back and toss the next pebble with a little more force this time.

TINK.

Finally, the curtain shifts, and my stomach erupts with nerves. A silhouette comes into view, so I take a few steps backward. The curtains open, followed by the window, and it's her.

She balances herself with her hands on the window seal. "Sam?"

I can't help but smile because, my God, this actually worked. And she looks stunning. I haven't seen her since Dexter's. She never changes.

"What in the world are you doing?" she yells down in a whisper.

"Maria, please come outside so we can talk."

"Sam, I can't," she looks at her ring. "I'm getting married tomorrow."

"I know. That's why I'm here. Please," I plead, "you owe me an explanation."

Looking down at me, her eyebrows pinch together. "You're right. I do. Give me five minutes and meet me in the shed. It's unlocked." With that, she shuts the window and disappears.

I turn around and make my way to the shed that rests at the back of the yard. With a shaking hand, I grab the handle to the door, and it creaks open. On heavy feet, I step in, and the smell of grass and mildew assaults my nose. I know exactly where the light is, so I look ahead and the string hangs from the light bulb on the ceiling. I tug it, and light fills the space. It looks the exact same from what I remember. And it's the memories that are making me unsteady on my feet. This used to be Maria's and my make-out spot. We would sneak in here sometimes … okay, a lot of times … and with roaming hormonal teenage hands, we would get lost in each other.

The sound of her approaching pulls me from my thoughts. She steps in and closes the door behind her, immediately filling the small space with a thick humidity. I watch her every movement and try to memorize it all since I don't know if this will be the last time I see her. Her hair is in a high ponytail, she's wearing a white t-shirt and navy-blue pajama shorts, no make-up. She's never looked more beautiful.

"It's been a while since we've been in here." It comes out rough and husky. I know she is thinking about the past just as much as me.

A sly smile creeps on her face, and her cheeks turn pink. "Those were some good times."

We both stand there glancing around the space, trying not to look at one another. Neither of us sure where to start. Since I'm the one that showed up at her window, I guess I should say something.

"What happened, Maria?" I ask, the question coming out in a whisper. "Please tell me the truth."

She looks down at the steel floor, not wanting to make eye contact.

She shakes her head and turns on her heels. "I can't do this." But before she walks away, I grab her wrist and pull her to me. Under my grasp is the watch I gave her.

She still wears it.

I wipe the thought from my head as my hands land on her arms, and I hold her tightly, but not too tight. Inches separate us, tears begin rolling down her cheeks.

"Fine. You don't have to tell me because I think I already know. But I have a few things to say." She nods, and I let go of my grasp. With a sniff, she uses her hand to hastily brush away her tears. "Don't do this, Maria. Please don't. I love you and I know you love me." She sucks in a breath as her eyes pierce me, full of pain, her brows furrowed.

"Sam, please don't," she begs. Her hands betray her request and land on my arms. Her grip tightens, not letting go, even though she knows she should.

"Don't what? Tell the truth?" Memories of us in this shed flood my mind, and I want to recreate every one of those moments. This is only the second time I have held her since *The Chad* letter. All I want to do is kiss her within an inch of her life and show her how much I love her.

But I won't. That doesn't stop our foreheads from coming together like magnets. Our breathing is getting heavier.

"Don't marry him," I whisper. "Marry me." I do not know where that came from, but it's how I feel. It's what I want. Her head whips back, and I find myself under the scrutiny of her piercing eyes.

"Sam, I can't—"

"Yes, you—"

"No. I can't." With determination, she shoves me away and steps backward toward the door. My arms suddenly feel empty. I put my hands in my pockets to stop myself from reaching out to her again. "My parents are finally in a good place, Sam. Financially." She swallows hard, taking her time to gather up with the right words.

This is excruciating.

"Plus, Nate's dad just gave my dad a huge promotion and a raise to help, in spite of his disability." She pauses again. "Nate loves me, Sam."

"Not as much as me." My body rises from confidence in my statement.

"But he does. And I can't hurt him."

What did she just say?

My jaw is on the floor.

I huff out a breath and turn my eyes toward the ceiling. "So, you can't hurt him, but you had no problem hurting me."

"That's not what I meant," she retorts as she reaches out to me, sensing her statement hurt me. I step back, hitting my legs on a bicycle behind me.

Neither of us speak for a few minutes. She takes this as her cue to leave and turns, grabbing the handle to the door. "Do you love him?" I blurt out, not ready for this reunion to end.

She pauses, not answering me, so I continue. "You said he loves you, but you didn't mention if you love him."

She turns, drawing her attention back to me. She's picking at her nails. "It's not about being in love with him."

"Oh, *really*? Because last I checked, people should be in love when they get married, Maria. How is that fair to him? How can you marry someone you aren't in love with? Please, make it make sense."

"It's everything!" she shouts, causing me to flinch at her outburst. She paces in the little floor space she has beneath her feet. Four steps up. Four steps back, still going to town on her nails. "It's my parents spending way too much money on this wedding when they are just getting back on track. It's my dad working for his dad. Mr. Connelly would fire him, Sam. It's about Nate and how this would look for him—"

I hold up my hand. "Whoa, whoa, whoa." She stops pacing and stares at me, motionless. I take a deep breath to steady myself and get my anger under control. "How would this look for *him*? Did you seriously just say that? Is any of this about you, Maria, and what you want? Any of it?"

Her eyes drop again as she wraps her arms around herself, seeking a sense of security. "It's complicated."

"Famous last words."

The silence returns to this humid box, neither of us knowing what to say or what will happen next. My brain is racing with a million thoughts. It's obvious where her head is, but I need to know if I can reach her heart. I'm not ready to give up on us. Not here in our shed.

Without a second to think, I rush, grab her by the waist, and pull her toward me. She lets out a yelp but doesn't resist. Her eyes immediately land on mine, and her arms wrap around me. "Maria, what do you want? Right here, right now, in our shed, in my arms." We are both panting. "What. Do. You. Want?" She doesn't answer, biting her lower lip in contemplation.

I decide to continue because she needs to know the truth. "Because I can tell you what I want. You. Every day, all day. You, in my life. You, with my ring on your finger. You, waking up next to me every morning. You, carrying my children." She lets out a gasp, and the tears return, spilling over her lashes, landing on her cheek in a silent cry. "Only you." I wipe away her tears with my thumb and cradle her face in my palm. Her skin is both cold from the tears and warm from the heat in this shed.

God, I want to kiss her so badly. But I won't cross that line. She belongs to someone else. "Maria, this isn't about me. This isn't about Nate or your parents. Choose yourself. Choose *us*." I plead with her. I beg. "*Please.*"

Time seems to stand still as I wait for her answer.

Suddenly, though, her body answers for her as she goes rigid and stiff. Her hands slowly make their way to my chest, and with a gentle touch, she pushes. I uncoil my arms from her waist as the realization of her decision comes into clear focus, and we both take a step back. The heat is now replaced with a cold, chilly distance.

"I know you won't understand, Sam. But I can't be selfish with this. Too many people are involved. And I do love you, Sam. I do." The tears are now pouring down her cheeks, unstoppable. "So much it hurts. What I want more than anything is to leave this shed with you and start the life we talked about years ago. But I can't." She pauses, trying to collect her thoughts. "I'll always remember us. I'll never forget." She brings her hand to her mouth and sobs. "I'm so sorry."

With that, she turns around and slams right into the shed door before stepping back, opening it, and running out into the night.

I fight it. I fight it harder than I have fought anything.

I swallow the tears.

My God. What kind of hold do these people have over her? Or is this Maria just being the people pleaser she is?

It's clear that I won't receive answers to these questions in the near future. Which sucks.

Stepping out of the shed, I roll my shoulders and try to get myself together as I retrace my steps back towards Big C's car. He watches me approach. With each slow and heavy step, regret weighs down on my heart. As I reach for the door handle and before I get in, I turn to look at the house one last time.

I. Am. Done.

With a burst of energy, I yank open the car door and throw myself inside, slamming it shut as the vehicle rocks from the force.

"Didn't go well?" Big C asks as he turns the ignition, the engine roaring to life. He pulls the gearshift into drive, and the car lurches forward. We drive down the road when I answer.

"You can get my room ready." His head whips in my direction.

"I'm coming to Georgia."

Chapter Thirteen

JUNE 2001

I'm squished into the corner of a bustling reception hall, the lively chatter of my friends and family ringing in my ears. We have decorated the large room within an inch of its life, thanks to my mom. She strung lights everywhere. Gaudy centerpieces rest on the tables, napkins with our names and wedding date embossed in gold adorn the table that houses our monstrous cake. The guests wear gorgeous party dresses and their best suits. Every guest is here to celebrate us.

Nate and Maria. Mr. And Mrs. Connelly.

An eager energy fills the room with laughter and conversations of old friends catching up. Faint dinner music plays softly in the background. My stomach churns. The rustling of my dress is filling my ears. A wedding dress that, at one time, I thought was gorgeous. But now it's constricting, binding, and suffocating. As if I'm trapped, a prisoner in this life that I have chosen for myself.

And that's because I am trapped. The officiant's utterance of those magic words, 'I now pronounce you man and wife,' sealed my fate.

I am now officially Maria Connelly.

Sure, I could have bolted. I thought about it from the minute I woke up. I assume most brides wake up on their wedding days, happy and excited. Full of elation over the life that they are about to form with their fiancé. Thoughts of forever plastered across the smiles they have. Not me. I woke up with only one thought in my head.

Sam.

Not my fiancé and now husband, Nate.

But Sam.

He knows I'm getting married today. After seeing him last night, holding him, and hearing him say that he wanted to marry me, my head hasn't been where it needs to be.

I wonder what he is doing right now?

When the officiant said, 'Should anyone present know of any reason why this couple should not be joined in holy matrimony, let him or her speak now or forever hold your peace,' my lips trembled as tears brimmed because I am the person who should have spoken up.

Me.

With a smile on his face, Nate locked eyes with me. He thought my tears were for him and a reflection of my happiness. Just like everything else, I let him believe that lie.

I hurt Sam deeply last night. Again. I saw the pain etched on his face. More than anything, I wanted to grab his hand and run out of that shed and leave it all behind. But I couldn't. At this point in my life, I can't choose myself. When I told him that too many people were involved, I meant it. I couldn't do it to my parents. Maybe I'm a little traumatized from the entire experience with Chad, but I honestly was afraid of what Nate would do. He hasn't laid a finger on me. But would he? Could he?

Plus, Nate's father is a powerful man in the community. What would he do to Sam in retaliation? I know what he would do to my dad. He has the power to ruin my father. He is ruthless. I didn't want to risk it and find out, which factored into me walking away from Sam. For the third time.

Does he hate me? My stomach drops with that thought.

A hand lacing his fingers through mine breaks up my thoughts of Sam. I look up and my husband is giving me a small smile. I glance at our interlaced hands. I have to admit that Nate does look handsome in his black tux and white bow tie. Every strand of his dark blonde hair is flawlessly styled, and the lingering scent of his signature aftershave fills my nose. It's earthy, like a forest.

I look down at our joined hands as he traces his thumb along the top of mine. Nate's hands are soft. But they don't feel like Sam's.

I force a fake smile back at Nate. A habit at this point. He squeezes my hand. "You ready for this, Maria?" he asks, his eyes brimming with excitement. Nate has never given me any kind of term of endearment. No 'honey,' no 'babe,' no 'love.' I mean, I would have taken a 'pookie.' It's always just been Maria.

Maybe I don't deserve one.

I nod at his question and turn my attention to the dance floor and what is about to happen. Nate must pick up on my uneasiness because he leans in and whispers in my ear. "Relax, Maria. Let's just eat, dance some, and appease our parents. Then we can get out of here and have some real fun." I turn to look at him, and he waggles his eyebrows.

Suddenly, the lights dim. A strobe light coming from—I don't know, somewhere—starts sporadically pulsing different-colored rays over the hall. Then, out of nowhere, an urge to cough fills my lungs. Is that smoke? Dear Lord, a smoke machine. Am I at a club or at my wedding?

"LADIES AND GENTLEMEN! Are you ready to make some noise?!" the DJ screams into the microphone. He's holding onto his headphones with one hand, the other on a turntable. Our guests roar and clap over C&C Music Factory's "Everybody Dance Now."

"I CAN'T HEAR YOU! I said, are you ready to make some noise?" Louder screams and claps this time as C&C's volume increases also. I glance at Nate, who is no longer looking at me. Instead, he is pointing, laughing, and engaging with his already too drunk groomsmen. These guys started drinking at the wedding venue, which continued in the limo. Then the booze made its way to the park for pictures. All of them, including Nate, are three sheets to the wind.

Without warning, one of them sprints towards Nate, leaping onto his back and shaking him violently.

"Let's get this party started, man!" He exclaims as he high-fives my husband.

The DJ announces our bridal party couples one by one. Nine couples total. Normally, it's the girl that wants a huge bridal party. Nope, that was Nate. The DJ introduces one frat buddy after another to our wedding guests with their escort. Girls I had to pretend to be friends with to fill our bridal party quota.

Now it's our turn.

"THE MOMENT YOU HAVE ALL BEEN WAITING FOR! Without further ado, it is my honor to be the first to introduce you ... MR. AND MRS. NATE CONNELLY!"

With those words from the DJ, Nate and I sashay onto the dance floor. My too-tight dress is swooshing and swaying with each step. The room explodes into hoots and hollers. I see my mom, her table-issued disposable camera in hand, snapping away in our direction. I give her a huge smile that I know she will love. My dad is standing next to his new girlfriend, grinning with pride. Nate raises our joined hands up into the air and lets out a huge, "WOOHOO!"

We make it to the center of the room for our first dance, and I know Nate is thriving. His smile reaches ear to ear as he waves at everyone. Never once looking at me. And that's because Nate loves attention. Any and all attention. Now, it's on him, and he is relishing it.

His proposal was proof of how much he adores people focusing on him. And what is the most attention-grabbing proposal out there? Asking your beloved to marry you at a NBA game, on the big jumbotron. So, what do you do when you are a people pleaser and an arena full of twenty-thousand Cavs fans are screaming 'JUST SAY YES! JUST SAY YES!' over and over as your boyfriend is on bended knee?

You say yes.

Even if you gave your heart to someone else as a teenager. I was supposed to meet Sam the next morning at Bistro 1845. We made the plans via our letters. As soon as Nate got on one knee, I knew that date wouldn't happen, and the letters that I loved so much would stop.

Sam wrote to me immediately after. His letter and letters that followed were begging me for an explanation. And I never replied. I couldn't. But I should have.

I wasn't ready to marry Nate. Far from it. I knew he wanted to get married. He talked about it all the time. But for him, it was more wanting the life that his parents had. A wife waiting on her husband hand and foot, doting on her man twenty-four seven. A spotless house that doesn't look lived in. Piping hot dinners waiting on the table at the stroke of five, not a minute later. A wife who looks dinner party ready when her husband walks in the door. Not a hair out of place. A wife who can never speak her mind or seek her own interests. Why? Because her sole focus in life is her husband.

He wanted Mayberry. And for some godforsaken reason, I led him to believe that I would give him that. And worse yet, I wanted it too.

That's how I ended up in the middle of this reception hall, my husband holding me in his arms as we sway and dance to Faith Hill's "There You'll Be." Our bridal party is lining either side of the dance floor. Nate is, of course, nodding, waving, and smiling at the entire audience of people. He's beaming.

Good grief, he thinks he is a celebrity.

Without warning, he spins me. The crowd eats it up. Camera flashes surround us. We are dancing in sync, not missing a step. Never faltering. Perfection.

Nate's soft hand is on my lower back. His touch, which at one time felt like something I needed, now feels empty and foreign. And it has for a long time.

It makes me think of Sam's arms from last night. They felt warm, comforting, and full of promise.

I turn my attention up to Nate. The song is halfway over, and our first dance as husband and wife is almost a memory ... and he still hasn't looked at me once.

I turn back to our friends and family, plastering on the fakest smile I can muster. Trying my hardest to push down the raising need to scream.

The photographer taps Nate on the shoulder. "Let's get a close-up. Nate, lean into Maria and press your cheeks together." We do as instructed. "Perfect," she says as she takes a few steps backward. She places the camera up to her face. "Now, on the count of three, look right here"—she points to the camera lens—"and smile as if this is the happiest day of your life!"

We hold our pose. Both of us flashing our biggest smiles. The smiles that will be framed and grace our parents' fireplace mantels for years to come.

"One, two, three!" The bright flash fires.
And one face bursts before my eyes.
My Sam.
Then the flash disappears.
And so does Sam.

Chapter Fourteen

OCTOBER 2002

Sam

"**L**et's get married!"

Erica's fork stops mid-bite as she looks at me, stunned at my outburst in the middle of this run-down BBQ joint in downtown Atlanta. Her fork hovers for a brief second before returning to her plate.

"I'm sorry … what?" she asks, confused by my—oh, I don't know what you call it—a semi-proposal? She stares at me, blinking as the chatter of other diners fills the air.

"You heard me. Let's get married," I reiterate because I am dead serious.

And look, I know this sounds confusing. It was just over a year ago when Maria, for the third time, shattered me completely. As I left her house that night—the night before her wedding—a newfound determination filled my heart.

It was twofold.

    1. Never let Maria affect me again and get over her as fast as possible by any means necessary.

    2. Start a new life in Georgia.

It turns out number two was a lot easier.

I spent the day of Maria's wedding stone cold drunk. My plan was to black out and not remember the whole day. I was pretty successful.

Then, one week later, I had my whole life packed up in about ten different boxes, shoved into my car. I didn't renew the lease on my apartment and left the furniture. The car was so packed that I couldn't see out the rearview window. A twelve-hour drive later, I was in Georgia. Determined to start fresh and ready to move on.

Jasmine and Big C were kind enough to let me stay in their spare room above the garage till I got on my feet. I went to bed every night feeling stronger with a renewed sense of purpose ... but also with Maria's ring and letters tucked away under the bed.

I said I felt stronger. That doesn't mean I wasn't still weak.

Removing Maria out of my thoughts and heart was the hardest thing I have ever done. Thankfully, my PhD program provided a constant stream of work, keeping my mind occupied. Ricky, on occasion, would try to give me updates on her, but I told him I didn't want to hear it. I needed a clean break. And that is what I was doing here in Georgia. I put five states plus six hundred and eighty-five miles between us.

Was it hard? Yes. Was it necessary? Definitely yes.

Then, one night about four months ago, at a local brewery, I bumped into one of the most outrageous and sexy women I have ever met. The one sitting across from me right now, mouth hanging open from my declaration.

Erica.

We were both there with friends, touring the micro-brewery. During the whole tour, I couldn't tear my eyes away from her. Don't ask me how to make beer. I have no clue. But I can tell you what Erica was wearing that day. Denim shorts frayed on the ends, a skintight red tank top, and Doc Martens. She was tan, irresistible, and took my breath away. After the tour, I made sure to sit by her at the tasting table. We connected instantly, and the conversation continued at the bar, then at her place. It was the first time since Maria that I looked at a woman with lust and desire. This goes way beyond attraction.

And it felt amazing. Almost like a drug.

And let me tell you, she is the anti-Maria. Exactly what I need in my life right now. Maria is soft, whereas Erica is rough and hard. Maria is a planner and overthinker. Erica is spontaneous and borderline dangerous. Maria has green eyes, she's tall, with long blonde hair. Erica's eyes are almost black. She is shorter, with a dark brown pixie cut, which sometimes is purple.

And she has her faults. Mainly, too much alcohol. Okay … a lot of alcohol. Her third beer is resting right in front of her, almost empty.

Her adventurous side is the reason I have blurted this out right here in the middle of this restaurant. I fell hard and fast for Erica. Mostly because of what she brings to my life. A life so different from the one I had in Ohio.

Do I love her? I *think* so. Yes. Yes, I love her.

The love I feel (or think I feel) for Erica is new and fresh. It's like reckless abandonment. We have so much fun together, it's ridiculous. Granted, most of that fun is attached to alcohol and the bustling energy of our favorite bar in town, Morning Ale.

But this desire to start from scratch and begin a whole new life is pulling me toward Erica. And by pull, apparently, I mean asking her to marry me.

Add given what happened on 9/11, it feels like the entire world is changing. So, I might as well change with it.

Plus, Maria decided to drive a wedge between us via a wedding ring. So, why shouldn't I do the same?

"Look, I know it sounds crazy," I continue. "But we connected so quickly."

"Is that what that day in the brewery was?" she asks, raising her eyebrow, her question dripping in sarcasm.

That first meeting was … something. Electric sounds like a good word.

I reach for her from across the table. Her dainty hand with chipped black-painted fingernails intertwine with mine as soon as we touch.

"I love you, Erica. And I feel like there isn't a reason to wait. We've talked about it." She nods her head in agreement. Heck, we talked about spending our lives together and what adventures we could have after only one week together. (How a wild life will fit into my career path as a psychologist? No clue. I'll cross that bridge when I get there.)

I press on because she is chewing on her bottom lip. This is something she does when she has some kind of hair-brained idea that normally ends with us hungover the next day. "I am at your place almost every day, anyway. We spend pretty much every waking moment together. We have so much fun, it should be illegal." She laughs at this one.

I pull her hand up to my lips and kiss her knuckles as I stare into her eyes. Both of us letting the enormity of the moment sink in. "I don't have a ring."

"I don't need one," she counters, her lips ticking up into a sly smile.

With a playful grin, I run my thumb gently across her left ring finger, noticing the soft feel of her skin. As I stare at her hand, I find it difficult to make eye contact when I finally gather the nerve to ask. So, I don't. "What do you say? Erica Richards, will you be my wife?"

This isn't who I planned on asking. This isn't who I wanted to spend my life with.

But life had other plans. And I want—no, I need—a different life. And I could have that with Erica.

I raise my gaze to meet hers, holding my breath as I do.

"Yes, Sam. I will absolutely marry you."

See, here's the thing with Erica. Once she gets something in her head, she wants to act on it. ASAP.

Which means we got married the next week. On a Tuesday, no less.

Total insanity.

Big C and Jasmine were there as our witnesses. It was at the historic courthouse in downtown Atlanta. Not my first choice, but, hey. This is new to me.

My mom wasn't happy about it all, and honestly, I have barely spoken to her about it. Truthfully, I don't want to hear what I know she is going to say. And I know she'll be right.

Since nothing about this whole marriage is traditional, Erica wore black pants with the skintight black lace top that I love. I wore my best khakis with a button-down black shirt.

Yep, we got married wearing black. Total insanity. Erica reminded me that it's not the color of the clothes but the meaning behind the day. She's right.

The night I asked her to marry me, I went back to Big C's and broke the news. He was ... well ... let's say that he was skeptical.

"Sam, are you freaking kidding me right now? What are you thinking?" he exclaimed as we stood in his kitchen drinking whiskey.

"It's spontaneous, I know."

"Spontaneous? It's stupid. You've only been dating for like what ... three months?"

"Four."

"Well, then. That makes everything better," he scoffed.

"Okay, mom." His lips curled into a brief grin as he shrugged off the slight dig at his genuine concern for me.

"That's the other thing," he continued with his lecture. "What about your mom?"

"I know, I know." I hang my head in shame. "Mom is livid about this whole thing."

He gave me a knowing look.

We stood there in silence for quite a while. I knew he wouldn't take this well. He hasn't been a huge fan of Erica's since we met. He says that she brings out the worst in me. I know he's right. But at that moment, in his kitchen, I didn't care.

He turned his attention back to me, his brow furrowed with concern. "Sam, does this ..." He stopped and looked down at his glass and let out a long breath. "Does this have to do with Maria? She got married, so now you have to. Be honest."

"What! No!" I yelled as I threw my hands in the air. "I know you think this is just a rebound."

"Heck, yeah, I do." He took a sip of his drink, wincing as it went down. "The first beautiful woman to bat her eyelashes at you now that Maria is out of the picture once and for all, and BAM! You want to marry her." He shook his head, gripping his glass. "This is so ridiculous."

"I really care about Erica. I need this, C. I need to start a new life. Erica makes me happy. She makes me feel alive for the first time since I got *The Chad* letter from—"

"God! Would you stop calling it that!"

I ignored him. "For the past seven years, it's like time has stood still. I'm stuck back in '95 and the day Maria destroyed me ... I'm trapped in that moment in time. So, I need ..." I stopped to collect my thoughts. Whatever the reason, getting my best friend's approval was crucial. "You and Jasmine have been wonderful to me. But I need to move on." And he knew this. His sole purpose in pressuring me to move here was so that I could start over and forget Maria once and for all. That night in our shed, she made her choice. Without a doubt, her future is mapped out and meticulously planned.

Awesome. Good for Maria. But now it's time I make some life decisions of my own.

Albeit it, crazy ones, but still.

I needed to start living my life and move on from the past.

He continued to stare straight ahead, rolling his rocks glass in his hand. He finally spoke up. "Is this your way of asking me to be your best man because, if so, you suck at it?" A wave of laughter passed between us, instantly easing the tension. He didn't agree with this decision, but he will be there to support me.

Erica's arm snaking around my bare chest pulls me from the memory. Her touch, heck, her whole body, makes my skin feel hot with need. We are lying in the king size bed of this small hotel's honeymoon suite. A thin white sheet covering our bodies. The ugly floral comforter is in a heap on the floor, along with our black non-traditional wedding attire and our two champagne glasses. The room reeks of alcohol, with three empty bottles of bubbly and wine resting on the table in the corner. As I run my fingertips up and down her arm, a low moan escapes her lips. "God, that feels good," she whispers, sounding content.

The rise and fall of her chest is slow and steady, a clear sign of how relaxed she is.

"Are you happy?" I ask as I take in the smell of her hair. It's musky. Erica has never been one for anything "girly." Another contrast with Maria.

Don't think about your ex while your new wife is in bed with you on your wedding night. You idiot.

Turning towards me, her eyes are brimming with desire, while her messy hair and smeared makeup are proof of what we just did. "Yes, so happy."

I plant a passionate kiss on her swollen lips as I turn her onto her back and climb on top of her. I rest my elbows on each side of her head, caging her in with my arms. Our lips break apart as I stroke her forehead with my thumb. We lock eyes, and time seems to stand still. Finally, she tilts her head to kiss me, and the world fades away again. And again. And again.

I get lost in my new life.

And my need to move on.

Chapter Fifteen

January 2004

Maria

Bursting through the door, I toss my purse onto the counter, and in a flurry, shed my jacket and shoes. I carefully hang them in the coat closet, making sure that it's orderly. With a sense of urgency, I decide the kitchen should be my starting point since Nate will see this room first when he comes home. I check Sam's watch that still rests on my wrist. It's five-fifteen. Nate is going to be here any second, and I just got home.

"There is no way I am going to get everything done in time, let alone start dinner," I say in a panic, my head hot from the anxiety. I'm also sick to my stomach. Is it from the baby or knowing that the house won't be perfect when Nate comes home?

Who knows at this point?

I barely had a moment to catch my breath on this busy day. It started with a dentist's appointment. Then I had lunch with my mom, followed by grocery shopping and my monthly OB appointment.

Yep, I'm pregnant. Four months, to be exact.

The doctor kept me longer because my blood pressure was above normal. Which was high because I was running late, knowing the race to get the house ready would await me when I got home.

But I can't think about how nauseous I am right now because I'm home an hour late and already behind.

In a frenzy, I dash through my house, hurling breakfast dishes into the dishwasher, wiping down the kitchen counters, and emptying the trash.

"God, I'm running so behind." I drag the full—and heavy—trash bag to the bin outside and heave it in. Racing back inside, panic consumes me as I realize I only have minutes left before he pulls in.

In my head, I'm trying to prioritize what needs done because I won't be able to make the entire house "Nate ready" in time. Once the kitchen is taken care of, my attention shifts to the living room. I tidy up the throw pillows, fluffing them and arranging them where they need to be, followed by neatly folding the blankets.

As I survey the open living space to make sure I have missed nothing, a wave of nausea hits me. I cover my mouth before I barely make it to the half bath that sits off of the kitchen. The contents of lunch with my mom splash into the toilet with force.

So gross.

It hits me again.

"God, how much did I eat?" I wipe my mouth with the back of my hand as I brace myself to stand, flushing the toilet as I do.

When I found out I was pregnant, my doctor told me that this morning sickness would last only the first three months. Well, that was a lie. Because now I'm four months along and the barfing hasn't stopped. Plus, it's definitely not only in the morning.

As I stand at the sink, cupping water into my hand to drink and rinse this taste out of my mouth, I hear the door that leads to the garage from the kitchen open and close. My heart rate spikes as I anticipate the first words that will come out of his mouth. I know exactly what they will be.

"Where's dinner?" Nate calls from the kitchen as I hear him throw his keys on the kitchen counter.

Yep, knew it.

Not "Hello," not "Hey honey, I'm home." Instead, I got "Where's dinner?" I grit my teeth together, and with a quick swipe of my hands on the towel hanging from the rack, I move to leave the bathroom. *Oh, wait!* I straighten the towel meticulously before stepping out to give him an answer he won't like.

This is my life now, and I need to accept it.

As soon as we returned from our honeymoon, Nate's controlling behaviors surfaced. I knew he wanted a perfect 1950s type of life and was a clean freak. However, I had no inkling that he would be like this. When we were dating, Nate liked having control, but he always respected my boundaries. For the most part, he played a supportive role in my life, giving me the freedom to pursue my dreams. No one cheered louder as I walked across the stage at college graduation. In that moment, I felt a sense of pride radiating from him, as if he truly appreciated my accomplishment of finally getting my degree. But now I realize that what concerned him was his reputation.

It's almost like he was hiding his true self because here's how things work around here.

Nate leaves for work at seven-thirty sharp every morning. When he wakes up, his coffee needs to be ready (in his favorite mug, cream with two spoonfuls of sugar) sitting at the breakfast nook table next to his two fried eggs and a slice of toast with Smuckers grape jam. While he eats, I get his lunch ready. His lunch is the one thing he isn't particular about. After he finishes his breakfast, he takes a shower while I iron his work clothes, which are then neatly arranged on the freshly made bed. I take care to starch his shirt and pants, making sure they are perfectly creased. Which he inspects when I'm done. In the beginning, I had to re-iron more times than I like to count. I have it down to science now. While he gets dressed, I wipe down the glass shower door because Nate doesn't like streaks or mildew. It has to sparkle.

When he's ready to leave, I always make sure that I'm standing at the door, his lunch in hand. He kisses me goodbye and leaves as I stand and watch him drive away. He beeps as soon as he turns onto the street.

And I can finally breathe.

But not for long, because then I am on the clock. No matter what I have going on for the day, the house must be spotless when he comes home, and dinner needs to be hot and ready to eat. Plus, I have to make sure that I look put-together and ready to greet my husband after his long day of work. Which means a full face of makeup, a cute outfit, and not a hair out of place. With how I have been feeling lately, that last one has been difficult.

The evenings are when I can truly unwind and enjoy some peace and quiet since Nate works out. And that only lasts until around nine o'clock. Which is when he wants sex.

The weekends are somewhat better, but not by much. Nate takes charge of our plans, leaving me with no input. However, there are two seasons that I love. Fall through the first half of winter, because he spends every Sunday with his buddies watching football. And the summer, because he golfs with his dad at the country club. These are the times when I get to embrace my true self. I relish in them.

Then there is our home. Nate made all the decisions when we were building the house, from the color of the walls to the style of the furniture. He generously let me pick out the curtains and artwork, half of which he changed. And when Nate wanted to start a family, he told me to quit taking my birth control. So, I did. Even though I was nowhere near ready to become a mother.

Three months later, I was late, and the pregnancy test told me that my life was now forever going to be tied to Nate Connelly.

The simple truth is, I have no control over anything in my life, just like it was with Chad.

At least Nate doesn't beat me.

Granted, my life could have been different ... and better. If I just had left the shed hand in hand with Sam. Still, I couldn't help but feel scared. Not of how Sam felt about me. That much, I was sure of. But scared of how my family would react. I knew what the consequences of choosing Sam would do. And I couldn't do that to them. So that meant sacrificing my own happiness. And Sam's. Yet, again.

Recently, I heard that he relocated to Georgia and got married. I'm happy for him. I am. When I heard the news, though, it felt like a sharp, painful stab to my heart. And the wound is still healing. Not that I have any right to feel that way.

This is my life. The one I chose. I know I should accept it. But the guilt about what I did to Sam will always be there. And so will the love.

I shake the thoughts of Sam from my head. I can't think about him right now because I need to walk out of this bathroom and face my husband. With determination, I take the cold doorknob into my hand, but not before checking my appearance in the mirror. I fix my hair, trying to smooth out any out-of-control strands, suck in a breath to calm my nerves, and step out.

As soon as I open the door, Nate's eyes find me. "There you are." He strides in my direction and places his hand on my stomach. "Are you feeling okay?" he asks, his voice dripping with genuine concern as he places a kiss on my temple, his lips cold from the outside air.

It's in these small moments that I see his tender side. They are brief, but I cherish them. Ever since I got pregnant, Nate has been more attentive and sweeter. At night, he rests his head on my stomach and talks to our baby. I'll run my hands through his hair as he does. It's easy to overlook his controlling tendencies and witness the husband I had hoped he would become. The small amount of love I have for him will spark. Then I'll look up and see a thin layer of dust forming on the dresser, and I remember.

Because there can't be dust. Ever.

Right now, though, he is being sweet Nate. Some days, I'll take what I can get. I rest my hand on top of his, both of us cradling our child through my body. "This little munchkin is doing a number on my stomach today."

"Well, we can't have that." Nate smiles as he gets on his knees and takes my small, protruding belly into his hands. "Now you listen here, little one," he says, talking to his child. "Your momma needs to make us dinner, so calm down some. We can't have dinner being late all the time now, can we? Listen to your Dada."

And Control Freak Nate is back.

He places a small kiss on my stomach and gets back to his feet. Taking my chin in his hand, he lifts my mouth to his and kisses me. "Take your time with dinner, Maria. I can hit the treadmill while I wait." He slaps my butt as he walks away, heading to the workout room in the basement. Relief washes over me that he's going to work out because now I can race upstairs to straighten up while dinner cooks. I head to the refrigerator, the cool air hitting my face as I reach in to grab the chicken I bought earlier in the week.

"Oh, and Maria," Nate calls from the basement. I hang my head in defeat as I walk over, and he's standing at the base of the stairs. I make sure to flash him my fakest smile. "Remember, don't eat a full plate. We don't want you gaining too much weight during this pregnancy. I'm going to want my hot wife back sooner rather than later." He winks and disappears.

Little does he know that he never had the real me to begin with.

Chapter Sixteen

SUMMER 2004

Sam

"Are you ready for this?" Erica asks, her voice filled with readiness as I lift the trunk open and retrieve our two suitcases, setting them down on the ground before slamming it closed.

"I guess so," I reply nonchalantly with a shrug as I study the house I grew up in. I grab both bags. It still looks the same, just more dated. My mom tries her best to keep up with everything, but I can tell that it's becoming more difficult for her as she gets older. The paint of the light blue cape cod is chipping, and there are more weeds in the flower beds than normal. I make a mental note to help her with some things while I'm here.

Taking a quick sip from her water bottle, Erica joins me in walking toward the front door. She nudges me in the side. "Oh, come on! It won't be as bad as you think." My eyes briefly meet hers, and she responds with a sly wink.

Erica is under the impression that I don't want to take a vacation. And that's because I lead her to believe that. She is the one who pushed for the trip home. I would have preferred to go camping and relax on a hike during the day and Erica in my arms at night.

Nevertheless, she insisted on meeting my mom, curious to see where I grew up and get a glimpse of my childhood. Her eagerness to learn about my life before we met is evident.

After we were married almost two years ago, I told her about Maria. Of course, there was some jealousy, which was to be expected. But oddly enough, ever since we decided to take this trip, her curiosity about my past life with Maria has been growing. Which is unusual since Erica is always so self-assured. The woman exudes confidence in spades, which is so sexy. But this is different. There seems to be no end to her questions about Maria.

And to be brutally honest, I wasn't keen on coming home for a week this summer. This town, this place, is filled to the brim with countless memories ... all of them tied to my past relationship. Thanks to Ricky's updates (which I started listening to ... don't judge), I know she still lives here. Still married and now with a kid, no less. Nate's kid.

And how does Ricky know this information? I have no clue. He is worse than a bitty old church lady with gossip. More than likely, it's from mutual old high school friends, who I'm sure he still parties with. But I don't ask. Mostly because I don't want to look too interested (even though I am) and give myself away. Besides, it's better that I don't know.

And something else about Erica that has changed. Her drinking. I stopped completely (other than some whiskey shared with Big C) because it was interfering with my PhD work, and I can't let that happen. I've worked too hard for this to let hangovers and partying get in the way. Plus, I'm thirty years old. There comes a time when it needs to stop.

But Erica has compensated for my lack of the bottle. In the past, we would only drink when we were together and out with friends. But now, I'll see her occasionally slipping something into her coffee in the morning. When we grocery shop, she always has some form of alcohol in the shopping cart. And, for example, like right now, I'm pretty sure the bottle she just took a swig out of isn't full of water. It's tucked away in her bag, and she pulled it out when we had about an hour left on the road.

Don't get me wrong, I love her. But I'm worried.

Curiosity gets the best of me, and I want to know what's in that bottle. We have made our way up to the step that leads to the front door. "Hey hon, do you mind if I take a swig of your water before we go in? I have cotton mouth." I extend my hand out, willing her to give it to me, hoping I'm not drawing the wrong conclusion about my wife.

That she is a functioning alcoholic.

"What?! No way! Keep your germs to yourself, mister." She chortles.

"So, I can kiss you and touch you, but I can't drink after you?" I raise my eyebrow, confused yet understanding what's going on.

She nudges me. "Stop stalling and walk inside to see your mom. I can't wait to meet her!" She tucks the bottle away in her purse while also grabbing a pack of gum. I watch her as she unwraps a piece and pops it in her mouth, trying to mask the smell that I know is already there. "Here," she passes me that pack, "this will help your cotton mouth."

I grab a piece and give her a tight smile. "Thanks." She thinks I don't notice the small yet nervous side eye glance she gives me as she smooths down her shirt.

"Gosh, I'm so nervous," she says, her voice trembling slightly as she lets out a small breath. I grab her hand and open the door to my past, knowing full well why she's nervous.

And it's not because she is meeting my mom.

After the awkward mom-meet-my-wife-of-two-years introduction, we settled in. Now Erica is taking a nap. Gearing up, more than likely, for our planned night out at Dexter's meeting with Ricky and some friends. I'm sure she's tired from the drive. Plus, the three glasses of wine she had at dinner.

Now, it's just my mom and me sitting in the living room catching up. "Well, she's lovely, Sam," my mom says as she takes a sip of her hot tea, the steam rising from the cup as she drinks. I notice the hint of doubt in her tone and something else. Is it indifference?

"Thanks, Mom, she's pretty amazing," I reply, glancing up toward the steps as if I can see her through the walls. "So, you like her?" I inquire, praying that her reply will be what I need it to be. Our quick wedding didn't sit well with my mom. To be fair, she didn't talk to me for a week after, and we never discussed it. In hindsight, I regret not including her. It would have been better if we had waited a few more days for my mom to arrange her work schedule and join us in Georgia. But I knew that if I waited, even only a day or two, I would have backed out. And at the time, I needed to marry Erica. Sooner rather than later. Looking back, I see the selfishness in my decision.

"She's different," Mom replies while resting her cup down on the coffee table.

I know what she's saying without her saying it. "Different from what? Or, should I say, who?"

"Oh, Sam, stop. You know what I mean. She showed up to meet her mother-in-law for the first time in *that* outfit. She's not who I would have expected you to be attracted to, that's all."

I knew my very conservative mom would find an issue with what Erica wore to meet her for the first time. I tried to convince her at the hotel this morning to change. She decided on baggy cargo pants, a cropped skintight Rolling Stones tank top that showcases her belly button piercing, and combat boots. Her pixie cut is currently neon green at the tips, and her makeup is darker than usual.

"There is nothing wrong with what Erica is wearing." I retort, feeling defensive. Mom suppresses a laugh. We sit in silence for a moment, then I continue. "Mom, before Cara and now Erica, Maria was the sole girl I had been romantically involved with or found myself genuinely interested in." I know Maria is the 'who' my mom is referring to. And I get it. My mom loved Maria. Her decision to end it left my mom devastated, as she had adored her. But right now, I need to defend my wife. "And yes, Erica is not the type of woman I gravitate to, but that's what makes her so appealing to me. It was time for me to branch out and live a whole new life. Erica gave me that."

My mom releases a deep, exasperated sigh and, with a gentle touch, places her hand on my forearm. "Sam, honey, if you say she is a good person, then I believe you. I trust your judgement, and I'm sure we will become friends." Hearing her say this brings an immediate sense of relief, causing my tight shoulders to loosen and relax. My mom's approval means everything.

She pats my arm before quickly retracting it to grab her tea again. "Do you plan on catching up with Maria while you're back?"

"Mom, come on. Why would I do that?" Not that I haven't fantasized about running into her while I'm home, but I'll keep that thought to myself.

Mom shrugs. "I just thought maybe for old times' sake. Friends catching up. I mean, it can't hurt to say hi. You guys were a big part of each other's lives." She sips her tea, as if her suggestion is completely innocent.

No matter how hard I try, I can't help but give in to my curiosity. "Why are you asking me this? Have you seen her? Have you talked to her?"

"Well," she sits her cup down again and stands to retrieve her purse. She reaches in, pulls out a Post-it note, and hands it to me. "It turns out her mom and I are a part of the same book club, so we have been hanging out more lately. She gave me Maria's email address. Her and I have been emailing on occasion and—"

"Wait, hold on." I raise my hands in protest. "You have been communicating with my ex?" How is this happening? Somehow, I knew coming home would thrust Maria back into my orbit. Little did I know that it would be via my mom.

I stare down at the Post-it note still in my mom's hand.

Against my better judgement, I take it and read. Mariathepoint90@aol.com.

"I mean, only a few emails back and forth." She pauses as I stare at the address, the meaning behind it loud and clear. The Point, our spot in Pittsburgh. 90, the year we started dating.

"I think you should email her and meet up when you're here," my mom says, pointing to the yellow square piece of paper.

"Mom, I'm married." I bite back. "And so is she."

"Geez, Sam, don't say it like that. I don't mean for *that* reason." *Thank God.* I didn't think Mom meant it that way, but still. "Look, you never got closure. I know you still love her. You two need to hash some things out in order to move on."

"I have moved on."

She tilts her head in disbelief. "Have you? Because I know you, Sam. When you try to avoid hurt, you run to something that is the opposite of the thing you are missing. Do you remember when dad left?"

I nod because I do remember. My dad left us for another woman and family when I was thirteen. I loved playing football with him. That was our thing. So, when he left, I took down every football poster from my room and trashed them. I gave my football (the one Dad got me as a gift) away to my cousin and then quit the team. Instead, I dove headfirst into baseball. Why? Because my dad hated baseball. Therefore, it was my new favorite. But deep inside, I didn't love it. It just wasn't football. And it was a distraction from the hurt.

Is that what I'm doing now?

I shake that thought from my mind. "I remember," I whisper, my head now flooded with memories I had buried.

"Look," my mom inches closer to me on the couch. "All I'm saying is, get together with her and talk. Hash out everything. It's the only way you can move on in a life with Erica and finally release Maria from your heart. You owe Erica that, don't you think?"

She's right, I do.

"Ahem!"

I freeze. My mom and I both turn in unison, toward the direction of the stairs, and there stands my wife.

Dexter's was a blast, as usual. If Erica heard any of my and my mom's conversation, she didn't lead on. It was fun to catch up with old friends, hang out with Ricky, and let loose. And of course, it was really fun for Erica. As nights go with her lately, she's passed out. I practically carried her up the stairs to my childhood bedroom. Thank goodness, my mom was asleep and heard nothing, since Erica is always loud when she is drunk. By the time I had her on the bed, she was out cold.

Now I'm lying here staring up at the ceiling, at four in the morning, wondering if I should do the one thing I know I shouldn't do.

And that's email Maria.

I can't help but replay my mom's conversation in my head. She's right, I run away when I'm hurt or scared. You would think that my schooling would have clued me into my own tendencies. But no. It took the one person who knows me the best, other than Maria, to see this in myself. My mom is right. I need to talk to Maria. And this has nothing to do with seeing her again.

Nope, not that at all.

But I have so much to say to her. With the decision made, I ease myself out of the bed, careful not to wake Erica. Not that she is going to stir. She will probably wake up in the morning still a little drunk and hung over. The worst way to wake up.

On light feet, I make my way downstairs to the office where my mom keeps her computer. I flip on the power switch and sit and wait for it to turn on. Meanwhile, my head is stirring with what to say in this email. The room is eerily quiet. The hum of the computer and the air conditioner kicking on are only adding to my eagerness.

Finally, the home screen comes into focus, and I dial into the internet. As that happens, I wipe my hands down my pajama pants. They are sweating with nerves and anxiety.

As I wait, I grab the Post-it note. Before we left for Dexter's, I placed the note on the desk. Subconsciously knowing what I was going to do.

Once everything's connected and ready to go, I sign into my AOL account. With my head feeling hot, I click on the 'write' button for a new email. The blank email template stares back at me. I wait for a beat or two and then I type.

Date: July 2, 2004 04:40 am

To: mariathepoint90@aol.com

From: sam0574@aol.com

Subject: Hey!

Hey there!

It's me, Sam. You're probably wondering why you're getting an email from me or how I got your address. Well, it was from my mom. I'm in town for the next week and I was wondering if maybe we could meet. Just to say hey and catch up. Only if you want. No pressure. Just reply and let me know.

Hope to hear from you soon,

Yours,

Sam

That brief email took me a half hour to compose. I kept typing, then reading, then backspacing, then retyping. I stare at the screen, happy with my words and hit send.

There, it's done.

I get up and walk away to use the restroom and get a glass of water before shutting down the computer. As I sit my glass in the sink and leave the kitchen, I hear three words coming from the office.

"You've got mail."

There's no way.

What is she doing up at this hour? *She has a baby, you idiot.*

I race back into the office and practically fall back into the chair. The wheels slide across the plastic carpet covering. I adjust myself, and staring back at me is a new email from Maria. Without a second to think, I click on it, the anticipation killing me.

Date: July 2, 2004 05:01 am

To: sam0574@aol.com

From: mariathepoint90@aol.com

Subject: re: Hey!

Hi Sam!

I have to admit, seeing your email was a shock. And yes, I can meet with you, but the only time I can is today, actually. We are going out of town in two days.

Would that work for you? I don't know what your plans are, but I'm taking Brielle for a walk in the park at one. She has a hard time napping, so this has been our routine.

Let me know if that works for you. I usually go to rose garden at Mill Creek Park.

Talk to you soon,

Love,

Maria

I can't stop the huge grin that stretches across my face because this time is perfect. My mom wants to take Erica shopping and out to lunch so they can spend some more time together and get to know each other.

Without time to think or second-guess whether this is a good idea, I compose my response.

Chapter Seventeen

THE PARK

Maria

W ell, this day took a turn I wasn't expecting.

While I was up at the crack of dawn this morning, nursing Brielle and checking our flights online, I heard the familiar notification of an incoming email.

From Sam.

The surprise made my heart leap out of my throat. Once I opened it and read it, I reread it again. Then a third time because I was in shock. Sam was emailing me, and he's in town.

And he wants to see me.

The spike of adrenaline I got when I read his words reminded me of the excitement I felt opening his written letters. I mean, of course I would meet him. This could be a chance to catch up, and I can properly apologize for hurting him the way that I did.

So, without a second to think, I replied.

And now here I am, standing at the entrance to the pavilion at Mill Creek, the warmth of the sun on my skin as I wait for him to show. The longing I have to see him has turned my head into a furnace. As I run my hands down my flared tan dress slacks, I can't help but wonder if I look okay. It took me the longest time trying to decide what to wear.

With a ton of pent-up energy, I shuffle my feet, the strain of the pointy four-inch heels I'm wearing pinching my toes. My perfectly pressed white button-down blouse is driving me crazy, with its pristine fabric clinging to my body in the heat. My hair, pulled back into a neat chignon, offers a welcome relief from the sweltering temperature. That doesn't stop a bead of sweat from running down my back. Honestly, this whole getup is suffocating on a scorching day like today, but Nate always insists his wife look flawless at all times.

His words, not mine. I kid you not.

One thing is for sure, I do not look like I'm dressed for a casual walk in the park. A woman who is about to take charge in a boardroom as CEO? Yes, that's how I appear at the moment. But Nate wants nothing less.

I watch the parking lot as cars come and go, and I realize that I have no idea what Sam drives these days. So, I watch and wait, my hand resting on the stroller, rolling Brielle back and forth. Finally, a silver Saturn pulls in, parks, and Sam gets out, looking incredible as usual. He's wearing jeans and a navy-blue t-shirt as he exudes an aura of confidence and style. And I know he's not even trying, which is what makes him so great. Plus, he's wearing walk-in-the-park-appropriate attire.

With each confident stride, determination becomes more pronounced on his face. I'm surprised he hasn't smiled yet since I'm grinning from ear to ear. As he approaches, I lift my hand in a friendly gesture, but he walks right past me as if I'm invisible. My smile fades as I track his movements. His eyes scan the area eagerly, trying to find me.

He walked right past me and didn't recognize me. Do I look that different? I guess I do. The Maria he knew and loved wouldn't leave the house to go for a walk in the park in this getup.

He didn't know it was me. The thought sends a quick pain straight to my chest.

Shaking my head to dismiss these thoughts, I call out to him before he gets too far away from me. "Sam!" At the sound of his name, he spins around to see who called him. His head tilts to the side in my direction, and I become aware of the obnoxious oversized sunglasses I'm wearing. I lift them onto the top of my head so he can see my face. As soon as we lock eyes, he realizes it's me.

"Maria?" he asks, walking over, still unsure. He pauses, standing directly in front of me. "Wow! I didn't even recognize you." With a perplexing expression on his face, he scans me up and down, trying to decipher something. His eyes hold a blend of confusion and admiration. "You're so dressed up. I mean, don't get me wrong, you look fantastic. But just ... *really* dressed up."

"Yeah, well, Nate likes me to look good no matter where we are, so ..." I say as I shrug. As Sam processes this revelation, his eyebrows furrow in a perplexed manner. He shakes it off, smiles, and stretches his arms out, more than likely wanting a hug. We both let out an awkward snicker, the tension palpable between us. As we step forward to hug, our heads collide instead.

"Ow!"

"Oh, geez!"

We both exclaim simultaneously. I rub my forehead as our laughter fills the air. Sam steps back, foregoing the hug because I am sure he is feeling this awkward tension as much as I am. He puts his hands in his pockets, clears his throat, and diverts his attention to Brielle, peacefully asleep in her pram.

That's right, a freaking pram. I wanted a practical stroller, but of course, Nate vetoed it, saying he didn't want his wife looking like a soccer mom. Whatever that means. So my mother-in-law bought this pram like we live in the turn of the century England or something. I hate it. It's ridiculous and impossible to get in and out of the car. But again, what can I do?

"So, who is this little one?" His voice softens as he peers at my daughter, and I realize we haven't said hello to each other yet. It also occurs to me that this is our first time seeing each other since the shed, and a wave of regret washes over me. The day I made the second worst decision of my life when it comes to Sam.

I watch him stare at my daughter; his eyes filled with curiosity. "This is my angel, Brielle," I answer, my response dripping with pride. I may not have chosen the right life partner for myself, but one thing is certain. That decision brought me Brielle, and she is my life. I wouldn't trade her for anything.

Sam's gaze shifts from me to my daughter, his eyes filled with … what I don't know. Once again, I struggle to read his face as he studies her. It's killing me, since it's my only gateway to his thoughts. And I am not about to ask him what's going through his head right now.

He appears … sad.

"She's gorgeous," he says as he admires Brielle and touches her small delicate hand. "Congratulations, Maria."

"Thanks. She's pretty amazing." Our fingers brush briefly as he pulls his hand away at the same time I lean forward to adjust her blanket. This quick light touch floods my whole body with heat.

And it shouldn't.

He turns back in my direction, a slightly awkward smile playing on his lips, as he slips his hands into his pockets, then back out again. Sam, who is always so confident, looks nervous and unsure. "She looks just like you."

And he's right, she does. She bears no resemblance to Nate.

I nod in agreement. We stand at the entrance of the park, taking in our surroundings, purposefully avoiding eye contact with neither of us talking. The silence lingers, and the tension in the air is almost suffocating, even though we are outside. It's a beautiful day. The sky is blue and full of big, puffy clouds. Birds are singing as people mill around us, enjoying the park's beauty.

But this awkwardness between us is new.

And I don't like it.

After what feels like an eternity, he finally makes a move, his attention drawn to my shoes. "So, will you be able to walk the path in those shoes? Because, I mean, we can get coffee somewhere instead," he says, thumbing behind us.

I possess a hidden talent he is unaware of: the ability to walk flawlessly in heels with little to no effort.

All because Nate makes me wear them.

"Nope, I'm good." I grab the handle of the pram and start forging ahead to prove my point. I put my sunglasses back on to shield my eyes from the intense midday sun. Sam falls into step beside me, and the uncomfortable silence settles back in.

Being with Sam is doing a number on my heart. There's an undeniable feeling of being loved and secure that washes over me whenever I'm near him. Despite what Nate offers me … a vast roof over my head, a big bank account, fancy clothes, and frequent vacations … none of it compares to Sam.

But this silence is sucking the life right out of me, so it's time to bridge the conversation gap. I finally gather the courage to do so. "I was really shocked to get your email."

His shoulders slump, and he remains fixated on the ground. "My mom gave me your email address, and I thought that since I was in town, it might be nice to catch up. You've been emailing my mom?" he inquires, his gaze not leaving the ground, oblivious to my longing for his beautiful brown eyes to meet mine.

"Just a few times. You know how well your mom and I got along. And after, well …"—he nods his head, knowing what I'm about to say as I let out a long breath—"everything. I missed her. She was like a second mom to me."

"She loved you." He pauses as if this conversation is drudging up the past that he is trying hard to forget. "Has she seen pictures of Brielle?"

As we continue to walk along the path lined with colorful flowers, the gentle breeze brushes against my face. Glancing down at Brielle, I double-check to ensure she is well-wrapped and protected from any potential chill. He breaks the staring contest he was having with the ground, his eyes observing Brielle with an expression bordering on anguish.

And I know why.

He wishes Brielle was ours. From the beginning, our plan was to get married and build a future filled with little footsteps in our home. Sam wanted two kids, and I always wanted three. Our lighthearted banter about it became a recurring inside joke, with us pretending it could make or break us.

Little did we know what *would* break our relationship.

Me. Young, stupid Maria who can never stand up for herself. Just thinking about that time causes a dullness to form in my chest, followed by a lump in my throat. I push it all down before I continue.

"She has. I sent her one recently." He hums in response. "I heard you got married." Without saying a word, he nods, his eyes never straying from the path ahead. It's slowly killing me that he won't look my way. This tension and tight conversation is driving me nuts. The way we used to be with each other has dissolved, fading into the distance like the passing years. Breaking the ice is essential, and I have to figure out a way to do it.

"What's her name? Cara?" I ask, nudging him in the side with my elbow. My face breaks into a smile as I pose the joke disguised as a question. His head snaps in my direction, and our eyes finally lock. I lose the smile, unable to determine if he's mad, or...

Oh, geez. Did he marry Cara?

In the few emails that his mom, Elizabeth, and I exchanged, she avoided any mention of Sam's wife. And I didn't ask. She only mentioned that he was married, leaving the rest of his personal life a mystery.

Suddenly, the open air around us fills with the best sound—Sam's contagious laughter. It's so infectious that before we know it, we are both in hysterics.

Mission accomplished, tension is now broken.

"I guess that's a no?" My question comes out in short bursts of laughter.

He shakes his head, regaining his composure. "No, I didn't marry Cara."

Thank God!

He continues. "Her name is Erica. And I'm not sure why the thought of marrying Cara made me laugh so hard, but it did." A breathy huff escapes his lips. Coming to a sudden halt, he swivels around to confront me. "Can we start over? I feel like this started off ... strange."

"Sure," I say with a genuine smile. With a giggle and a small wave, I offer a second greeting. "Hi, Sam."

"Hi." His face breaks into a large, toothy grin. "Can we maybe try that hug again?"

You bet. He doesn't need to ask me twice.

Stepping towards each other, butterflies dance in my stomach at the thought of holding him again. Our arms wrap around each other, and it feels like....

Coming home.

And it shouldn't. My home is with Nate and Brielle. It's a safe and secure home that is partially full of love. Brielle did that. But Sam … I know that if I had a home with Sam, love would be causing the walls to burst.

God, he feels so good. Wait! No, he doesn't. This does not feel good.

In an instant, Sam tenses up, as he withdraws from our hug. The embrace is quick, as friends. A gesture I am grateful for because touching Sam, though only slightly, is … dangerous.

We start back on the path, and I can't help myself. I need to know about the woman he married.

Is she pretty?

Is she good to him?

Is she better than me?

Why am I doing this to myself?

"So, tell me about Erica," I inquire, as I bite the side of one of my nails, nervous about his answer. Plus, I'm still reeling from a three-second hug.

He gives me a curious look, his eyebrow lifting in response. "You really want to know about my wife?"

I shrug, trying to be nonchalant, and failing. "Sure. I mean, that's what friends do when they catch up, right?" I'm still nibbling on my nail, and I can't seem to stop.

He pauses, almost as if he is reluctant to talk about her. But why?

"Well, she's the complete opposite of you," he starts.

My finger drops from my mouth. What does that mean? Never mind, I don't want to know.

He continues, his voice remains steady. "We met at a brewery in Atlanta and dated for four months before getting married."

My feet come to an immediate halt. I'm unable to continue walking due to the shock coursing through me. Four months? He only knew her for four months before marrying her. I can't wrap my head around this. I'm not sure if I'm hurt because he didn't propose to me after years together. Or if I'm floored that Sam did something this … spontaneous.

As Sam takes a few more steps, he becomes aware that I'm no longer beside him and stops, pivoting to face my direction. His head tilts as his eyes scan me with interest. "Shocked you, didn't I?"

After a few seconds, I find my footing and take fast steps to make my way back up to meet him.

"You did." I pause, the silence hanging heavy as I gather my thoughts. I clench my fists around the handle of the pram. "She must be pretty special if you married her so quickly." My voice trembles.

Am I hurt? Or is this jealousy? Whatever this emotion coursing through me is, I need to get it under control.

"It definitely was quick. But she's great, and we have a lot of fun together."

"I'm happy for you, Sam, truly." And I mean it. If we can't be together, his happiness means more to me than anything. And if Erica makes him happy ... so be it.

But why didn't he ask me? I push that thought down. Deep, deep down.

With a slight frown, he purses his lips together, deep in thought. "So, how are things with you and Nate?" His voice carries a hint of sharpness, adding an edge to his question. The last time we saw each other, he was begging me to choose him and not Nate.

"You really want to know about my husband?" I ask, throwing his question back at him.

He barks out a hearty laugh. "You're right. I don't."

"And besides, the only thing you need to know about Nate is lying asleep in this pram. I got the best part of him."

A small, knowing smile plays on his face as he glances in my direction. "Do you like being a mom?" he asks as we approach a bench. He motions for us to sit down with a sweep of his arm. *Yes, please, because my feet are killing me in these shoes!* We sit down, positioning Brielle right beside us.

"Being a mom is unlike anything I have ever experienced. When the doctor placed her on my chest, it was like she filled a hole in my heart that I didn't even know was open. I never knew love for another human could feel like that, ya know?"

"Well, actually no, I don't know. Not yet, anyway."

I sit back and cross one leg over the other, settling in for what I hope is a long conversation. It's nice talking to my friend again. "Do you and Erica want kids?" I've never been so invested in an answer to a question. And why should I care? He has every reason to start a family with his new wife. But still ...

"Honestly, we haven't talked about it. But you know how I feel about starting a family." He shrugs. "I've always wanted one."

When he says this, he returns his attention to Brielle, and his eyes reflect a bittersweet combination of affection and sadness, piercing my heart. Looking at her is really bothering him. "I have no doubt you are an amazing mother."

My heart aches at his words.

All I wanted was to experience motherhood with Sam by my side. Instead, Erica will be the mother of his children. This realization is almost too much. And I need to remember that it was me who got us here.

This conversation has to change back to something that doesn't remind me of the stupid mistakes I made to implode my life. I gently pat him on the knee, feeling the warmth of his leg through my hand. "So, tell me about school. I want to hear all about it."

As his face lights up, he unloads, and the weight of the day lifts. At last, we have returned to a state of comfort and ease with our conversation. Our laughter fills the park, carrying with it the joy of years past, as if no time has gone by. We talk about stories of our shared history; I tell him about Brielle's birth; he walks me through his schooling. It's so easy.

An hour later, I know it's going to be time for Brielle to eat, and even though I don't want to, I need to get going. We make our way back to the pavilion, taking slower steps, neither of us wanting this to be over.

"Hey Sam, would you mind waiting with Brielle?" I ask before our time together is over. "I really need to use the restroom. It'll just be a minute, promise."

"Of course not. Go right ahead."

As I turn and head to the pavilion, I can feel his stare burning into me. But I won't turn around. I can't.

As soon as I take care of business and leave the pavilion, I am met with a sight that stops me in my tracks. A sharp intake of breath fills my lungs because there, standing on the sidewalk, holding my daughter, is Sam. He's swaying and humming a soft tune as he stares at her with soft eyes. Instantly, I'm sick to my stomach, so I clutch my abdomen. The sight is too much. Feeling the cries ready to escape my mouth, I cover it with my other hand.

Brielle should be his daughter. We, Sam and I, should be her parents.

Fearing that he saw me, I turn on my heels and make a beeline for the bathroom, where I lock myself in the stall I just left.

And sob.

Chapter Eighteen

Sam

Trying not to make a sound, I tiptoe into the house, hoping not to wake my mom or Erica. Also, secretly hoping Erica isn't awake because I'm not sure I can look her in the eye right now.

Ever since Maria and I spent the afternoon together, my mind has been in a haze, unable to focus on anything else. I shouldn't have met her. Mom thought it would give me closure. It didn't. I got no answers as to why she left me in the shed, and Maria didn't offer any. And I didn't ask.

Instead, it opened a part of my heart that I thought I had closed with Erica. It wasn't until I held her daughter that I almost lost it. But then I remembered the promise I made to myself ... to never cry over Maria again.

Brielle's wails began as soon as Maria stepped away, as if she sensed that her mom was gone. The loud cries stabbed my heart. I made a pathetic effort to console her, of course, but it didn't work. So, I made the last-minute decision to pick her up.

My nerves were in overdrive as I reached into that obnoxious stroller thing. With gentle hands, I lifted her to my chest, adjusting her blanket along the way. Something about cradling her, knowing she was half Maria's and not mine ... not ours. The realization did a number on me. Brielle is gorgeous and everything I pictured when I would think about Maria and me starting a family. A girl that would look just like her and a boy who would look just like me.

Maria took longer than I thought, and before I knew it, Brielle was asleep in my arms. I rocked her and hummed a lullaby my mom would sing to me. She was out like a light.

Gotta say I was quite proud of myself.

I should have laid her back in her stroller, but I didn't. I continued to stare at her, taking in her delicate features, watching her sleep without a care in the world. Her eyes fluttered as she slept. But then reality came crashing down around me. *I can't get attached to this baby.*

She isn't mine.

Maria walked out of the bathroom just then, with bloodshot eyes, and I knew she had been crying. I'm pretty positive she saw me with Brielle, and it affected her like it did me. We stood there, time standing still as we exchanged a silent, lingering stare. The unspoken words and feelings hanging in the air.

Once we parted ways—and awkwardly, at that—I called Ricky, and I hung out at his place until right now. He didn't ask questions. He's known me long enough to recognize that something was off. I called Erica and told her that Ricky and I were going to hang, and she understood. Apparently, she and my mom were having a great time, which made me happy since that was the focus of this entire trip.

Somewhere, more than likely this afternoon, my focus changed.

On light feet, I walk into my old bedroom, and lying asleep on my childhood bed is my wife. She looks so peaceful and gorgeous. Her clothes are crumbled up on the floor. Yet there is one thing that stands out in the room.

The smell of alcohol.

Knowing my mom, she went to bed right after she and Erica got home. She is not a night owl but will be awake at the butt crack of dawn tomorrow. So, this makes me wonder what Erica did, or where she went, after my mom went to bed.

After brushing my teeth and stripping down to my boxers, I pull back the covers, but then something catches my eye. Erica's water bottle resting on the nightstand, half full. Or half empty, depending on how you want to look at it.

I need to know if my suspicions about what she was drinking when we arrived are valid.

Other than Erica's soft snores, the room is eerily quiet, as I grapple with my decision. I won't be able to sleep until I'm sure. While making my way around the bed, I curse under my breath as my toe meets the unyielding bed frame.

Dang it!

I've stubbed my toe, and the sharp sting is forcing me to clench my teeth. The motion must have stirred the bed because Erica moans and turns onto her side. Motionless, I stop, my body tense, as I pray for her to stop moving and fall back asleep. After a few moments, she does, and I cautiously move forward and reach her side of the bed.

I grab the bottle and unscrew the top, smelling it, then taking a quick sip.

Vodka. I knew it.

While placing it back, I consider discarding it. But then she would know that I discovered it, and I need to proceed with caution. Our marriage may not be what it was in the beginning, but I care deeply for her, and I want her to know that I am on her side and want to help.

I tip-toe over to my side of the bed and get in, the mattress sinking in with my weight as I turn to face my wife. The sudden movement jolts her awake, and she slowly opens her eyes. "Hey," she whispers, "when did you get in?" As she leans in closer, her warm breath skates against my skin before I plant a gentle kiss on her lips. As I breathe in, I detect the unmistakable odor of alcohol.

"Just now. Did you and Mom have fun?" I ask, trying not to let my disgust and disappointment show.

She nods. "We did. After she went to bed, I got a cab and went to Dexter's to hang out. That place is great."

I stare into my wife's eyes, and they are glassy and lacking focus. Drunk eyes. Sad to say, I have seen them in her more and more lately.

"Hey, I forgot to ask you. Am I the first girl you've ever had in this bed?" She slurs her words and shimmies her body to get closer to me.

I bark out a laugh. "Why are you asking me that?"

She shrugs her bare shoulder. "Oh, I don't know. Just wondering if Maria was ever in here."

"Of course, Maria has been in my childhood bedroom."

She rolls her eyes. "You know what I mean. Has she ever shared *this* bed with you?" she asks as she bites her lower lip, waiting for my answer. An answer I will not give her tonight and risk a fight.

"It doesn't matter, sweetie. That's my past." I need to say it out loud to convince myself more than her. "It's late. Go back to sleep."

I move my hand to her face, caressing her soft cheek. I could always count on this woman to go above and beyond for me. Our marriage is happy, and I'm content. But none of that means it's working. Something has changed along the way. And I know what it is.

Her drinking.

I look into her eyes and search for a glimpse of what I see and feel when I look at Maria. But it's not there. I know that after I moved to Atlanta and tried to move on, I said I was fine. But after spending time with Maria today, I know the truth of the matter.

It's like Erica is a placeholder. I realize that sounds harsher than it should. I love Erica in my own way … but she isn't Maria.

Being with Maria today, one thing became glaringly clear: I will always love her. And I shouldn't. I know that. It's not right. I mean, our attraction should have faded over time. So then why does it feel more powerful?

And look, I am a good guy. I may love Maria, but I would never act on it. Not when I'm going to bed every night with Erica and Maria is cranking out kids with Nate.

But I can't let her go. So if that means friendly correspondence back and forth, like before, then so be it. Erica drifts back off to sleep as I play this over in my head. With this new choice, I can't help but feel a rush of excitement and a surge of energy.

So I march back down to my mom's study and start the computer up. And before I know it, my fingers are flying over the keys, talking to Maria again.

Chapter Nineteen

THE EMAILS

Date: July 3, 2004 01:36 am

To: mariathepoint90@aol.com

From: sam0574@aol.com

Subject: Me again

Maria,

Hey! So I know that we just hung out today but I feel like we left kinda in a weird place. Which honestly seems to be our thing lately.

Anyway, I have a crazy idea. And feel free to say no. I wouldn't be upset and would completely understand. What would you say to writing and keeping in touch again? As friends, of course. We are both married and adults (and you're a mom, which is still crazy to think about, by the way). After spending time with you today, I realized that I missed you. Missed having you in my life. I miss my best friend. And I have a sense that you feel the same way.

So what do you say? Can we write again? Well, email. Let me know. And I hope you guys have fun on your trip and Brielle loves the ocean.

Yours, Sam

P.S. I gotta ask...why did you wear that to the park today?

Date: July 3, 2004 06:47 am

To: sam0574@aol.com

From: mariathepoint90@aol.com

Subject: re: Me again

Sam,

Of course we can write! I would love that! I miss talking to you. I think one thing that we established today is that, despite everything, we are still great friends. I could use one right now.

And I feel like I need to apologize. The afternoon went so well and then I made it awkward after I used the bathroom. I'm sorry about that.

Anyway, in regards to your question about my outfit ... will the same "no questions about our significant other" rule apply here? Because in order to answer your question, I will need to break that rule.

You see, Nate expects certain things from me as his wife. And one of those things is how I look when I leave the house. And that means wearing outfits similar to what you saw me wearing yesterday. And you're right, that getup wasn't me. But I need to keep him happy so that our home remains happy. For Brielle.

I know that you probably won't understand and that's okay. I made the bed that I have to lie in night after night. I accept it and roll with it.

Anyway, I gotta go for now. I hope you enjoy the rest of the visit with your mom.

Love, Maria

Date: July 10, 2004 11:23pm

To: mariathepoint90@aol.com

From: sam0574@aol.com

Subject: What's up

Maria,

So, I hope your vacation went well. The visit with my mom was good. She and Erica spent a lot of time together and I feel like they really got to know one another, which is amazing. It felt so nice to be home, if I'm being honest. Atlanta is great because of Erica and school, but it isn't home.

I think you and I are old enough now that we can talk about each other's spouses without it getting weird. Like you said, we are friends and friends talk about each other's lives.

So on that note, I do have some news to share. Erica shocked the pants off of me yesterday and told me that she thinks she may be pregnant. As soon as we got home, she took a test and, well, it's positive. I'm going to be a dad! The timing is just crazy. You and I were at the park just a week ago talking about being parents and I'm about to become one myself.

One thing I worry with Erica and this pregnancy is her love of the bottle. She drinks ... a lot. I need to keep an eye on the situation. She promised me that she won't touch a drop when she's pregnant. But I can't be with her 24/7.

Anyway, when I read what you wrote about Nate wanting you to dress a certain way, that concerned me, Maria. That sounds controlling. I don't like it.

Why does he care what you wear to take Brielle for a freaking walk? Anyway, Sorry I asked. It's none of my business, really.

Your, Sam

Date: September 17, 2004 8:07am

To: sam0574@aol.com

From: mariathepointe90@aol.com

Subject: re: What's up?

Sam,

Sorry it's been a couple of months since I've written. Things have been kinda crazy around here. Nothing bad in particular, just life, ya know. Nate has been very stressed out at work and he's been a bear to be around, so I'm trying hard to just keep him happy. Finally, things have started to settle down, so here I am. Then Brielle got really sick with a summer cold that turned into a horrible upper respiratory thing. It took weeks for her to get better. The scariest few weeks of my life. You just wait and see! Speaking of which....

Congrats on the baby news! I'm really happy for you, Sam. I have no doubt that you will be an amazing father. I mean, just seeing you hold Brielle told me that. Plus, you're well...you.

How has Erica been feeling? I had the worst morning sickness. And it lasted way more than three months and was definitely not just in the morning. It was horrible. So I hope Erica is fairing better.

I'm sorry to hear about her drinking and I truly hope that she is holding onto her promise. The life of your unborn baby is in her hands. She's growing a human, your human, and that needs to be taken seriously. So please keep on with her about that. I would hate for anything to happen.

So you talked at the park about your PhD program. How soon until you are done? That has to be coming up, right? I really wish Nate would allow me to work. I miss having a sense of purpose and something to call mine. Not that being Brielle's mom isn't the best most rewarding job in the world, but I need to step away from time to time. Maybe I'll talk to Nate about it again. I really hope he lets me.

Anyway, write soon. This email thing is great so far. I love having you back in my life again.

Love, Maria

Date: December 27, 2004 7:04am

To: mariathepoint90@aol.com

From: sam0574@aol.com

Subject: How are you?

Maria,

So, just like my subject line says, how are you? Things here have been good. Erica is 6 months along now, which is hard to believe. So far, and from what I can tell, she has been true to her promise and not drinking. But you are the only one that I have confessed this to, I worry. A lot because I just don't trust her. I hate even thinking that she would be capable of drinking while growing our child. I honestly can't think about it anymore.

To answer your question, I should have my official PhD in 6 months. Things are going to be very hectic around here, let me tell you. I'm in the final workings of my dissertation and that has been keeping me busy. Add in being a new parent and things are going to be tough.

I hope that you were able to get a job or find something that is just for you. Maria, stop putting everyone else ahead of yourself. And I know, of course Brielle needs her mom. That's not what I meant. What I mean is, you will never be the mom Brielle needs if you hide your true self from the world. Because the woman that was all dressed up in those ridiculous clothes and pushing that pretentious stroller was not—is not—you. If Nate can't see that, well, maybe you need to show him. And maybe it's time that he accepts it. Don't change for him. Or anyone. Not even me. I can't write about it too much because I will get upset. All I know is this, if you were my wife, I would want you to be just...you. There's no one better. Just my two cents. Sometimes I just want to ask you why are you with him?

Anyway, write soon.

Yours, Sam

P.S. I've been waiting 6 months to say that to you. Please don't be mad.

Date: April 27, 2005 11:42am

To: sam0574@aol.com

From: mariathepoint90@aol.com

Subject: re: How are you?

Sam,

Hey! It's me! I know, I know … I took forever to respond again. And it's not because I am mad at you. Far from it. I need to hear stuff like that. It's just hard to talk about it, especially with you. I wish you would take the time to hear me and understand.

I'll let you know a few things about Nate and me. He is controlling. I am told what to wear (we've already established this), what Brielle has to wear, what to make for breakfast, lunch, and dinner (because GOD forbid I put on even one pound of weight), who I can hang out with, where we vacation, and finally when we are having our next kid. He wants to start trying. My whole life and existence is in his hands.

I am grossly unhappy; I hate myself for walking out of the shed that day. Because deep down I know that my life would have turned out so much different. The life I would have had with you.

But my hands are tied. Just know and accept that they are. And you asked me why I'm with him. You know why. It's my dad. And now it's Brielle. I feel trapped and sometimes like a caged animal. I can't believe I am in a similar relationship that I was in with Chad. And it's all my fault.

I could ask you the same thing though Sam. Why are you with someone who, more than likely, drank while pregnant and is an alcoholic? Why Sam?

Love, Maria

P.S. Did Erica have the baby? Is everything ok?

Date: April 27, 2005 2:12am

To: mariathepoint90@aol.com

From: sam0574@aol.com

Subject: I'm Sorry

Maria,

Ok, message sent and received. I don't live your life and walk in your shoes. I had no right to ask that question of you and I apologize. We are friends, and for that reason alone, I should support you. I'm so sorry.

To answer your question, I don't know why I am with Erica anymore. I honestly don't. At this point it's out of obligation. Kinda like you feel staying with Nate. I get it.

And now on to the best news...I AM A FATHER! Erica had the baby a month ago. I know I should have written and told you, but just like I thought, my life has exploded with responsibilities. We have a baby boy and his name is Michael, after Erica's brother who passed away. We call him Mikey and he is the cutest. I'll try to attach a pic to the email. I've never done that before, so hopefully it works.

And I had no ungodly clue that babies wake up at all hours of the night. Which is why I am responding to this at 2am. Erica doesn't really get up with him much, so it kinda falls on me. Don't get me wrong, I love it. But it's a lot.

And on that note, he's crying again. Let me go and get him. Write soon.

Yours, Sam

P.S. Also, how does so much crap come out of such a little human? Like seriously!

Date: July 3, 2005 3:16pm
To: sam0574@aol.com
From: mariathepoint90@aol.com
Subject: I have some news…

Sam,

I'm pregnant. And I don't want to be. The thought of sharing another child with Nate is terrifying to me. I should be happy. I act happy around friends and loved ones. But internally I want to scream. Don't judge me. I love this baby, I do. I know that it will be just another part of my life that he will control.

I'm not looking for advice or even your pity. I just needed to get that out there.

Love, Maria

P.S. Can you believe it's been one year exactly since we met at the park? Brielle is walking now.

Date: November 11, 2005 5:32am

To: mariathepoint90@aol.com

From: sam0574@aol.com

Subject: I also have some news....

Maria,

So, I have some news as well. You are friends with Samuel Harper, PhD. That's right, I am officially a psychologist. And I have you to thank for it. Ultimately, you were the one that suggested I do this, which got me thinking that I could. So thank you Maria. Thank you for always believing in me.

You would think that since I am officially a psychologist now, that I would be able to shell out advice to you and also to help me with my life. The irony is pretty comical.

Since you got some things off of your chest, I guess I'll do the same. On the night of graduation, Erica got so hammered. Her drinking has increased tenfold. Which has caused us to drift further and further apart. We fight constantly. I'm beginning to think the spur-of-the-moment decision to get married to someone I only knew for four months was not the best life choice. The only good thing it brought me was Mikey.

I hope your pregnancy is fairing better than Brielle's and that you are accepting it now.

Keep in touch.

Yours, Sam

Date: February 17, 2006 11:45pm

To: sam0574@aol.com

From: mariathepoint90@aol.com

Subject: re: I also have some news...

Sam,

I have read and reread your email about a thousand times and I am so freaking proud of you! And I deserve no credit for your success. I just nudged you and you flew. Have you found any work yet? I'm sure any practice would be happy to have you. I can see you doing so much good for your patients and I can't wait to hear all about it.

So how is Mikey doing? He has to be what like 10 months now? Isn't it crazy how fast time flies when you have little ones. My Brielle is growing like a weed and attached to my hip. Which bothers Nate to no end. She's also very close to my parents but not to his. It's a whole thing. Maybe if Nate and his family weren't so cold and frigid, Brielle would warm up to them more. We fight about it all the time and I am so tired of being stressed.

And if you're ready for another little bit of good news ... I am a mom again! Mason was born the beginning of this month and he's perfect.

My pregnancy went well enough. But full disclosure ... after he was born, I had a hard time bonding with him. And it's not because I don't love him, I do. I've never felt depressed before and I don't know what is bringing this on. I don't feel like myself. Nate is oblivious, as usual. You are the only one I can confide in about this. I'll be okay ... it's just hard. It's just that ... well, I won't say. There's no sense in dreaming or thinking about what might have been.

There's no point.

Love, Maria

∞

Date: April 25, 2006 3:14pm

To: mariathepoint90@aol.com

From: sam0574@aol.com

Subject: Are you ok?

Maria,

Are you ok? I'm serious. I didn't like the tone of your last email. You sound so sad and depressed even. I'm very worried.

Please find something that makes you happy, Maria. Anything. It can be as simple as a TV show, or a nice long hot bath, or maybe that job we talked about. I feel like I am losing you. The spark that I love so much about you, seems lost.

Please, I am begging you.

Yours, Sam

P.S. I found a job working for a psych group here in Atlanta. I love it.

Date: August 13, 2006 8:22pm

To: sam0574@aol.com

From: mariathepoint91@aol.com

Subject: re: Are you ok?

Sam,

So you were right in your last email. I was a mess. Not sure I would use the word depressed, but I was close. Your email hit a nerve. You were right. I needed to find something for myself. And one of the easiest things I can change right now is how I dress. I haven't worn jeans in over ... honestly I don't know how long it has been. So, even though I wasn't feeling like myself, I went and bought some jeans. Three pairs! Nate was furious, but I wore them every dang day and slowly, I felt like the old Maria was coming back. My choice in clothes is still causing issues, but when it comes to Nate, everything is an issue.

How did both of us end up in these marriages? Do you ever think about that?

Love, Maria

Date: August 14, 2006 5:21am
To: mariathepoint90@aol.com
From: sam0574@aol.com
Subject: Yes, I think about it

Maria,
Yes, I do. I think about it all the time.
Yours, Sam

P.S. Maybe we need to take a break from emailing. Plus, Erica and I are getting a divorce. Well, a dissolution actually. It's a long story.

Date: August 14, 2006 6:49am

To: sam0574@aol.com

From: mariathepoint90@aol.com

Subject: re: Yes, I think about it

Sam,

If not writing is what you need, I understand. But I will miss my friend.

And I am so sorry about your marriage ending. This has to be so hard on you. You know you can talk to me about it. Or not. Whatever you need. I'm always here.

Love, Maria

Date: October 1, 2006 12:20am
To: mariathepoint90@aol.com
From: sam0574@aol.com
Subject: I won't stop

Maria,

We don't have to stop writing. If I'm being honest, when it comes to you, as soon as we get close all over again, I'm afraid you will leave me.

And I know you won't. I know that. But it's always there. Maybe it always will be. And look, I know I have no right to say that considering I started this whole communication thing, this go around. I just want to be honest.

Okay, subject change. Mikey is like a freaking machine. He's like 18 months now and has so much energy I can't keep up. It's insane. I haven't updated you in a while so I thought maybe I should. Erica hasn't really bonded with him. It's sad to see. Just like Brielle is attached to you, Mikey is all about his daddy. Which I love, don't get me wrong. Little dude can hang with me everyday. But, he needs his mother. And she isn't there, even on the days that she is supposed to be. She's always out. Always drunk. I don't know how to make this better or fix it. I know that I can't fix her, she needs to do that on her own.

I feel so lost.

Yours, Sam

Date: October 1, 2006 10:14am

To: sam0574@aol.com

From: mariathepoint90@aol.com

Subject: I wish I could help

Sam,

Your email broke my heart. I wish Erica knew how good she had it with you. How fortunate she was to have been your wife. Like what is wrong with her?? Can't she see that she was married to the most amazing person? I would give anything...

Nevermind.

Anyway, it sounds like all you can do at this point is be there for Mikey. Raise him to be loving, caring, and a good man, like his father. It sounds like Erica needs to sink or swim. She has to help herself, but you need to be there for yourself and Mikey.

Write soon.

Love, Maria

P.S. I will never leave you again. Ever.

Date: January 30, 2007 2:10am
To: mariathepoint90@aol.com
From: sam0574@aol.com
Subject: Thank you

Maria,

So I hope you are doing well. My life has been pretty hectic but I'm rolling with it. Your last email...well...it made me so happy. I am trying very hard to be the type of role model that Mikey needs and deserves. I hope that I can achieve that.

Just the other day, I was thinking about us. The odd situation we find ourselves in. Can you believe we started dating 17 years ago? You wrote The Chad letter 11 years ago. Or that we are in our 30s. I used to dream about what our lives would be like in our 30s. And I promise you, it wasn't corresponding via email.

Do you think about what could have been? Or is it just me?

Yours, Sam

Date: January 30,2007 3:33am
To: sam0574@aol.com
From: mariathepoint90@aol.com
Subject: re: Thank you

Sam,
I do. I think about it every day.
Love, Maria

Chapter Twenty

EARLY 2007

Sam

My *God, if I wake up one more time tonight, I'm going to lose it.*

In a huff, I roll over and check the alarm clock on the nightstand. It's flashing twelve o'clock. *Good grief.* A nasty cold front blew through, and the power must have gone out briefly at some point during the night. The wind has been relentless waking me up a dozen times, so it would be nice to know how much sleep I have left.

I haven't been able to get my and Maria's last two emails out of my mind.

I printed off her last one, as I always do, and placed it away with the others. Along with her handwritten letters and her ring. It's all tucked away in a Nike shoebox under the bed in the spare bedroom. Do I get them out from time to time and read them? Maybe.

Okay, yes, I do.

As I read them, I question everything about my life. I know I shouldn't. I know that I need to let her go because this isn't healthy. My schooling tells me this. But each time I get into my email and see one from her, I can't walk away.

I need to stop thinking about this because I have a seminar tomorrow morning. Plus, I need to know the time, which means I need to get out of bed.

Ugh. This is so annoying.

I throw off the blankets and pull on my pajama pants. As I walk toward the hallway, the house is eerily quiet as it always is this late at night. My bladder warns me to make a pit stop at the bathroom first. As soon as I step out onto the carpet and turn right to head toward the bathroom, I look left and notice that the light is on in the spare bedroom. Erica must be here for her time with Mikey. Tomorrow is her day, per our parenting agreement. She still has a key to the house and occasionally, when she is up for it, she will let herself in and sleep in the spare bedroom. That way, she is here when Mikey wakes up. It's worked out pretty well.

When she actually shows. Plus, she has to spend her time with Mikey here, and she can't drive him anywhere. Why? It's simple. I don't trust her.

It's odd, though, that she would have the light on. I'm assuming it's late, so she should be sleeping. Or perhaps she just arrived, in which case, I should be polite and say hello. Curiosity gets the best of me, and I head toward the bedroom. The soft carpet under my feet masks my approach. With each step, I try to be as silent as possible, not wanting to disturb either Mikey or a potentially sleeping Erica.

I walk until I'm inches away from the door but stop because I hear sniffling and the russeting of papers. Is she crying? *What in the heck is she doing in there?* I round the corner of the threshold and ...

CRAP!

There sits Erica in the middle of the floor. Her legs are criss-crossed, hair sticking up on end, bloodshot eyes, mascara streaks down her face, and Maria's letters and emails scattered around her. The Nike box is open, and the ring box is resting on the bed, standing out like a sore thumb.

The ring.

The ring box keeps pulling my focus, as if it holds some kind of magnetic power.

In an instant, memories of the day I bought it start rolling in my head like a movie.

It was right after the day she got the job at the warehouse. We were so excited and thought that this job was exactly what we needed to start our life together. Little did I know that it would lead to our demise.

We went to the mall to buy her some professional work clothes. While strolling past store after store, we passed the jewelry store that I had frequented dozens of times without Maria's knowledge. I was eyeing a ring that I knew she would love. A simple one and a half carat round diamond. Understated yet dazzling. Just like Maria. But I needed to know if she would love it like I suspected she would. So, I played dumb and pulled the let's-just-go-in-and-look act. She bought it. And while browsing, she picked out *the* ring. I never told her what I was planning. But that night, I went back and maxed out the one and only credit card I had to buy it for her.

When everything imploded, I could have returned it. But I didn't.

It was her ring.

Erica immediately senses my presence, and her head shoots up. Her eyes meet mine, snapping me out of the past. They are glassy and somewhat crazy looking.

The temperature rises in my head, and the room starts to spin. Because if she is reading those emails, then she knows that Maria and I were communicating while we were still married. Erica always felt threatened by Maria during our whole marriage. Her curiosity about our relationship sometimes was relentless. And that's because, deep down, she knew.

This isn't going to be good.

Chapter Twenty-One

Sam

As I shut the door behind me, the tension builds in the air, and I suck in a deep breath. Plus, I don't want this confrontation to wake up Mikey.

I glance at the ring again, wanting to snatch it off the bed. Erica looks so desperate right now, I'm not sure she wouldn't do something with it. Like flush it. I turn to face her. "Erica, let me explain—" She immediately starts reading from the letter in her hand.

"*—I was with Cara for a whole year, and she never made me feel what I felt for you.*" She lays it on the pile, searching for another one. "Who in the heck is Cara?" she asks, head down, hysterically flipping through papers and envelopes.

The fact that we never once talked about Cara is proof of how little we truly know about each other. And how we never should have gotten married in the first place.

"Erica please, let's—"

"A-ha!" She finds the one she was looking for. "Here it is! This one is great, it says, or *you* say, '*All I know is this, if you were my wife, I would want you to be just...you. There's no one better.*'" She tosses the letter and starts frantically searching for another one.

With no defense here, I run my hand down my face in frustration. I'm at a loss for words, unsure of what to say or do.

"I got it!" She grabs the one she was searching for and shakes it as she stands to face me. "This one is my personal favorite. Especially since you wrote it just six hours ago."

I step toward her to grab the email, and she yanks her arm away, moving from me as she does. The crunch of Maria's letters coming from underneath her feet.

She gives me a piercing glare, then reads. "It says, although, you already know this, *'Do you think about what could have been? Or is it just me?'*" She peers at me with furrowed brows and eyes brimming with tears. "And of course, let's not skip her reply. Let's see what she says in return, shall we? But again, you already know." The snarky side of her personality is coming out in full force. "She says, *'I do. I think about it every day.'*"

"We aren't married anymore, Erica. What I wrote in an email hours ago is none of your business." I know it's a weak defense. I know. But I need to say something. Anything.

She takes two determined steps towards me. We are face to face now. Her chest is heaving from anger. "What about the others, Sam? Hm?" She cocks her head to the side. "The emails you wrote to her while we were *married?* What about those?"

I can't look her in the eye because she's right. With a heavy heart, I turn my head up to the ceiling and release a long, weary breath.

She shakes her head in disbelief, crinkles the email up, and heaves it onto the bed. It lands right next to the black velvet box. Erica whips the ring box off of the gray comforter and grabs my wrist, shoving it into my hand. "Here, take it. This shouldn't be tucked away in a shoebox under a bed. Go give this to the love of your life. I'm sure she thinks about you every day!!"

With that, she steps around me, grabs the doorknob, and yanks the door open as it slams against the wall. She storms out of the room and starts making her way into the kitchen. I open the box, and the ring is staring back at me. Relief floods my body.

It's still here.

I couldn't part with it. The ring I went into debt for, just because of how Maria looked at it that day in the mall. The one I never had the chance to give her.

The box snaps shut as I close it. Setting the ring box down on the bed with a groan, I take a second to scan the floor. Sixteen years of letters and emails litter the carpet. Taking a brief moment to regain my composure, I am immediately greeted by the sound of glasses clashing and the pouring of liquid.

Marching into the kitchen. I'm ready to deal with this once and for all. Not just the letters and Maria, but Erica's drinking. Her love of the bottle ended our marriage. Yes, I shouldn't have been communicating with Maria. That's on me. But even if Maria wasn't in the picture, I know for a fact that our marriage would have ended. Erica always chose booze over Mikey and me.

I stand there and watch her fill a rocks glass with whiskey, a healthy four finger pour, and down it like it's water. She unscrews the cap of the whiskey and before she has a second to pour, I grab the glass.

"You are not having any more to drink. We need to talk about this." Her large purse sits open next to the bottle. Which means she brought this with her. Since I don't trust her, I never keep alcohol in the house.

"Okay, great," she slaps her hands down on the small kitchen island. "Let's talk about it. Who in the heck is Cara?" Her eyes are wide and wild, and her hands are shaking.

This is what she wants to begin with? This woman will always confuse me.

"I dated Cara off and on after Maria and I broke up." She bobs her head, taking in the information she is hearing for the first time.

"Why didn't you tell me about her?"

"Seriously, Erica? This is about Cara? After what you found, you want to talk about a relationship that didn't pan out?"

She leans over the counter and looks me square in the eye. The closer she gets, the more I can smell the whiskey on her breath. "I want to talk about everything," she says through gritted teeth. She pulls back. "Did you love her?"

"Who? Cara?" She nods. I pinch the bridge of my nose, trying to soothe the headache I can feel coming on. "On some level, yeah, I guess I did."

"But not as much as you loved Maria." She raises an eyebrow.

"No. Not as much as Maria."

We stand on either side of the island, squaring off, neither one of us talking. I take her in. The rise and fall of her chest, her dilated pupils, her thinner frame, and her pale skin. She is a far cry from the woman that captivated me that day in the brewery. The one who made me want to throw caution to the wind and make an impulsive life choice that I am now deeply regretting.

"Did you love me as much as you loved Maria?" There it is, the million-dollar question. The words come out soft, as if it pained her to ask it. More than likely, it did. Her years' worth of insecurities about Maria bubble to the surface with that question.

I lower my head and shake it in disbelief because if I give her the answer she is searching for, she won't like it. So, I deflect. "How did you know that box was under the bed?"

She throws her hands up in the air. "That's the answer to my question? Come on, Sam." I don't say anything in reply.

She rounds the island and marches into the living room. I follow her, the smell of alcohol lingering in her wake. She turns to face me, hands on her hips. "Fine. I saw you putting papers in it a few months back. I decided to leave it alone. Give you your privacy since we aren't married anymore.

"But something ate away at me. My gut was telling me I should look. So once I got here tonight, I got up enough nerve and, well ... let's just say I was blown away." She pauses. "You always told me that she was your first love. Which is fine. But you didn't tell me you proposed."

"I didn't. She broke up with me the night I had planned on asking. And why does this matter now, Erica?"

She purses her lips into a fine line, and her whole body is tight and wound up. "Why does it matter?" She pauses for a quick second. "Because I still love you, Sam, and you know who didn't break up with you? ME! I didn't break up with you," she jabs her finger into her chest. "I married you!!!" she screams.

"Shhh, you are going to wake Mikey!" I implore in a soft whisper.

She points to the hallway, ignoring my plea about our kid. "Those letters and emails, Sam. Those were between two people who are in love. Look, I get the ones that were from when you dated and before we met, but what hurts is that you kept them the whole time we were married. Why? Why keep them?"

I'm trying hard to think straight. Do I tell her? I owe it to her, the mother of my child, the woman I once shared a life with, to be honest with her.

"I kept them because Maria was a huge part of my life for a very long time. I would have married her if she hadn't ended things. My formative years will forever be linked to her."

"And you went and saw her when we went to your childhood home?" I look away. "You didn't think I had a right to know that you went and met up with your ex. And not just any ex, the love-of-your-life ex?"

"You're right, I should have told you."

"Tell me the truth, Sam." She gets closer to me, and she is in my face again. "Why did you meet her? Why did you write to her?"

I stand there and stare my ex-wife in the eye. Searching for the woman that I met and fell in lust with. And I realize that she is gone. Long gone. I lost her a long time ago to the bottle. I'll answer her question. But I have a few of my own.

"Because I will always love her." As soon as the words leave my mouth, her palm comes into contact with my cheek. Flesh smacking skin echoes through the air, tossing my head to the side, leaving a sting.

I let out a huff and rub my face. I look at her, and she raises her chin, proud of herself. And honestly, I deserved it.

"Yes, I love Maria. And I always will. But I need to ask you, who or *what* are you in love with, Erica? Because I know it wasn't me. Or your son." I decide right here and now that it's time we have this conversation. She knows why we split. But we never had an open and honest discussion about it. Now is as good as a time as any.

She takes in a sharp intake of breath, obviously shocked that I have turned the tables on her. "Every single day." I march back into the kitchen, grab the bottle of whiskey, and hold it out to her. "You choose this over Mikey and me. Every single day."

"Don't you dare turn this around on me!"

"This bottle"—I slam it down on the counter—"has nothing to do with Maria or the way that I feel about her. This is all you. Should I have been emailing Maria? No. It hurt you, and I'm sorry for that. But your drinking is something we should talk about."

"Right now?"

"Why not?" I shrug. "You were awfully eager to dive into my shortcomings at"—I look at the clock on the wall, finally getting the time—"four a.m. Let's talk about yours."

She stands there staring at me, and tears form.

"What are you accusing me of?" she asks in a whisper.

"You're a drunk, Erica. Or I believe the technical term is 'alcoholic.' And it's affecting your relationship with Mikey and ended our marriage." I stop to take in a breath, my hand on my hips as I gawk at the tan Berber carpet, trying to gather my thoughts. I meet her eyes, and tears are streaming down her face now. "You know what? Forget about our marriage and relationship, which is over obviously. What about Mikey? You never hold him."

She scoffs and starts storming back to the spare bedroom. I've hit a nerve. I'm hot on her trail, talking to her back as she walks. "When it's your time, you don't do anything for him!" I tick accusations off on my fingers. "You never bathe him, never spend time with him, never put him to bed, never eat with him, play with him—"

"ENOUGH!" she screams as she turns in my direction, pointing at me. "How dare you accuse me of not loving my son! I love Mikey!!"

"Do you? Because other than giving birth, how have you been a mother to him? I am basically a single father, Erica. And you know what? I love it. Because I love him!"

She walks over to the dresser, stepping on the letters, and grabs her jeans. With anger, she shoves her legs into the pants. "Great!" I throw my hands up in the air. "Where are you going? We need to talk about this and figure this out."

She's now dressed with her coat on and running out of the bedroom. I follow her and watch her grab her purse and keys. I make a desperate attempt to snatch the keys from her hand, but she quickly evades my grasp. There is no way I am letting her drive because I have no clue how much she has drunk tonight. "Give me the keys, Erica!"

"Geez, Sam! I'm not going to drive! Give me some credit, will you? I'm going for a walk to ... I don't know ... cool down. Also to get away from you!"

"And go drink, no doubt," I accuse. And I mean every word of what I've said to her tonight. She needs to know how her behavior is affecting us.

After making her way to the door, she grabs the handle, and before she leaves, she looks back at me. "You know what, Sam, you're free. Go be with Maria. Or Cara. It doesn't matter anymore. Don't wait up for me."

"HAVE I EVER?!" I scream as she storms out. I watch her walk out into the windy night, and then I slam the door. My chest is rising and falling rapidly as I anxiously expect the sound of Mikey's cries. Thank goodness my son can sleep through anything because our screams have been replaced with nothing but the hum of the furnace.

Out of the corner of my eye, I see the whiskey resting on the counter. Walking over to the bottle, I yank it off the sleek corian surface, the glass cool to the touch. I drag my tired legs over to the sink and tip the bottle as the brown liquid waterfalls into the sink. I watch it spiral down the drain, a perfect reflection of the demise of my marriage.

After I empty the rest of the alcohol, I head back to the scene of the crime. I stand at the spare bedroom door's threshold and look at the floor. It's littered with Maria's letters and emails. I get on my hands and knees and put the letters away. I have a feeling she sat here and read every single one of them. A heavy wave of guilt crashes over me.

I'm sure these recent emails hurt her. But I can't explain this pull when it comes to Maria. I need her in my life, even if it's only via an email address and as friends. Once I have them tucked away back in the Nike shoe box, I sit on the floor with my back resting up against the bed. I reach behind my head and feel for the softness of the black velvet box. It hits my fingertips so I pull it around. I open it, and the diamond stares back at me.

It slowly sinks in that this is the only ring I have ever bought for a woman. My ex-wife didn't wear one. She never wanted to. As I look at the orange box sitting on the floor before me, I realize that its contents, along with this ring, held a greater importance in my life than Erica ever did.

I sit the ring back where it belongs. In the box, where I keep Maria.

The woman I will always love.

Chapter Twenty-Two

Sam

The throbbing in my head intensifies as I make my way home from the seminar. I can't stand them, plus the ongoing situation with Erica is causing me so much stress that my head is ready to explode.

Since this morning, I've been making constant calls and sending numerous texts to Erica. Texts like:

> Are you ok?

> Make sure you're at the house at 6. We need to talk

> Please answer me Erica.

It's strange that she hasn't responded to any of them, which is not like her. Even when she is cranky or we are fighting, she will always reply with an *OMG! Stop texting.* So her silence speaks volumes. She's completely pissed and has every right to be. But also, we need to sit and talk like adults and make some changes and decisions. No matter how those may hurt the other. Forget about the situation with Maria … I don't trust her with Mikey.

And he is the most important thing to me right now. After the fight, I knew she wouldn't come back to take care of Mikey while I was away. So, I planned for him to spend the night at Big C and Jasmine's, so I don't need to worry. We aren't related by blood, but they are family all the same, and Mikey adores them because they spoil him rotten. The thought of Big C turning into a huge softy around my son brings a smile to my face. A nice distraction from the difficult discussion I know lies ahead of me.

I exit the highway and decide to stop and pick up some dinner. As a kind gesture and a measure of good faith, I order Erica's favorite burger from a little joint called The Fearless Spoon. The smell of greasy French fries and ground beef permeates the interior of my car as I pull into the drive. Instead of the usual growling, my stomach churns with a mix of dread and nerves, drowning out any hunger pains.

The first thing that catches my eye is her car, sitting undisturbed in the driveway. She stormed out on foot after our fight, leaving me wondering where she disappeared to, but since her car hasn't moved, I know she hasn't driven anywhere. Which brings me some measure of relief since I'm pretty positive she has been drinking the day away. Especially after our argument. Plus, that means she's here and ready to talk.

I tightly grip the handles of the brown bag that house the takeout containers and make my way inside.

Steadying my breath, I insert the key into the lock, hearing it click as I turn it. I'm so tired of constantly feeling on edge around Erica. I never know what to expect with her anymore.

The old door creaks on its hinges (I really need to WD40 that thing), echoing through the house as the smell of stale beer mixed with sweet grapey wine hits my nose. Not her drink of choice, which is odd. Whiskey and vodka are the norm.

I let out a moan. *God, she has my house smelling like a homeless drunk.*

The foul smell is a clear sign she is here. Or was here? Which means she got my texts about meeting to talk.

It's late, and the room is shrouded in inky black darkness. The curtains are drawn, so I flip on the light switch and take in the scene before me. Empty beer bottles are strewn across the floor. A few half full wine bottles—no glasses, which is odd—are resting on the couch. On the coffee table, an open pizza box sits open, it's half-eaten slices now cold.

What happened here today? Thank goodness I sent Mikey to C's.

Erica and I have fought before—both during and after our marriage—and she has gotten drunk after, but this is next level. I sit the food down next to the pizza box while I kick off my shoes. As I peel off my coat, I toss my keys and wallet next to the food. I bend over to collect the empty beer bottles, clinking together and echoing in the quiet room. "Erica!" I call out as I pick up bottle number six, making my way further into the living room. As I wait for her to answer, the clock ticks rhythmically.

Tick … tick … tick

There's only silence.

I step further into the house. "Eric—what the heck!" My sock instantly becomes saturated as I step onto a wet spot on the floor. A wine bottle sits in front of a red-soaked spot on the carpet. Is that an entire bottle of wine spilled out?

"Erica!"

Tick … tick … tick

I sit the bottles on the end table and peel the soaked dress socks off, thrusting them onto the couch. My head is spinning with a million questions. It's obvious she went on some kind of bender after our fight. More than likely buying this while I was at the seminar and coming here to drink away her feelings about what happened. But why here? Was she hoping to maybe see Mikey?

None of this makes sense.

The guilt builds in my stomach, coupled with rage due to what I just walked into.

A thought pops into my mind, and I race to the spare bedroom, hoping she didn't do something to the Nike box. I immediately get on my hands and knees and peer under the bed. The orange box sits undisturbed where I left it. "Erica!" I call out again.

Tick ... tick ... tick.

No answer.

Engulfing the house is an eerie quietness, as if it's holding its breath. My nerves are suddenly on edge because if she isn't here, then where is she? Because she is in no condition to be out and about if she drank this much. We may not be married, but I'm not a monster. I care about her well-being and would hate for something to happen to her.

My emotions are being pulled in two different directions. I'm starting to get irritated. I pick myself up and let out a huff because now I have to search for her since she's being a brat and not answering me. Judging by the chaos in the living room, it's safe to assume she's passed out in my bed. This isn't my first go-around with her. Before the divorce, more often than not, I'd come home, Mikey in my arms, to Erica passed out on the couch or in the bed. But now that we are divorced, I wonder if she stumbled in there so drunk that she didn't realize where she was.

As I walk down the hallway, my footsteps echo off the walls. Stepping inside, I look at the bed, undisturbed and still made. Instead, the bathroom light is gleaming, casting a warm glow onto the far wall where Mikey's picture hangs.

I march toward the light. "Erica, I know you're in here. Why haven't you—" The question stops on my tongue. Because there, in the tub, full of water, where Mikey takes his nightly bubble baths, is my dead ex-wife.

Nothing prepares you for this. Nothing.

I'm staring straight ahead at a family photo of us smiling and happy when the coroner wheels the gurney past me. Erica zipped up in the black plastic. They stop in front of me. "Would you like a minute alone with her?" the overweight, balding man asks me. I take a second to ponder his question. My answer comes quickly as I shake my head, and out the door she goes into the waiting ambulance with its doors open wide.

After pulling her from the bath water, I whispered my goodbyes as I cradled her, cried from the shock, and pleaded with her for forgiveness. Forgiveness I will never get.

The words "I'm sorry" spread throughout the small bathroom, too numerous to count. How do you apologize to someone who will never hear your remorse?

I called 911 and held her as I waited to hear the sirens. Her skin was cold, wet, and pale.

I know deep down what caused this. Me, I did this to her. I should never have let her go out into the night. I should have called her, or maybe had Big C or Jasmine come and check in. I should never have been emailing Maria.

There's no going back now.

Erica is gone. Mikey no longer has a mother. Erica's father lost his daughter. Nothing will ever be the same.

I watch as they drive away. Once the ambulance turns the corner, I shut the door. The heaviness and guilt in my chest are too much as I crumble to the floor.

"How ya doing, man?" Big C's huge hand grasps my shoulder as he sits next to me on my couch, his weight causing the cushion to sink. He's yanking off his tie and chucks it across the room. It sails through the air and lands on the Lazy-Boy. "God, I hate those things," he says as he hands me a bottled water.

I grab it from him, swiftly unscrew the cap, and gulp down a mouthful. "I'm dealing." He nods.

Neither of us say anything for a few minutes. My intense stare locks on the framed photograph. C turns and looks over his shoulder. "Where's Mikey?"

I peek down the hall toward his room, then pivot my focus back to the picture. "Jasmine is putting him down for his nap."

Erica's memorial service was this afternoon. It was small, spiritual, and the worst hour of my life. Ricky flew down for it, as well as my mom and sisters. They are all still at the funeral home, collecting the flowers and donating them as I asked. I don't want any part of this day to remain with me.

Memorials, funerals, life celebrations, whatever you choose to call them, they're the same. A final way to say goodbye to a loved one or friend. They are depressing and awful. I hate them.

Before this happened, I agreed with the mantra of "Death is a natural part of life."

That's the biggest lie ever told.

Anything that happens in life that is 'natural' brings us joy. The birth of a child, marriage, watching your kid take their first steps, having grandchildren ... those things bring happiness. Death is nothing but sadness. Right now, what I'm feeling is anything but natural.

"Eventually, you are going to have to stop blaming yourself." C takes a swig of water.

I scoff. "Eventually, sure. But not right now."

"Guilt will eat you alive if you let it. Trust me, I know." He's right. I know he's right.

C and I sit in silence, the weight of our emotions palpable, as I can't tear my eyes away from the picture, for some unknown reason. Memories of our life together play on a loop in my head. Meeting her at the brewery, the proposal and ceremony, then retracing the steps of our marriage, trying to pinpoint what went wrong. And when? What could I have done differently? Would Mikey have his mom if I made better choices?

I'll never know. And the not knowing is the worst.

"Are you going to stay here?" C asks, ripping me from my thoughts.

As I glance down, my eyes zero in on the unsightly wine stain, a reminder of that night. "Nope."

"Your room is still free. If you're interested. Jasmine and I could help with Mikey until you find a place. We will set it up and make it kid-friendly. Whatever you need."

Like I said. Family.

I turn to take in my friend who has been there for me ever since I walked into Dexter's late on a Friday night, spilling my guts about Maria. "Thanks, man. Tonight too soon?"

"Nope." He smacks my knee as he stands up. "Take your time packing." He walks back toward Mikey's room, and a few minutes later, he and Jasmine appear. I stand and hug them both, grateful for their friendship.

"I'm going to let Mikey sleep. Plus, my mom, sisters, and Ricky will be back soon. I'm sure they will help with packing up some things. We will be there in a few hours."

Jasmine hugs me again. "No rush, okay. We will be there waiting."

I release my grip, and Jasmine exits the house, making her way towards their car parked outside. Big C stands there staring at me, concern etched on his furrowed brow. "I'm fine," I reassure him. "We'll be there soon. I just need to take care of a few things first." He nods in silence as he brings me in for a hug, slapping me on the back.

"Don't be long." He releases his hold on me, then follows his wife.

"Thanks, man."

As I close the door with a gentle click, the void within the house becomes huge.

I know what needs to happen next.

On heavy feet, I trudge over to the computer, turning it on. With a quick login, I find myself staring at my inbox, hesitating for only a moment before my fingers start typing.

Date: February 8, 2007 4:11pm

To: mariathepoint90@aol.com

From: sam0574@aol.com

Subject: This is it

Maria,

Erica died. I don't want to get into specifics but, it was due to her drinking. I know what you're thinking and what's going through your head. And to answer your question, no, I'm not okay.

Maria, as much as I love our emails, I can't write to you anymore. Erica found our letters the night before she died. She got drunk because of it and well, the rest is too painful to talk about. She was really hurt.

I was selfish to continue to write to you while I was married to her. And please, don't blame yourself. I was the one that started this go around.

I am a single father now and that is where my focus needs to be. I am all the family Mikey has here. I can't be distracted by my feelings for you, or wondering when your next email will come.

Please don't be upset with me and please don't respond.

Yours, Sam

I hit send and immediately wonder if it was too harsh. But this is how it has to be.

My days of being selfish are over. My one and only focus needs to be on Mikey. He's all I have left of Erica. And she left me the best part of herself.

For that reason alone, Maria needs to stay in the past.

Chapter Twenty-Three

2009

Maria

"Hey, Maria! Can you come in here for a sec?" Nate calls from our bedroom as I sit on Mason's floor, folding what feels like thousands of pairs of toddler socks. He's playing with his trains, his hair still a mess from sleeping, his sockless feet looking cuter than ever.

A groan escapes my mouth because I know I need to get up and answer him. If I don't, he will march in here demanding to know why I didn't run to his beck and call. "I'll be right back, bubba." I ruffle Mason's hair as I peel myself off the floor, groaning because my abs are still sore from my workout the day before. The soreness causes Nate's words from last week to ring out in my head. *"Your stomach hasn't quite recovered from Mason. Have you been working out the way you should be?"*

Truth be told, I haven't been. And I know how Nate feels about me looking fit and trim. I've only heard him remind me every day for the last eight years. Never mind the fact that his stomach resembles more of a wash tub than the washboard it used to be. But I keep my thoughts to myself and do as I'm told.

Ever the trophy wife.

I trudge down the hallway, bracing myself for what task he feels I need to accomplish today. Who knows what it could be? Scrubbing the kitchen floors, pulling out the furniture and cleaning underneath, vacuuming the drapes. It could be anything.

I'm basically Cinderella, who has birthed his children at this point.

As I make my way around the corner towards our bedroom, I follow the soft glow emanating from the en suite bathroom. Water sloshes around as he runs his razor through the sink. He slyly grins when he sees me through the reflection of the mirror. "Hey, you." There is a playful look in his eyes, which is unusual for seven a.m. I ready my thoughts about the chore he is about to throw at me.

"So, I was thinking maybe we could go away this weekend. Just you and me. No kids. What do you think?"

Okay, I was not expecting that.

"Seriously?" I cock my head, my eyebrows shooting up in surprise.

He wipes his face down with a wet washcloth, ridding his skin of any remaining shaving cream, and tosses it on the vanity, not bothering to ring it out first. He sits his razor on top. White foam is everywhere.

"You look so surprised? Is it so shocking that I want to spend some quality time with my wife?" He's walking into the bedroom now, a towel wrapped around his waist, his wash tub on full display.

"I mean no, of course not." I answer quickly because I know better than to not agree with him.

If I'm being honest, a weekend away sounds like heaven. The kids are older now, and my mom or dad could keep them for the weekend. They would love it and will probably fight over who gets them.

"I was thinking my parents could keep the kids," he interjects into my thoughts as he whips off his towel and pulls on his boxers. Of course, *his parents.* "Then maybe we could head to Finger Lakes for a couple of nights. I'll find us a cabin." He looks at me and waggles his eyebrows.

"Wait, I thought you had a conference this weekend with your department for work?"

He walks over to me and wraps his arms around my waist. He glances down at me, and for a fleeting moment, I see the Nate of old. There was something about that Nate. He pulled me in like a gravitational force. That Nate was sweet, attentive, and made me feel sexy for the first time since Sam.

Desire fills his expression.

Locked in an intense moment with my husband, the idea of escaping to a secluded place and rediscovering each other feels incredibly enticing. The thought spreads through me like a warm blanket.

His lips brush over mine, then he pulls me in for an embrace, nestling his nose into my hair. "It got canceled," he whispers. He tugs me closer, and the smell of his aftershave fills my nose. I melt into him, craving this attention and need from him. "God, you smell good," he purrs.

Even though this feels nice and familiar, it also is ... strange. I'm not understanding where this new tender Nate is coming from. He isn't affectionate toward me anymore. Sex is more of a routine and, of course, only when he's ready. I never seem to be a part of the equation. This has been an ongoing thing since Brielle was born. My body has changed after giving birth to two children. At thirty-four years old, I'm no longer the twenty-something he fell in love with. All lean and young.

Now, there are stretch marks, cellulite, sagging boobs, and dark circles under my eyes. And trust me, I know because Nate loves to point it out.

I try my best to put that aside and relish in the tenderness that Nate is offering right now. "That sounds nice. Let's do it." The words spill out of my mouth at the prospect of reconnecting with my husband. This could be a good thing. A new beginning.

He pulls back. "Really?" I nod my head in agreement. "Yes!" With a strong grip on my face, he leans in for a forceful kiss that unexpectedly fills me with laughter. "Okay, I'll have my secretary make the arrangements today."

He slaps me on the butt as he grabs his shirt and shoves his arms through the sleeves. His fingers are working the buttons when Nate of the here and now comes back. "So, start packing today, and we can leave right after I get home from work. I'll have my mom pick up the kids around noon." He's pulling on his pants now. "And don't pack that black lace nighty. It shows off too much of your stomach. You can't wear that until you get"—he points to my abs—"that in order. You worked out last night, right?"

I nod.

"Good. Keep it up. You'll be back to yourself in no time." He winks at me as if he's paid me the ultimate compliment. With a heavy heart, and the initial excitement now gone, I turn to head back to the never-ending pile of toddler socks. "Oh wait, Maria." I shift my weight, grab onto the door frame, face my husband, the supposed love of my life, and give him a tight smile. "And make sure to give the bathroom a deep clean today. I really made a mess of it this morning."

I sigh. My Nate is back.

Suddenly, folding socks sounds a lot more appealing than the Finger Lakes.

The weekend ended up being a bust.

We arrived at our cabin at ten that Friday night. Nate passed out on the bed by ten-thirty, claiming the long drive and a stressful week at work did him in.

The next morning, while on a hike (a hike that was supposed to help with my weight loss), he got a phone call. His face lit up when he saw who the caller was. He stepped away, and when he returned, he told me that we had to head back home because his conference was now back on.

Yeah, okay.

We drove five hours home and picked up the kids. As soon as we pulled into the driveway, he kissed me on the cheek and off he went to his "conference."

I know full well what's going on. And I'm choosing to ignore it. One day, when I have enough courage, I will confront him.

But not now.

Currently, I'm back in Mason's room, folding yet another basket of laundry as him and Brielle play in their playroom, waiting for my husband to return home. Also, trying to put out of my mind what I know is happening.

My husband is cheating on me. The signs are there, flashing their warnings. The late dinners with so-called colleagues. Weekend conferences. Unnecessary overtime. The smell of perfume that isn't mine on his clothes. He thinks he's being slick about it all. However, as of right now, it's only suspicions on my part. The proof will come. I need to remain calm and wait.

Although those thoughts taunt me daily, I choose to ignore them and move on.

Music from the radio in our bedroom is traveling through the hallway. I chose a soft pop/rock channel to help with my emotions. The songs are soothing and upbeat. I need that right now. Although angry screaming death metal might mirror my current mood as well.

Brielle's and Mason's laughter is coming from the room on the other side of the wall. No matter how crappy my marriage is, or how horrible Nate makes me feel, those two little humans make it all worth it.

A song I'm familiar with starts to play. "Lucky" by Jason Mraz and Colbie Caillat. My body immediately sways with the beat. But it's the lyrics that send a shockwave through my system. Lyrics about being in love with your best friend, seeing them in your dreams, coming home again.

Only one person has fit those lyrics for me.

Sam.

I stand up and walk to the bedroom as Jason and Colbie sing in harmony, letting the lyrics fill my thoughts and wrap around my heart. We were fortunate to share a love that went beyond romance and made us the best of friends.

My chest fills with the same familiar pain that always accompanies thoughts of Sam, and I know what follows that pain.

I sit on the edge of my and Nate's bed, and the tears well up in my eyes as the duet continues.

I pull my body into itself as I wipe my running nose on my knees. Snot smearing the dark denim. It's been two years since the email from Sam. The one he told me not to respond to, and for obvious reasons, I understood his request. Erica died. How or why, I have no clue. But he needed to be a dad to his son. I would have been a distraction. I get it and would never fault him for making his son his sole focus. It's those types of qualities that made me love him so much.

But does he still feel that way? Even though I'm living this life, getting those emails from Sam always was a bright spot for me. I feel like I need that again. To cope with the absolute mess that my life has become.

I peel myself off of the bed and head toward the computer. I peek in on Brielle and Mason, and they are fine. Happily playing with one another.

The comforting sound of the computer coming to life starts to get my adrenaline going.

With a click of a button, my email opens. I type.

Date: June 30 2009 4:45pm

To: sam0574@aol.com

From: mariathepoint90@aol.com

Subject: Hi

Sam,

Hey! I'm not sure if this is the best idea or not, but two years have passed since your last email and I wanted to check on you to see how you are. Plus, I never got a chance to tell you how truly sorry I am about Erica's death. And I am Sam. I can't imagine how hard that must have been on you. I wish there was more I could say, just know that I am thinking about you and hoping that you found the comfort and help you needed to cope.

I heard it through the grapevine that Ricky flew down for the service and that it was small and nice. I hope that it was. The mother of your child deserves that.

I've been thinking about you a lot lately. I'm worried about you. And Mikey.

Do you think that we could maybe start emailing again? Only if you want to. I miss our communication and seeing that I got an email from you.

Just let me know,

Love, Maria

Before I chicken out, I hit send.

Will he write back?

My heart leaps at the thought. *I hope so.*

Chapter Twenty-Four

THE LAST EMAIL

∞

Date: July 1, 2009

To: mariathepoint90@aol.com

From: sam0574@aol.com

Subject: re: Hi

Maria,

Hey. Thanks for reaching out. I would be lying if I said hearing from you wasn't nice. It was.

Thank you for the condolences. It's still hard. Very hard. Raising Mikey on my own is so difficult. But I'm getting by. My days are spent at work and my nights are spent raising my son.

With that said, I can't email you anymore Maria.

We need to let each other go. Once and for all. The choke hold you had on my thoughts affected my life in a way that I never imagined. Writing to you again will be a constant reminder of Erica and her death. So please, I am pleading with you to stop writing to me. Try to forget me and what we had. Try to work on your marriage (if it's still bad). Try to stand up for yourself. But mostly, try to find some happiness. That's what I'm trying to do.

Sincerely, Sam

Chapter Twenty-Five

Maria

I read, then reread his email dozens of times, fighting back the tears.

Upon reaching my breaking point, I hit delete, power off the computer, and, with a profound sense of sorrow and loss, leave Sam in the past.

Chapter Twenty-Six

2012

Maria

There it is, staring back at me. Finally, proof that Nate is a cheater and a liar. It's taken three years. I was patient, and I knew that, eventually, I would have what I needed to confront him. I'm holding his phone in my hand, and the text message is staring back at me.

> Mona: Hey you. Can't wait for tonight. I'll be in Room 405. Knock twice so I know it's you.

So gross. And Mona? No clue who that is.

I heave his phone onto the bed, wanting it and his betrayal out of my hands. Nate told me he had a dinner meeting with the department heads. I knew it was a lie. Everything he says is a lie. No engineer has as many meetings or business trips as Nate does. He recently got a new phone from work, and he keeps it locked via a code. The phone never leaves his side. He unlocked it at dinner the other night while I was gathering up our plates, so I got to see what he typed over his shoulder.

0601

Our wedding month and year. What a pig.

I knew, given time, he would trip up. Tonight is the night. He left the phone in his work pants instead of with him or locked in his briefcase. He's in the shower since he just got done with his nightly workout, and I'm ready to confront him.

The bathroom goes quiet as the shower turns off. The door opens and Nate steps out as steam billows out behind him. His eyes land on me sitting on the edge of the bed. Stone-faced. Normally, when he showers after his workout, I'm either with the kids or watching TV.

He cocks his head to the side. "What's with you?" He doesn't wait for me to answer, as he whips off his towel, leaving it on the floor. He crosses the bedroom and goes to the dresser. Opening and closing the drawer, grabbing his boxers, putting them on as I watch his every movement. I wonder what I saw in him all those years ago in college, mad at myself for not seeing it then.

He turns back around. "Seriously, what's wrong with you?" He jams his legs into his pajama pants.

"Who's Mona?" I surprise myself with how calm my voice is and how brave I'm being. It's freeing.

His back is to me, holding his t-shirt. His body becomes rigid at the sound of Mona's name. He freezes for a moment, then pulls the shirt down his frame. "Mona? Should I know her?"

By the time he turns around, I'm holding out his phone to show him the text message.

The color drains from his face. He looks mortified but then quickly regains his composure, placing his hands on his hips. "Mona," he pauses as he leans forward and gets closer to my face, "is the best sex I have ever had." I have no idea what comes over me because before I know it, my fist comes into contact with his stomach.

He lets out an oomph and then laughs in amusement. As if this is the funniest thing he's ever experienced. "Your lack of working out shows with that punch. God, you're so weak."

I stand and shove him away as I march toward the door, but with lightning fast speed, he cuts me off, slamming the door shut.

"You are such a liar. I've known for years that you have been cheating, but that text is the proof I need to leave you!" I scream at him as I back away because he is stalking toward me like I'm his prey. My body trembles uncontrollably because I have no clue how this is going to go. Flashes of Chad slamming my head against the door and punching me in the face fill my mind.

The fear in my heart is overwhelming.

"Oh, Maria. You aren't going anywhere." His dark, menacing eyes burrow into me. I'm now up against the bed again. The back of my knees hit the mattress, causing me to sit. He towers over me, knowing he has the upper hand. "You know, my cheating is all your fault."

My mouth drops open in shock. "You can't be serious? My fault?"

"Oh, yes. Maybe if you were taking better care of yourself, I wouldn't have to go elsewhere." He pauses to let the accusation slap me like he was hoping it would. It worked because what I heard was, *"You had my two kids and now you are a fat slob, so I'm not attracted to you anymore."*

He continues. "So, here's how this is going to work. Everything stays the same." His voice is almost calming and soothing. Which makes it more intimidating. "You will continue to enjoy this life that I provide for you and the kids. You will continue to cook and clean and be the beautiful, doting wife to everyone else on the outside. Nothing changes."

I hear the words coming out of his mouth, but I still need answers. "How long has it been going on?"

A cocky laugh escapes his throat. "With Mona? Oh, I don't know, a month maybe? But before that there was Leslie"—he starts ticking off his conquests with his fingers—"than my first secretary, gosh, what was her name? Kyla was it? No, wait ... Lily! That's it!"

"You're unbelievable," I whisper out, tears pooling in my eyes.

"Oh, I'm not done. Then there was Michelle, Rhonda, my second secretary, Keesha, Belinda—"

I lower my head. "Please, stop." I'm so stupid. This has been going on for our whole marriage. How did I not know? Because he hired Lily six months after we were married.

The maniacal laugh that next escapes his mouth sends chills down my spine. As if this is a joke to him. "Let's get something clear." He returns, towering over me again. "If you leave me, your dad loses his job, and I will make sure he never finds another one. If you leave me, I will make your life miserable and take *my* kids." The mention of Brielle and Mason makes me flinch as he inches closer to me, knowing he has full control of the situation. We are practically touching noses at this point. His face is so close to mine, the smell of mint toothpaste on his breath dances around my nose. "Do I make myself clear?"

I nod.

I agree because he's scaring me.

I agree for my dad.

I agree because I'm not one hundred percent sure he won't take my kids from me.

I agree because it's what I do.

He places both hands on the side of my face and gently pulls my head forward, kissing me on the forehead. "I'm glad we have an understanding."

He turns and leaves the bedroom, his shoulders back, full of confidence.

While I slide off the bed and the gravity that is my horrible life pulls me onto the floor.

And I sob.

"Did you see what Amanda was wearing yesterday when she picked her kids up? My God, what a slob. Leggings, a Nirvana t-shirt, and flip-flops. She looked medieval," Josie quips, followed by a cackle, which Lola, Gabby, and Camila imitate. The five of us are sitting in a row of pedicure chairs for our weekly pampering. A little ritual that started with these women who live in my cul-de-sac about a year ago.

I hate it.

But since their husbands golf with Nate, he wanted me to join in. I have never met females as fake and gossipy as them. Amanda, the supposed outcast of our little clique, is, in my opinion, the most genuine of us all. And the most beautiful woman I have ever seen. And for that reason, Josie, Lola, Gabby, and Camila hate her.

"Oh, come on," I counter, admiring the hot pink color currently being painted on my toes. "She is actually really nice, if you guys would get to know her." I look over, and four sets of eyes are glaring at me. As if I said Amanda murdered one of their kids.

The queen bee Josie speaks up first. "What's with you, Maria? You haven't been yourself lately."

Ha! These women have never seen or known the real me. Honestly, only a handful of people have seen me for me. But at the end of the day, these women are the only friends I have, and I need to play the part.

Plus, when I found out about Nate a month ago, I have always wondered if I could confide in them about this because I need to talk to someone. Anyone.

I decide to put aside my reservations and confess, lowering my head in shame. As if I'm the one that should be embarrassed. "Well, actually, Nate has been cheating on me. For our whole marriage. It was pretty devastating to discover." I raise my eyes to meet theirs, followed by a long pause.

"And?" Lola asks, expecting me to continue. Her retort confuses me. *Isn't that enough?*

"And it hurt me. Deeply," I add.

Four blank stares glare back at me. I look back down at my toes, and my pedicurist gives me a pitied, tight smile. I mean, geez, at least she gets it.

"Maria, honey," Josie starts. "All husbands stray." Lola, Gabby, and Camila shake their heads in agreement. They are acting like Josie said, 'All men like football.'

"Wait," I say. "Your husbands have slept with other women?"

"Yep."

"Of course."

"I mean, obviously."

"What's the big deal?"

All four of them answer me at once.

Whoa. Like, what the heck? I realize this little community isn't what people said it was, and I knew these women were fake, but dang. To know that your husband cheats and to look the other way. "And it doesn't bother you?" I ask.

Camila barks out an amused laugh. "Why would it bother us? Everyone wins. He gets what he wants, and I get to spend his money. Plus, I get what I want." She waggles her eyebrows. I'm pretty sure I get her meaning. "It's just something we don't talk about. But, honey, everyone knows."

I stare at them in disbelief. Camila is sitting next to me, so I decide to direct my next question to her since Lola, Josie, and Gabby have moved on to a new conversation. Probably trashing Amanda's new Audi.

It also doesn't escape my notice that none of these women have offered an ounce of support.

I lean in and lower my voice. "So, you sleep around also?" I inquire.

"Oh, you better believe it. There's no way he gets to have fun and I don't." She looks down at her feet. "Hey, make sure the polish is even this time. Last week, it looked like a toddler painted them." The pedicurist only nods. She continues talking to me. "You should find yourself someone."

"Um, no. That's not happening. I'm not a cheater."

"It's not cheating, Maria, if he's doing it as well."

"Yes, it is, Camila. I know Nate sleeps around, but the vows I said on our wedding day, I take very seriously. I wouldn't do that."

This conversation takes me back to when I actually considered cheating. The thought of letting Sam go was unbearable. But I couldn't do it. Regardless of what was happening in my life at the time, there was no way I could be that disrespectful to Sam. I hurt him enough as it is. My biggest life regret. Although marrying Nate is a close second.

Our emailing shouldn't have happened either. Looking back, I understand it was wrong. The strong emotional bond between Sam and me makes it really hard to communicate when we're in relationships. It doesn't matter how friendly we try to keep things, our feelings always get in the way. Every time. No matter what my life is like with Nate, I will never stoop to that level. Ever.

"Whatever, it's your loss." She shrugs and turns her attention back to the other girls, obviously annoyed and bored with me.

I sit in silence as I contemplate and make a few choices. One, I will not be joining them next week. Or any week after. Two, I'm going to call Amanda to see if she wants to have lunch tomorrow. And three, Nate may be a dog and a liar and a cheater, but that's not me. I'm not that person.

And finally, four. I have to wait this out. Until I can figure a way out of this mess.

Hopefully, someday soon.

With a renewed sense of purpose and my head held high, I leave Josie, Gabby, Lola, and Camilla to their gossipy ways.

Determined to find a life worth living. For myself and my children.

Chapter Twenty-Seven

2014

∞

Maria

"Hey, Daddy," I say as I greet my father with a hug. He's come over to watch the kids while I run some errands and grab some lunch with Amanda. It's Saturday and, of course, Nate is golfing or sleeping with another woman.

I don't care either way.

It's been two years since I found out about him. And he wasn't wrong. Nothing has changed. Nate is going about his life as if he didn't destroy me. Also, the girls were right that day at the salon.

No one talks about it.

But that doesn't mean I don't think about it. Or discuss it ... with Amanda. She has become my best friend these last two years. We have a lot in common, and she quickly became like a sister to me. The other wives hate us both now. Which Amanda and I find a lot of amusement in.

Nate wasn't happy about it. He would rather control me and have me buddy up with the fake clique from the neighborhood. But, like I said, I'm beyond caring at this point.

Which is where my mind is with him. Amanda and her husband don't operate like the other couples in the neighborhood. She has helped me to see what a loving and stable marriage can look like. Which has also shown me how far removed from that ours is. Nate doesn't like Amanda's husband Elias. For obvious reasons. Elias isn't a man whore. Or a control freak. Or a manipulator. He loves, adores, and respects Amanda. As a marriage mate should.

Amanda has also guided me on how I need to talk to my dad about the whole situation. Nate threatened me that day with two things. However, lately, I have gained enough confidence to handle the situation myself when I leave him. I am a wonderful mother, and he won't be able to take my kids away from me.

Another behavior surfaced with Nate that really sent me over the edge. He directed his controlling tendencies towards the kids.

That was the last straw. You can mess with me, but not my children.

Did I mention that Amanda and Elias are both lawyers in family law? Those two together are a force to be reckoned with. So yeah, Nate is in for a fight if he tries anything. Because Amanda pulls no punches. The woman is as tough as nails. And I love her for it!

But now, I am worried about my dad. I know that if I leave Nate, he and his father will make sure that my dad loses his job. A job that, for the first time in his life, he could handle and excel at. I saw a confidence in my dad that I had never seen before.

Despite the hardships my dad and I have faced, we have finally found ourselves in a good place. Same is true of him and my mom. They are friends now, who support each other. I don't want to mess any of that up. But I also can't assume that everything will go haywire. My dad is a different person than he was nineteen years ago when he was a gambling addict. He's changed for the better. So, I need to tell him what's going on so that we can work this out together. Because at the end of the day, my dad only wants what's best for me.

"Hey, sweetie," he says as he walks into my home and peels off his shoes. He removes his coat and hangs it in the coat closet, making himself right at home. "Where are those beautiful grandkids of mine?" He's darting his eyes over the house, looking for them. I take a quick glance at this man who raised me. He's older now, mid-sixties. His hair is gray, and his beard makes him look like Santa Claus. As aging does to a person, he's lost some pep in his step. But also getting older has been a blessing for him. He's happily married now and is the best grandfather to my kids.

"They are watching a movie right now." His excitement is contagious, and I can't help but smile as I watch him. Whenever he's with my kids, his face lights up with pure joy.

"Well, bring them out here to see their Papa," he retorts, rubbing his hands together with a wide grin on his face.

I rest my hand on his forearm, a nervous smile replacing the happy one I just had. "I will. But, Dad, can I talk to you first?"

He can see the tension and hear the seriousness in my voice because his brows furrow immediately. "Sure, pumpkin. What's wrong? You're not sick, are you?"

I lead him to the couch, and we both sit as I take his hands in mine. My dad's large and protective hands. The ones that used to hold me when I was a baby and when I crossed a parking lot as a kid. I can feel their warmth, and in this moment, I know he would protect me. "No, Dad, I'm not sick." He lets out a long breath in relief. "Well, no. Let me rephrase that. I am sick. Sick and tired of my marriage to Nate."

He shakes his head because I'm sure this has thrown him for a loop. We have painted a picture of the perfect and loving family so convincing that my parents believed the lie. "What? Maria, what is going on?"

For the next ten minutes, the current state of my marriage vomits out of my mouth.

I tell him about Sam and the shed the night before the wedding.

I confess to him how unhappy I have been since day one.

I tell him how I felt pressured to marry Nate to protect him and his job.

I tell him how Nate can't keep it in his pants (his signature nostril flare came out for that one).

I tell him everything.

As soon as I finish, he is blinking rapidly and having a staring contest with the wall. "Dad, please say something."

His breathing is getting heavier, and I see a single tear travel down his cheek. "Maria, I am so sorry." He looks at the ceiling, trying to compose himself. "I have failed you as a father. First with that idiot Chad. You left Sam for him to help your mother and me financially, and I have never forgiven myself for that." He turns to face me. Now I'm the one crying.

"I know you are, Dad. And I let that go a long time ago."

"And I don't deserve your forgiveness. So, there is no way I am going to be the reason for your unhappiness now. Honey, why didn't you tell me that Sam came to win you back the day before your wedding?" he asks, agony etched on his face.

"Because I was young and stupid. I thought I was doing the right thing. You were getting back on your feet, and I didn't want to be the reason to mess that up."

"Maria, you wouldn't have—"

I cut him off because I need to get this off of my chest. "Plus, you and Mom did so much, paid for so much, with the wedding. When Sam came to me, all I could think about was disappointing you guys. And I was worried about how Nate would take it or what kind of retaliation he would have brought? I should have put myself first. It was confusing and scary, quite honestly."

He nods in agreement. "Well, the days of you putting everyone else above yourself are over. Do you hear me? No more." He shifts his weight on the couch. He's fully facing me now. "What does my Maria want?"

I let out a heavy sigh, the weight of my frustrations escaping with each breath. "A lot of things. I want to be able to wake up each morning and not worry if I cleaned the kitchen the way my husband demands. I want to live without the constant concern of who my husband is sleeping with or what diseases he could bring back to me from his antics. And I want love. I want a love like the one I had with Sam." A pain shoots straight to my heart at this last admission.

"Well, that sounds pretty attainable, if you ask me." Dad's lips tuck up into a small smile.

"But you'll lose your job, Dad."

He shrugs his shoulders. "So."

"But, what about—" He puts his hands up in protest.

"No buts." He adjusts himself on the couch, his posture straighter, his chin up. "I'll quit. Or better yet, I'll retire. I need to spend more time with my family, anyway."

"So, you'll retire? Just like that?"

"Just like that." He grins at me and pinches my chin the way he would when I was a kid. "Anything for you. Now, let's go get those grandbabies of mine." He stands with purpose, slapping his hands on his legs. Before he heads to the kids' rec room, he peers down at me. "Oh, and do me a favor, will you?"

"Anything, Daddy."

"Beat Nate home, okay."

He winks at me as he walks away, and I know full well his meaning.

Chapter Twenty-Eight

2015

Maria

The gavel hits the round wooden disk that sits beside the judge, echoing throughout the empty courtroom. That sound means only one thing.

I am officially no longer married to Nate Connelly.

I'm free.

I peer over at Nate, and he is putting on his winning smile, shaking hands with his lawyer, and then hugging his parents. Followed by a hug and wink for his current girlfriend.

He wasted no time.

After my conversation with my dad a year ago, Amanda got the ball rolling. A week later, while Nate was at work, I packed up my and the kids' things and moved in with my mom. He came home to a note and divorce papers waiting for him. Along with a sink full of dirty dishes, a trash can that was overflowing and smelled, an unmade bed, a load of his clothes in the washer (no doubt collecting mildew since they had been in there for about forty-eight hours), and a dirty bathroom. Of course, as retaliation, he made sure the entire neighborhood knew it was *him* who kicked *me* out. That *I* was the reason *he* was miserable. Poor Nate.

Whatever.

The opinion of his friends means nothing to me. Not anymore.

As I stand here, lots of feelings wash over me. Sadness at the end of a marriage I tried hard to be perfect at. Anger that Nate forced this by not being able to keep his hands to himself. Bitterness toward him, which I don't think will ever really go away.

A sense of loss, because even though he was who he was, a small part of me loved him.

But mostly relief that this is over and an immense amount of pride in myself. For being brave enough to put myself and my children first. To stand up for me. Probably for the first time in my whole life.

I'm free.

But the new me is now a single mom of two and a divorced forty-year-old woman who now has to start fresh.

Thanks to Amanda and Elias, I have been able to accomplish exactly that. They have helped me in so many ways. And for that reason, I tear my eyes away from my past and turn to my friends, hugging them both.

"Thank you for everything," I say as I wrap my arms around my best friend.

"Anytime." Amanda pulls back and smiles sweetly at me. I turn my attention to Elias. He brings me in for a hug as well. We break apart, and I see him grab Amanda's hand as they lace their fingers together.

"So, what's next for you?" he asks. I shrug as I watch Nate leave the courtroom, his arm slung over his girlfriend's shoulder. The way he would always do with me. Nate and his family didn't so much as give me a second glance.

Good riddance.

"Well, right now, I'm going to pick my kids up from my mom's, grab some pizza, and watch a movie back at the condo."

My condo. The first home that is truly mine. I haven't vacuumed the carpet in over a week, there's a layer of dust on just about every surface, and dried toothpaste on the bathroom sink.

It's unbelievably liberating. "You sure you don't want to get some dinner with us? We can celebrate," Amanda singsongs.

"No, I'm good. I really just want to be alone with my kids tonight."

"Okay, call me tomorrow, though." I smile as she kisses me on the cheek. We say our goodbyes, and I watch her and Elias walk hand in hand out of the courtroom. Right before the doors close, they sneak a quick peck on the lips, and a desire swells in my chest.

I want that.

I need that.

A love where you can sneak secret hand holds, longing glances, and kisses as a way to tell the other person, 'I'm here. I got you.'

I had that once.

As with everything in my life, my thoughts always seem to drift to Sam. I'm sure he's married or with someone by now, happy. Which, if that's the case, I'm happy for him.

I gather up my purse and coat and walk toward the doors, eager to open them. My new life waiting on the other side.

I push the grocery cart to the meat case and stop in front of the chicken. I sent Brielle and Mason off to the cereal aisle to pick what they want for the week. Knowing my kids, they will have Cinnamon Toast Crunch and Lucky Charms in their hands.

"Maria? Is that you?" The deep male voice is coming from beside me. I turn and see Sam's best friend, Ricky, smiling back at me.

"Ricky, hi! Yep, it's me." I come from around my cart, and we embrace in front of the pork chops.

He squeezes me tight and shakes us, which causes me to let out a soft chuckle. A surge of deep nostalgia fills my chest as he finally lets go, and I take in the sight of him after all these years.

"It's so good to see you," he says, full of sincerity. "It's been forever. How are you?" Ricky looks exactly how I remember him. Still basketball tall and thin, with the same goofy smile and charisma that always attracted the ladies. He gives me a once-over. "You look fantastic." And he's still a shameless flirt.

"Well, thank you," I giggle, a hint of embarrassment coloring my cheeks as his compliment reminds me of how long it has been since a man has noticed me. "I've been good. Better than I have in a really long time, actually."

"Well, that sounds like a story waiting to be told." His voice is filled with intrigue.

"Nothing to tell. I just got divorced."

His eyes droop in sadness. "Oh, I'm sorry. That must have been hard."

"Oh, trust me, I'm not. It's hands down the best decision I have ever made."

"Well … then, good for you!" He nudges me in the arm, and a genuine smile comes across his face.

"How about you?" I nudge him back. "Anyone special in your life?"

His laughter fills this corner of the store, causing me to snicker in return. "Me? Gosh, no. You know I will always be the constant bachelor. Best life ever."

A snicker escapes me effortlessly, as I expected nothing less than this. After a few beats, a thought pops into my head. *Should I ask him about Sam? Are they still in touch? Is it a good idea to ask?*

Then I remind myself. I am the new Maria who doesn't back down, and I conquer my fears. So I muster up the courage, curiosity hanging on my tongue, bursting to come out.

"So, do you still keep in touch with Sam? How is he these days?" The question comes out shakier than I wanted. So much for trying to exude confidence.

He pauses and doesn't answer right away, shifting on his feet. I can tell he is trying to gather his thoughts, probably deciding what to share and what not to share about our mutual friend. And the love of my life, the one that got away. Whatever he is. Or was.

He smiles, hesitant and unsure. "I do, actually. Sam is great. He moved back home, just last month."

With this new information, my face feels hot, and butterflies erupt in my stomach. Sam being in the same city as me is creating a whirlwind of thoughts and emotions, but I have to keep my cool.

"That's great. I'm glad to hear it. Please tell him I said hello," I squeak out, sounding like a hyena.

Nice to know that even the thought of Sam still gets me tongue-tied.

He gives me a quizzical look, and then the same flirtatious Ricky grin appears. "I will. It was nice to see you again, Maria. Take care of yourself." He offers me a soft wave as he wheels his grocery cart away.

"You as well." I glance over my shoulder and watch him turn down the soup aisle.

As I refocus on the chicken, my knees almost give out. The thought of Sam being this close to me for the first time since our walk in the park is doing crazy things to my head. I replay my conversation with Ricky, and I realize he didn't mention Sam's relationship status.

A glimmer of hope stirs inside of me, but I can't get excited. He could be with someone.

I shove aside thoughts of Sam as I see my kids approaching with their hands full of cereal boxes. They drop them into the cart. "Seriously, guys?"

"Yes, seriously," Mason quips. "I'm a growing boy." I raise my eyebrows at him as I pick up some chicken breast and toss it in.

"Mom, who was that guy you were talking to?" Brielle asks, her lips pursed together.

"Oh, that was Ricky. Just someone I went to high school with."

"You're not going to date him, are you?" She crosses her arms over her chest and crinkles her nose. "You were giggling an awful lot."

"What?! Ricky?" I scoff at the thought. "God, no. He's the biggest player ever."

Brielle unfolds her arms as her shoulders relax. "Okay, good. Because I don't need a new stepdad right now." My eyebrows raise at her confession.

"Me either," Mason chimes in. "Come on, Brielle, let's go get some cookies."

With that, both of my kids race off to buy some more junk food, leaving me with my thoughts.

Whether Sam and I reconnect or I find someone else, one thing remains unmistakably clear.

I may be focusing on my own happiness for the first time in my life, but I know that this isn't just about me. Brielle, Mason, and I are a package deal. A team.

A sobering thought, for sure.

The exchange with Ricky and the mention of Sam causes me to think of the last email he wrote me. I try to recall it to mind as I compare bacon prices. It was so final. But it was his words at the end that I never forgot. About finding happiness and standing up for myself.

I know he would be proud of me.

If only he knew.

Chapter Twenty-Nine

2015

∾

Sam

"Where in the world did I put those navy blue shorts?" I ask as I stand in my boxers, searching one of the packing boxes marked 'Clothes' that sit in the living room.

"How should I know?" Mikey replies from the kitchen as he plates his breakfast.

Mikey and I have been home for a month now, and I'm still not unpacked. Boxes are strewn haphazardly across the living room of the small house I bought, stretching into the hallway and taking up space in the kitchen. They are everywhere and probably collecting dust. At this point, I have to chalk it up to pure laziness on my part. "Here they are!" I pull them out and hold them up in the air, victorious.

It's Saturday, and Mikey and I have wasted no time getting into a routine. Mostly for him, but also for me. And that means dropping off Mikey at baseball practice while Ricky and I meet at the gym to get in a quick game of racquetball.

Moving back home was the best decision. With Erica gone and Mikey getting older, I knew he would need a female influence in his life. Big C and Jasmine moved back two years after Erica passed. For a long time, it was just Mikey and me. Being his sole parent meant not a lot of time for socializing or dating for this dad. Plus, it meant handling everything with my son by myself.

Mikey's first day of school, all his T-ball games, his concerts at school. All of them I experienced alone. We were getting into a rut, and I was feeling lonely and homesick. Plus, memories of Erica were everywhere. I could tell both of us needed a change, so I found a job as a psychologist for a local hospital, and we moved pretty quick. Now Mikey has my mom and Jasmine. And of course, mom's thrilled to have us back. If I'm being honest, it has been great for everyone involved.

At one time, Georgia felt like a new beginning for me. But slowly, it morphed into a prison, and I knew it was time to break my son and me free. It sounds so cheesy to say, but there's no place like home.

"Dad, when are you going to unpack your stuff?" Mikey asks with a mouth full of bacon. "I mean, seriously?"

Okay ... so my kid is more organized than me, and his room was unpacked and set up in mere hours after arriving. Sue me.

"I'll get to it." I glance up at him, and he's glaring at me. "Eventually." I sit the shorts down over the back of one of the barstools and take a sip of my coffee.

"You need a wife," he says nonchalantly as he takes a bite of his toast.

Coffee sprays out of my mouth and lands on the counter.

"Eww. Gross, Dad. You just spit coffee on my toast."

"What did you say?" I wipe the coffee off my mouth with the back of my hand.

"You need a wife. Or a girlfriend maybe." He shrugs, eating his toast with the coffee spray on it. Ten-year-old boys are gross.

"I'm fine, Mikey. I definitely do not need a girlfriend. Or a wife, for that matter." I grab a paper towel and wipe up my mess. "Trust me."

There's a long pause as I clean up the kitchen from our breakfast. He's watching me, and I can tell he wants to say something. He steps closer to me with purpose. "Even though you and Mom were divorced, and she's gone, she would have wanted you to be happy, Dad." The mention of Erica stops me in my tracks. Mikey doesn't know the whole truth about the circumstances of his mom's death. He knows about the drinking, of course, but the details of that day I've kept close to my chest.

I don't respond to the mention of his mom. "So, if I did date someone, would that bother you?" I mean, he brought this up. I guess now is as good a time as any to ask this. Realistically, I know that I'm not in any position to start anything with a woman. But also, I'm forty-one years old and not getting any younger. Eventually, the right woman will come along and when that happens, I need to know his thoughts about it.

He shrugs as he steps around me and brings his plate and OJ to the sink. "I mean, it might be strange at first, but I would be cool with it."

"Really?" I turn to face him.

"I mean, sure. You deserve to be happy, Dad." My kid is the coolest. I grab him by the back of the neck and pull him in for a hug, kissing him on the top of the head.

"Thanks, kiddo," I whisper.

He wiggles away. "Okay, that's enough of that." I snicker as I rough up his hair.

"Head upstairs and grab your stuff so we can get going." He runs away to his bedroom as I load the dishwasher and take in the possibility of dating again. To be honest, my last three long relationships didn't exactly work out well. Cara is the only one that ended on amicable terms.

I wonder what she's up to these days.

Erica ... well, we know what happened there.

Then there's Maria. The one relationship I would probably still be in if she hadn't ended. My whole body floods with warmth at the mere thought of her name.

I shake the image of her from my head and shut the dishwasher door. Snatching the shorts from the chair, I walk the short distance to my bedroom to get dressed. And just like the thousands of times before this one, I can't rid Maria from my thoughts. I've been thinking about her more and more lately, due to how I left things in my last email. Something I deeply regret. I was curt and rude to the one person that has always meant the world to me. But in my defense,

I was hurting, grieving, and harboring massive amounts of guilt about Erica's death.

That guilt has faded with time. It doesn't cloud my thinking every time I think about Mikey's mom and the good times we did have together. It doesn't hang over my head every time I look at our son. Therapy helped with a lot of it.

The psychologist sought out a psychologist. Something I should have done a long time ago, if I'm being honest.

He helped me to see that if Maria and I weren't communicating, Erica would have met the same fate. She was too far gone. The alcohol consumed her. It was her addiction. Just like Maria was mine. We were having a full-blown emotional affair. The guilt may be gone, but I still have regret. What Maria and I were doing wasn't fair to anyone involved. Her, me, Nate, Erica, and our kids.

Therapy helped me to see that as well.

I grab my gym bag and notice that I'm running a little late. "Come on Mikey! We need to get going. We will tick your coach off if you're late again!" I yell out as I wait for him by the front door.

As I check my watch again, I wonder if Maria's kids are in any sports.

I lower my head. Everything in my life, every thought, always circles back to her.

WHACK!

The hollow blue ball slams against the scuffed up white wall in front of Ricky and me. It bounces back and hits the floor, way out of Ricky's reach. He dives for it, his body hitting the lacquered hardwood with a thud. He rolls over onto his back, his breathing labored. "I'm too old for this."

I offer my hand to him, and he takes it as I yank him up to his feet. "Good game, man."

He lets out a snort. "Yeah, good for you. You won again." A satisfied smile crosses my lips.

We drag our tired, sweaty bodies to the bench that sits against the back wall of the court. I reach into my bag and grab the Gatorade waiting for me, popping open the cap and chugging the ice blue liquid. We sit in silence, our breaths ragged, as we both towel off and attempt to cool down.

Ricky is the first to speak after our breathing is under control. "I forgot to tell you who I saw at the grocery store last week."

I'm bending at the waist, fishing my street shoes from my bag. "Oh, yeah. Who?"

He stops what he's doing for a split second, almost as if he's preparing for my reaction. "Maria."

The sound of her name snaps me up, and my mouth falls open. "My Maria?"

He smirks. "My Maria? Hmmm ... interesting." He takes a drink of his Gatorade.

"You know what I mean." I forcefully throw my empty bottle into my bag.

We finish bagging up our stuff and disinfect the bench as we exit the court, the next couple waiting patiently for us to leave. "All yours, man." Ricky holds the glass door open for the pair. We walk down to the entrance of the gym. "You're dying to know details, aren't you?" He lets out an amused hum. His entertainment at my expense is grating on my nerves.

"No." I lie. I am.

"Liar." We walk out of the gym and head to his Jeep. He hits the unlock on the key fob as we climb inside. My mind is racing, and Ricky is staying silent, allowing me the time to process this. Suddenly, it's like I'm back in high school, wanting to know if the girl I like asked about me.

Oh, screw it. I need to know.

He's sticking the key into the ignition when the question spills out. "Did she ask about me?"

"Oh, aren't you cute?" He turns to me, fluttering his eyelashes, mocking me.

"Fine. Forget I asked." I cross my arms over my chest, sulking like a lovesick teenager. And internally hoping he doesn't forget it.

"Do you want me to pass a note to her in class?" A smug smile plays on his lips. *God, he's loving this way too much.*

"Shut up."

He lets out a long exhale. "Honestly, I'm afraid to tell you what she said."

"What? Why?"

"Because I know you, Sam." He starts the Jeep and kicks it into reverse, backing out of the parking spot. He pulls out onto the street when he continues. "You will want to contact her."

"You don't know that."

"Oh, trust me, I *do* know that." We stop at our first intersection, waiting for the signal to turn green. "She's divorced."

Those two words hit me like the truck that passed in front of us. *Maria's single.* For the first time since she wrote *The Chad* letter, we are both single at the same time. A small smile crosses my lips.

"See!" He points to me. I turn to him, surprised by his outburst. "Right there. That smile." He shakes his head. "I knew I shouldn't have told you."

"What?" *God, he knows me so well.* "I'm happy for her. Nate treated her like a slave. I'm glad she's free of him."

"Mm-hmm."

"You never answered my first question." I need to know. If Maria is single and didn't ask about me, then I know she's over me. And I can forget this whole thing. But if she did....

"You are so pathetic." He's shaking his head as he turns towards the school so we can pick up Mikey. "Yes." A smile is playing on his lips. "She asked about you. She wanted to know how you were and if we still talk. Which is funny because you will never be rid of me."

I chuff. "And not for a lack of trying." I can't decide if I want to ask more because ... obviously I do. "What did you say?"

"I told her you moved back home."

"What did she say?" Good grief. I *do* sound like a high schooler.

He rotates his head to face me. "She said to tell you hi."

"That's it?" I'm trying hard to not let my disappointment show.

He shrugs and looks out the window. "That's it."

Great. Now I'm analyzing and overthinking every aspect of this situation. She asked about me; she knows I'm back home, she's divorced, and she said to tell me hi. It all sounds so insignificant. But for me, it's huge. I thought with my last email to her that I had messed everything up. Maybe not.

We sit quietly as we drive the rest of the way to the school and wait for Mikey to come out from his practice. "I wonder if I should contact her?"

He lets out an exasperated moan. "I knew it," he mutters under his breath as he turns to look at me. "Don't." The word comes out stern, as if it's a warning.

"Why not? It would be nice to hear from her again," I retort. That's all this is. Keeping in touch with an old friend. Reconnecting after six years. No big deal.

"Yeah, right. As if that's the only thing you're after."

I let that accusation hang in the air for a moment "How did she look?" I inquire, raising my eyebrow in curiosity. Ricky has always thought Maria was hot.

He gives me a huge dose of side eye, then he smiles. "She looked good. Really, really good." In Ricky-speak, that means she looked hot. *Why? Why does she have to look good?* Thoughts of Maria as a hot mom are dancing in my head, and it's causing some intense reactions inside of me. He continues. "You know, she asked *me* if I was seeing anyone."

My head jerks in his direction, and my heart bottoms out. Why would she ask *him* if he's seeing anyone? "Did she ask if I was single?"

"Nope." His grin is maniacal.

I know Ricky. He's instigating me. He is well aware that this will get under my skin. My body is rigid now because, I mean, Ricky is a good-looking guy. He has no problem finding dates every weekend. Maria is single and so is he. Maybe she saw him and realized she was interested. I shift in my seat at the thought.

"Look at you." He grins in amusement.

"What?" I ask between gritted teeth.

"If contacting Maria is only friendly, as you claim, why does it bother you so much that she asked me if I was single? Which, by the way, relax, dude. I would never do that to you." My shoulders sag in relief. "But seriously, she said that she *just* got divorced. Which tells me it's fresh. Who knows where her head is at? Don't contact her and confuse her. I know you care, but it's not the right time, and you know it."

He's right. I'm making this about me. If Maria left Nate, or if he left her, she needs to take the time to put herself first. Heck, that's the advice I gave her in my last email to her.

"You're right."

"Always."

We watch Mikey run towards us. "Besides, I just moved home myself. I need to get settled and make sure Mikey is adjusting." Ricky only nods in understanding.

As Mikey heaves his bag into the back seat and jumps into the Jeep, our seeing-Maria-again conversation ends. Ricky and I listen as he raves on and on about how great practice was. I'm trying to pay attention, but my mind travels back to Maria.

How will I know when it's the right time to reach out to her? Will there be any visible sign or signal?

Would it be a good idea to get in touch with her?

I rest my head on the back of my seat.

All this uncertainty sucks.

And to make it worse, I realize how much I miss her.

Chapter Thirty

November 2016

Sam

The morning breeze blowing into my car feels amazing as I sit here waiting to go to work. Despite the change of season from fall to winter, the refreshing coolness of the air is a welcome addition as it seeps into the car. If nothing else, it's definitely jolting me awake. I received a text from my office manager telling me that my seven a.m. patient canceled last minute, so I have some time to kill before I start this Monday morning. And by time to kill, you would think I should be preparing for my next patient or reading a book. Something else more productive. Instead, I'm sitting here in the parking lot, scrolling through Instagram.

Somehow, my eleven-year-old convinced me I need to be cool and join the social media app. I'm a forty-two-year-old man. Why in the heck do I need to be on social media? I refused for the longest time until I relented. Now I find myself looking at nothing and yet everything at the same time, scrolling along. A post about laying ceramic tile piques my interest. Something I've never done in my life. But this guy makes it look easy.

Hmmm. That's a cool way to install...

Female laughter rings out catching my attention. I glance up to see a group of women walking toward the employee entrance of the office that sits next to the wing of the hospital where I work. It's a physical therapy slash gym that opened about a month ago.

This same group of women always walks in together every morning. Carrying their coffee and all of their belongings they think they need for a day of work. I mean, seriously, why do women carry so much stuff with them?

I shake my head as I scroll through Instagram once again. Out of nowhere, a distinct voice grabs my attention.

"Hey, Richelle, you dropped your badge." My head whips up because I'd know that voice anywhere. Then I see her.

Maria.

What in the world? When did she start working there?

I can't believe it's really her. It's as if a ghost from my past has reappeared to haunt me, uninvited.

She's dressed in black scrubs, a gray hoodie hugs her body, and her blonde hair, still long, is up in a high ponytail, swaying with each long stride.

Dear Lord, she looks incredible.

Something else stands out as well. Something I can't un-see.

She's wearing my watch. Still, after all this time, she wears it. That has to mean something. Right?

Or maybe it means it's a good watch, and she likes it. I need to stop reaching.

She's trailing behind the other gang of women, and it makes no sense why I haven't seen her before today if she works so close to me? With each passing moment, I watch her intently, my heart sinking deeper into my stomach. Ricky wasn't lying. She looks ... so good. She's older now, but somehow still looks like she's twenty. Which is very unfair to the other representatives of the female race. Her legs are a mile long, as I remember them, and her body looks amazing. Nothing about her appearance is making this easier.

Everything fades to black around me. The chirping morning birds disappears, and the only thing I hear is my beating heart hammering out of my chest.

"Oh, thanks, Maria," the other woman, Richelle, I'm assuming, says as she grabs the badge from Maria's hand.

"Sure. You're welcome." Maria flashes her the smile that I miss so much.

I can't take my eyes off of her as the two of them resume walking toward the employee entrance, which I now realize I'm parked right in front of.

CRAP! I scoot my body down on my seat and pull on my sunglasses. I can't risk her seeing me. Not yet anyway. My head and heart are in no position for that encounter. So instead, I'll eavesdrop and watch like a creeper. Good plan.

"So, how is your first week going so far?" Richelle asks.

Ah! Thank you for getting answers to my questions, Richelle. Maria has only been here a week. No wonder I haven't seen her yet. My first patient is typically at seven every morning, so I'm in my office by the time she arrives for work. Unfortunately, it's also the appointment that has the most cancellations. Like today.

"Great! Can't complain. Everyone has been nice, and it works well with my kids' schedule, so that's a plus. And the pay is great." Maria taps her badge on the entrance lock, and the door releases with a clank. She opens it, holding it open for Richelle as they enter.

"We should have lunch…" The door slams shut on whatever Richelle was going to suggest, which I'm assuming was going to be lunch. I exhale deeply, feeling a rush of relief, and then sit up straight in my seat.

This is the first time I have seen Maria since 2004. Twelve years and she still looks the same. She sounds the same. Walks the same. Does she still smell like coconut?

I groan and pinch the bridge of my nose, trying to compose myself. That was a lot of information and feelings to have thrown at me first thing Monday morning.

That day after the gym, over a year ago, when Ricky told me he spoke to Maria, it took every ounce of my willpower to not contact her. But Ricky was right. It wasn't the right time. So gradually, I tried to force myself to forget. Well, not forget entirely. I could never forget Maria. But, I did begin to date.

Not only did I join Instagram, but Ricky convinced me to join a dating app. Total disaster and waste of time. I arranged to meet a woman for dinner that I was talking to, and shocker … she stood me up. I deleted the app the next day, vowing that my lot in life is to stay single.

Soon, that unreasonable outlook changed, and I did start seeing an old friend. It's not serious, but it could be. We are taking it slow and keeping things casual, seeing where it goes. Honestly, when I'm with her, I forget about Maria in a way no other woman has ever been able to do. Even Erica.

But seeing Maria now ... is this the universe or God telling me she and I should talk? Can we give this another go? Is that what I want? Could I trust her again? And would she even be interested? Especially after the last email I sent her.

Baffling how quickly my current relationship gets tossed out the window with only one glance at my past.

Maria's little encounter with both Ricky and this Richelle gave me some insight into her world. I make a list in my head. She's divorced (best news ever), she's working again (and I assume as an exercise physiologist since it's the rehab gym), she seems to be surviving since it pays well, and she looks incredible.

I bite back a smile because these are good things. Not only that, she looked happy and healthy. These revelations make me wonder if she took the advice I gave her years ago. To put herself first. I hope so.

Without warning, a thought pops into my head. *Is she on Instagram?* In a rush, I grab my phone as if it's going to walk away from me, and I open the app. I hit the search button and type in 'Maria Connelly.'

Nothing.

Clearing it out, I type in her maiden name 'Maria Bryant.' The results stare back at me. *Of course!* There's a thousand Maria Bryants. With a moan of frustration, I toss my phone into the console.

I check my watch and roll my head back against the car seat head rest because it's time to go in and start my day.

As I gather up my stuff, I walk the opposite direction to my building. Away from Maria. I haven't made any decisions yet whether I will approach her. Eventually, I'm sure I will. But for whatever reason, I don't feel ready. For the moment, it's comforting to know that she is so close.

The usual Monday morning work buzz is going strong as I make my way to my office. Beginning my usual morning routine, I sit my stuff down and check my emails and patient schedule. But my mind keeps wandering back to the leggy blonde I saw fifteen minutes ago. A smile crosses my lips as I swivel in my chair and look out the window.

I really hope my seven a.m. cancels again. *I wonder what she will wear to work tomorrow?*

The next morning

The appointment canceled, so I decide to park a little further away, under a tree shaded from view. Today, she is wearing pink scrubs, and her hair is down. I saw her pull in, and she drives a blue Honda Civic.

The following week

She's rushing today and is later than normal. She's talking on the phone, and it sounds like she's arguing with Nate about the kids. I can see her frustration as she hangs up before she walks in and wipes a tear from her cheek. My heart drops seeing her upset. I miss being the one to wipe away her tears.

A month later

It's pouring rain, and she doesn't have an umbrella, so she's running into the building. Water splashes up onto the bottom half of her scrubs every time she stomps on a puddle of water. How she made that look graceful and beautiful is beyond me.

After the new year 2017

She's taking her time getting out of the car today. She arrived earlier than normal. Just like me, hoping I could catch a glimpse. Her head is down, and she's scrolling on her phone. She lets out a laugh but doesn't look up from whatever has her attention. I try to rub away the pain that I'm feeling in my chest, because I really hope it's not another man.

The next week

It's the pink scrubs again. Pretty sure these are my favorite.

Two weeks later

She and that Richelle are walking in together. The cold is bitter today. Her puffer jacket is back, and she has the cutest hat on. One with the fuzzy ball on top. Her hair is cascading from underneath it. Richelle's hands are waving in the air, gesturing with anger. Maria is listening kindly, bobbing her head in agreement with whatever Richelle is in a huff about.

The next week

She isn't here today. I overheard Richelle tell the other girls that she has the flu. I hope she's okay.

The next day

I watch as she drags herself out of her car, holding a tissue in her hand. Her nose is red, and she's coughing as she walks slowly into the building. I remember she likes soup when she's sick. I hope she's eating soup.

Friday the next week

I woke up this morning with a renewed sense of purpose. I'm going to approach her today. Sitting and stalking her is now becoming too much to bear. I need to talk to her. Plus, it's creepy, so there's that.

Mikey couldn't resist poking fun at me for taking so long to do my hair, playfully imitating my careful movements.

"Why do you keep messing with your hair today, Dad?" he asked while I ran my fingers and combed through my mop a hundred times this morning as he copied me, laughing along the way. "You're going to work. It's not like you have a date." He thinks he's so cute and clever.

If you only knew, Mikey. If you only knew.

Now I'm sitting under my tree, waiting for her blue Civic to pull in. On Wednesday, I decided it was time to approach her. I mean, what's the worst that could happen? She'll be nice, of course. We will exchange a few pleasantries, maybe a hug, and catch up on our lives. Then be on our merry way.

Easy.

So then why are my palms clammy? On instinct, I rub them down my dress pants as I see her car approach and park in her usual spot. She gathers up her things, finishes up a phone call, shuts her door, and points her key fob at the car. The horn beeps to let her know it's locked up as she turns on her heels and walks toward the building.

With my stomach in knots, my mind racing, and a heart full of hope, I step out of my car and call her name.

Chapter Thirty-One

MARCH 2017

THE PARKING LOT

Maria

"Brielle, I don't know where you left your math book." I internally moan as I look both ways at the intersection I'm stopped at. "You're thirteen. And old enough to keep track of this stuff yourself." I see the coast is clear, so I make the turn onto the street my building is on.

"I'm going to get in trouble if I can't find it." She poses this to me as if it's a threat. It's not.

Teenagers are so fun.

"Did you check the dining room table?" I offer as some sort of solution. Knowing full well it's not there since I ate breakfast at the table this morning. I pull my car into my usual spot and turn off the ignition. She grumbles into my ear, and I can practically hear her eye roll as I turn around to grab my lunch bag from the back seat.

Out of the corner of my eye, I see the same black car parked under an enormous tree across the lot. He gets here early sometimes, but then I won't see his car for a few days. The tree branches cast a shadow, obscuring my view of his face, but a sense of being watched always hangs over me. I wonder where he works. At the hospital next door, or maybe in my building.

God, I hope he's not some pervert. I gotta admit, my trust issues with men are currently at an all time low.

Plus, I wish I had someone waiting at home to tell this stuff to. Even though Nate was ... well ... Nate, it was nice to have a sounding board. Now, I have no one.

I asked Richelle about this guy a few weeks back, but she didn't seem fazed.

"Oh, I've noticed him. I'm sure he's harmless," she shrugged when I asked her. But something seems almost familiar about his silhouette. I don't know what it is, and I can't seem to put my finger on it. Like, I know him somehow.

I shake the thought from my head, avert my eyes from the mystery man, and step out of the car. The phone is still up to my ear. I can hear Brielle lifting things, and it sounds like she's rummaging through her bed, on the hunt for the math book. I heave my backpack from the back seat and there, staring back at me, is her book.

Son of a....

With my body tense and full of frustration, I break the news to my daughter. "Brielle, it's in the car."

"WHAT! Why is it in the car?"

The winter air bites at my back as I bend over to pick up the book, staring at it, wondering if I should take it to her at lunch or force her to reap the consequences at school. I toss it back in the seat.

"I don't know, B. It's not my book." I only use her nickname when I'm irritated with her. Which, since she turned thirteen, is a lot. I'm standing outside my car now, my puffer coat doing nothing to protect me from the cold winter air swirling around me. "Maybe you will remember next time. I can't bring it to you since I'm at work."

"Fine," she huffs out. "I guess I'm going to get detention then."

"I guess so." She doesn't respond. There's only silence. "Alright, sweetie, I gotta go or I'm going to be late. I'll see you at home."

"Bye, Mom." The line goes dead. I shake my head, thinking about where my life is now raising teenagers. It's different, that's for sure. I throw my phone into my purse, quickly gather my things, and lock the door.

As I make my way to the employee entrance, the sound of a car door shutting startles me from behind.

CRAP! Is it the tree shadow creeper man?

"Oh, my God," I mutter to myself.

The sound of crunching feet on pavement, only steps behind me, spurs me to quicken up my pace.

"Maria!"

I stop dead, my feet frozen in place. Because I know that voice. I would know it anywhere.

No wonder the tree man's silhouette felt familiar.

It was Sam.

I turn slowly because he has caught up to me now. When I do, I'm met with my past and what was supposed to be my future. Our eyes collide, and suddenly, Brielle's math crisis is in the rearview mirror because the only thing I see right now is Sam.

The skin around his eyes shows signs of aging, but the longing remains unchanged. His stare would always send warmth throughout my whole body. Which is still the case because I feel like I need to peel this coat off.

Did the temperature rise in the last five minutes?

He has a few days' worth of stubble growing, which totally works for me. Maturity has reached his hair and beard because it's scattered with gray strands. Let's just say the years have been kind to him because he is rocking this whole salt-and-pepper dad vibe.

"Hi." His voice shakes with nerves, and he gives me a soft wave while clearing his throat. "Hey," he says again.

I'm completely dumbfounded, and it seems my ability to speak has gone out the window. I haven't seen Sam since Brielle was a baby and we spent that day in the park. And I haven't heard from him since his last email after his ex-wife's tragic death. A very curt and final email.

As I blink in disbelief, a wave of shock washes over me.

Questions swirl in my head like a tornado. What is he doing here? Does he work here?

I should probably say hi instead of standing here staring at him. "Hi, Sam." We both let out a nervous laugh and go in for a hug. Despite my open-armed approach, it becomes clear that he only wanted a handshake as his palm was outstretched.

"Oh, okay." He jolts back with surprise, then wraps one arm around my shoulder. My bag and purse are slung over the other. I don't know where to put my hands, so I give him a quick double pat on the back. The whole thing lasts only seconds. We pull apart and take a step backward, both of us studying the ground, not wanting to make eye contact.

Most uncomfortable almost-hug ever.

There was a time when hugging Sam felt natural and easy. We would fit like a glove and melt into each other. The world, our emotions, or problems could never penetrate the bubble we would create in each other's arms. I miss his arms around me. But that hug? That hug was full of unshared history and awkwardness.

God, I hate that we went from what we were to ... this.

His hot breath floats in the cold air as he exhales. He forcefully slides his hands into the warmth of his coat pockets. "How have you been?"

I bob my head as if it's a toy. "Good. Great, actually. And you?"

He kicks a piece of gravel with his shoe. "Good."

Silence hangs in the air for a beat or two, and I turn to face the car under the tree. It's empty.

I have to know, so I jut my thumb toward the empty car. "So, are you the guy that's been hanging out in your car for the last few months?"

He holds his hands up in surrender and laughs. "Guilty."

"Well, at least I know you're not some creeper."

He raises an eyebrow. "You sure about that?"

The sound of our laughter cuts through the tension, instantly lightening the mood.

But I need to know if my sixth sense about being watched was accurate. A slow smile builds. "Have you been watching me?"

He lifts his left shoulder and gives me a slight grin. "Guilty again."

I shake my head, a smile playing at the corners of my lips. I should be mad that he didn't approach me sooner. Or that he stalked me for months. But oddly enough, I'm not. It's kinda heartwarming and comforting to know that he has been this close.

Caught up in the moment, he can't help but join in with laughter, helping to ease some of the awkwardness. "I'm glad you're not mad."

"No, I'm not mad." It's impossible for me to resist smiling when I look at him.

"Good."

"I am wondering why you didn't say hi sooner, though?"

He peers off into the distance, collecting his thoughts. "I wasn't sure if I was ready. Or if you would want me to." As his focus returns to me, a faint smile forms on his face. "But my lack of self-control won out."

"Oh." The heat rises in my cheeks, which I'm sure is now a nice shade of pink. "Sam, I will always want to talk to you."

His brown eyes pierce mine with so much intensity that I can't help but feel vulnerable. We stand in silence for a second or two, the tension between us palpable, until he finally breaks it with a nervous throat clearing. "Um ... so, how are your kids? Brielle and Mason?"

My toy bobble head returns. "Good. Great, actually. Getting big."

"Crazy how that happens, huh?"

"And how is Mikey?" I want to add 'since his mom's death,' but I stop myself.

"He's good. I mean, the move has been really great for him. Living in Georgia became"—he stops, gathering his thoughts—"too hard."

"Too many memories?"

Sam tears his eyes away from me, a flicker of sadness crossing his face. "Something like that," he whispers. As soon as he says those three words, he furrows his brows and his shoulders tighten, revealing his unease. Every word carries a weighty significance and a hint of sorrow.

I hope one day, he will share with me the untold story that has been haunting him. I mean, if we continue to talk after today.

"I was sorry to hear about you and Nate," he says, directing the conversation back to me, each word sounding forced and unnatural. There's no doubt in my mind that he loathed Nate. Our emails from back then showed as much. But his sympathy is sweet, even though I know he's just saying it out of kindness.

A playful grin spreads across my face. "No, you weren't."

He breaks into laughter. "You're right. I'm not." Our eyes meet, and a spark of connection passes between us. "He wasn't good enough for you."

Sam's right. Nate wasn't good enough for me. Of course, Nate wouldn't agree with that. According to him, I should have woken up every morning, thanking my lucky stars that I was his wife. But all I have ever wanted was to wake up with the prize of a man standing in front of me.

The worst decision I ever made. Letting Sam go.

I can't decide if I should tell him that Nate cheated on me. Maybe he would feel like it's karma.

It probably was.

And besides, now is not the time.

Immediately, I am catapulted to that fateful day when I was standing in front of him, just like we are now, and I handed him the Dear John letter. Looking back, I can't believe I was that stupid. There is nothing I want more than to rewind, go back in time, and warn that terrified girl. My heart aches to scream at her, to plead with her not to let Sam go, to prioritize her own well-being, and to caution her about what's coming.

But I can't.

Before I word vomit all of this out of my head, I decide we need a swift subject change. Because like everything Sam and me, we always veer off course into the realm of guilt, shame, and shared history. I can't do that this morning.

"So, do you work here?" I flick my thumb at the hospital behind me.

"I do. Since we've moved back. Almost two years now."

"And you work as a psychologist?" I bounce up on my toes, anticipating his answer.

He glances down at the ground and nods in agreement, not wanting to brag on himself. "Mm-hmm."

A surge of pride courses through me, causing my face to beam with happiness. "I am so proud of you, Sam."

His cheeks turn a rosy shade, and there's a sense of joy knowing that I caused it. "Thanks. I owe it all to you."

"Stop it. I just nudged you. You did the work. You deserve the credit."

My phone buzzes in my purse, and I know it's Richelle wondering where I am. Or knowing her, wondering who I'm talking to because she is probably watching me from the breakroom window. I glance at my watch to see the time and to get an idea of how late I'm going to be. I can feel Sam's stare tracking my movements.

As I move my hand downwards, Sam's fingers curl around my wrist, pulling my hand towards him. I step closer as he carefully examines my watch. In a tender reminder of our past, he runs his thumb under the watchband, the sensation instantly bringing me back to that dance floor at Dexter's eons ago. The gentle caress causes goose bumps to erupt on my arm. I gasp in surprise as this brief meet-up takes an unexpected twist. As it always does.

"You still have it?" he asks, his eyes glued to the watch.

A pit forms in my stomach. "Y-yes."

"Why?" His brows pinch together, and his eyes are full of intensity as he studies me.

"You know why." Somehow, and I can't pinpoint when, it's not just me who has inched closer. My racing heartbeat fills my ears, and I can't help but wonder if he can hear it, too. He looks down at my hand and gives it a gentle squeeze before releasing it. His touch lingers on my skin.

Sam takes a deliberate step back, trying to create some distance between himself and me. And I hate it. "I better let you get into work."

I give a slight nod of agreement because he's right; I need to get in there and start my day. This whole little emotionally charged reunion has already made me late. So, why does being out here with him seem so much more important? As if this is a start. Of what, I don't know.

But a start.

He opens his mouth to say something, then stops. I tilt my head in curiosity, silently begging him to say whatever it is. He rubs the back of his neck and finally speaks. "Before you go inside, can I get your number?" My head jerks in shock at his suggestion. This seems to catch him off guard as a skeptical expression skates across his face. "I mean, only if you want to."

And just to show him how much I want to, I start rummaging through my massive purse to find my phone. I tap on the unlock code, feeling the smooth glass beneath my fingertips, and hand it to him. "Here. Type in your number."

"You sure?" With hesitancy, he takes my phone from my hand, our fingers brushing slightly. It feels like fire, a burning sensation that leaves me breathless and in agony.

Why does every touch from him feel like this? Even after all this time.

"Of course," I say.

He exhales in relief, and I watch his fingers type in his number, a grin etched on his face. His hands look like they always did. Still strong but older and more weathered. The same, but better. Memories of how they felt when he would touch me flood my brain.

"Here." He hands it back to me, snapping me back to the here and now. I attempt to compose myself as I type out a quick text and then add him to my contacts. His phone dings from his back pocket.

"Is it too much to ask for a hug redo? That last one … well … we can do better." This entire exchange is taking me back to the park when Brielle was a baby. I'm hoping this hug redo tops that one. He knows he doesn't have to ask twice, but it's sweet that he does. We can do better. We always have.

With a grin, I set my bags down, extend my arms, and we both dissolve into nervous laughter, the sound filling the cold air around us. In one swift motion, he seizes my forearm and draws me toward him, holding me close. His hands tightly clasp my back, the pressure of his fingers sending shivers down my spine. My hands wrap around his shoulders, then his neck, and I can't stop pulling him tighter, holding onto him with purpose.

God, he feels so good.

His nose nuzzles into my hair, and the warmth of his breath skates against my skin as he exhales, warming me from the cold. He smells my hair, like he always used to, and a soft moan escapes his lips. This only spurs me on as my face brushes against his neck, and I inhale deeply, taking in his familiar, comforting smell. His hand glides up to my head with a gentle touch as he weaves his fingers into my hair. Then his calloused finger traces a path down my neck, sending a tingling sensation through my body.

Nope, not awkward anymore, because the one man I do trust, more than anyone, is back in my arms again.

I have no idea how long we have been standing here, holding one another, but it's obvious neither of us wants to be the first to let go. And I really wish I wasn't wearing this massive coat. It's too much clothing because I feel like I can't get close enough to him.

This is the first time we have embraced like this since that day in the shed before my wedding, and it feels like no time has passed. Yes, we hugged in the park, but it was quick. Like how you hug an old friend whom you haven't seen in a while. But this hug ... this hug feels like it's full of promise and hope. As we immerse ourselves in the moment, the sounds of the world fade into silence. Our history feels ancient and non-existent. We stand there, locked in an intense embrace, so tight it feels like the last time.

I don't want this to be the last time.

After a final squeeze, the weight of Sam's arms drops, and they fall to his sides as he steps back, catching his breath.

I clear my throat to get my breathing under control because that ... that was ... everything. "Better?" I choke on the question, my voice now hoarse.

A soft hum escapes from him. "Much."

I pick up my bags and take steps backward, still facing him. "I'll talk to you soon, Sam. It was nice seeing you again."

Neither of us wanting to turn away from each other, we are both walking backward in sync. "I'll text you." He smiles, and it sounds like a promise. I hope it is.

Making it to the entrance of my building, I wave, turn, and tap my badge to unlock the door. I step inside and look back. His eyes remain locked on mine. "One more thing," he hollers out.

"Yeah."

"I've missed you."

It's an admission I wasn't expecting. But also, one I didn't know I needed to hear.

I rest my head on the door as I hold it open and take him in, standing so close to me, thrust back into my world unexpectedly. "I've missed you, too." Because I have. So much.

He gives a small wave as the door shuts, the sound echoing in the hall, and I can finally breathe. I collapse against the cool door, and within seconds, Richelle is at my side.

She curses, then asks, "Who in the heck was that gorgeous man?" her tone full of curiosity.

I continue to stand there, staring at the floor, trying to get my bearings.

"He's—" I stop to consider my answer. "He's a start."

Sam

Is it too soon to text? Probably. But I'm going to do it, anyway.

As I walk to my building, my body still buzzing from the best hug of my life, I grab my phone from my back pocket and add Maria's number to my contacts. I hit the message button and type.

> Me: I hope you don't get into too much trouble for being late.

Do I want to do this? My finger hovers over the send button as a yearning builds. Without a doubt, I want to do this.

Send.

I shove my phone back into my pocket, since I'm sure she won't answer right away. Who knows, maybe her work doesn't allow her to have her phone with her.

As I enter my building, keyboards clicking, phones ringing, and the usual morning chatter fills the air as I greet the staff. When I round the corner to my office, my phone dings.

A sudden feeling of euphoria rushes through me, making me feel like a teenager again. I throw my bag onto my desk, its weight causing a thud that echoes through the room as I pull out my phone. However, this text is not what I expected.

> Cara: I hope you have a great day at work. Can't wait for tonight. I've missed you these last few weeks.

Rubbing a hand down my face, I feel the rough texture of stubble against my palm and sink down into the comfort of my office chair.

Cara.

Cara and I reconnected after my dating app debacle and is the woman I have been seeing. She moved back home, and since then, we have gone out a few times, keeping things between us lighthearted, fun, and friendly.

Then I saw Maria.

And everything changed.

Cara, at one time in my life, meant a lot to me. I would venture to say that I loved her. We dated twice and had a lot in common, and we still do. Our friendship and relationship were always easy, uncomplicated, and freeing. So, when we started texting, then started hanging out, I thought that this is the direction my life should be going. We aren't official, but could be.

Then I hugged Maria.

I quickly type out a text. I don't want to cancel on Cara just because of this encounter with Maria. That wouldn't be fair. And Maria and I ... well ... we aren't anything at the moment. All we have is an intense history, a recent five-minute (albeit emotionally charged) conversation, and each other's phone numbers. That's it.

Honestly, I probably shouldn't have asked her for her number. So dumb. *Why did I do that?*

I finish out the text, not wanting to overthink this.

> Me: Thanks! You too. And tonight should be fun.

I heave my phone onto my desk, and it hits with a thud, the landing echoing in the room. A sudden wave of guilt washes over me. Because tonight will be fun. It always is with Cara. But, I don't know if I *want* it to be fun. And I know why.

Because I just held Maria in my arms. If I hadn't let go, I'm pretty sure I would have kissed her. That's what she does to me. I also know, without a shadow of a doubt, that she would have let me.

As I try to shake thoughts of kissing Maria out of my mind, I sit down and log onto my computer, the keys clicking beneath my fingertips, getting me into the right frame of mind. While going through my patients' charts for the day, my phone pings, interrupting my concentration. I raise my eyes from the screen and fix my stare on my phone. The thought of picking it up fills me with apprehension, as if my world has instantly become complicated.

Which woman will it be?

Which woman do I *want* it to be?

With a mix of excitement and anxiety, I turn my phone over, my head hot and dizzy.

> Maria: I got wrote up. But it was worth it. <heart emoji>

I smile.

Then quickly frown.

What am I going to do?

Chapter Thirty-Two

The Text Messages

March 2017

Maria: I know we only saw each other yesterday, but is it too soon to ask you on a lunch date? <fingers crossed emoji>

Sam: That depends.

Maria: On what exactly?

Sam: Will you wear your pink scrubs?

Maria: I can. <Blush face emoji>

Sam: I'll be there.

∞

May 2017

Sam: What am I going to do with you?

Maria: Whatever do you mean?

Sam: You need to stop looking so beautiful in scrubs. It's not fair to the rest of the medical community.

Maria: I can't make any promises. <heart emoji>

∞

June 2017

Maria: Can you meet for lunch today? I was thinking that small diner we used to love back in the day.

Sam: Sounds great. But we can always try something new.

Maria: I thought it would be nice for old times' sake.

Sam: No, you're right. It would.

Maria: I will always think about the time that we went there on a dare dressed up in chicken suits.

Sam: Good times.

Maria: LOL! It was all Ricky's fault.

Sam: No. If I recall, it was yours for losing that bet.

Maria: True.

July 2017

Sam: Lunch was nice yesterday. <heart emoji>

Maria: It was.

Sam: I love watching your face light up when you talk about Brielle and Mason.

Maria: They are my life.

Maria: I would love for you to meet them someday.

Sam: Hopefully. Someday. Maybe.

September 2017

Sam: Sorry. That was mean.

Maria: Yes, it was.

Maria: …

Sam: Were you going to say something?

November 2017

Sam: How have you been? It's been 6 weeks since I've heard from you.

Maria: Sorry, yeah. I've been busy.

Sam: You avoiding me?

Maria: Maybe a little.

Sam: I'm so sorry I brought up Chad and Nate. That was rude and insensitive.

Maria: You know I can't stay mad at you for long. But maybe it's best that we don't bring up our past relationships in conversation.

Sam: Agreed.

Maria: Are you okay still…with us talking and reconnecting?

Sam: I am. It's strange. It brings up a lot of memories
and emotions. But I like it.

Maria: Me too.

Sam: Wanna get lunch tomorrow? My treat.

Maria: Of course.

∞

December 2017

Sam: I didn't want to say this in person, but you looked beautiful yesterday.

Maria: Seriously? My hair was dirty, thrown up in a messy bun, and I had no makeup on.

Sam: I noticed.

Maria: Then how on earth can you say I looked beautiful?

Sam: You were you. I loved it.

Maria: <blush face emoji>

∞

January 2018

Maria: I hate my boss.

Sam: The worst. Wanna talk about it? Over lunch?

Maria: Definitely.

Sam: Our diner?

Maria: Meet you at our booth. Regular time?

Sam: Sounds good.

Maria: Do you think we will ever gravitate toward dinner?

Sam: Are you asking me out?

Maria: Maybe. <heart emoji>

Sam: I don't know if we are ready for that yet.

Maria: Sounds like I need to up my flirting game.

Maria: To help change your mind.

Sam: Your game is on point.

Sam: Trust me.

March 2018

Sam: I am exhausted today.

Maria: Haha. Staying up till 2 in the morning texting your ex will do that to you.

Maria: FYI … I can't keep my eyes open.

Sam: I can't believe we talked that much.

Maria: It was so nice.

Sam: It was.

Maria: I can't believe it's been a year since you approached me in the parking lot.

Sam: Time flies when it's spent with those you care about.

$$\infty$$

May 2018

Sam: Did you like that bottle of wine?

Maria: I did. It was delicious. Is it from that winery we used to visit?

Sam: You remember that place?

Maria: Of course I do. I was never allowed to taste test anything because I was 20 and you were 21. That would always bum me out. LOL!

Sam: I was there the other night and ordered it. I thought of you. Thought you might like it. So I bought you a bottle.

Maria: It was a nice surprise to find it resting by my car after work.

Maria: The other night, huh? A date?

Sam: I was having dinner with a friend. With the weather warming up, we ate out on the patio.

Maria: Well, thank you. I wish I could have shared it with you. It made me think of drinking wine together in your old apartment. Even though, technically, it was against the law for me. Haha.

Sam: Good times.

Sam: But also the past.

Maria: Sorry, I know bringing up that time must be hard.

Sam: I hate thinking about that time.

Maria: I don't. Because it's time I spent with you.

∾

Maria: I got so sick from the steak salad at lunch yesterday.

Sam: Ugh. I'm so sorry. Now, I'm happy I changed my mind and got the chicken.

Maria: Consider yourself lucky. Being sick and alone sucks. I know you don't like talking about the past but it did remind me of that night I got the stomach flu senior year when my parents were away for their anniversary. And how you never left my side.

Sam: I remember

Maria: I threw up all over your new Nikes. <puke face emoji>

Sam: Ha! That's right. I kinda forgot about that.

Maria: If you were mad, you never showed it.

Sam: I could never be mad at you.

Maria: Lord knows I've done plenty to make you mad.

Maria: This may be a loaded question but, do you still think about any of it?

Sam: Think about what?

Maria: Us. And how we ended.

Sam: I don't think this is a conversation to have over text.

Maria: You're right. Sorry.

∞

Maria: I haven't seen or heard from you in a while. I miss you. Lunch tomorrow?

Sam: Um … sure.

Maria: You sound hesitant. Are you sure?

Sam: Yes, of course. Our booth?

Maria: I'll be there.

∞

Sam: I'm sorry, I have to cancel lunch today.

Maria: Bummer. Everything ok?

Sam: Yeah. I just kind of forgot that I had a prior commitment.

Maria: It's ok. I understand.

Maria: Wanna try for next week?

September 2018

Maria: Hey, are you alright? I haven't heard from you in a few weeks.

Sam: Yeah. Sorry. I'm good. Just busy.

Maria: Ok. Just wanted to check. Lunch tomorrow?

Sam: I can't. I have patient appointments through lunch.

Maria: Ok. Maybe next week then.

Sam: I'll let you know.

Sam: I can't do lunch this week.

Maria: Ok. You must be busy.

Sam: Yes

Maria: Well, let me know when you're free

Sam: …

Maria: It's been so dramatic at my place lately. Brielle and her friends are fighting. So. Many. Tears.

Maria: Any advice? I may need a professional.

Sam: I don't specialize in pediatric psychology.

Maria: Um. Ok. So formal. Is everything alright?

∞

> Maria: Hey! Just wanted to text and say Good Morning.

Maria: I haven't seen you much in the mornings. Or heard from you. It's been a couple of weeks.

Maria: Have you changed your number? If this isn't Sam, please let me know.

❧

Maria: Sam, are you okay? I don't want to seem like a crazy ex-girlfriend here, but why haven't you been texting me? I'm worried.

Chapter Thirty-Three

LATE OCTOBER 2018

Sam

> Maria: Sam, are you okay? I don't want to seem like a crazy ex-girlfriend here, but why haven't you been texting me? I'm worried.

Maria's text from yesterday stares back at me as I swirl the scotch in my glass, the amber liquid coating the sides as I do. I ordered it about thirty minutes ago and still haven't taken a sip. My mind is elsewhere. Dexter's is especially quiet tonight, which makes sense since it's Tuesday. I texted the guys and asked them to meet me for a drink.

Mostly, I need their advice. Because I have a huge decision to make.

Over the past year, Maria and I have been messaging each other, grabbing lunch together, and gradually rebuilding our relationship. We would see each other in the parking lot, and I loved it. If I'm being honest, it has been nothing short of amazing. Having her back in my life again brings a sense of completeness that I didn't know I needed. Being together feels like all the missing pieces have finally come together. It's relaxed, it's easy.

But then, as soon as the texting stops or lunch is over, the confusion settles in. There are plenty of reasons why.

For one, Cara and I have gone from casual to official. That was over the summer, so it feels wrong to keep this up with Maria. I've already done the emotional connection thing with Maria while in a relationship. And we all know how that ended.

And two, she keeps bringing up the past, which for me, when it comes to us, is full of hurt. Full of memories of being given *The Chad* letter on her doorstep. Of pouring my heart out in a shed, begging her to choose me. And her choosing Nate instead. I don't want to go through the same heartache again.

Plus, I brought Cara home to meet Mikey, which was a huge step and was the exact moment I knew I had to let Maria go. Did Mikey and Cara hit it off? Meh.

Mikey said that she seems high maintenance. And he's right, she can be. But just like how Chandler told Monica on *Friends* ... I like maintaining her.

With my decision made, I arranged lunch with Maria, intent on telling her. But of course, the second I saw her, all reasonable thoughts got tossed out the window.

When we would meet for lunch, it was nothing but friends catching up with some flirty banter thrown in. It was wonderful having her in my life again. We would go months sometimes without seeing each other, and then we would meet again, and it was like no time had passed.

As time went on, occasionally, our hands would meet across the table. I never kissed her, but we always hugged once we would depart. Each hug getting longer and longer. Kisses on the cheek followed. And let's be honest, we all know what would happen next. And I'm not sure I'm ready for that. Do I want to feel her lips on mine again? Absolutely! Am I ready for the relationship that would follow? No. No, I'm not.

But then again, maybe I am.

Overwhelmed, I click off my phone and bury my hands in my face, feeling the weight of the world on my shoulders. *I am a complete head case right now.*

A huge meaty hand wraps around my shoulder. "Hey, man." Big C saddles up to the bar stool next to mine and sits. I give him a nod as he waves over the new bartender. A beautiful, tall, statuesque woman that Ricky is going to salivate over as soon as he gets here.

She places a napkin down in front of Big C. "What can I get you?" she asks and flashes us a smile that I'm sure will get her a lot of tips.

"I'll have whatever is on tap," C answers in his signature low, deep voice.

She gives C a once-over, glancing up and down his body. "You look like a Yeungling kinda guy."

Big C smiles. He never smiles. "How did you know?"

"Lucky guess." She pats the bar and winks at him. "Coming right up, cutie."

Yep, lots of tips coming her way.

"Ricky is going to love her," C says with a low chuckle.

"Ricky is going to love who?" Our tall, flirtatious friend enters the chat. He sits on the other side of me and waves his hand to get the bartender's attention. A mischievous glint appears as a devilish grin spreads across his face. "Never mind. I know who you mean."

A small, stifled laugh escapes my lips. I may be in a crap mood, but no one can pull me out of one quite like my oldest friend.

A napkin materializes in front of Ricky as well as Big C's beer. "What can I get you?" she asks with that same smile back on full display.

Ricky leans his elbows on the shiny lacquered bar as his eyes roam over her whole body. "You're new."

She must recognize Ricky's type because, immediately, the smile falls. "Funny, I didn't see that brand on the ordering sheet last week." She pops her hip out, resting her hand on it. "Wanna try again?" Little does this poor woman know that Ricky is a big fan of snarky and sassy.

"Sure," Ricky retorts. "I've never seen you here before." The evil grin is back. *Good grief, Ricky.*

She leans her elbows on the bar, mirroring Ricky's stance. Her white tank top stretches across her chest, which Ricky notices. "Look, the only thing you are getting from me is a drink. I don't date customers," she says with some bite as she pushes herself off of the bar and looks him square in the eye while also trying not to smile. "Especially patrons so much older than me."

Ricky's eyes pop open in surprise, and his jaw hits the floor while Big C and I choke back a laugh. I don't think I have ever seen him so gob smacked before. She rejected him with the one thing that he hates the most. Being reminded of his age. Even though he is forty-four, Ricky remains steadfast in his commitment to thinking and behaving as he did in his twenties.

She *is* good. This woman had him pegged almost immediately.

Ricky's shoulders sag in defeat. "I'll have a Budweiser."

"Coming right up." Her smile returns as she taps the bar and winks. Brutal.

Ricky turns to face us. "Well, that sucked."

Big C stretches his body across the bar to address Ricky. "Losing your touch?"

"Ha! Never." She returns with his beer, and Ricky can't help himself. "Can I at least get your name?" he asks as he takes a slow drag through his grin.

She walks away, ignoring him. But then halfway down the bar, she pauses and looks over her shoulder. "It's Rachel."

He turns to face us, satisfied. "I'll have her number by the end of the night."

Shaking his head in disbelief, Big C lets out an incredulous chuckle. "You are a legend, man."

Ricky laughs as he takes in the bar atmosphere. "They are really sprucing this place up."

Big C nods in agreement. "Yep. They are adding on and putting in loads more pool tables. The owner wants to start running tournaments here."

"I saw Givens Construction was doing the reno. I used to work for them. Good guys," I add.

Ricky directs his next question at me. "So why the meeting of the minds? What's up?"

I let out a deep, audible sigh. "I've reconnected with Maria."

With a grin spreading across his face, Ricky slaps the bar with a satisfying thud. "Yes! My man! It's about time."

"Whoa, whoa, whoa," Big C interjects, his head shaking with disbelief. "What about Cara?" His question slices through me.

"What about her?"

"What do you mean, 'What about her'? Are you still together?" It's a valid question. My friends' expectation is building as they wait in silence for my answer.

I finally take a sip of my drink, and I sigh, dejected. "Yes."

In an instant, Ricky's excitement evaporates into thin air, his tone laced with seriousness. "Okay, that's not cool."

Big C chimes in, "Tell us what happened."

For the next fifteen minutes, I spill my guts and tell them everything. Starting with seeing her in the parking lot, the lunches, the texts, Cara and I. All of it. "Guys, I have no idea what to do," I finally confess.

We all sit here quietly, listening to the rumblings of a less-than-packed bar on a Tuesday night.

Ricky eagerly breaks the silence and speaks first. "Well, for starters, ghosting her is not okay. I mean, this is Maria we are talking about."

"I know."

Sometimes, in the last year, Maria and I would go a month or longer without talking or texting. But when one of us initiated a text conversation, the other would always respond. So, I'm sure she is wondering what is going on.

Big C hangs his head low. "I'm sorry, but I gotta say it."

"Go ahead," I encourage. "Let me have it."

He looks me in the eye, his brows furrowed, stern and serious. "I have no clue what you see in her."

Okay. Was not expecting that.

Out of nowhere, a defensive feeling washes over me. "Maria is the love of my life. You know this."

"Dude, what the heck?" Ricky asks C because he knows. He has been there since day one when it comes to Maria and me. Starting in high school.

Big C leans forward again to address Ricky. "Oh, I don't know. Maybe because all she's done is break his heart, string him along, remind him of the past every chance she gets. It's sick." *I mean, it's not like I haven't started our communications in the past.*

Ricky looks indignant. "Oh, and as if Cara is that much better. I'm pretty sure her body and looks mean more to her than Sam. She's actually canceled a date because she had a nail appointment." *Yep. She did that just last week. But I love that she cares how she looks.*

Big C claps back. "Cara has never left Sam. Or broke up with him for a dude with a Vette." *Also true.*

My head ping-pongs back and forth between these two as they argue about my love life.

Ricky is practically sitting on my lap as he stretches over the bar to argue with C. His voice is raising. "We know her reasons. She's suffered from those mistakes. Plus, Mikey doesn't really like Cara." *Fact. Mikey isn't a fan.* "Can't say I blame him." My head whips around. *Wait, Ricky doesn't like Cara?*

Big C doesn't back down, his voice booming as he points his finger in Ricky's direction. "Got that right. Cara would never do to Sam what Maria did. When her and Sam are together, he is her world. Every man wants that." *He's not wrong.*

Ricky rolls his eyes. "Please. Except when she's getting her nails done. We all know Maria is the one. If she wasn't, they wouldn't be doing this same old song and dance." *Yep. We can't seem to stay away.*

C lets out an amused chuckle. "That is a lot of romantic talk from the guy who can't keep a woman." *Okay, that might have been too far.*

Ricky's nostrils flare. "Says the guy who had to settle for Sam's sloppy seconds." *Oh, crap. Not good.*

The tension in this bar just skyrockets as Big C's shoulders tighten. He rises slowly from his bar stool. Ricky does the same, his eyes dark with anger. This situation went from zero to a hundred fast, and I need to diffuse it quickly because, let's face it, Ricky doesn't stand a chance.

As I plant my feet firmly on the floor, I reach out my arms, creating a physical barrier between these two. "Guys, enough!" My voice erupts with frustration as I look back and forth between the two of them. "Stop!"

I see C's shoulders sag in defeat. With purpose, we all sit down. Both Ricky and C stare straight ahead, their breathing labored from what almost transpired.

I take a second before I scold my friends like children. "As much as I appreciate your concern and somewhat *weird* passion about my love life"—who knew they were so invested—"you're not helping."

Big C speaks first. "Sorry, man."

Ricky follows. "Yeah. Sorry."

After that awkward display, I feel like I need to defend myself. And my feelings for both women. I address Big C first. "Look, I know you're a fan of Cara, but Ricky has a point. Maria is the love of my life. I have been in love with her since I was sixteen. No one knows me better, and other than you two, she is my best friend. She's incredible, she's smart, she's fiercely loyal to those she loves, even to her own detriment. It makes me sad that you never got the chance to know her or see what I see."

"Remember whose fault that is," he says flatly as he finishes his beer.

He's right.

I turn to Ricky. "And I know if I wasn't interested in Maria all those years ago, you would have gone for her."

He chuckles. "You better believe it. She's amazing."

"She is." I stop to gather my thoughts. "But so is Cara." Ricky's eyes meet mine, and I can feel the weight of his attention. "She is probably the most independent, confident woman I know, which is so sexy. When she loves someone, it's with everything she has. And yes, she's into her looks, but, when I'm with her, she makes me feel like I am her world. And she's funny as hell." Ricky grins. "I really hope you find that someday. With someone."

Big C lets out a long breath and points in Rachel's direction. "Maybe with her. Because she keeps looking over at your sexy self."

"I knew it!" Ricky exclaims. As we burst into laughter, the atmosphere becomes light and carefree once again. Ricky finishes his beer and slams it down on the bar. "I'm going in."

With rapt attention, Big C and I watch Ricky walk over to Rachel with his usual swagger. She's wiping down the bar as he sits in front of her. We can see him mouth something to her but can't make out what it is. Her big, toothy smile returns as she leans against the bar, giving Ricky her full and undivided attention. I'm pretty sure she is going to break her own 'no dating customers' rule.

Shaking my head, I turn towards C. "How does he do it?"

He shrugs. "Like I said, legend."

We sit in silence as I finish my drink and ponder what to do with the catastrophe that is my life. Big C must sense my tension. "So, what are you going to do?"

"I honestly have no clue."

"Well, you need to decide quick. What you're doing isn't fair to either of them. If you keep this up, you'll lose them both."

I hang my head in defeat at his truth and decide to speak my truth as well. Pain fills my heart as the words spill out. "I don't trust her."

He stands and pulls a twenty from his wallet, placing it down on the bar. "Well, then. I think you have your answer."

I watch him as he leaves, ducking his head as he walks out the door, knowing he's right.

The pain in my chest is telling me how much this is going to hurt.

Chapter Thirty-Four

EARLY NOVEMBER 2018

I t's been two weeks, and I still haven't texted Maria back.

I realized a decision had to be made after that night at Dexter's with Ricky and Big C.

And I've chosen Cara.

Day after day, I crafted a text to Maria, my words carefully chosen as I would ask her to meet me. Then, I would delete it. Deep down, I know that as soon as I do this, she will be out of my life. Probably forever. And the thought of that is … heartbreaking. Because despite everything, I'm going to lose my best friend.

Instead, I have chosen avoidance.

And look, I know that I am being a world-class coward right now, but I don't want to face the music. For the past fourteen days, I have arrived at work early so that I don't run into Maria. I've totally ghosted her and when she finally sees me, she is going to be mad.

Kinda like the way she looks right now as I pull into the parking lot at work, and she is standing right next to where I usually park. Arms crossed over her chest, hip cocked out to the side.

Oh, God.

Why is she so beautiful, even when she's mad?

I pull the car into the spot under the tree, grab my bag, and get out. It's six-forty-five in the morning. Way before her shift starts. Which also means she came here this early on purpose, wanting answers.

With the day just starting to break and me not quite ready to face the music, I get out, shut the door, and hit the key fob to lock it. A loud chirp fills the air, adding to the palpable tension. Maria's eyes study my every move. Finally, she speaks.

"I'm trying really hard to not be mad at you right now, Sam. Why have you stopped talking to me? Are you okay? Is Mikey okay?" She's equal parts mad and concerned, which is making me feel like garbage. Here I thought she was furious with me, but it turns out she actually thinks something might be wrong with me. Or Mikey.

God, I'm such a jerk.

"I'm fine, Maria. Mikey is okay as well."

She throws her arms up in the air. "Then what the hell, Sam!? What's going on?"

I can't look at her, so I turn my attention to the yellow parking lines, noticing that they need repainting. Shaking my head in frustration, I reluctantly come to terms with the fact that I have no choice but to do this. "Maybe we should get in my car and talk."

She inhales sharply as the color drains from her face. "Um ... okay."

Unlocking the doors that I just locked, I walk to the driver's side. I hear Maria open and shut the door. By the time I put my bag into the back seat, she is already in the passenger side, waiting and watching.

I turn to face her as I rest my hand on the steering wheel to brace myself. "Maria, I'm sorry, but I can't text you anymore or meet for lunch."

Her head jolts back in shock. "Why?"

I take a second to work myself up, bracing for whatever happens next. "Because I'm seeing someone."

She lets out a small gasp. I understand why this is a shock. My texts and our lunches together have never led her to believe otherwise. Quite the opposite, actually. By her reaction, I realize I should have told her.

Plus, well, there's Cara.

"I think it would be—"

"For how long?" she interrupts as her eyes narrow.

Crap! *I was really hoping she wouldn't ask this question.*

She asks again. "For. How. Long?"

I steady myself as I prepare to answer. This is going to hurt, which is making me feel terrible. "We've been seeing each other for a year."

Her chin quivers, and tears pull in her eyes. "You have *got* to be kidding me?"

"Maria, let me—"

She holds up her hand to stop me. "So, when we hugged that day—the day *you* approached *me,* by the way—when you text me I was beautiful, and during our many lunch dates, when you would hold my hand and hold *me,* you were seeing someone?"

The hurt look on her face is killing me. But I need to be honest. "Yes." It's all I can muster.

"Okay ... wow." She pauses as the rising sun casts a soft glow to her face, adding to her gorgeous features. "Need I remind you that you were the one that started this?"

"You don't."

"Obviously, something has changed. You've been ignoring me for weeks, out of the blue. So what is it, Sam?"

"Maria, I ..." The words won't come out. I can't tell her. Having her sitting here, her eyes pleading, knowing my decision is going to hurt her, is making this way harder than I expected. "Cara and I—"

"Cara? Seriously?" she questions with disgust and now I'm defensive.

"Yes, Cara. We have history, and we reconnected recently."

"Not recently, Sam. A year ago. That's far from recent." She crosses her arms over her chest. "Does she know that you and I have been texting, getting lunch together? Reconnecting?" She uses air quotes with that last word.

I shake my head no.

"*Wow.*" She lets out a sarcastic chuckle. "I never pegged you as a cheater, Sam."

This makes my blood boil.

"I didn't cheat on Cara. We were casual. She was seeing other people also. It was nothing serious until recently, which is why I'm doing this." I pause. "But let me ask you. How did it feel riding in that shiny red Vette? Or spending Chad's money? You are the reason we are in this situation to begin with, Maria. You. Don't forget that."

The words vomit out of my mouth before I can stop them. And I regret them immediately because it looks like I just smacked her in the face. But honestly, that statement has been brewing inside of me for a while now. Ever since I read *The Chad* on her doorstep. Add to that her obvious disdain for a woman she doesn't even know ... maybe it's time we have this conversation.

Her breath catches, and I can feel the sharpness of my words cutting through her heart. "I can't believe you just said that to me." She turns to look out the window, and I see her wipe a stray tear from her cheek. She keeps her eyes fixed on the outside world as she continues. "I explained to you why that happened. You know how much I regret what I did to you."

"Do I?"

Her head whips around, her green eyes narrow, now full of anger. They burrow into mine. "You should!" She yells as she points her finger at her chest. "Sam, I am full of so much regret over that decision that I am practically drowning in it!" Her hand is shaking now. "How can you not know that?!!"

"YOU BROKE US!" My raised voice reverberates through the small space, causing her to flinch. "You destroyed me! You destroyed us!"

"You think I don't know that?!" The energy inside the car is palpable, surging and charging the more we scream at each other. "I BROKE MYSELF! Can't you see that? My decision that day affected me just as much as it did you! And trust me, I understand."

"You understand? How could you possibly understand how I felt—"

"Nate cheated on me." She says it so matter of fact that my head whips back in shock. "For almost our whole marriage. So yeah, I understand what's it like to be left and betrayed by someone you love."

I really want to feel sorry for her. I do. But right now, I can't. My anger and repressed hurt are getting in the way.

"We wouldn't be in this situation if you had just TALKED TO ME! Brielle, Mason, and Mikey ... they could have been *our* kids!" I pound my chest. "We could have had a life, but you threw it away! Not once, but twice!" *Finally,* I am saying out loud what I have been holding in for years. Not writing it in a letter, an email, or a text. These are words I need for her to hear. I get my breathing under control before I continue. But she speaks before I have time to.

"Are you trying to hurt me? Is that what this is?" She adjusts herself in the seat as if she is trying to get away from me, though she has nowhere to go.

Is she right? Is that what I'm doing? She hurt me, so now I hurt her.

With her back pressed up against the car door, her chest is rising and falling from her labored breathing. If she could sink into the tan leather of the seat and disappear, I'm sure she would. "Hurt me, push me away, force me to run away so this is easier for you to end." She points between the two of us. "Whatever this is? Or was."

We both stare at each other, and she places her hand on her stomach. More than likely feeling as sick as I am over the turn this conversation has taken. "Maria, when you started talking about the past in your texts and when we would talk over lunch about maybe a future, my anxiety kicked in. I can't take a chance on you hurting me again. There's a trust issue, and I can't allow myself to open back up to you. I'm sorry, I just can't."

"Hmm. Okay." She nods in response, her hair gently swaying with the movement. Then her eyes lock onto mine as her jaw tenses. "I'm going to start by saying this. How *dare* you put the blame on me for this past year? I did nothing wrong. This is all you. I think we can both agree on that, can't we?"

"Yes." She's right. All she did was show up and be herself. I can't blame her for my shortcomings here. "I'm sorry."

"You should be." She's biting the side of her lip. Something she does when she is really mad. Also, she's picking her nails. "I know you blame me for everything. Maybe even Erica's death." The mention of Erica's name makes me wince. "But I need for you to know how much I blame myself. Not a day goes by ..." She's out right crying now, and it takes her a second to catch her breath. I reach for her hand. She yanks it away.

"Maria ..."

"No! Let me finish." Her tear-filled eyes meet mine. "Not a day goes by that I don't think about how the decisions I made affected us. Affected our future. Giving you that letter, marrying Nate, all of it haunts me. Hell, I ended up in not one but two abusive relationships because of it. Every day, Sam. I live, breathe, and sleep with regret." She pauses, her eyes scanning the surroundings as she gathers her thoughts. "I may never be able to forgive myself. But in order for us to ever have a chance, I need for you to forgive me. To trust that I would never do that to you again. And it's obvious you aren't there yet."

She's not wrong. I haven't let it go. I haven't forgiven her.

And I don't know if I ever will.

"You're right," I whisper back. Because it's the truth.

She wipes her cheeks and turns her whole body away from me to leave, grabbing the door handle, but stops. She's fiddling with something, but I can't tell what. Without turning and with her back to me, she peers out the window, workers streaming into their jobs the only view. "I'm done asking for your forgiveness and trust, Sam." She straightens her back as if saying this gives her the strength she needs to leave my car. "I wish you and Cara the best. Have a nice life."

I avert my eyes, unable to watch as she opens the car door and steps out. It slams shut, causing me to flinch. She confidently strides in front of my car, her shoes crunching against the pavement. As she marches back to her car, her blonde hair catches the gentle morning light. Without a glance in my direction, she gets into her car and drives off, leaving me alone with my thoughts.

I rest my head back on the seat as a burst of anger fills my chest. In a fit of rage, I pound on the steering wheel and scream, the intensity of my emotions finally breaking free.

I should have never opened up this can of worms with her. The consequences of stopping to talk to her that day are present in my mind. She wouldn't have known I was so close and been none the wiser.

Ignorance is bliss. I realize that now. The only thing I've accomplished is hurting her.

At the same time, I understand the importance of moving on and embracing new beginnings. I can't take the chance of Maria hurting me again.

I don't trust her. And I won't be able to forgive her until I feel I can trust her again. When will that be?

No clue. And now, after this ... I'll never know.

Also, I have Mikey to think about. There is no way I can introduce him to her, and then she decides to leave me for someone else. Because, without a doubt, I know my son would fall in love with Maria.

He is my son, after all.

I refocus my thinking and decide to forge ahead. *Maria is my past. Cara is my future.*

Without warning, my mom's thoughts from that visit home years ago pop into my head. Am I doing it again? Running in the opposite direction of what I want to avoid the hurt? To avoid dealing with what is really plaguing me? And then, in turn, sacrificing my happiness?

Probably.

But I can't psychoanalyze myself right now. I've made my decision, whatever the reason, and I have to follow through. I round my shoulders and reach around to grab my bag from the backseat. When I do, the light catches on something resting on the passenger seat.

Her watch. My watch. *Our* watch.

She left behind the watch I gave her at graduation. She promised me that day she would always wear it. And she did. Every time I have seen her since, she was wearing it.

Until today.

With a shaking hand, I pick it up, the metal still warm from her wrist. I study it, feeling its smooth texture as I roll it in my hand. I stop and purposely flip it over, the inscription staring back at me. Words I felt at the time.

They are just words. But they are *my* words. To her.

Yours, Sam.

I honestly don't know what to do with it. This is a chaotic mess that leaves me feeling lost. How do I feel about her leaving it behind? Hurt? Is this closure? Am I happy?

I have no clue. These conflicting emotions are doing a number on me, and it's all so complicated.

Complicated. That's what my feelings are toward Maria. And maybe they always will be. There's no making sense of this situation. No matter how hard we try, our relationship is muddy.

A big muddy mess.

Not wanting to deal with this right now, I open the glove compartment and toss the watch in, slamming it shut.

Shutting the door on my past.

I shake my head vigorously and rub my hands over my face, attempting to make sense of the whirlwind my life has become. I open the car door and step out. *Why does this hurt so badly?* The heaviness in my heart is overwhelming, and I must find peace and remind myself that this was the best decision for me.

And I know just how to do that.

I get my phone from my back pocket and open up my messages, finding my and Cara's text thread. I focus my attention on the screen, typing out a text.

> Me: Hey gorgeous. Have a great day today. Dinner tonight? <heart emoji>

I hit send, satisfied with myself. The prospect of tonight already stirring something inside of me.

But with each step I take, my heart hurts more.

Something doesn't feel right. A sinking sensation floods over me as I press my hand against my chest, as though it's caving in on itself.

If Cara is my future, then why does everything feel so wrong?

Chapter Thirty-Five

EARLY 2020

Maria

I reach over to the end table, the scent of the wine wafting towards me as I take a sip from the glass. The red Merlot burns slightly on the way down. Unlike the glass of Pinot I had right before this.

It's a typical Saturday night for me. On the couch, legs covered in my favorite fleece-lined blue fuzzy blanket, and I'm catching up on some shows I recorded during the week. On the TV for tonight's viewing pleasure, *This Is Us*.

Brielle is out with her boyfriend Tony, and Mason is at his buddy's house. And here I sit, hanging out with the fictional Pearson family, wishing Jack Pearson was my husband and not Rebecca's.

"I need a man like Jack." Maybe sending this out into the cosmos will make it happen.

From my lips to God's ears.

My dream scenario plays out in my head. He would be here sitting next to me, with some scotch. Nestled under the blanket together, our bodies intertwined, radiating heat and closeness. His arm would be slung over the back of the couch as I rest my head on his chest. We would wait until the end of the show and start making out like teenagers.

My head hits the back of the couch, and I remember I had that once. With Sam. I try to rid the thoughts from my brain because I need to forget. Anytime I fantasize about what my life would be like with a loving and caring husband, the man in my thoughts is always Sam.

But he is with Cara, and I haven't talked to him since that day in his car a year and a half ago.

It still hurts.

After that day, seeing him occasionally in that stupid parking lot weighed on me. As hard as both of us tried to prevent a run-in, we would see each other now and then. Our schedules lining up to arrive or leave at the same time. He would ignore me, or sometimes, I would get a small wave with a sad, forced smile. I never waved back.

Other times, I would hide in my car and watch him. I would see him walking into work, talking and laughing on the phone. Probably with Cara. Sometimes, I wouldn't see him for a month or two, and I could feel myself getting better. Then BAM! There he'd be, and the pain would come bubbling to the surface again.

Richelle wanted to key his car or slash is tires. I had to reign her in more times than I can count.

I couldn't take it anymore, so after a year, I put in for a transfer to the office clear across town. Because of my seniority, they granted my request without asking any questions. It devastated Richelle, but she understood.

I thought that not seeing him would help ease the pain of losing him ... again. It did, but only slightly. And that's because I found Cara's Instagram. Her account is public. I think the woman loves the attention. And because I enjoy torturing myself, I constantly look at it. Her feed is full of pictures of her posing in the mirror at the gym, sweaty after a workout. Or modeling short little dresses in front of a full-length mirror in her bedroom. Or after she gets her hair done. Where? You guessed it, in front of a mirror, of course.

Trust me, I've looked at Sam's Instagram as well. He rarely posts. His last photo was one day after our fight in the car. A picture of them, in a dimly lit restaurant. The caption said, "To new beginnings with this amazing woman."

If he was trying to make a point, he succeeded.

However, he has never unfollowed me. Which is interesting. Not that he would see much since I never post. My life to too boring.

The last picture of the two of them in Cara's feed pops into my head. They were on a beach together with her svelte, toned body in a red bikini, kissing him on the cheek as he holds his phone out for the selfie. His six-pack abs, big beaming smile, and clear happiness were on full display.

I grimace at the thought and finish the last of the wine in my glass, shaking it in the air, getting every drop. I sit it down with semi-aggression, let out a small burp, and pull my concentration back to my show.

It's a sweet episode. Kate and Toby are trying to adopt. I'm happy for them. Especially now since they have finally got into a routine of raising their blind son. A new baby would be good for them. They are such a solid couple...

"God, Maria, snap out of it!" I need to get a grip on myself. I'm thinking about Kate and Toby as they are real people and my friends. These fictional characters hold a stronger place in my heart than any real person.

"I'm so stinking lonely."

Truthfully, since my divorce, then the whole supposed Sam reconnection, I haven't been me. I can't help but feel a deep sense of satisfaction in myself on both occasions, though. I took a stand, advocating for myself and what I needed. Pride fills my heart every time I think about it.

But also, life has become so mundane. I'm forty-five years old, and all my life consists of is my kids (whom I adore), my job, and my Saturday night dates with the TV and a good cabernet.

Pathetic.

Brielle and Mason have more of a social life than I do.

Doubly pathetic.

I wonder what Amanda and Richelle have going on tomorrow. Maybe a girls' brunch is in order. We haven't had one in a while, and I need to get out more. I pause my show before I reach for my phone lying on the coffee table in front of me. I type out a group text to my two best friends.

> Me: Hey ladies! Anyone up for brunch tomorrow? Say 11 at Nikki's. My treat.

Their replies come almost immediately.

> Richelle: YES! That sounds awesome. I've been craving their chicken and waffles.

> Amanda: I'm there.

> Me: Perfect! See you both then.

I sit my phone down, pleased with myself that I'm at least attempting to get out. On a normal Sunday, you can find me at home cleaning my house. However, a mimosa with some pancakes and girl time sounds downright divine.

I'm mentally picking out my outfit for tomorrow as I readjust myself and snuggle back into the couch. As soon as I hit play, Jack kisses Rebecca.

I groan at the TV.

"Will you please stop looking at her Instagram? You're torturing yourself, and it's not healthy," Amanda pleads as she raises the flute glass to her red-tinted lips and sips her strawberry mimosa. We are at Nikki's, enjoying brunch and each other's company out on their closed in patio dining. The tall heaters are ablaze on this chilly February day, spreading a comforting heat throughout the space.

"I know. I know," I say as I continue to scroll through pictures that I have looked at thousands of times. After I crawled into bed last night, I opened up Cara's page because, of course, I did. She had posted a new picture only an hour before. A black-and-white of their hands intertwined, resting on his thighs. The caption read, 'Nothing better than a quiet evening with my man.'

Whatever.

One thing that caught my attention was the absence of a ring on her left finger.

Thank God.

"You need to stop. You're borderline obsessed. It's been a year and a half now, Maria. You need to let go." Now it's Richelle's turn to chastise me as I hold my phone in my hand, scrolling. I ignore her because I know she's right. As I pass the pictures from last year, a tightness builds in my chest. Him, Cara, and Mikey at Cedar Point Amusement Park, standing in front of the entrance. One big happy family.

"That's it!" Before I can react, and with lightning-fast reflexes, Amanda grabs my phone out of my hand.

"Hey!" I reach across the table to try to retrieve it as she yanks her arm away. She taps a few times on the screen and hands it back to me.

"There. Done."

I look at the phone, and it's back to my home screen. My kids and I smile back at me. "What did you do?"

"I blocked her account. And I know you can unblock her, but I'm begging you not to. I'm worried about you, Maria. Constantly looking at those pictures is doing nothing but making you more depressed than you already are."

I raise my voice in shock. "I'm not depressed!"

Richelle raises an eyebrow. "Really?"

"Yes, really. I have my kids, my job, you guys, my ..." I trail off because, well, that's kinda it. But I need to clarify. "Honest, guys, I'm not depressed. I'm lonely. That's two different things."

Amanda reaches across the table and rests her hand over mine, empathy etched on her face.

I elaborate. "You guys need to understand. There is this pull with Sam and me. I can't explain it. I know he hasn't been mine for a really, really long time, but he will always *feel* like mine. As if we belong together. We've done this same back-and-forth for so long now, and he was my best friend. And just when it feels like it's our time, Cara happens. And now, it feels like I've lost him forever.

I know that sounds stupid and juvenile, but it's the truth. So, seeing him with her, looking happy, is like a knife to my heart."

Richelle reaches for my other hand. My girls. My friends. My support. "That doesn't sound dumb." Her tone is soft. "It sounds like you still love him."

A single tear leaves my eye and trails down my cheek. "I always will." I shrug.

Amanda squeezes, then lets go of my hand and takes a bite of her salad. "You need to date someone," she says with her mouth full as she points her fork at me. "And I know just the guy."

Richelle starts clapping. "Yes! Who is it?"

"Mm ... Mm. Nope. I do not want to date anyone." I sling myself back in my chair and cross my arms over my chest in defiance.

"Why not? I'm not talking about getting married. Just go out with the guy and see what happens. You need to get off your couch, turn off the TV, and kiss a really handsome man."

"Ooooo ... handsome, huh?" Richelle leans forward and rests her elbows on the table, placing her chin in her hands, waggling her eyebrows.

Amanda gives her a side glance. "Very, very good looking. If I wasn't a happily married woman, I would be interested."

Richelle looks my way. "That's high praise coming from her."

I look between the two of them and sigh in defeat. "Ugh. Fine. What's he look like?"

A satisfied smile crosses Amanda's lips as she gets her phone and unlocks it. "His name is Geoffrey, with a G."

"Seriously? *Geoffrey with a G*?" I ask mockingly. She can't be serious.

Richelle lets out a snort beside me. "What?" Amanda asks, her eyes darting between the two of us.

"He sounds pretentious." I take a sip of my mimosa, feeling like I'm going to need it to get through this.

"Hey now, don't be a snob. He didn't choose his name." Amanda slaps my arm, then goes back to searching on her phone.

"Okay. Fair point."

She continues her scrolling. "He's a partner at the firm, and he's divorced with no kids."

"So, he has baggage?" I ask.

Amanda raises her eyebrow. "And like you don't?"

I lift my glass to her. "Touche." I down the rest of my drink to ready myself for this.

Amanda arches one eyebrow. "Anyway, here." She flashes her phone in my face, and staring back at me is one of the most handsome men I have ever seen.

My eyes widen. "Oh."

"I wanna see!" Richelle grabs Amanda's arm and pulls it towards her. "Wowzers. Hello there, Geoffrey with a G. He really has a whole Channing Tatum vibe going on, doesn't he? I wonder if he can dance?"

I snicker at this because Richelle isn't wrong. He does look exactly like Channing. Which one hundred percent works for me.

"See what I mean," Amanda continues. "Maria, he is the nicest guy. Honest. You are my best friend, and I wouldn't set you up with a tool. Get this ... his wife cheated on him with his cousin."

We crinkle our noses up at this. "Gross," Richelle says. I'm an expert on cheating spouses. At least we would have that in common.

"He was devastated for the longest time but has bounced back and is ready to start seeing people again." She's staring at me now, eagerness written on her face, wanting the green light to set me up with Geoffrey with a G. But for some reason, I'm hesitant.

"I don't know, you guys."

"Look." Amanda sits her phone down. "What is Sam doing right now?" She jams her finger into the table.

"Why are you asking me that?" I'm annoyed with where I know this conversation is going.

"He's probably out having breakfast with Cara. Or maybe kissing her across the table at whatever restaurant. They might be doing some kind of domestic thing, like refinishing a dresser or grocery shopping. I don't know! My point is, he has moved on. The two of them are vacationing together, spending time with Mikey. He's happy. So why can't you be?"

I sit back in my chair again and ponder what Amanda said. She's right. Why am I sitting around my house in my pajamas, watching TV, drowning my sorrows in wine when I could be out having a good time? Me and Geoffrey with a G. Sam and his abs are having fun with Cara and her red bikini. More than likely, not giving my miserable existence a second thought. He made his choice.

Now it's time for me to make mine. I choose myself. I need to start living and move on.

Sam is my past. I am ready for my future.

"Let's do it." The words spill out of my mouth before I have a second to take them back.

Richelle lets out a screech and leaps out of her chair to hug me. A satisfied smile crosses Amanda's lips. She is already typing something into her phone.

"Wait, who are you texting?"

"Who do you think? Geoffrey." Her thumbs are flying over the keyboard.

"Wow. You work fast," Richelle says as she sits back down in her seat, taking a bite of her waffle.

"You're already texting him? This is happening too fast." Amanda has always been efficient. And yet again, it will be at the expense of my love life. She helped me end one relationship. It makes sense for her to start a new one for me, I guess.

"Full disclosure. I already told him about you yesterday, and he has agreed to meet you for dinner next Friday night. And don't worry. I sent him that pic of you from your employee end-of-year party last December. You had on that one-shouldered pink dress and your hair was swept over to the side. You looked amazing that night."

"Oh, my God." I bury my face in my hands. Because I can't believe she has done this. But also relieved she showed him that pic because I was feeling good that night. That dress made my legs look a mile long.

She sits her phone down on the table. "There, done. I just sent him your number and told him to text you."

"You're unbelievable," I say as I shake my head.

"You love me and how proficient I am."

She's right, I do. Amanda was my savior when I divorced Nate. I got everything I wanted and then some because of her and Elias.

Seconds later, my phone pings with an incoming text.

"Dang," Richelle quips. "He is interested! I like a man who works fast."

I give her a pointed look and lift my phone to read the incoming text.

It's him.

> Unknown Number: Hey Maria. This is Geoffrey. I work with Amanda. She gave me your number and insisted I text you right away or, and I quote, "Heads will roll." Lol. She's ruthless. Anyway, I would really like to take you to dinner this Friday if you're free. No pressure. Or we can just text first to get to know one another. Whatever you're comfortable with. Just let me know. Look forward to hearing from you. Soon, I hope.

My cheeks feel flushed from reading the text. I can picture him, sitting on his couch, casual, in a t-shirt and sweats, barefoot, looking Channing-esque, typing out this text to me.

It isn't overly flirty. He said nothing inappropriate. He's actually putting the ball in my court and being a gentleman, which is ... considerate. And really sweet.

"You're blushing!" Richelle exclaims. "Let me see." I hand my phone to her, and she reads. "Ahhh ... he seems genuine!" She hands me back my phone. "Say yes."

Amanda doesn't ask to read it. I look over at her, and she winks before taking a roll to butter it. She doesn't need to read the text because she knows what a good guy he is. Like she said, she wouldn't set me up with a tool.

I look between my two friends, and I know what I'm going to do. I type out my reply and hit send before I rethink this.

"Alright, Geoffrey with a G. Let's see what you got."

Chapter Thirty-Six

2021

The Restaurant

Sam

"Wow." Cara glances around at the restaurant, her eyes roving all around in wonder, taking in the ambience. "This place is something else."

The speakeasy/restaurant, a converted 1920s bank, has been on Cara's must-visit list for months. When it opened back up after COVID-19, I booked us a table right away.

The ceilings soar above us, creating an expansive atmosphere, and the intricate wood carvings along the walls are impressive. Soft leather couches line the open second floor, providing a relaxed spot for those who want to enjoy a drink. The smooth texture and polished sheen of the marble-like columns create an air of sophistication. Black table cloths drape over each table along with a lone candle as a centerpiece. In the basement, there is a bank vault which is rented out for private parties. As soft jazz music fills the air, other patrons engage in lively dinner conversations.

"Mm-hmm," I mutter, not able to take my eyes off my phone. I strain to catch her words as she debates the menu, trying to figure out what to order. But my focus is on Maria's Instagram page, neglecting everything else around me.

Her once quiet page was full of information. And thanks to my decision in the car three years ago ... I'm completely in the dark when it comes to her life. Naturally, I became obsessed by scrolling on it non-stop. Acting like a jealous, obsessive high schooler.

How am I back at this place?

That place being my thoughts consumed by her. And not the incredible woman sitting across from me. My girlfriend of four years, Cara. Which is why we are at this fancy, over-priced restaurant. It's our anniversary, and I have a feeling I know what Cara is expecting tonight.

A proposal.

Yeah ... that's not happening.

Not as long as my heart is still halfway with Maria.

Cara and I were going strong in the beginning. I left Maria behind and dove in headfirst with Cara. As I always do when I'm trying to avoid something that hurt me. We had a blast, and I fell in love with her all over again.

Well, kinda love. It's love, but not the all-consuming kind. I had that once, so I know.

There were vacations, road trips, romantic dinners, and quiet evenings spent at home. All of it was amazing.

About a year ago, when Cara started dropping marriage hints, is when I checked out. Her wedding talk was a trigger for me. It made me realize that I wasn't ready to travel down the marriage road again with a woman, only for the sole purpose of avoidance.

All the marriage talk made me realize that deep down, Cara and I don't belong together. Plus, the long stretches of time apart followed by the constant togetherness due to the pandemic began to wear on us. On top of that, Maria's Instagram became a noisy hub of activity, overwhelming me with details about her life. There were pictures of her kids, her with the kids, scenic pictures, and then the ones that hurt the most. Her with another man.

Why am I doing this to myself?

I continue to scroll and size this loser up as Cara goes on and on about how her friend told her the calamari was 'top notch' here. In every picture, Maria looks stunning, and I can't help but feel a surge of jealousy as I examine this adonis of a man.

He's a guy who fills out a suit with his gym-bro body, probably one of those meat heads who can bench 315 lbs. His jawline is so perfectly defined, it looks like it's been carved from solid granite. In the pic of them at Marshall Lake on what I am assuming is this dude's boat, I'm pretty sure he has a twelve-pack. Maria, well, she was wearing a black bikini and a tan. And wearing it well.

I keep scrolling.

And his name—don't get me started—Geoffrey with a G. He is the epitome of male attractiveness. And to make it worse, I'm sure he's a nice dude and not a horrible human. Because after what Maria had gone through, she wouldn't settle for anything less.

Plus, he looks identical to a celebrity, but I can't seem to put my finger on who.

Brad Pitt? No. Charlie Hunnam? No, that's not it. Ryan Rey—

"Um ... earth to Sam?" Cara's voice cuts through my obsessive thoughts, bringing me back to the present as I peer across the table at her. The small candle centerpiece flickers in the darkened restaurant, illuminating the irritated look she is giving me. She flicks her head and eyes to her right. I glance up to see our waiter staring at me, his arms behind his back, waiting for what? I have no idea.

"Oh, yeah, hi." I put my phone down, greeting the young, skinny kid who towers over our table. He's wearing a white pressed dress shirt, a black tie and pants, with an apron around his waist. He looks twelve. Then again, everyone looks young to me these days.

"What would you like to drink this evening, sir?" He whips out a bottle of wine from behind his back, showcasing it to us both. "May I recommend our newest Shiraz?"

Is this kid even old enough to offer alcohol to people?

I gesture to Cara. "Why don't you go first, honey?"

"I already did." She deadpans, her face devoid of emotion.

"Oh." With an irritated demeanor, the waiter places the bottle on the table, letting out an exasperated sigh. I was so engrossed in Maria's Instagram that I didn't notice this kid sneak up on our table. Or hear Cara place her drink order. I square my shoulders and clear my throat as I allow myself to embrace the present moment. I'm pretty sure I'm coming across as the world's worst date right now. "No wine for me, thanks. I will have a Glenlivet on the rocks." The waiter picks up the bottle of wine, nods, and scurries away.

Cara takes the fancy folded napkin from the table and fans it out, placing it on her lap. "What's with you tonight, Sam? You haven't torn your eyes away from your phone since we got here." When I meet Cara's eyes, there is a mix of frustration and genuine concern. If she only knew what was holding my attention on the phone, she would be way more upset than she is right now. But she's right. I need to focus on her. It is our anniversary, and I'm being an insensitive jerk.

"I'm sorry, honey." I extend my hand across the table, the smooth black tablecloth brushes against my forearm. With a soft smile, she reaches out and takes hold of my hand. "Work is getting to me. You have my full attention now, though."

Our conversation flows with ease, as it always does. Our drinks and food arrive, and the aroma of the crispy calamari Cara ordered fills my nose. Things seem to be back on track.

As we wait for our entrees, Cara excitedly begins sharing every detail about her friend Zoey's wedding. She rambles on and on about Zoey's dress, the centerpieces at the reception, the tuxes the men wore. Then she starts in on how Zoey and her husband went to Fiji for their honeymoon. Want details? Well, I can tell you all about it because Cara won't stop. I make sure to nod and throw in a big 'Wow' every so often. Next is her asking me when I remarry, if I would want a church wedding or one in a barn (neither), and would Mikey be my best man? Or Big C? Ricky?

Marriage and weddings. It seems like that's the only thing on her mind these days. And I know why. I know what she wants and expects from me. I also know that I am not ready to give her that.

Why can't we talk about something else? Anything else.

As if on cue, our food arrives, offering a welcome distraction from her wedding ramblings.

With a steak knife in hand and my mouth watering, I cut into my New York strip doused in garlic butter. Out of nowhere, Cara gasps in shock, her fork crashing down onto her plate, stopping me mid-slice. "Oh, my God!" she exclaims.

"What?" My eyes dart across the restaurant, trying to notice anything unusual.

She lowers her head, her voice barely a whisper. "Don't look now, but Channing Tatum's doppelgänger just walked in."

"Wait, who's Channing ..."

"Shhhh!" She waves her hand to shoosh me as a couple walks past our table to be seated diagonally from us. The enormous man, with his hand resting on the bare back of his date in her navy blue dress, guides her towards their table. With her blonde sleek hair swept to one side, she walks confidently, her dress revealing hints of her toned legs. And when he pulls out her chair for her, and she turns to hang her purse on the back of it, I almost choke on my tongue.

It's Maria.

With her gym-rat-meat-head-celebrity-look-alike boyfriend.

In my full line of sight.

Lucky me. This restaurant is so dark, and with her back to me, I didn't recognize it was her when they walked past.

Maria flashes him a huge smile and giggles at something he whispers in her ear before he rounds their table and sits down. He's a guy, so I'm sure he made some sort of comment about how good she looks in her dress.

Jerk.

Maria has my full attention as Cara turns her head, trying to catch a glimpse of them without being noticed. "I seriously cannot get over how much he looks like Channing Tatum. I swear I thought it was him at first." With a shake of her head, she laughs lightly while taking a sip of her drink. For the life of me, I can't place who this Channing is.

"I have no clue who Channing Tatum is."

Cara looks like I just slapped her. "You're kidding me?" I shake my head, still trying to figure out who this actor is. "You know ... *Magic Mike, Dear John, Step Up*." She stares at me eagerly, hoping that the mention of these movies will jog my memory. They don't.

Cara digs her phone out of her purse and starts searching for what I'm sure is pics of this amazing Channing Tatum. As she does, I glance over at Maria and catch her and Geoffrey exchange a knowing look. It's a look shared by two people who truly know one another and have a connection. A knot forms in my stomach, tightening with each passing moment.

The waiter, who had seemed annoyed with me earlier, now stands over their table, presenting the same bottle of wine with a newfound cheerfulness. They must take him up on the wine offer because the kid is uncorking it, pouring it into their glasses.

"See!" Cara shoves her phone in my face, drawing my focus away from the happy couple. And staring back at me is Channing Tatum (yep, they could be twins), on a stage, looking like a Chippendale dancer.

"Wait, I know who that is." I stare at the picture, trying to make sense of it. "Isn't he a stripper? Or an actor? I'm confused." You have got to be kidding me. Maria's boyfriend looks like *that* guy.

Kill me now.

Cara glares at me. "He's an actor, silly. But he played a really good stripper in *Magic Mike*." She takes one more quick look at the photo, shivers, and shoves it back in her purse.

I hate Channing Tatum.

"I told you he looked like him." Oblivious to my inner freak-out, Cara takes a bite of her cajun chicken pasta dish with a satisfied moan. "This is so dang good," she says with her mouth full. "We are definitely coming back here."

Why? Why does Maria have to be dating that guy? And, of course, he is better looking and more put together in person. Plus, why does she keep popping up in my life? Does the universe hate me? Is God punishing me? Is this karma?

Stupid small towns!

The sudden clinking of glasses jolts me, causing me to redirect my focus quickly towards their table. They are both drinking from their wine goblets. As soon as they finish, he leans forward, his hand stretching across the table to meet hers. He lifts her hand to his mouth, pressing a delicate kiss onto her knuckles. He says something to her, and her laughter is like a knife to my heart.

I want to throw up.

I used to make her laugh like that.

Witnessing them together is taking a toll on me emotionally, and I know why. The only other time I saw Maria in person with a man was at Dexter's when she was dating Nate and we danced. That night, she looked unhappy, uncomfortable, and out of place. But tonight, she is stunning and alluring. Her face is beaming with joy and confidence. She's laughing and touching him ... because she wants to. She looks genuinely happy.

The way she used to look with me.

And I hate it.

Plus, she looks so phenomenal in that dress, that it's nearly impossible to avert my attention from her.

Cara starts talking about what kind of fall decorations she wants at her condo this year as I zero in on Maria's smooth leg when it crosses over the other. Her black strappy high heels and red-painted toenails doing nothing to help curb this desire to touch her.

I clench my hand into a tight fist and grit my teeth in frustration as I glare at my untouched steak. My body language gives me away, and Cara quickly notices my obvious tension.

"Is your steak okay? You've barely touched it," she asks as she pierces a piece of her chicken.

Ugh. I need to tell her who that is. If she finds out I kept that from her and didn't say anything, well, that would be bad.

I ready myself to deal the blow. "Cara, Channing Tatum's date over there..."

"Yeah?" She doesn't glance at me and continues to chew her food, while gathering more pasta on her fork.

"That's Maria."

She stops chewing, and I see her throat bob as she swallows her bite. She sets down her fork and reluctantly turns to the happy couple.

Ever since that day at the mailbox at the apartment all those years ago, when she saw my excitement at getting Maria's letter, she knows exactly who Maria is. And what she meant to me.

Both Cara and I watch them.

They are engrossed in their animated conversation and devour the bruschetta they ordered, savoring it. Geoffrey takes a piece of bread and brings it to Maria's mouth. She opens her perfect lips and takes a bite. He wipes away something from her chin with his thumb. My nostrils flare.

I force myself to look away, and when I do, Cara's eyes pierce through me like daggers.

She wipes her mouth with her napkin. "Wow. Jealous much?" Frustrated, she slams the black square cloth down on the table.

"What?! No, of course not."

"Yeah, okay, Sam." She pushes away her plate, done with the pasta she was devouring minutes ago.

"It's just weird seeing her, that's all."

"Mm-hmm." She shifts in her seat. "Or is it because you still love her?" Her eyebrow raises with this loaded question I wasn't expecting her to ask.

I'm tapping my finger on the table to release this frustration coursing through me. "Cara, you know what Maria meant to me."

"You're right, I do. You've always been honest about her. But that's not an answer to my question. Plus, I know you've been stalking her Instagram." I freeze as she nonchalantly shrugs. "I've caught you looking."

Busted.

Leaning forward, I prop my elbows on the table and interlock my fingers. "If I'm being honest, yes. Some part of me will always love her."

As Cara slumps back in her chair, the weight of my confession washes over her. I should give Cara all my attention while on this date. She deserves it. But no matter how hard I try, my eyes insist on gravitating towards Maria's table. Meat-head Geoffrey brushes a piece of hair behind her ear. I wince.

Seeing her with another man is stirring up a mix of unexpected sensations in the pit of my stomach. I can't seem to control my emotions; they're like a storm raging inside me. Jealousy, rage, and sadness course through my veins. But mostly anger and regret for letting her leave my car that day. I was a coward.

Because, of course, I forgive her. We both have made mistakes in this tangled web that we have created. I could have fought harder for us. I should have. She deserved more empathy for what she was dealing with, both with Chad and Nate. The corners people backed her into, I'm sure, felt suffocating, leaving her no room to maneuver her own life.

Plus, she was young. So, so young.

I can't imagine what it must have been like for her to find out Nate was unfaithful for their whole marriage. That must have been devastating. And with Chad, she had no life experience to help her make hard choices. How can I possibly hold any of that against her? It's not fair.

I need to give my therapist a fat tip. Again, he helped me to see what I was missing.

As I stare at her and *Geoff,* acting like they are the only two people in this place, I realize ... I may have lost her. For good.

The actual pain in my chest is too much.

Out of the corner of my eye, I see Cara studying her phone, its screen illuminating her face. She sets it down gently. It wasn't until now that I realized how much time had passed without us saying a word. She gives me a pointed look, and I can feel the weight of what she's about to say. "Sam, we have been together for four years," Cara begins, choking out the words, while my gaze remains fixed on Maria. "And you have never looked at me the way you are looking at her right now."

This declaration quickly brings my attention back to her. "How am I looking at her?"

She wraps her arms around herself, and her chin quivers slightly. "With desire, longing ... and love."

As the waiter comes to gather our plates, we sit in silence, our eyes locked in a wordless conversation. He offers us boxes for our leftovers and then dessert.

We deny both.

As the waiter leaves to get us our check, Cara continues. "You've been distant for months. I can feel things changing between us. This is the third time we have tried to make this work. I'm thinking three strikes and we are out. Honestly, we both have kinda checked out lately."

At this point, I'm not sure who is breaking up with who. But either way, we both know that this is the end. She sees it. I see it. We've been forcing this for far too long.

A heavy silence hovers over our table as the harsh truth lingers in the air. As long as Maria is alive and well on this planet, I will never be able to fully commit to another woman.

While we wait for our check, Cara confirms my suspicions about the whole evening. "You know, I was hoping you were going to propose tonight, wishing I was wrong about where this was heading."

"We never talked about that. I never lead you to believe—"

She raises her finger to stop me. "Yes, you did. Maybe not in words. But you did." She pauses for a moment, before continuing. "I've been talking about it so much lately because I thought maybe that was where you were. But then something changed in you, so I kept bringing it up, hoping I could get some kind of signal about where your head was at. I guess I got my answer tonight."

I extend my hand across the table, pleading with her to take it. She hesitates for a moment before shifting forward in her seat and resting her hand on mine, tears pooling in her eyes. I lightly rub my thumb over her smooth skin. "I'm so sorry, Cara."

"For what? Wasting my time or being in love with another woman?"

"Both. But mostly for not being the man you deserve."

She gives my hand a firm squeeze before releasing it. "Thank you for saying that," she says, her voice laced with a sadness.

Movement from Maria's table catches my eye. They both rise from their seats, getting ready to leave. *Geoff* pulls his wallet from his back pocket, opens it, and throws money on the table like the cool guy I'm sure he is. As he glances at his watch, a look of urgency crosses his face. They must be in a rush.

What are they in a hurry to do?

Never mind. I don't want to know.

As Maria takes a step to leave, our eyes lock. She halts mid-step. A small gasp escapes her mouth. For a moment, her entire body is rigid, but then she relaxes as a gentle smile graces her lips. And when her eyes light up with the slightest twinkle, it's almost as if she is happy to see me. I scrub my hand over my mouth to hide the smile crossing my lips at her reaction. But then her gaze shifts to Cara, and the smile fades as she lowers her head, her shoulders slumping.

My heart sinks.

Geoffrey senses her sudden lack of movement and leans down, lips moving as he speaks. His words and voice are barely audible over the bustling crowd and soft music. Probably asking her what's the matter. She says something in return as she juts her chin in our direction. He follows her line of sight, then instinctively adjusts his stance, squaring his shoulders. He then slings his arm around her back and locks eyes with me, his glare intensifying.

He knows exactly who I am.

Moving in closer to her, I watch his lips moving as he whispers something in her ear, and she nods in agreement. He drops his arm, and they lock hands as they walk straight toward Cara and me.

Looking like a team.

"Oh, God," I say, my eyes dropping to the ground, bracing myself for what will be the most awkward conversation in history.

"What?" Cara questions, turning in her seat. "Oh." She straightens up, getting ready for whatever is headed our way.

Without any more time to wrap my brain around this, they are standing right next to our table.

Chapter Thirty-Seven

Sam

"Hi, Sam," Maria says with a warm smile, and a tremble in her voice. She's nervous.

"Hey, Maria. Nice to see you." My eyes zero in on their intertwined hands.

Geoffrey grips her hand tighter.

My stomach twists.

Maria turns to Cara and extends her hand, her palm open and welcoming. "You must be Cara. I'm Maria. Nice to meet you finally."

Cara kindly takes her hand while also shooting me a look that I can't read. It's a cross between pity, humor, and possibly shock that Maria knows who she is. I can't place it. "You as well." Cara looks at Geoffrey and offers him a handshake. "And you are…?"

With a strong grip, Geoffrey clasps her hand and shakes it warmly. "Geoffrey Reynolds. Nice to meet you." His hand returns to Maria's, not offering me a handshake in greeting.

Fine by me, dude.

Cara blushes as soon as their hands touch. He probably has this effect on every woman he comes in contact with.

Because, of course, he does.

Cara takes the lead in the conversation, which I am grateful for. As a friend should. And it occurs to me that this is what we are, and perhaps we have been for quite some time. Friends.

Instead, we have been pretending to be something we aren't

Cara's face lights up, and she excitedly points her finger toward Geoffrey. "Has anyone ever told you that you look like…"

"Channing Tatum," Maria answers for him. With love, she looks at him, her eyes beaming with adoration as she rests her hand on his chest. "Yeah, he gets that a lot. But I think he's more handsome than Magic Mike, if you ask me."

Geoffrey lifts his chin in response to her compliment, and he pulls her close, his arm now securely around her waist.

I grab my scotch, the ice cubes clinking against the sides of the glass, and down it in one gulp. Cara's eyebrow arches as she watches me.

Maria's attention shifts to Cara again. "Did you enjoy your dinner? We only stopped in for a quick glass of wine and an appetizer. I've always wanted to eat dinner here, though."

Maria's smile is stretching from ear to ear. Her fake smile. I've seen her flash it before when she is trying to be nice, but deep down, she wants to cry.

"It was delicious. You should try the Cajun Chicken Pasta if you come back," Cara answers. Maria nods, and an awkward silence hangs in the air.

This small talk is sucking the life right out of me. I shift in my seat to relieve the tension pumping into me.

Cara gives me a side glance and clears her throat before trying to resume the conversation. "Maria, I love your dress. Where—"

"I haven't seen you at work in a while," I quickly interrupt while studying the square cubes left inside my rock glass, turning it in my hand. "Did you quit?" I force myself to look away from my empty drink and glance in her direction. She sucks in a breath as my question hangs in the air.

"Wait, you two used to work together?" Geoffrey questions, pointing his finger back and forth between the two of us.

Interesting. She never told him that part. A small satisfied smile crosses my lips as I wait for Maria to answer both him and me. As she narrows her eyes,

I can almost feel the intensity radiating from her. "No, we would just see each other in the parking lot. Sam is a psychologist at the hospital next door."

"Psychologist, huh?" Geoffrey's eyes focus on me at the mention of my line of work. "I've been looking for a new therapist. Do you—"

"I'm no longer accepting new patients," I lie through gritted teeth because I would rather quit my job and be homeless than take him on as a patient. Or have him see any therapist in the department.

"Ooookay."

Maria's lips form a thin line, revealing her frustration. "To answer your question, Sam, I didn't quit. I transferred offices. Things were becoming complicated and a little hard to deal with, so I thought it was better to move on."

She's moved on, alright.

She continues. "Apparently, even after dozens of apologies, there are some things that are unforgivable, so I decided not to wait around."

Ouch. I guess I deserved that one.

Cara interlaces her fingers together, resting them on the table, and comes to my rescue with a subject change. "So, what is it that you do for a living, Geoffrey?" Her lips curl up in a flirtatious smile.

Boy, Cara is really interested in all things Geoffrey, isn't she?

Before replying, Geoffrey studies Maria intently, his brows furrowed, looking confused, at her answer to my question. He shakes his head in frustration, then looks directly at Cara. "I'm in family law and a partner at Reynolds, Ghizzoni, and Weston."

"A lawyer. Wow! Impressive."

A lawyer. I mean, why not at this point? What other line of work would the perfect man be in? A lawyer or doctor are your only two options. Or a professional athlete. And by the looks of his body, he could pull that off as well.

"It's not that impressive," Geoffrey continues. "It's a lot of work. And dealing with people's family problems can really drain you."

Maria's hand shoots back up to his chest again. I guess she can't keep her hands off of him. She can probably feel his bulging pecs through his suit. "Don't be modest, honey. He's the best family attorney in the state, if you ask me."

Well, we didn't, Maria. My inner eye roll is huge.

I can tell muscle man Geoff is over this conversation because he uncoils his arm from Maria's waist and grabs her hand. "Well, it was nice to meet you both. Maria and I need to get going." He looks lovingly down at her and winks as a playful smile crosses his lips. "My place, right?"

Shoot me now. He knows what he's doing. I hate him. My hand tightens around the glass.

"Of course." Maria turns to us both. "Sam, it was good to see you again. Cara, it was a pleasure meeting you. Enjoy the rest of your evening."

They are already turning to leave, not wanting to get away from us fast enough, when Cara says, "Likewise." We both watch them exit the restaurant.

"Well, that was awkward," I say, rubbing my hand down my jaw, hoping to release some of the tension radiating throughout my whole body.

Cara and I sit in silence as we wait for the check—which is taking forever—the awkwardness from the last five minutes hanging in the air. Waiters and waitresses pass us by, oblivious to the dining disaster that just happened.

While we wait, I glance at the beautiful woman who has been nothing but wonderful to me. I met her the day she moved into her apartment. She has floated in and out of my life for close to twenty-five years. And with that thought, I can't help but wonder if I will regret this decision. "One last drink together?" I ask.

She glances at her phone, then sheepishly answers. "Okay." I flag down the waiter, and within minutes, another scotch and a glass of wine appear at our table.

For at least a half an hour, we drink and chat like friends do. A friend who you shared adventures with, confided in, and loved. In this moment, I realize I will miss Cara. She's truly a remarkable woman. Only, not the woman for me. I hope she finds happiness and love.

After we wait for our check for a second time, a notification sounds from Cara's phone. She glances at it, stands, and retrieves her purse and shawl from the back of the chair before pushing it into the table. With a swift motion, she drapes her shawl over her arm. "Wait, the check hasn't come yet," I say, my confusion evident in every word because she knows we haven't paid yet.

With a gentle smile, she walks over to me and leans down, brushing a sweet, affectionate kiss against my cheek. Her lips are warm but not as familiar as they were before. She wipes away the lipstick mark she left. "Take care of yourself, Sam."

"Cara, hold on. How are you getting home?" I stand and pull a Geoffrey, throwing cash on the table.

"I called an Uber while you stared at Maria's legs. It's here, and I'm leaving," she informs me as she stands a little straighter.

"Don't be ridiculous. I can take you home and we can talk—"

"It's better this way. There's nothing left to say."

I nod in agreement, my eyes meeting hers, silently conveying my respect for her decision. This is her way of letting go, not prolonging the painful breakup goodbye on her front porch.

Not wanting to prolong this goodbye any longer than necessary, I pull her in for a heartfelt hug. She hums as soon as her chin rests on my shoulder. "I wish you the best, Cara. You deserve everything," I whisper into her ear. As we pull apart, she calmly places her hand on my cheek, her palm soft against my skin. Her touch lingers for a moment before she lowers her hand, then takes a step around me and walks away.

I watch her leave out the exit door and observe her from the window. She gets into the Kia Optima that was waiting for her and drives away. Gone from my life, for the last time.

As I take a step to leave this godforsaken place, my attention immediately shifts to a flash of a bare back, long legs, a blue dress, and golden blonde hair outside. Maria's waiting on the steps of the entrance, tapping her foot impatiently.

Holy crap! *What is she still doing here? And where is Geoffrey?*

I bolt out of the restaurant as if it's engulfed in flames. Within five seconds flat, I'm right beside her, my hands in my pocket. She turns to see who is standing next to her and flinches before quickly refocusing on the road ahead.

"I just saw Cara leave. Alone. Trouble in paradise?" she asks.

I hold my breath, knowing I have to accept whatever she is prepared to serve up.

"Well, truthfully, we broke up tonight. Right before you and Geoffrey came over to the table."

Her head snaps to meet mine as I catch her eye. I raise my eyebrows and shrug. A few more seconds pass, and I turn away, roaming the busy street, looking for her perfect lawyer boyfriend. "So, why are you out here alone? Where's *Geoff* the lawyer?" I ask.

She clears her throat, trying to shake off the nervousness. "Um ... *Geoffrey's* car won't start. So he's with the tow truck guy while I wait for an Uber."

"I can take you wherever you need to go." I offer this up faster than I intended. But man, I hope she says yes.

She turns away from me. "Yeah, okay. That wouldn't be the best idea," she laughs out.

She's probably right.

We both stand there, taking in the chaos of car horns and bustling footsteps in the busy street. A burning need to know more about Channing 'Geoffrey' Tatum consumes me. So I ask. "Are you guys serious?"

I try to will her to look at me, but she doesn't glance in my direction, busy searching for her ride among the traffic. "Not that it's any of your business, but we have been seeing each other for about a year now. We have plans for him to meet the kids next week."

Not good. That means it's very serious. Maria wouldn't introduce just anyone to her kids.

I try to keep my cool, even though my heart is drowning in disappointment. "Wow. That does sound serious."

"What happened with you and Cara?" I swear I heard a touch of happiness in her voice.

"You. You happened." The confession hangs in the air, as she slowly turns her head and her eyes meet mine, brimmed with unease. A massive shot of adrenaline shoots through me, a reminder of the intense connection we share.

Her lip's part to say something, and my eyes zero in on their perfect shape and pinkish color. With each passing moment, her breath becomes more rapid. Then she blinks, checks herself, and averts her attention while shifting her feet.

I can't tear my eyes away from the mesmerizing curve of her spine in that stunning dress. With an impulsive urge too strong to control, I pull my hand from my pocket. With a featherlight touch, I lightly skim down the surface of her spine, ending on her lower back. Goosebumps erupt on her skin. It's the same spot where I had seen Geoffrey's hand earlier as he guided them past our table. I want nothing more than to remove the memory of his touch from her head and replace it with my own.

Her breath hitches when my fingers graze her smooth skin. "You can't say those types of things to me, Sam."

My thumb rubs in small circles ... the way I always used to. Her eyes flutter close.

Tires rolling on pavement breaks up our intimate moment, diverting our attention to a Chevy Blazer pulling alongside the curb.

"That's my ride." She takes off down the steps, faster than she should be able to in those heels. I can't stop staring at the enticing contours of her back and the toned definition of her legs as she walks away. Shaking off my daze, I sprint to catch up as a surge of adrenaline courses through me. My hand reaches around her, grabbing the door handle just seconds before she does.

She looks up at me, and tears brim her eyes as we part ways yet again. Like we always do, "I'm sorry about Cara." With a quick turn and a duck of her head, she tries to get into the car, but I reach out and take her arm.

This moment isn't over yet. Not by a long shot.

"Sam, don't," she pleads with me, her voice trembling. She sniffles as she turns to face me.

I'm not letting this chance pass by. I need her to have a clear understanding of where I stand. "It turns out some things are forgivable," I whisper. Her face softens at my confession and the reminder of our conversation in my car.

"You said you didn't want this." The words escape her lips so softly, I barely heard them as her eyes search mine and a single tear trails down her cheek. I swipe it away.

Ignoring her statement, I continue. "I know you are with Channing,"—she huffs out a chuckle with a hint of amusement at the use of this name— "but I want you to know something, and I'm not expecting anything from you. I just need you to know."

She nods. "Okay."

Leaning in, her hair tickles my nose. A gentle sigh escapes my lips as I mutter the words. "I'm all in." She sucks in a breath of air as I continue. "With you. It's only ever been you."

As I pull away, the electric tension between us is almost too much, and I can't breathe. Our faces are now inches apart. I watch her as she processes my revelation. More tears brim her eyes as she shuts them, trying to stop her emotions. Her breathing increases.

Something in this moment feels different. Standing here, outside a black Chevy, in the middle of the noisy city, our worlds have collided yet again. Staring at her, I can feel a seismic shift in my life, and the handful of times we have seen each other since the break-up, the significance of each floods my mind.

Our first meeting at Dexter's felt surreal.

The time in the shed before her wedding. Catastrophic.

That day we met in the park. Sad.

All our lunches together. Nostalgic.

When I let her go that day in my car. Loss.

But now, right now, the earth is moving me toward her. Pulling me back into her orbit. Right now ... feels ... permanent.

And I never want to leave this moment.

Yet, I know she needs to go. So, reluctantly, I release her arm. The second she's out of my grasp, I miss the feel of her skin. As I lean past her, the intensity of her stare pierces into me. I pop my head into the car, speaking directly to the driver. "Make sure she gets home safe."

He gives me a sharp salute. "Will do."

Without a word, Maria enters the car with a graceful slide. I close the door and step back. Our eyes meet through the glass, conveying a multitude of emotions. The driver pulls from the curb and makes a left. I watch the taillights disappear into the sea of cars.

Taking the love of my life ... to Geoffrey.

Chapter Thirty-Eight

∞

Maria

The lingering touch of Sam's hand on my back as the Uber arrived at Geoffrey's house made me aware of the choice I had to make about our relationship. No touch from one person should have this kind of effect on me. Especially when I am in a relationship with someone else. Heck, just seeing him made my stomach turn inside out.

Taking in the view of Geoffrey's cape cod, the house is undeniably stunning. But I know deep down that the man inside isn't where I belong.

The chemistry and connection between Sam and me is beyond words, and for the first time since I wrote the Dear John letter, the timing feels right for us. How do you describe a love so intense that it consumes everything? Love that surpasses the boundaries of time, space, distance, and broken promises?

It's simple. You don't.

Sam and I share a deep bond, our hearts intertwined, unbreakable. No matter how much we try to move on, date other people—even marry other people—somehow, we always find our way back into each other's lives.

I don't believe in soul mates. The idea that there is one person meant for us is misguided. To me, there's nothing more romantic than the knowledge that out of all the people living on this earth, someone has chosen you to be their person.

Love isn't something out of our control. It's a choice. And Sam has chosen me.

Now it's my turn to let him know that I want him. I need him. I love him.

But before anything else, I have to confront Geoffrey and have a tough conversation where I end things between us.

There is absolutely nothing wrong with him. This is going to be hard because he's such an extraordinary man. Geoffrey is undeniably gorgeous. A true gentleman, successful, kind-hearted, and brave. He is perfect in every way, but there is one flaw that he can't shake off.

He isn't Sam.

Our relationship started slowly, and that was because of me and the pandemic. I had a hard time going the distance with him due to my shattered heart. But eventually, Geoffrey snaked his way into my life, and my feelings grew. We connected and have the best time together.

I've tried with him. I did. But I haven't given my heart to him, not completely. And after tonight, I know why. As long as Sam is close and around, I'll never be able to love another man.

The way Sam glared at Geoffrey and clenched his fists at the restaurant left no doubt in my mind that he was burning with jealousy. If I'm being completely honest, seeing that reaction brought me satisfaction. Geoffrey saw it also because as soon as we walked away from his and Cara's table, he began bombarding me with questions.

"Did you know they were going to be here tonight? Is that why you recommended this place?" he asked as he led me away from their table. His question hung in the air, heavy with accusation. From the start, I was honest with Geoffrey about Sam. About my feelings, but not the full story.

I peered at him, a mixture of surprise and indignation crossing my face. "What! Why would I do that?"

"To make him jealous." As he led us to his car parked on the street, he didn't bother to glance in my direction. His strides were long, laced with anger, as I had a hard time keeping pace in my heels.

"I haven't spoken to him in three years," I said through gritted teeth. "And besides, who's acting jealous now?"

He was practically running, as if he couldn't get away from me fast enough. "Would you slow down!" I yelled.

He shot me a cold, disdainful glare as we reached his car, ignoring my pleas. "Of course, I'm jealous, Maria! You've told me all about him and what you guys meant to each other. How could I not be?"

He paused before opening the car door, glancing out into the night air, pondering his next words. He turned as his eyes met mine, and his lips tightened. "I want to be that person for you. I want to be the love of your life." The car door swung open, and I hesitated before I slid into the seat, letting his revelation wash over me. With his typical swagger and ease, he rounded the front of the car when the guilt hit me.

Geoffrey is a prize. A good, decent, and kind man who deserves to be the love of someone's life. He should have someone who adores him and makes him the center of their universe.

And that person isn't me.

From that point on, the situation went downhill fast, beginning with the car not starting. It refused to turn over no matter how many times Geoffrey tried, forcing us to call AAA in frustration and defeat. As we waited, he grew more curious, craving more details about Sam and me.

"You never told me that you guys worked so close. What happened? Why did you transfer?" he inquired.

I fiddled with the fabric of my dress, feeling bad that I never told him that part of the story. "I'm sorry, I should have. We were texting and spending time together. I thought maybe things were going to restart with us, but then he told me that he was going to see Cara exclusively. I walked away after that because I realized he wasn't ready to forgive me for the past."

"Well, that man in there"—he jammed his finger toward the restaurant—"hasn't moved on, that's for sure. And I won't compete for your attention, Maria. I won't. The question is, have you?"

"Have I what?" I knew what he was asking, but I inquired anyway.

"Moved on. From Sam."

The answer was easy. I haven't. I never will.

But I didn't say it.

With that loaded question hanging in the air, we sat in awkward silence as we watched the tow truck pull up, and before we knew it, the car was jacked up, my Uber was on its way, and we were ready to part ways.

He came up next to me and kissed me on the cheek, his hand resting softly on my arm. "I'll see you at my place." His lips felt warm on my skin as he pulled away and our eyes met, his forehead forming a wrinkle that wasn't there before. "Let me know what you decide."

He didn't have to tell me what he meant because I knew.

As I stood there, waiting for the Uber, my thoughts continued to waver. Geoffrey is a good guy. I should choose him. He told me he loves me, and he's been patient with me, understanding that I need time to process my own feelings and find the right moment to say "I love you" back. I feel ... something for him. It's close to love but not quite. And honestly, no love will be like Sam's. The comparison will always exist no matter who I'm with.

And what would the old Maria had done? Well, more than likely, she wouldn't have put herself first. She would have stayed with Geoffrey out of fear of hurting his feelings. But that isn't me now. There is no way I am pushing Sam out of my life again because of a lack of self-esteem.

The new Maria is saying yes to her happiness.

While I waited on the steps and contemplated everything, my attention was drawn to Cara sprinting out of the restaurant and jumping into a car that was ready and waiting. Not with Sam. Strange, to say the least. And then, moments later, Sam was at my side. Telling me he was newly single and—in so many words—that he forgives me. And that he's all in.

I mean, come on. What am I supposed to do with that information?

On top of it all, he grazed his thumb on my lower back, lightly rubbing in small circles. The way he always used to. I was a goner at that point.

Now, I'm sitting in this stuffy Uber that reeks of stale pizza, trying to decide on what to say to Geoffrey.

And Amanda because she is going to be maaaaaad.

No one is team Geoff/Maria (or Geria, our ship name, according to Richelle) more than Amanda. She set us up and says we are endgame. And we could have been.

But not after tonight.

The Uber sits idle in Geoffrey's driveway as butterflies erupt in my stomach. Getting out of the car, I thank my driver and take a moment to fix my dress and run my fingers through my hair. As I do, the passenger side window goes down. "Ma'am," his voice echoes through the empty street.

Curious about why the drivers calling me, I twist my body and lean forward to catch a glimpse of his face through the window. I cast a fleeting glance to the backseat, seeing if I missed anything. I bring my eyes back to him. "Did I forget to do something?"

He's an older gentleman, who looks to be in his mid-sixties, with salt-and-pepper hair and faded tattoos that run up and down each arm. He flashes me a gentle smile, his eyes crinkling with warmth. "No, ma'am. I know it's none of my business, and I have no clue what that man means to you." He points at Geoffrey's front door. I turn, and there he is, standing tall and motionless, waiting for me. His tie and suit jacket are discarded. I bring my focus back to this stranger, curious about where this is going. "But I used to look at my late wife the way that man who put you in the car back at the restaurant looked at you. It's rare and beautiful. If you're lucky enough to get it, don't run away from it."

His words are like a gut punch. This stranger, who is maybe a little intrusive, understood the situation by watching Sam and me for only a few minutes. Sam and I have been running away from and toward each other long enough. Heck, we have been stuck in this repetitive routine for more than two decades, and it's starting to wear thin. But now, Sam is running toward me. The question is, am I willing to go all in?

Yes. Yes, I am.

"Have a good night, ma'am." He tips his trucker hat to me, rolls up his window and drives away.

Now I'm alone, standing at the base of the driveway, staring at a man I am about to hurt. With equal amounts of fear and sadness, I head in Geoffrey's direction. The new wrinkle on his forehead is back because he knows what's coming. The clanking of my heels on his driveway, as well as sudden heart palpitations, are only adding to the dread. When I reach the steps, Geoffrey kindly shifts to the right, ensuring there is enough room for both of us on his narrow front porch.

"Hi." My greeting comes out strangled.

Geoffrey gives me a tight smile and shoves his hands into his pockets. His posture is rigid. "What's going on Maria? And please, be straight with me."

I flex my foot, balancing the weight on my left side with my heel, stalling, as I try to come up with the right words. Are there any 'right words' to break someone's heart with?

There aren't.

Without hesitation, I blurt out the first thing that pops into my head. "Geoffrey, I'm so sorry. I thought I was over him. I really did. But then I saw him ... with her and—"

"You'll never be over him." He interrupts, shifting his glance over my shoulder, not wanting to make eye contact.

I nod my head, feeling my hair brush against my cheeks. "You're right." A part of my heart will forever belong to Sam.

He finally looks back at me, his eyes full of determination, his voice low-pitched. "Maria, I won't settle for being someone's second option. I deserve better than that." His statement is steady and firm.

And true.

"You're right, you shouldn't." My hand stretches out as I take a step toward him, seeking his touch, but he takes a deliberate step backward. I retract my arm, feeling a sense of unease, and immediately grip my clutch, holding it protectively in front of me. "I won't go into the specifics of my complicated feelings towards Sam, but I want you to know that I care deeply for you."

"But not enough."

"No, I guess not. But you helped me more than you could ever imagine. When I met you, I was so lonely that my life felt almost painful. You helped me to see myself again and desired me in a way no man had in a long time. You brought me back to life again, and for that, I will always be grateful."

Looking downwards, his eyes scrunch together, like he's in pain. He probably is. "You brought me back to life also," he murmurs so softly that I almost miss it.

Gradually, his eyes come up to meet mine, revealing a flicker of longing. "Can I hold you, please? One last time," he whispers as he leans in closer.

I release the grip on my clutch and open my arms, inviting him in. As his hand wraps around my wrist, Geoffrey effortlessly removes my silver clutch from my grasp and tosses it onto the patio chair. He tugs me closer, his grip tight but gentle. His hand slowly travels up my arm, the touch becoming more tender, as if he's trying to etch this moment into his memory before it fades away forever. His eyes are intense and trail up my arm along with his touch. The tender feeling of his fingers sliding on my skin stirs something inside of me and when it does, I finally understand what Sam felt for Cara throughout the years. Because I am almost ready to forget my decision and pull him into his house.

We are chest to chest now. The moment our eyes meet, he delicately tucks a lock of hair behind my ear. His hand travels to the back of my neck and lingers there, causing goosebumps to explode over my body. I lean into him and inhale his scent as his other arm snakes around my back, his touch searing my skin. As I rest my head on his chest, I wrap my arms around his broad back, and we stand there in our embrace, saying goodbye with unspoken words.

Geoffrey and I discovered something with each other that filled a void we didn't realize existed. We were both hurting and lonely and helped the other breathe again. We gave each other the same gift.

I will be eternally grateful for that.

With the passing of a few minutes, Geoffrey's grip relaxes. But before he pulls away completely, his full and soft lips brush lightly with mine. It's sweet and sad, all in equal measure. He lingers for a moment, savoring our final kiss before breaking the connection and taking in my face, memorizing it. "To remember."

He slips away, and my body shivers with a sudden coldness as soon as he steps back. But even though I feel this way when I'm with him, his presence doesn't match the warmth and familiarity of Sam's.

"Stay right here," he says, his voice fading as he turns and grabs the doorknob, the sound of the clicking echoing into the night. "I'll get my keys and drive you home."

I nod and watch him disappear inside to grab the keys for his second car. Without realizing it, I had been holding my breath, and as I let it out, a sense of relief washes over me.

After a very tense and quiet ride home, we make it to my condo. Geoffrey squeezes my hand, a silent understanding passes between us, and without another word spoken, I exit the car.

Once I'm inside and settled for the night, I sit down at my desk in my room and fish out a blue-lined piece of paper and a pen. And without a second to spare and a plan in place, I write a letter.

Chapter Thirty-Nine

Sam

On tired feet and legs, I drag myself out of my office chair after a long, exhausting day. Granted, most of my job involves sitting and listening to patients talk about their lives. Then me trying to help and guide them through their problems.

My work is mostly mental, but that doesn't mean, on certain days, those patients don't weigh heavily on my mind. Also, our computers and phones went down, which was a major inconvenience. Talk about stressful.

Needless to say, I am looking forward to heading home and relaxing with a pizza, some scotch, and maybe a movie with Mikey.

I say goodbye to my workmates, their laughter and chatter fading into the distance as I walk to my car. My heavy footsteps echo against the pavement as I try to make a decision about my evening plans. I pull out my phone and shoot a text to my son.

> Me: Hey. How about pizza and a movie tonight? Unless you have other plans.

Which wouldn't surprise me. His social life is much more robust than mine, even when Cara was in the picture.

Plus, lately, I have been introducing Mikey to the movies that I loved growing up or were released long before he was born. I want to show him one of my favorites tonight. *Men in Black*. So I hope he doesn't have anything going on.

I swiftly slide my phone into my back pocket as I reach my car, parked in its usual spot, resting beneath the shade of the tree. For some reason, I never want to park anywhere else.

Well, I know the reason.

This spot will forever be associated with Maria, particularly the sight of her walking into work in those darn pink scrubs.

I shield my eyes from the blinding glare caused by the sun shining through the branches onto my face. As I wave goodbye to one of my workmates, who's parked a few spots away from me, I hit the unlock button on my key fob. The familiar chirp of my car unlocking fills the air.

"Looks like you might have gotten a ticket," she yells to me.

A ticket? Did I hear her right? What in the world could she be talking about?

"A what?" My voice echoes as I holler back at her.

She points, which directs my attention to the windshield. Something's pinned under the wiper.

What the heck?

"Thanks!" I wave back to her as she gets in her car, and I reach to grab whatever this is. I know we are allowed to park here. This is a shared lot between the hospital and the office building. The one Maria used to work in.

Unless they changed the parking arrangement and now this spot is off limits. A host of thoughts are running through my head as I lift the wiper blade and retrieve the white envelope without giving it a second glance. If it's a parking violation ticket from the hospital, it's strange that it would be in an envelope. Honestly, I'm too tired to care.

After the day that I've had, I don't want to deal with it, so I open the car door, get in, and throw the envelope into the passenger seat. Just then, my phone vibrates. It's Mikey.

After ordering the pizza, I toss my phone into the car's center console, ready to put this day behind me.

"So, K just goes and lives his life after reconnecting with his woman?" Mikey asks as the credits roll on *Men in Black*.

"That's right."

"And now J is going to take over?"

His excitement about one of my favorite movies is clear, and it brings a smile to my face. "Yep. So, you liked it?"

"Heck, yeah! It was awesome. Is there a second one? I want to see what happens." He stands, picking up the empty pizza box and our two soda pop cans.

"There is. How about next week?" I watch him carry everything into the kitchen, and I wonder how I got so lucky. Erica and I were a mistake as a couple. But it's crazy how that mistake created something so perfect, and for that, I will forever be grateful to her.

"Hey, Dad, what's this?" He's holding the envelope that was on my windshield.

I heave myself up from the couch and start walking towards the bathroom. "I think it's a parking ticket from work."

"But it has your name written on the front. And it says, 'Please Read,'" he yells as I walk away. The echoing of his question stops me because that is weird. *Why would I get a parking ticket with my name handwritten on the envelope?* I hardly glanced at it earlier, so I didn't notice my name or the written plea to read it.

With my curiosity piqued, I turn on my heels and head back toward the kitchen as Mikey extends the envelope to me.

As I take it from his hand, everything around me stops. In handwriting that I would recognize anywhere, my name stares back at me.

It's from Maria.

DAMNIT! Why didn't I open this earlier?

Thoughts of her have consumed me since Saturday. Right after I professed to her I was all in, I placed her in an Uber and sent her away to be with her hunky boyfriend. Hoping for any sign, message, or phone call from her, I clung to my phone on Sunday, making sure it was always within reach, checking it every five seconds.

But I got nothing.

Which leads me to assume that she and Geoffrey are still together.

So many times, I wanted to text her and apologize. I shouldn't have said that to her. Told her I was ready. Ready for us. She's in a relationship, for heaven's sake. And from what I could tell on Saturday, a happy one.

But there was no way I was letting her slip from my grasp again without telling her where my heart was at. And if I get nothing from her in return, I'm ready to accept that.

But now, this envelope is taunting me.

Mikey interrupts my internal rambling. "Are you going to open it?" I have no clue how long I have been standing here holding and staring at it.

As I flip it over, hope builds in my chest. My finger slips under the glued flap. Paper ripping tears through my ears as well as the heavy expectancy in the kitchen. I pull out a blue-lined piece of paper.

A letter. She wrote me a letter.

I unfold it and read.

Dear Sam,

I'm all in. Meet me at our spot. I'll be there.

Waiting all day if I have to.

Love always,

Maria

"Oh, my God." The words spill out of my mouth because I can't believe what I just read.

This is it.

It's our time.

After twenty-seven years, can this actually be happening?

"Who is it from?" My son's question brings me out of my thoughts. With urgency, I shove the letter back into the envelope and run over to the closet to get my shoes. I've only recently told Mikey about Maria. Not every detail, but enough for him to know what she meant to me.

As I shove my feet into my shoes, I answer him. "It's from Maria. I have to go to Pittsburgh."

I stand up, scanning the living room, my eyes darting over every surface, desperately searching for my keys and wallet.

Where did I put them?!

"Whoa. Like Maria, Maria? *The* Maria?" Mikey asks, following me around the room as I take my search on foot for my stupid keys.

I'm patting down my t-shirt and sweatpants now, as if they would be hiding in my clothes. *Seriously! Where are they?!* As I frantically search, I see Mikey out of the corner of my eye, reading the letter. "Wow, this is incredible!" he exclaims, his voice filled with excitement as he sits the letter back down and eagerly assists in the search.

"Yes, Maria! I have to drive to Pittsburgh, Mikey. She wants to meet me there." I'm lifting and throwing couch cushions. I can't think straight.

"Dad! Here they are!" I spin my head, only to see Mikey snatching them off the end table and flinging them towards me from across the room. Keys clank together as they soar through the air. I catch them. "Will you be okay here?" I ask as I walk toward him, a beaming smile on his face.

"Of course, Dad. Go!" I rest my hand on his face, grateful that he seems to be happy for me at this moment. "I can't wait to meet her."

"Me too," I choke out as my throat tightens. Because ... yeah.

"Wait, don't forget this." He reaches down and hands me back the letter. "Now, go!" Mikey yells as I run out the door, into my car, and toward the future that I have always wanted.

This hour-long drive into the city has been the longest of my life. The moment my car enters the Fort Pitt Tunnel, a wave of anxiety washes over me. My grip around the steering wheel is getting tighter by the second as I drive through. This tunnel has never made me feel more claustrophobic than right now. I just want to be on the other side, with the city in full view and Maria that much closer.

Driving through this mountain, my mind becomes a whirlwind of thoughts, doubts, and fears.

Is she still there?

What happened to Geoffrey?

Is this really happening?

As I exit the other side, the bright lights of Pittsburgh hit me in the face as I make my way to Point State Park. Where I know Maria will be waiting for me. At the Point, by the three rivers and the fountain.

Our spot.

I park, and it feels like I am being charged with electricity from the inside out. I'm in a desperate rush to get out of the car, but before I do, I quickly reach over and pop open the glove compartment. The watch is still there, untouched and silently ticking. I snatch it and forcefully stuff it into my back pocket.

Then I shut the car door and run.

Chapter Forty

Their Spot

Maria

Glancing at my phone, I check the time. Again.

9:15

Five minutes later than it was the last time I checked.

He's probably not coming.

I scan the area for any sign of him. Nothing. My shoulders sink in defeat. Instead, there is only the chatter and laughter of people milling about around me. They are immersed in their own lives, taking selfies of the city behind them, enjoying this windy yet beautiful night. Pittsburgh is glowing and lit up, the fountain is rising high, bright and majestic. The three rivers are in front of me, the water flowing and somewhat rough due to the wind.

And here I stand, waiting anxiously, my stomach twisted in knots.

Getting off work early today, I drove across town, the letter gently resting in my lap on my scrub pants (side note, I wore my pink ones).

I had to wait until today since I had no clue where he lived. Plus, I didn't want to do this over text. And thanks to his question at the restaurant about him not seeing me in the parking lot anymore, I knew he still worked here. I found his car, parked in its usual spot, a layer of pollen covering the windshield. With a careful glance around, I slipped the envelope under his wiper, ensuring no one was watching, before jumping into my car and driving straight here. That was at four-thirty.

As I wait and the minutes turn into hours—four, to be exact—doubts creep in about whether he was going to show.

I thought about texting him instead of writing a letter. But somehow, this moment felt monumental. A letter would take us back to our roots. Inviting him to our spot, the place where we promised to make huge decisions together, felt right. It would send a message to him that I want back what we had.

Additionally, it was me who caused our relationship to crumble. I wanted to be the one who made the initial move towards building a life together.

To show him that I'm ready for a future. With him.

A thousand and one scenarios are running through my head about why he isn't here yet. And the one that is the most prominent is ... he and Cara got back together.

And if they did, I only have myself to blame. Point each finger at me, please. Twenty-seven years ago, I made the life-shattering decision to walk away. No matter my reasons, I destroyed us. He never would have dated Cara in the first place if it weren't for me.

But after seeing him at the restaurant and hearing him say he forgives me, one thing became clear as the weight of decades of guilt lifted from my shoulders.

I am officially done. Done with waiting. Done making mistakes. Done feeling lonely without Sam. Done living my life without him.

I want him. I need him. I love him. Nothing matters more.

Once again, I glance at my phone to get the time.

9:31

I let out an audible sigh as I look out at the three rivers, feeling a sense of calm wash over me. Mentally, I resolve to wait until midnight. Then, I will walk away.

Forever.

A sudden burst of commotion catches my attention, prompting me to spin around and see what's happening. A group of teenagers are carrying on, laughing, jumping on each other's backs, collectively having a great time. I watch them and smile, reminiscing about the fun Sam and I used to have at that age. Before life veered off course and descended into chaos.

As they begin to make their way toward the fountain, my breath catches, because ...

There he is.

Standing just feet from me, a smile playing on his lips as soon as our eyes lock.

His all-consuming stare pierces into my soul, leaving me feeling exposed out here in the open.

As he strides toward me, a huge smile spreads across my face, unable to contain my joy. He steps closer, and his expression turns stoic. There is a fixed look of concentration. He doesn't look sad, mad, happy, or anything, really. If I had to put a word to it, I would say pensive.

Suddenly, I want to throw up.

Thanks to his words on Saturday, I know what he wants. And hopefully, because of my letter, he knows where I stand.

But for some reason, there is still this lingering fear that creeps up inside me. And that's because, after years of trying, we could never get this right.

As he inches closer, our shared history swirls in my head.

The Dear John Letter.

The shed.

The park.

Nate and Erica.

Our letters and emails.

The lunch dates.

His car and the watch.

Cara and Geoffrey.

All of it.

But now, right now, for the first time, nothing is standing in our way. There are no manipulative bosses, financial troubles, abusive husbands, troubled wives, past girlfriends in their red bikinis, or buff celebrity look-alike boyfriends.

Now, the possibility of us being together exists.

I'm having a hard time breathing as I shift from one foot to the next, unable to contain my anxiety. With only a few dozen feet separating us, the tears well up in my eyes as the wind whips my hair in my face.

He reaches me, and our eyes meet, intensifying the moment, neither of us saying anything.

Finally, he holds up the letter, the paper crinkling in his hands. "Someone left this on my car today."

A quiet chuckle slips out of me. "Weird. A letter, huh? Seems kinda old-fashioned."

He shrugs. "Or romantic." His lips curve into a smile as a light breeze stirs the air, causing the smell of his cologne to surround me. "Hi."

"Hey." My attempt to sound calm and cool fails in my breathy response.

His eyes roam down, then back up my body. When they meet mine again, a smug smile plays on his lips. "Nice scrubs."

I blush as he takes a step closer, his body filling my space, his voice laced with curiosity. "What happened with Geoffrey?"

"I ended it." With a contented exhale, he smiles, clearly pleased with my answer.

"And what about Cara?" I counter in return.

As his hand reaches out, his pinkie gently intertwines with mine. "I told you, we broke up." This one small tiny touch of skin on skin causes a volcano of electricity to erupt throughout my whole body.

I bite the side of my cheek. "For good?" Because, for whatever reason, they kept trying. He obviously cares.

"For good."

"Thank God."

He huffs out a laugh as he releases my finger and takes the letter, tucking it into the side pocket of my scrubs. My eyes track the movement as he grabs my wrist that was hanging at my side. He holds it, then tugs gently, coaxing me to step closer to him. Standing chest to chest, the warmth between us intensifies. I've never been this short of breath in my life. All I want is for him to grab me and wrap his arms around me. Encase me with his strength and security.

"Are we all in? Together?" His eyes scan mine, eagerness etched on his face as he waits for my answer.

Without hesitation, I give him the easiest answer I have ever given to any question. "Yes. All in."

With a swift motion, he reaches into the back pocket of his sweatpants and pulls out my watch. When I see it, my breath hitches. After I left it on his front seat, I couldn't stop wondering whether he would keep it or throw it away. As time passed, I regretted my choice of leaving it behind. For the longest time, it was the only thing I had left of Sam. Once it was gone, it felt like he was gone. I thought it was the end.

He delicately lifts my hand and slides the watch over my fingers and back onto my wrist. The clasp clicks into place. My body reacts instantly as he lifts my wrist, sending a shiver through me. His lips graze the sensitive skin on the inside, his eyes closing as he makes contact. His breath is warm, and I'm pretty sure I'm dying.

He opens his eyes, takes my hand, and rests it on his chest. Over his heart. It's thumping rapidly under my touch, and I know that whatever I am feeling is mutual. "Just like the inscription says, I'm yours, Maria. I have *always* been yours. I will always *be* yours."

Leaning in close, I whisper my response, my hushed words barely audible against the howling wind. "And you're mine."

In this moment, nothing else matters. I hear nothing. Not the commotion surrounding us, not the fountain shooting high, not the wind whipping through the air.

There's only us.

Standing here, peering into each other's eyes, it feels like we are back in high school again. Just two kids in love with nothing but a blank slate for a future. Right now, despite the lines around his eyes, the gray in his hair and beard, the creases on his forehead, he's still Sam.

My Sam.

His hands gently rest on either side of my neck, and even though he is exuding confidence right now, his touch betrays him. They are trembling. I bite my lip, anticipating what I'm hoping is going to happen next. He brushes his thumbs on my already hot skin. My arms wrap around his waist. We move on instinct and forget about our history, the bad choices we made that kept us apart. Everything disappears into the past.

He nuzzles his face against my hair and inhales. As the fine hairs raise on the back of my neck, a shiver runs down my spine and my eyes instinctively close.

"You are so beautiful," he whispers, his breath warm against my face. He sweeps my hair over my shoulder, his hand brushing my neck as he does. With a slow and deliberate movement, his plump lips start planting a series of tender kisses on my neck. I lean my head to give him better access. He works his way to my cheek, then the corner of my mouth.

The desire for his kiss consumes me. This building passion is making my breaths come in fast, as if I just ran a marathon. We haven't felt the touch of each other's lips for twenty-seven years.

Twenty-seven *really, really long years.*

He pulls back, and I moan in frustration. "You're killing me."

His thumb glides against my parted lips, and now I'm unsteady on my feet as if I'm drunk. "I know." He lets out an evil laugh. "Call it payback."

I grin, with his thumb still resting on my lower lip. "I hate you." He lowers his thumb.

The gentle rise and fall of his chest against mine causes heat to rise in my core. My grip tightens around him, as our heads tilt and lips draw closer with each passing second.

"No, you don't," he whispers. Faster than my brain can register what is happening, his lips crash into mine. I melt into his embrace with the surge of his mouth. The bristles of his beard scratch against my soft cheeks as he grips my head firmly.

I'm completely breathless.

His hands leave my neck and slide down the side of my body, gripping my waist. He pulls me closer to him, as if he is a man starved but also trying to keep me from escaping.

I'm not going *anywhere.*

Our lips fit together in a way our lives never could. With ease. Finally, we are coming together as one with each pass of his lips over mine. Every inch of my body feels like it's on fire. My arms grip his back tighter because I can't seem to get close enough to him. Clinging for dear life.

I'm pretty positive this is the kiss to end all kisses. It's sexy and sweet and rough and loving and toe-curling goodness mixed in one. Twenty-seven years of separation are pouring into this moment. This kiss. This perfect mind-blowing kiss. Our long-awaited dreams are finally coming true, filled with love, passion, hope, and excitement for the future.

The future is ours.

We are all in.

Have we been kissing for five seconds or five hours? No clue. Time is standing still.

Even though we don't want to part, we do. A soft exhale escapes both of us, our breathing now in sync as we rest our foreheads together, taking in the moment for what it is.

Us coming back together.

Sam's joyful laugh echoes through the air, filling the surroundings as he pulls me close in a tight embrace. I feel weightless as he effortlessly lifts me off the ground, twirling us around like characters in a movie. My own laughter erupts as he spins me, finally setting me on my feet and sprinkling kisses over my face.

This. Is. Happiness.

"Pinch me. Is this really happening?" he asks rhetorically. But this is the most real my life has felt in a long time. Gently taking hold of both my hands, our fingers intertwining, he keeps his stare fixed on me, intently, the way he always did.

I shake my head. "It feels like a dream."

Eagerly, he kisses me again, this one softer and more passionate, causing a ripple effect to course through my whole body. I feel it everywhere, and I can't wait to experience every one of his different kisses again. He pulls back, and his grin borders on evil. He knows what he's doing to me. "Did that feel like a dream?" He gives me another quick peck.

I try to form words. "Nope. That felt very, very real." My voice quivers, betraying my emotions. "God, I missed kissing you. Like, really missed kissing you."

He scans my face, taking in each feature as if he's seeing me for the first time. "Me too."

No one's kisses have ever compared to Sam's. Definitely not Chad's, not Nate's, and not even Geoffrey's, despite how he looked and how I felt about him. Sam is in a class all by himself.

Neither of us have stopped smiling. Joy is radiating off of Sam. His fingertips trace a gentle path down my neck, then my arm, before trailing back up again. All the while, never tearing his eyes from mine.

Before I overthink it, the words spill from my mouth, eager to be heard after being confined for what feels like an eternity. "I love you, Sam. God, I love you so much. I always have."

He exhales as his eyes close, and I can see the relief that flows through him at my admission. "I love you, too." The words are spoken with ease. As if they are the easiest eleven letters he has ever strung together. It feels so good to hear him say it. "And we are never letting each other go again," he continues. "Do you hear me? Never. Again."

My arms snake around his neck, feeling the warmth of his skin against my fingertips as he rests his hands on my hips, his touch firm and possessive.

"We are all in, Sam."

"All in."

Then he kisses me again. In our spot. A kiss that, for the first time, won't be the last.

It's only the beginning.

Epilogue

2024

Sam

The morning rays streaming in from our bedroom window stirs me awake. There's a gentle breeze coming in from the outside, making the light curtain blow with the wind. I adjust myself so that I'm more comfortable by turning on my side ... to face my wife.

Her unruly blonde hair cascades across her face, making it difficult for me to see her beauty. With a gentle swipe, I brush it off and just stare, taking her in.

My God, she is gorgeous.

Her left hand is resting on the white sheet. I reach over and grab it, her wedding ring grazing my hand.

I'm not sure I have ever been this happy. Every single day with her gets better and better.

After that day three years ago at the Point, we have spent every waking moment together. It was almost as if we were trying to make up for the years we were apart. Maria even transferred back to her old office so that we see each other every day and drive to work together. Then eat lunch together, drive home together, eat dinner together.

Because that is what we are, together.

Our kids were thrilled. After that day, we drove straight back to my place so that Maria could meet Mikey. This was important to me. And just as I predicted, he fell in love with her. Parting with her that night was so difficult. We went to our separate homes, then talked all night on the phone and, for the first time, made plans for the future.

The following day at work was a bear. But it was worth it.

Then, the day after that, I met Brielle and Mason. It's crazy because we meshed together perfectly. Mikey isn't Maria's, and Brielle and Mason aren't mine. But for some reason, it feels like we belong with each other. Like this is how it was supposed to be.

We are a family. Not in the traditional sense, but it makes sense to us.

Not long after we got back together, we heard another bit of surprising news. Our exes, Cara and Geoffrey, started dating. Apparently, they ran into each other at the gym (shocker) and bonded over their mutual hurt. One thing led to another, and honestly, we couldn't be happier for them. The match makes sense. Now they are married and, from what we have heard—through Ricky, of course—blissfully happy.

Everything worked out as it should have.

As I stare down at the diamond ring, memories of the day I proposed fill my mind. Only two months after we found our way back to one another.

I contemplated buying a different ring. But that original engagement ring was Maria's. It belonged to her, and there had to be a reason I held onto it for years. There were times in my life that I was broke beyond belief. That ring could have fetched me enough money to help me survive. But the thought of pawning it for cash never crossed my mind. Not once. I think because, deep down, I knew she would wear it someday.

So, on bended knee, at our spot, in front of the fountain, I asked her to be my wife. And despite knowing what her answer would be, my nerves were still shot.

She said yes.

Well, actually, she threw herself in my arms and screamed yes. After I slipped it on her finger, her mouth gaped open in shock.

Tears spilled from her eyes as she watched it glide over her finger. A perfect fit. "Wait. Is this the ring? You bought it? Our ring?" Her question trailed off into a whisper as I wiped the tears from her face. "How? When?"

"That day in the mall," I explained, "I went back after we went to dinner and bought it. Maxed out the one and only credit card I had."

"But you never asked."

I composed myself, knowing that the time had finally come to tell her.

"The day you gave me the letter, *The Chad*," I paused, bracing myself for the impact of my next words. "I was going to propose that night."

A sob escaped her mouth, and she buried her face in my chest. I pulled her close to me and let her cry. All these years later, and even after we made our way back to each other, I never told her this one truth.

I gently pulled her away from me so that I could see her face. "Maria, would you look at me, please?"

When she did, tears tracked down her cheeks. "I'm so sorry, Sam. I will never be able to forgive—"

To keep her from saying anything further and beating herself up, I gently pressed my finger against her lips. "Maria, I didn't tell you that to make you feel bad. That is the past." I pulled her hand up and kissed the ring. "This is our future. There is no turning back, no looking back. There's only forward."

She nodded her head in agreement, and then I kissed the crap out of her.

Something I do a lot.

We were married three weeks later. Seems fast, I know, but there was no point in waiting. Few people can say they had two quickie weddings in one lifetime. But this marriage was going to be different from my first because it's going to be my last.

Our ceremony was exactly what we wanted. Everyone that was important to us was there. Mikey, Mason, and Brielle, our parents, my siblings, Ricky and his new girlfriend (he's finally settling down), Big C, Jasmine, and the little girl they adopted, now their daughter. Richelle and Amanda, along with their husbands, rounded out the guest list.

It was small, intimate, and absolute perfection.

My favorite part ... watching Maria float down the aisle with Mason on one arm and Brielle on the other. A sight I gave up on ever being able to see. Yet there I was, watching her walk to meet me and become my wife. The one thing I have wanted since I was sixteen years old.

I cried.

I broke my promise that day to never cry over Maria.

Totally worth it.

We promised to love and cherish each other, in sickness and in health, until death parts us. I slid the wedding band on her finger. Five diamonds. One for me, her, Mikey, Brielle, and Mason. She placed my band on my finger, five diamonds as well.

Our family, with us always.

After that, we spent the next two weeks on our honeymoon. The first week we were in the mountains of Montana in a rustic cabin (my favorite), the second week was on a beach in Hawaii (her favorite).

I'll leave the details of those two weeks to myself. But yeah, it was fun.

Since then, we spend a lot of quiet nights together. Mostly, in front of the TV or in bed. Together, just the two of us. Then on the weekends, we venture out and discover new places, making new memories.

That may sound boring and mundane, and perhaps it's our age, but just *being* is enough for us.

All those years apart were torture. I missed her constantly. So now that we are together, that's what we want to be. Together.

Maria and Sam.

Sam and Maria.

All in.

Finally, Maria stirs, breaking me from my thoughts. Her eyes open, sleepy, green, and beautiful.

"Hi." Her voice comes out hoarse from the night's sleep.

"Morning." I swipe another stray of blonde from her face.

"How long have you been lying here staring at me?"

I trace my fingers up her arm, and goosebumps erupt on her smooth skin. "Not long enough."

With a subtle shift of her body, she closes the gap between us and plants a tender kiss on my lips. She moans, and her body sinks deeper into the bed. "What do you want to do today?" she purrs.

It's Saturday morning, so the entire weekend is ahead of us.

I shrug. "I don't know. Just be together, I guess."

"Mmm..." She smiles. "Sounds wonderful."

I roll her over onto her back and cage her in with my elbows on either side of her head.

I kiss her.

And we spend the morning in bed, as well as the rest of our lives ... together.

All In Playlist

- Unbreak My Heart (Weezer)

- I Had Me a Girl (The Civil Wars)

- A Year Ago (James Arthur)

- Just Another Girl (The Killers)

- Only Love Can Hurt Like This (Paloma Faith)

- Don't (Simu Lu)

- We've Got Tonight (Bob Segar)

- Would You Love Me Now? (Joshua Bassett)

- If I Didn't Love You (Jason Aldean, Carrie Underwood)

- Some Things I'll Never Know (Teddy Swims)

- Put A Little Love On Me (Niall Horan)

- Always Remember Us This Way (Noelle Johnson)

- Over You (Ingrid Michaelson, A Great Big World)

- Glimpse of Us (Joji)

- Love You Forever (Mikey Wax)

- Where It Says (Charlotte OC)

- Surrender (Natalia Taylor)

- From Where You Are (Lifehouse)

- Lucky (Jason Mraz, Colbie Caillat)

- Poison & Wine (The Civil Wars)

- Make It To Me (Sam Smith)

- Jealous (Labrinth)

- Kiss (Nicole Witt, John Paul White)

- True Love Will Find You in the End (Axel Flovent)

- All In (John Splithoff)

Acknowledgements

On a random day, about a year and a half ago, while having lunch with one of my workmates, *All In* was born. I had no idea, after Becoming Mallory, what my next book was going to be. But then, over a turkey sandwich (me), and chicken with broccoli (her), she told me about how, after a messy divorce, she and her first love found their way back to one another. In great detail, she relayed their love story to me. From the moment they started dating, until their reconnection, she had my rapt attention. Seriously, you couldn't make up some of the stuff she told me. It had the makings of a story you would see in movies or read in books.

I knew, while sipping on my iced tea, my next novel was born.

So, thank you Lisa and Steve. This book would not have been possible without you. Now granted, I took some liberties with the story (with their permission, of course). However, it's the overall feel of the book that I hope captures the love that they had for one another over many, many years. I will forever be grateful!

And naturally, I need to thank my family. They are my biggest cheerleaders, and I couldn't do this thing called writing and publishing without their support. I love you all so much!

To my Beta readers. All of you are the reason this book is what it is. Your feedback and criticism helped me see the deficiencies in this novel. You made the book better, and your presence graces its pages. I recognize your time is valuable, and I am grateful that you spent a part of your days helping me bring Maria and Sam's story to life.

To my editor, Nevvie. Again, you nailed it! I couldn't have done this without you. I hope you know you are stuck with me. Also, you are never allowed to stop editing. Just an FYI.

Finally, to all my readers. Thank you, thank you, thank you! I don't know what I have done to deserve your support. I simply hope that you continue to support me and stay with me for a long haul.

Because I'm not going anywhere.

About the Author

Elaine Evans has had a love of writing ever since she can remember. It wasn't until she hit middle-age that she decided to turn it into a career. All In is her second novel.

When she's not writing you can find Elaine exploring her other hobbies of reading, cooking, and photography. But more than anything, it is the role of wife, mother, and dog mom to her black Pomeranian, Vinnie, that she cherishes the most. Outside of the home, she works as a pediatric Medical Assistant, a job she adores. Elaine resides in Ohio with her family.

Elaine would love to connect with her readers! You can find her on Instagram, Goodreads, and TikTok.

instagram.com/elaineevanswrites

goodreads.com/author/show/1739279.Elaine_Evans

tiktok.com/@elaineevanswrites?_t=8iHsrNLlg11&_r=1

9 798218 467890